PERFECT DEATH

Helen Fields studied law at the University of East Anglia, then went on to the Inns of Court School of Law in London. After completing her pupillage, she joined chambers in Middle Temple where she practised criminal and family law for thirteen years. After her second child was born, Helen left the Bar. Together with her husband David, she runs a film production company, acting as script writer and producer. The D.I. Callanach series is set in Scotland, where Helen feels most at one with the world. Helen and her husband now live in Hampshire with their three children and two dogs.

Helen loves Twitter but finds it completely addictive. She can be found at @Helen_Fields.

By the same author:

Perfect Remains
Perfect Prey

Perfect Death

HELEN FIELDS

AVON

A division of HarperCollins*Publishers*
1 London Bridge Street,
London, SE1 9GF

www.harpercollins.co.uk

A Paperback Original 2018

1

First published in Great Britain by
HarperCollins*Publishers* 2018

A catalogue record for this book is available from the British Library

ISBN-13: 978-0-00-818161-1

TPB ISBN: 978-0-00-827874-8

Typeset in Bembo Std by Palimpsest Book Production Ltd, Falkirk, Stirlingshire

Printed and bound by CPI Group (UK) Ltd, Croydon CR0 4YY

MIX
Paper from
responsible sources
FSC® C007454

This book is produced from independently certified FSC™ paper
to ensure responsible forest management.

For more information visit: www.harpercollins.co.uk/green

Acknowledgements

My sincere thanks, in no particular order, to all who got *Perfect Death* from idea to book shelf, and who provided support for me during the process, often in the simple form of constant encouragement. If I forget anyone, please forgive me – that old chestnut about forgetting my head if is wasn't screwed on? Yup. That's me.

Helen Huthwaite, my editor, has done so much work on this book that it should probably be her name on the cover instead of mine. For all the help, patience, guidance (and for knowing what I wanted to say even when I didn't), you are a star. To Sabah Khan, Avon's publicist, thank you for never getting fed up with me (or at least for hiding it really well). And to the wider Avon and HarperCollins team – designers, marketing, sales (you guys rock), and everyone else who oils the machine – I am indebted.

To my agent Caroline Hardman and the Hardman & Swainson lovelies, for your support and good advice – thank you. The Wailing Banshee team produced animated GIFs, websites, promo films and handled all the tech for the books. I'm eternally grateful, and sorry for all the stupid questions.

A special mention to my friend Simon Gardner, son of the extraordinary writer John Gardner. Many thanks for giving permission for me to mention *The Liquidator* and Boysie Oakes. Your father was such a great talent.

To Andrea Gibson and Amanda Patchett who were my first readers for *Perfect Death*, I couldn't have made it through the first few drafts without you. Also, for the cups of tea, cocktails, meals, laughs, tissues, chatter and all round love.

For booksellers everywhere, particularly those who championed this series and got it into the hands of real life, flesh and blood readers. Thank goodness for all of you.

To Christine, Margaret, Ruth, Gabriel, Solomon and Evangeline for listening to me and hugging me. Then there's David (there's always David), who made me be brave and take a risk this year. You were right. You only regret the things you don't try. He also cooked, cleaned, drove, headed up my personal tech support team, changed lightbulbs, entertained the children and let me write. My best friend.

Helen x

For Sollie

Changing the world one great big smile at a time.
Remember this, my darling boy – there are no limits
to what you can achieve. None at all.
You take my breath away.

Chapter One

Lily's life was very nearly over, it was just that she didn't know it yet. He stroked the photograph of her he'd kept by his bed for the last few months. In it, she was bending over the edge of a pond, throwing bread for ducks, laughing, entirely unaware of her stunted future.

Much remained to be done before the evening, but he could allow himself a few moments with his box of treasures. He pulled the bottom drawer from his bedside table, putting his hands into the dark void beneath to grip the wooden container. He'd made it in woodwork at school – one of the few triumphs in a largely wasted period of his life – but then he'd moved around a lot, and academics had never come easily.

Sliding the lid off, he caught his breath looking at the scraps of lives contained within. A brooch, inlaid with semi-precious stones, in the shape of a sprig of heather. He remembered the back-breaking hours of gardening he'd had to do for that one, never allowed a rest to avoid the rain, yet it had been worth it in the end. Then there was the tiny silver letter opener, so well used and well loved that part of the swirling design on its handle had been worn away. A lucky coin, or so its owner had claimed, kept always in a pocket or a purse. Just went to prove there was no such thing as good luck. Finally, a tooth. More specifically a crown, dislodged in the torment and drama of those final moments when nothing had gone to plan. He liked the smoothness of its surface, the integral part it had played in the life he'd ended. Where did a body's energy go once death was complete? He thought back to his school days once more. There had been something about energy changing form but never ceasing to exist. Not enough knowledge to have passed a science exam, but he was pleased with the tiny pearl of wisdom. He wondered if it was possible to breathe a dying person's energy in.

Making a small space in the centre of the objects in his box, he imagined a new prize there. Its owner had taken more time to cultivate than the rest. Lily kept herself to herself, enjoyed family life, and worked hard. Soon he would have his memento of her, ready to savour among the others he'd worked so hard for.

He checked the tiny vial of cannabis oil he'd spent weeks brewing. Buying small quantities here and there rather than risking scrutiny for purchasing a massive amount in one go had been time consuming but worthwhile. Most of the process after that had been easy, snagging only when he'd tested it on himself and ended up sleeping so deeply that he'd missed work the next day. Not good. He had expenses. Such a complex calling required careful financing, and cash in hand jobs were in short supply.

Sliding the box back beneath the drawer space, he ran through the details once more in his head. His car was ready. All the lights were working – no point attracting attention from the police over something as ridiculous as a blown bulb. Everything had been handled with gloves. All his supplies. There wasn't one item touched freely. He'd watched enough true crime television to know that these days fingerprints weren't the issue. Skin cells could leave enough DNA to make a case against him. He didn't want to get caught. There was so much to do. So many more people that needed his attention.

All ready. He could even afford the time for a nap. Better not to be tired given all he had to do. Not just the physical aspects. Killing was hard work. Anyone who believed a human being perished in the few seconds portrayed in TV crime dramas was an idiot. Death, more often than not, was a slow striptease of a show. There were ways it could be done fast – gunshot, explosion, massive head trauma – but hands on, it inevitably took longer. Suffocation and drowning were the real time-heavy activities, and chances were that you'd end up injured yourself. Scratches, groin kicks, broken bones. He'd had enough of that.

Lying back on his bed, he closed his eyes. The anticipation was all a part of it. Rushing to the end point was like reading the final chapter of a book first. It was the build-up, the investment in the characters, that made the pay-off so thrilling. In the past he'd struggled to find the ideal victims, and now three had come along at once. He laughed. It was a brutal choke of a noise that exploded in the air like a firecracker. It was a cruel sound, but he wasn't a cruel man. Not unnecessarily. Only when cruelty was absolutely required.

Chapter Two

'Hey, sweetie, let me get you another drink.' Joe smiled at Lily as she returned from the pub toilets. Lily squeezed between a final pair of Friday night oblivion seekers, failing to notice the one staring at her backside as she turned side-on to get through. Fair enough, Joe thought. It was a body worth staring at and he wasn't going to start a fight over something so petty.

'Joe, it's my turn. You don't always have to buy,' she said as she dropped to the seat at his side. They huddled in the limited space, raising their voices against the increasing uproar of drinkers, music and the shuffle of feet on the wooden floor.

'Are you saving money for university?' he asked, gathering up their empty glasses.

'You know I am,' she replied, 'but that doesn't mean . . .'

'And are you going to bust your ass to become the best doctor ever?' Joe leaned down to kiss her. The crowd of girls sharing their table rolled their eyes, tutting, jealous beneath their masks of disgust.

'You're crazy.' Lily kissed him back.

'So am I doing the world a favour by helping Miss Lily Eustis save future lives without starting her degree an extra' – he looked at the ceiling, calculating – 'eight pounds forty-six in debt?'

'I give in,' Lily laughed, kissing him again then pressing her face into his neck as she blushed.

'Okay, you got me, I have a thing about women in white coats with stethoscopes. This is my way of secretly funding my own bizarre fetish,' Joe said. Lily mock punched his arm as he walked away. He didn't hear the woman staring at him whistle under her breath. He didn't notice as the girl sitting next to them looked daggers at Lily. They were a couple lost in each other.

Getting to the bar was like climbing a mountain. Drinks spilled down backs as people moved away with their hands too full. Positions were claimed and voices raised when one customer was wrongly served before another. Requests to change the music were yelled, and complaints made that someone was locked in one of only two cubicles in the ladies'. A beer pump ran flat. Joe stood patiently, quick to smile, to forgive the toe-treaders and elbow-jabbers. He had Lily, and she was everything he'd dreamed of.

In his car was everything they needed for the perfect romantic evening. Wood, firelighters, matches, a flask of liquor to warm them up, a sleeping bag. Even the weather had been kind. It would be cold but the rain was going to stay away. He'd even been thorough enough to check out their destination a few days ago. Edinburgh would spread majestically beneath them, its lights a reflection of the stars above, clouds willing. He would, at last, have Lily all to himself, and the time to show her what she really meant to him.

★　★　★

It was too cold for anyone to have been outside naked. That was Mark McVeigh's first – and most ridiculous – thought. The scene the drone camera was relaying back into his monitor was nothing like he'd imagined he might capture. The wintry frost and barren rocks, yes. A hard, blank sky with a horizon veiled in layers of fog, yes. A woman sprawled, one knee bent, one leg straight, one arm behind her head, the other slung out across the ground, no. Her long red hair was wind swept, a fluttering veil over her eyes. At her feet were the ashy remains of a fire. Abandoned at her side was a box of matches. He moved the drone closer, trying to convince himself that he might see her ribcage rise and fall. No joy. Mark directed the drone towards her face, hoping he wasn't about to be accused of some brand of perversion, and wishing to any number of deities that his gut instinct was wrong. Being wrong right now would be good. The drone copter was out of his eye-line over a ridge. He controlled its descent, careful not to bring it down directly over the woman in case she awoke, sat up and collided with it. Closer inspection brought no relief. The drone was fitted with a decent lens, and his screen was filled with shades of blue that had nothing to do with the frost or the winter-dead heathers. The blue was her lips, her open eyes, her veins and oxygen-starved skin.

Mark sprinted, knowing it was pointless as he exerted himself, but the idea of merely walking towards the dead woman smacked of disrespect. He took the ridge on his hands and knees, the longer, gentler pathway around the edge of the hilltop out of the question. He was bleeding by the time he could see her directly, a tableau on the ground, the good people of Edinburgh waking unaware in the distance, Arthur's Seat above them. Ignoring his skinned knees and cut hands, Mark flew down the scree slope, calling out to her as he went.

His drone was a grounded, whirring mess of plastic and metal a few metres away. He hadn't even realised he'd thrown down the remote. The mobile in his pocket was playing a game of cat and mouse with his fingers. Then he was at her side, kneeling on the frozen ground, pressing his fingers against her neck, aware that it wasn't possible for a body that colour to have a pulse. He ripped off his winter coat in spite of his certain knowledge that life had fled her flesh, in order to cover her nakedness. After that he called the police, giving the best description he could of their location within the mountainous landscape that stood regal over Scotland's capital.

Close-up, Mark could see she was younger than he'd thought, the freezing night having robbed her of the blush denoting her youth. Like him, he thought, she was in that teetering abyss between teenage and adulthood. A tiny diamond in the side of her nose sparkled with the first rays of morning winter sun, off-setting the blonde highlights artfully added to her copper hair. It was all he could do to stop himself brushing the hair from her face, but then he would see her eyes more clearly and he didn't want that. Mark stood up, peering over the ridge of the hill to check for approaching vehicles, but there was no clear view of any roads. In summer, free of corpses, it would have been a private and sheltered idyll. A waving patch of red in the scrub grass some twenty metres away caught his eye.

'I'll be back in a minute,' he said. It had seemed rude not to say anything, even to a dead body. Without his coat, the cold was already setting in. He forced himself into a jog to keep warm, wondering how long the police would take to arrive, given how hard the spot was to access. His own car was a mile away at the foot of the hills, the steep slopes and rocky tracks inhospitable to anything other than four-wheel drives.

The red object turned out to be a shirt, a warm one made from heavy cotton, perfect for nights by the fire and drinking in pubs. He picked it up, looking back at the girl, assessing the rough size as a match for her, coming up positive. A couple of minutes' walk further down the hillside he found a bra hanging off the edge of a rock, stark white, the metal fastener icy on his fingers.

Mark heard the helicopter before he saw it, the whap-whap of the rotors scaring wildlife and echoing off the rocks. The police circled, getting a location on the body and communicating the scene to the units whose blue lights became visible for the first time below. Mark carried the clothing he'd found back up the steep bank towards the girl.

A face appeared over the ridge, followed by two more. The one in the lead walked directly to Mark, holding out his hand.

'Good morning,' he said, his French accent clipped but still obvious. 'I'm Detective Inspector Luc Callanach. I'm assuming it was you who called this in?' Mark nodded. 'Let's get clear of the scene. How are you doing?'

'Don't really know,' Mark said. 'Better than that girl, I guess.'

Better than the girl, indeed, Callanach thought, hoping death had found her accidentally, wondering how much time he would spend staring at her face in photos on the incident room board. Did anyone ever sense it, he wondered, when they awoke on the morning they were destined to die? Did they take one extra glance in the mirror before they dashed from their homes to their jobs or studies, feeling that something in the universe had shifted? In a momentary burst of anger, he hated Scotland's chill air, its damp and greyness. The girl had perished in the freezing cold, watching her last breaths wisp into the air. It was no way to go. A bitter, stark and lonely passing. He could only hope she had been unaware that it was coming.

Chapter Three

Five months into her promotion, Detective Chief Inspector Ava Turner was still suffering from chronic impostor syndrome. It wasn't having so many people under her command, or the meetings she was expected to attend, nor the new office. It was simply that she no longer felt able to hang around in the incident room, drinking coffee and dissecting the day's events, having a bit of a laugh when circumstances allowed it. What she liked even less was the pressure of balancing the public well-being with Police Scotland's magically shrinking budgets. It felt as if the word 'no' had become her go-to response recently. Could they afford another expert for a certain case? No. Could the Major Investigation Team have a few more uniformed officers to help with enquiries? No. Could they trial some new software technology to filter CCTV footage? What the hell do you think the answer to that is? It wasn't that Ava regretted taking the promotion. It was more that every step up the ladder turned her dreams of doing good and solving crimes into something that felt more like a dripping tap of disappointment.

Whilst her professional life was being lived in an increasingly public space, her private life had taken on a positively desolate quality. The women and men from MIT felt the distance between themselves and their Detective Chief Inspector was too great to invite her for their occasional trips to the pub, and Ava would have felt obliged to make an excuse even if an invitation had been extended. Her peers were too busy with children or spouses to want to socialise after work. The youngest of her rank in her mid-thirties and as yet unmarried, Ava had no such distractions. Her best friend was in the throes of a new relationship hotter than a Carolina Reaper chilli pepper and would be unavailable until either she or her latest girlfriend remembered that the rest of the world was still functioning beyond their bedroom door. The price of success, apparently, was endlessly long evenings. Ava stared at her office phone, knowing better than to want it to ring, understanding that her need to be occupied could only come at someone else's cost.

Detective Sergeant Lively, in his late fifties and unaware of the concept of political correctness, appeared without knocking. Ava considered reminding him that announcing his intention to enter was commonly considered good manners, but was too pleased to have company to issue any sort of reprimand.

'Did you find DI Callanach?' Ava asked.

'I did. We checked the men's toilets first. He's usually to be found not far from a mirror. Surprisingly though in this instance he was out doing some actual detective work, ma'am.'

'Thanks for that, DS Lively. If you've finished your jibes you might like to tell me what case your commanding officer is attending,' Ava said.

Lively grinned. He and Callanach didn't have the best of relationships to begin with although more recently they'd settled for casual avoidance and occasional insults. 'A body's been found in the hills up at Arthur's Seat. There'll have to be an investigation but initial reports are that no foul play was involved. The pathologist has been to the scene. There are no obvious injuries or signs of violence. The body's been taken for autopsy. Only outstanding matter is identification. Once the victim's name is ascertained and the family has been informed, looks like it'll be a straight forward case. Nothing to bother you with, I'm sure.'

'Even so, would you ask DI Callanach to brief me once he gets back? I'd like to keep up to date with it,' Ava said. She looked at the mug in DS Lively's hand. 'I don't suppose there's any chance that's for me?' She smiled.

Lively took a long sip. 'Sorry ma'am, I'd have made you one, only I know that's frowned upon these days. Wouldn't want anyone to think you expected the rank and file to make you coffee. Flies in the face of modern policing, that does.' He left.

Ava leaned back in her chair, cursing the adrenalin her body had generated at the mention of a new investigation. It was a sick and sad indictment on policing that they should become bored rather than delighted when they had nothing to do, but there it was. It was tragic that a soul had perished up on Arthur's Seat, and Ava was grateful there was no suggestion of criminal involvement, but she needed something to occupy her other than signing off on the annual MIT dinner.

Some humorist had arranged for it to take place at a French restaurant this year – a sarcastic homage to DI Callanach, she imagined – his half-French half-Scottish ancestry still the butt of as many jokes as when he'd joined Police Scotland from Interpol a year earlier. Even his accent had paled into insignificance compared to the mickey-taking he'd had to endure when his squad had found out about his history as a model. Callanach had the sort of face it was hard not to stare at, and women regularly did. His dark eyes, long eyelashes, strong jaw and olive skin were never destined to fit in with the crowd, a fact Ava found constantly amusing when they socialised. Or when they used to socialise, Ava corrected herself. Since her promotion they'd played an awkward game of saying they really should do something together soon, never defining what or when.

She had one hand on her phone to call Callanach for an update as it rang in her fingers. She snatched it to her ear. 'Turner,' she said.

'Goodness me, could you not answer the phone like that, please? I'd rather not have people contacting the Major Investigation Team feeling as if you're mid-crisis before they've even introduced themselves. We're not mid-crisis, are we?' Detective Superintendent Overbeck asked.

'No, ma'am,' Ava said. 'Sorry. I was just about to . . .'

'Good, good. I have the shortlisted applicants for the open Detective Inspector position. I thought you should have a chance to look through them before we interview so I'll email the list to you this afternoon. If you could let me have your thoughts some time tomorrow that would be helpful. You were invited to drinks with the City Fellows this evening but I gather you're not attending. Why is that?'

'Oh, that's this evening? I've got a physiotherapist appointment. Didn't want to take any time off work for it, so I arranged it in the evening. It'll be another month if I cancel tonight,' Ava said, glad the Superintendent was quizzing her by phone rather than in person. In spite of years watching other people lie convincingly during interviews, Ava still hadn't honed that particular skill.

'Fucking right you shouldn't take time off work for a quick massage. Too late to change it now I suppose, but in future you need to remember that this is how the game's played. Don't miss the next one. And keep the overtime levels low again next month. We're within budget for once, which means I'm not getting shit from the board. I'd like to keep it that way,' Overbeck sniped.

'Yes, ma'am,' Ava said, already talking to a dead line. She dropped Dr Ailsa Lambert, Edinburgh's Chief Pathologist, an email asking for an update on the body at Arthur's Seat, then allowed herself the guilty pleasure of checking what films were on at the cinema. She preferred the reruns of old classics that occasionally made the late night showings, but right now she'd settle for anything mindless with a large popcorn. Luck was with her. There was an 11pm showing of Sergio Leone's *Once Upon a Time in The West*. Ava had a date with Charles Bronson, which was an improvement on another night home alone, and was close to a lottery win compared with the City Fellows' drinks party. There was tedious, then there was being called 'dearie' by eighty-year-old men who felt entitled to ask you to fetch them another drink just because you happened to be a different gender to them, and who wanted to talk golf handi-caps while you stood silently and looked impressed. Detective Superintendent Overbeck might have become adept at playing those promotion inducing games, but Ava was both less tolerant and less ambitious.

Her door opened again and DS Lively reappeared.

'Would you give me a break?' Ava sighed. 'If you've come to taunt me about the coffee, can I recommend . . .' She caught the look on his face. The usually sour, perpetually hard-done-by grimace was slack but his neck was drawn in tight, his throat working hard but producing no sound. DS Lively was, she realised, doing his damnedest not to cry. 'Tell me,' she said.

'It's DCI Begbie,' Lively said. 'I'm sorry.'

Ava stood up, knowing what the look on her detective sergeant's face meant, needing to hear him say the words anyway. 'Stop apologising, Lively, and just say it.'

'Ma'am, I'm not sure what happened. His car's been found. Too late to do anything. The Chief's dead.'

Ava felt a stab of pain in her chest. She was winded, crushed, the sentiment producing a remarkable physical effect. Her former commanding officer and decades-long friend was gone.

Chapter Four

Out at Gipsy Brae recreation ground, north of the city, the wind sliced sideways. It carried away voices and notebooks, whipping hair and leaving the landscape stark. The road had been cordoned off before the entrance to the park. Ava sat in her parked car, delaying the walk to where Begbie's vehicle was lit up in the distance. The recently retired Detective Chief Inspector George Begbie had been a policeman's policeman. Crabby at times, long-suffering, straight to the point and a champion of victims. In all the years Ava had worked with him, she never once saw him lose sight of what mattered. Somewhere at the heart of every case, someone had been hurt or had lost something. The Chief had fought for those people with all his considerable might, ignoring the brass bearing down from above, paying no attention to the press, oblivious to the politicians. He'd been as sharp as a pin and never expected a single officer to work more hours than he himself put in.

It was Begbie who had saved Ava from the misogyny that might have cost her a career as a detective, giving her a post on the Major Investigation Team, promoting her against more obvious candidates, even suspending her not long ago while her name was cleared regarding a breach of protocol. She knew it had hurt him to do that. They had evolved from colleagues to firm friends over late nights at crime scenes and early mornings when they were short-staffed. Even as a junior officer, Begbie had never excluded her from meetings, seeing her potential. If the rest of the squad liked and admired him, Ava had loved him like a favourite uncle. One who had occasionally shouted at her and made her work three days straight without sleep but, nonetheless, he was most of the reason she'd stuck with a career in policing. She didn't want to believe he was gone.

Ava locked her car and went on foot, wondering why George Begbie, who favoured warm pubs and comfy chairs, had chosen this barren place to say his final goodbye to the world. Staring out across the North Sea with Cramond Island to his left, Granton Harbour on the right, and nothing but vast grey skies reflected on icy water, it was a horribly bleak ending for such an oversized personality.

Ava hung back at the top of the small road that led down to the sea allowing access for caravans and maintenance trucks, now also to Begbie's ancient Land Rover. He had parked it away from the footpaths, facing the waves. No one would voluntarily have gone close to a lone male sitting in a vehicle, especially such an intimidatingly large figure. Ava put on a white suit, shoe covers and gloves, for what little good it would do. A determination of suicide had already been made, subject to autopsy. A snake of piping had been disconnected from the car window and lay still on the grass, malevolent even now. Tenting had been erected to protect the scene – more from prying eyes than to preserve evidence – and the busy silhouettes of Scenes of Crime Officers were bustling.

Walking down the gentle grass slope, hands in pockets, Ava was mindful that the light had gone from the day and soon a full lighting rig would be required to process the scene. A young Sergeant, his uniform immaculate, face a picture of concern, walked towards her.

'Do you have your ID on you, please?' he said.

Ava handed it over, too tired to explain who she was.

'Major Investigation Team?' the officer asked. 'I'd hardly have thought this was your territory.'

'Sergeant, if you've finished telling a Detective Chief Inspector where she should be and what she should be doing, perhaps you could chase that dog walker over there off this grass. And you address me as ma'am or DCI. Now get going.'

'Yes, ma'am,' he said, pulling his coat up around his neck and heading off into the wind.

Ava took a deep breath. She hated rudeness, particularly the brand that grew from superiority. If Begbie had taught her nothing else in all the years he'd been her commanding officer, it was that rank came with a responsibility to be kind and to listen. She reined in her emotions.

'Where's Dr Lambert?' Ava asked a passing Scenes of Crime Officer.

'Busy elsewhere,' the officer said, stepping around Ava to take a new pair of plastic gloves from a box. Ava took her by the arm.

'She's busy? The deceased is a former Detective Chief Inspector. He spent twenty years attending crimes scenes like this and now he's not a priority? I want to know what happened here. There's no way George Begbie committed suicide.'

The officer clenched her jaw, pulled her arm out of Ava's grasp and took a step away.

'A minibus skidded on a patch of ice and left the road half an hour ago, carrying eight children. Two of those are fatalities. Dr Lambert is making that the priority. If you'll excuse me.'

'I hadn't heard,' Ava said to the Scenes of Crime Officer's back. 'I'm sorry.'

'DCI Turner?' a voice said from behind her. A man stepped in offering his hand as the SOCO retreated. 'I'm Chief Inspector Dimitri. Never had the pleasure of working with George Begbie but I understand he was well respected by his men. Why don't we let forensics do their bit? I always feel like a spare part while they're processing. We could wait in my car if you like.'

'That won't be necessary but I appreciate the offer,' Ava said. 'I'd like to see the body in situ, though. I take it this is your patch.'

'I was assigned to deal with it, although it seems unlikely to be an ongoing police matter.' He paused and looked towards Begbie's car. 'I've lost people I worked with and it's hard. The trick is not to turn it into a crusade. As soon as you start overthinking it, you lead yourself in all the wrong directions. I'm not trying to put you off, but the best thing to do really would be to leave it to us. You can count on me to look after him, and any information you want, you only have to ask.'

Ava glanced at the Chief Inspector she'd heard of but never met in the flesh. He was so softly spoken that she'd found herself craning her neck forward to listen. Close-up, she realised his eyes were so pale a shade of blue that they were hard to look away from. His hair was white but not by virtue of his age. She guessed him to be in his mid-fifties although his face appeared sculpted from some organic material that didn't age. Before she could respond to his suggestion, a stretcher appeared from the vicinity of the car with a body bag on it. It was carried to a waiting van for transportation to the city mortuary. Whatever assumptions had been made at the scene, there would still have to be an autopsy.

'Let me walk you back to your car,' Chief Inspector Dimitri said.

'No need.' Ava shook her head. 'I'd like to inform George

Begbie's wife myself, if you don't mind. I appreciate your officers will follow up and take a statement from her. But tonight . . . I know her. He'd have preferred it to come from a friend.'

'I understand that,' Dimitri said. 'The facts, those few we have, are that a couple walking the coast path were aware of the sound of the engine, walked past to cut up to the road and noticed the hose running from the exhaust. They wrenched open a door – apparently the rear passenger side was unlocked – but by then it was too late. They called for an ambulance and police. The first responders asked for a plate check and that's how we ID'd him. I'm afraid to say it all looks tragically standard, if you can think of it that way. There's a bottle of whisky, empty, on the front passenger seat. The radio was playing. No signs of a struggle, broken windows or door locks.'

'Thank you,' Ava muttered. 'I appreciate your kindness. My squad will be devastated. You'll let me know what you conclude?'

'Of course. He's in good hands, I promise,' Dimitri said.

Ava nodded, shoved her hands down deep into her pockets and walked away, pausing before climbing into her car to look back down towards the crashing sea, a force as destructive and brutal as the news she was about to deliver to George Begbie's wife.

The Begbies' house was out east of the city at Portobello, where St Mark's Place met Argyle Crescent. A traditionally built home, with stone graduating from brown to black by years and precipitation, it stood out from its neighbours by virtue of the miniature turret rising at one side. Ava remembered the Chief joking about how his home was literally his castle, and it looked exactly like a tiny replica of one. He and his wife had loved the place, moving there a decade ago and as far as Ava knew they had been planning to remain there for the foreseeable future. A future that had been stopped firmly in its tracks. The house had been filled with warmth and laughter whenever Ava had visited in the past. This trip would mark the end of all that. It would never be the same again. Not for her, and certainly not for Glynis Begbie once Ava had delivered the dreadful news. She waited in her car a while as Mark Knopfler sang of jackals and ravens, half expecting Begbie's wife-cum-widow to step out of her front door, a sixth sense leading her onto the street and into Ava's path. She didn't appear. Ava clicked off the radio, made sure her clothing was tidy, and walked the few steps up the front path to the door.

'Ava! How lovely to see you, my darling. George didn't warn me or I'd have baked. Honestly, that man. So distracted all the time . . .'

'Glynis,' Ava cut in. There was a second when she said nothing, that television moment as Ava always thought of it, where somehow just the physical presence of a police officer unexpectedly on the doorstep was all the omen required to trigger knowledge and grief. It didn't come.

'Come on in, quickly now. You'll freeze out there. Probably just my age but I feel the cold all the time these days. Give me your coat. I'll call George on his mobile and get him back. He'll kick himself if he misses you.'

'Glynis,' Ava said again. 'Let's sit down.' There it was. That fractional falter of her smile, the double blink before she responded.

'Of course. Come into the lounge. Forgive the mess, I was just writing some cards. Are you sure you wouldn't like a cup of something hot?'

Ava sat down on the sofa and waited until Glynis had perched on an armchair.

'I'm sorry to have to bring you this news, but George has been found dead in his car. The initial indications are that it was suicide.'

Glynis' mouth slackened, her brow drew in. There was a

19

small shake of her head. Ava had seen it too many times, that moment of defiance, the refusal to accept the news of a death. She waited for Glynis to speak. It was always a question first. Where? When? How? Most often in a suicide: Why?

'Something was wrong,' Glynis said, her voice a thin tremor in the air.

Ava stared at her. 'His heart again? Had his doctor given him bad news?'

Glynis shook her head. 'Not that George told me. As far as I knew he was recovering well. But for the last couple of weeks he's been, I don't know, sullen. Not like him at all.'

'I'm sorry to ask this, but did you suspect he might be a risk to himself? Had he talked about it?' Ava asked.

'No. No, I'd have told someone. Where is he now?'

'On his way to the . . . he's going to Ailsa Lambert's office. She'll take good care of him,' Ava said.

'It's too late for that, isn't it? His dinner's in the oven. Plenty of green veg. Nothing high in fat or sugar. He hated it, the diet since his heart attack. Still, he always cleared his plate without complaint. Before, we used to have a cream cake every Friday, as a treat, you know. Hasn't had one for six months. I think that was the thing he missed most.'

'Glynis, let me make some calls for you. You should have your family here.'

'I'd like to go and see George first if you don't mind. There'll be an autopsy if I'm not mistaken?'

'Yes,' Ava whispered.

'How did he do it?' Glynis asked, her mouth a tightly pressed trembling line across her face.

'Car exhaust fumes,' Ava said. Glynis tried to rise from the chair, wobbled, took her seat again. 'Let me get you a glass of water. Don't try to move.' She walked to the kitchen and began opening cupboards to find a glass when feet shuffled in behind her.

'Would he have suffered? I want the truth, Ava. I was married to a policeman for thirty-five years. There's no point lying to me.'

Ava ran the cold tap to make sure the water was fresh as she thought how to answer the question. George Begbie's wife was no fool, and the detail of the cases MIT handled wouldn't have passed her by. Such was the baggage that came with marrying a police officer.

'Headache, nausea. He'd have felt faint. Probably there'd have been a sense of panic if he was still conscious when his body recognised it was starved of oxygen. He may have had chest pains, especially given his medical history. Possibly some sort of seizure at the end,' Ava said. 'I'm so sorry. I wish . . .'

'Please don't,' Glynis said. 'I'll take that water now.'

Ava handed her the glass and leaned back against the kitchen cupboards rubbing her temples.

'You said something was wrong. Can you be any more specific?' Ava asked.

'There were a few late night phone calls. A couple to his mobile, at least one on the landline. He never told me who they were from. Made a joke about it to distract me. Then a package was left on our doorstep once when we were out shopping. No label. I told him he should call the police. He knew he was still a target given the number of people he'd put inside. He took the package to his shed, told me it was some rubbishy free samples. I always knew when he was lying.'

'And you think whatever it was might have been enough reason for him to have . . .?' Ava broke off.

'George hated suicides. Said it was the cruellest thing to do to another human being. If you're right and that's what he did, then I have no idea who the man was I've been living with for more than half my life. I'd like to go and see him now please.'

★　★　★

21

They arrived at Edinburgh City Mortuary half an hour later. Dr Ailsa Lambert met them at the door, greeting Glynis with a hug. Ailsa held back her own tears as she showed them into the autopsy suite. There was a body beneath a sheet on a steel table.

'I'm sorry I can't offer anything more appropriate than this room. Everywhere else is in use. Are you sure you're ready to do this, Glynis? I can formally identify him. You don't need to make this your last memory of George,' Ailsa said.

'I need to,' Glynis replied, crushing a handkerchief in her hand and staring at the concealed bulk of the man she had loved for decades.

Ailsa pulled back the sheet to reveal naked head and shoulders. There was an intake of breath from Glynis. Ava reached out an arm to put around her shoulders, tempted to look away but there was no scope for cowardice when Glynis was having to be so brave. Still, it was dreadful to see. Death was never so final as when you had to stare it in the face. Ava hated the slackness of the Chief's jaw and the way the flesh of his cheeks had rolled back towards his ears, as if his body couldn't be bothered to pretend to be human any more. Life had literally deserted him.

'Why is he so red?' Glynis asked.

'Carbon monoxide poisoning can do that after death,' Ailsa said. 'Can you confirm that it is George?'

'It is,' Glynis said. 'Oh God, it really is.' She turned around and walked through the door into the corridor. Ava let her go.

'Have you had a chance to have a look at him, Ailsa? Can you give me any information?' Ava asked.

'I've had a few minutes, that's all. It's been a busy day,' Ailsa said, covering Begbie's face once again with the sheet.

'I heard,' Ava said. 'I'm sorry. You must have a lot of families needing you at the moment.'

'I do, but George was my friend. I was working with him

22

when you were still in school. Never thought I'd be asked to perform his autopsy. But the symptoms are classic suicide by inhalation of carbon monoxide. That cherry red colour of his skin? Means he had to have breathed the gas in. If you're looking for me to tell you someone killed him and posed him there, then I can't. He has no injuries. He wasn't restrained in the car. He hadn't defended himself.'

'Nothing?' Ava asked. 'Really Ailsa? You knew him better than me, and I know the Chief wouldn't have taken this way out.'

'You don't know anything of the sort. People break, Ava. They get bad news, they suffer a loss, they stop working and find their lives suddenly empty. They look in the mirror one day and find they got old and that scares the hell out of them.'

'It's cowardly,' Ava said. 'It was beneath him.'

'Suicide is the most human and lonely of acts. It's not for you to judge him,' Ailsa said.

There was a pause. Ava reached a hand out to the huge man beneath the sheet, drew it back again and turned to the wall.

'I know. I'm sorry. I didn't mean it, Ailsa. I just feel like I failed him somehow. I should have visited more often after his heart attack. I should have made sure he was coping. I just carried on, always too busy.'

'When there's a suicide the people left have a tendency to make it about themselves – what they didn't do, or say, or remember. It's not about you, Ava. It's not about Glynis, or their children, or anyone else. It's about the place George found himself in. I'm not expecting to find anything in the autopsy to be honest, although I'll be liaising with his doctor to check any recent diagnoses. His body was unmarked except for this.' Ailsa walked around to lift the sheet from the left side of George Begbie's body. 'Here, on his inner wrist – you can barely make it out now because of the reddening – but it looks like letters, albeit clumsily drawn. Capital N next to a small c. I suspect they've been scratched into his arm.'

'Means nothing to me,' Ava said. 'N c. I'll check it out. I'd better get Glynis home now. She's been more stoic than I'd ever have expected, although of course she's in shock. That combined with being the wife of a long-serving police officer. She probably spent years half-expecting that knock at the door. It'll take a while to sink in. She'll need to contact the rest of the family, too. Let me know, would you, when you have the full autopsy results.'

'Of course. You should go home and get some rest, too. If days like this teach us anything, it's that you never know what's coming. Every moment counts.'

Chapter Five

'I w-want to volunteer,' the man said, his Adam's apple working almost completely independently of the remainder of his body.

'You know they won't pay you, right? There aren't any proper jobs going at the moment,' a woman wearing clothes more usually seen at an eye-assaulting runway from London Fashion Week told him.

'I know that. I'm not here for the money. I just really w-want to help. It's a good thing you do here,' he said.

'You've got some alternative means of funding yourself that allows you not to have to work for money, do you?' the woman asked, looking from his haircut down to his shoes in a manner that signalled disbelief.

'I w-work somew-where else as w-well,' he mumbled. 'I just thought that a few hours a w-week might be a contribution. Even if I'm just making coffee or filing paperw-work.'

She sighed, pulling a sheet of paper from a drawer and clicking the end of a pen as she waited for him to finish the sentence.

'I can take your name but I'm not sure there's anything for you.'

'That's fine, Sian, I'll take it from here thank you,' another woman said, placing a gentle hand on fashion disaster's shoulder and smiling softly. 'Why don't you come into my office? I'm Cordelia Muir. You are?'

'Jeremy,' he said, feeling the weight lift as he followed her. She was somewhere between forty and fifty although good bone structure, careful moisturising and a trim figure made it hard to guess precisely. The media had listed several different ages for her, all to be taken with a pinch of salt, but they were universally agreed on the good her charity was doing in a variety of African countries. Crystal was a clean water initiative that relied on educating communities in how to build wells, then funding them to teach their neighbouring village so that a network of safe, sustainable water systems spread like a life-giving spider web, changing lives and securing futures.

'So, Jeremy, I have to say it's very generous of you to offer to volunteer. Sian does our day-to-day administration and she has a fairly rigid view of the world, but she doesn't mean any harm. I hope she didn't put you off, but she was right to point out that we can't pay you. We have limited resources and I make sure that as great a percentage of donations as possible reaches its intended destination. I'm not much of a one for expensive offices or endless amounts of staff.'

'That's w-why I'm here,' Jeremy said, head down towards his lap. 'I read that about you. It's the reason I'd like to help. You seem . . .' he blinked a few times, chewing his bottom lip. 'You seem good.'

'That's very kind of you,' she said. 'And if you're serious about helping then I'd love to have you here. Can you tell me a little bit about yourself?'

Jeremy flushed, took a deep breath, and steeled himself to make eye contact as he spoke.

'Twenty-five,' he said. 'I like to help people.' He spoke slowly, deliberately, every word considered. 'I w-was fostered. Nice people. I'd like to give something back. Other times I do some gardening w-work. Not much call for that in w-winter.'

'I guess not,' Cordelia said softly. 'I know what you mean about wanting to put something back. I was lucky. My parents were both Kenyan but from wealthy families. They moved me here when I was just four, at a time when racial integration was still a work in progress. My father worked in the finance sector. I was sent to a decent school, had holidays abroad, got through university without any debt. After my degree I sailed into the corporate machine, making piles of money for people who didn't need any more than they already had. I suppose I got fed up and wanted to find more of a purpose, and here I am. Doing something to improve the lives of people in Africa felt like joining up the ends of a circle for me. You know, I think you're going to be a real asset around here. What matters to me more than anything is working with people who have a positive attitude and the desire to do good. Why don't you come in next week, spend a few hours getting to know what we do and where you can fit in, and if you like us we can make it more regular? In the meantime, fill in a personnel form with some details and the name of a referee if you have one.'

'I do,' Jeremy said, allowing himself a small smile and a nod.

'How about I make you a coffee before you go, just so you can experience how badly I do it. Everyone here will be delighted to have someone other than me in charge of the kettle.'

She handed Jeremy a form requiring basic details – address, National Insurance number, telephone contact, next of kin for emergency purposes – and a pen, then she disappeared out to rattle cups and teaspoons around in a sink. He filled the form in quickly then glanced around Cordelia Muir's office. A family photo took pride of place on her desk. She was with her children. An older girl and a boy, taken a little while ago judging by the changes in Cordelia. Research had told Jeremy that her daughter was away at university while her son was attending sixth form college in Edinburgh. He wondered if she would mind him picking the photograph up, watching her through the glass partition as she opened the fridge door to put a carton of milk away.

'You have beautiful children,' Jeremy said as she walked back in holding two mugs.

'Thank you,' she replied, putting the steaming liquid down in front of him, showing no concern about him holding the precious image. 'My husband passed away a couple of years ago. He was terminally ill when we had that photo taken. My daughter has coped better than my son. Randall is only seventeen. I think boys need a man around to help them through those transitional years.' She smiled.

'My father died when I w-was two,' Jeremy said, putting the photo back down on the desk. 'He and my mother were in a coach crash. My foster parents tried their hardest but teenage years are tough. I w-wasn't very forgiving.'

'I'm sure you were no worse than any other teenage boy, and it must have been harder for you than most. Your parents would have been proud of you now.' She smiled. 'You've filled in the form already? Wonderful. How about you come in Monday morning? I'm starting a new project and I'd appreciate some help with it. Nothing very glamorous I'm afraid, but I'd love to have you here.'

Jeremy beamed, taking a sip of coffee with shaking hands.

'That w-would be great,' he said. 'Thank you, Mrs Muir.'

'Cordelia. First name terms only in here,' she said. 'I feel as if fate brought you to us, Jeremy. I'm a great believer in fate. Welcome to the team.'

★ ★ ★

DI Callanach was waiting in Ava Turner's office at the police station. He stood as she entered.

'Luc,' she said. 'What's the news on the body at Arthur's Seat?'

'Nothing much yet, ma'am,' Callanach said, sitting once she'd waved him back into his chair.

'Could you please not call me ma'am? I mean, yes in front of other people, but not when it's just us. You know I'm uncomfortable with it.'

'I'm uncomfortable without it,' he replied. 'I heard about the Chief. I wanted to see how you're doing and check if there's anything I can help with.'

'You want to get falling down drunk with me later, make sure I get home safely, hold my hair while I throw up then sit next to me all night to make sure I don't choke?' Ava put her head on the desk in front of her. 'God, I'm sorry. I don't know where that came from. Does everyone know?'

'Sergeant Lively knows,' Luc said. 'So it might as well have been publicly broadcast. And I will, if that's what you need me to do.' Ava looked confused. 'Hold your hair and make sure you don't choke.'

'I'm sure you have better things to do with your evening,' Ava said, guessing he probably didn't. Callanach had model looks that never failed to turn heads in public, but a false rape allegation made by a coworker during his time as an Interpol agent had made him reclusive in his private life. 'I have work to do anyway. Tell me about the girl at Arthur's Seat.'

'Her name's Lily Eustis. Nineteen years of age. In a gap year before university mainly because she was working to save money for her tuition fees. She was due to begin studying medicine next September at St Andrews. Her family has been notified. Mum, dad, one sister. I responded to the call but it's not looking like a matter for the Major Investigation Team. Initial findings are that cause of death was hypothermia.'

29

'How did she get all the way up there?' Ava asked.

'We don't have the answer to that yet. She doesn't own a car, lives with her parents. Apparently, she went out last night to meet a friend at a pub, and didn't come home. That's unusual but not completely unknown, although the parents say that normally she'd have phoned to let them know where she was staying.'

'Have you spoken to the friend?' Ava asked, scribbling notes.

'No one knows who it was. Parents suspect it was a male but they're not certain. Her sister has been calling Lily's friends but none of them have any further information.'

'Let's keep it with MIT for now. Ailsa should be doing Lily's autopsy as a priority. Keep me updated.'

Callanach stood up. 'Why don't you let me drop you home later?' he said. 'You can leave your car here. I'll pick you up and bring you back in tomorrow.'

'You think I'm incapable of driving now? I'm sad, Luc, not drunk,' Ava said. She sighed. 'God, I'm sorry. I'm not handling this very well. It was good of you to offer but I'll be fine, really. I have to update the squad about the Chief's death. They'll want what details I've got. Can you organise everyone into the briefing room for 3pm?'

'I can,' Callanach said. 'The drone footage from Lily Eustis' death will be available by then. I'll organise a copy for you to see after the briefing.'

'Good, then we can visit Ailsa at the mortuary together.' Ava's phone rang. Callanach made his way out. 'Hold on, Luc,' she called after him. 'You're sure?' she asked the person at the end of the phone. 'You checked her identification? No, don't show her up yet. I need to talk to him first. He's in my office. Give me five minutes. I'll call you back.'

Luc stood with his back against Ava's door, hands in his pockets, head to one side.

'Is it Astrid?' he asked. 'I knew she wouldn't leave me alone forever but walking in here, after what she did . . .'

'It's not her,' Ava said. She knew how hard it would have been for Luc to have faced Astrid — the woman who had set him up on a false rape charge. In many ways, seeing the woman waiting for him downstairs was going to be even worse. 'Luc, I don't know what's happened. She hasn't offered any explanation for why she's here, but your mother is downstairs.'

Luc ran a hand through his hair, looking for words but finding none.

'I don't want to see her,' he said finally, as Ava made her way around her desk to stand nearer to him.

'I understand,' Ava said. 'You've every right to feel like that. She abandoned you when you needed her . . .'

'It wasn't just abandonment. You couldn't possibly understand. I was accused of a rape I didn't commit. It was devastating. I wasn't even sure I had the strength to make it through to the trial. My mother was the one person who should have known, without question, that I didn't do it, that no part of me was so monstrous. When she left as I was going through the trial preparations, I even started to doubt myself. There were times when I thought that maybe I had raped Astrid and just invented another reality in my own mind. How could I have been innocent when my own mother couldn't bear to stay with me and support me through it?'

'Luc, I'm sorry this has come as such a shock. But she's here. Downstairs, right now. There must be a good reason why she's come. Don't you want to find out what that is?'

'Not particularly,' he replied.

'Do you want me to go down and talk to her first?' Ava offered.

'She changed her mobile number,' Luc said. 'I phoned her, left voicemails, texts. I emailed. I wrote letters. Every silence I got in return was a nail in the coffin of our relationship. It was months, Ava. Months from when she left to when the court case collapsed and I was told I was free to go. Even if I could understand why she wasn't able to support me before the trial, she's had more than a year to contact me since it ended. There's no excuse, no possible explanation for treating your own child like that.'

'Luc, please. I lost my mother. By the time I knew she was dying it was too late to get the years back when I'd been too busy, too obsessed with myself to spend time with her. I never had the chance to forgive her for all the petty, perceived slights of growing up. I don't want you to make the same mistake,' Ava said.

'Ava, this is my life, not yours. And these aren't perceived slights. These were body blows. I'm not making any mistakes,' he said.

'I get it. Really, I do. But go down there and face her. If nothing else, tell her how you feel. Find an ending to it all. There'll come a day when you need it,' she said. Luc walked towards the door. 'So you'll speak with her?'

'I'll treat her exactly the same way she treated me,' he said. 'I'll let her talk to her heart's content. She can beg for forgiveness, tell me she needs me, whatever. Then I'll cut her out of my life forever.'

Chapter Six

'I can't stay indoors any longer, Christian,' Lily's sister, Mina, whispered into her mobile. 'I'm getting out of this house once my parents are both asleep. Can you meet me?'

'Mina, your parents need you. If they wake up and find you gone, they'll be terrified,' he said. 'You know I'll come if you need me, but I'm not sure it's the right thing for you to be going out in the middle of the night.'

'It's suffocating me. Lily's room's right next to mine. Mum insists we keep the door wide open, as if shutting it pushes her further away. But I walk past it and see something of Lily's – a scarf, a pen, a bloody hair band for God's sake – and it starts again. Sometimes I feel like I'll never stop crying.'

'All right, I'll be there. Wait in the bus stop up the road from your house. Just do me a favour and leave your parents a note explaining that you needed a break. It's not fair to risk them finding an empty bedroom,' Christian said.

'You're right. I will. Just please come.' She rang off.

Christian went to shower and change his clothes. He'd spent the earlier part of the evening in a dive bar that held open mic evenings with a covert smoking room at the back and now his clothes reeked of cigarettes. Mina would hate it and he wanted to be able to comfort her the way she needed. Pulling on a denim shirt and black jeans, he wrapped a scarf around his neck and grabbed a thick duffle coat. He grabbed a book on the way out, throwing it casually onto the back seat. *The Legend of Sleepy Hollow* was one of next term's texts for Edinburgh University's Masters in US Literature course. Mina was always fascinated with what he was reading.

His car was the typical student vehicle. It had scraped through its most recent vehicle check, had the lowest insurance policy available and inside you could pretty much see the springs coming through the seats but it was functional and avoided breaking down, most days. Before he left his flat, he made two hot chocolates, put them in reusable takeout mugs (Mina was ever conscious of the environment), and picked up a bag of marshmallows he'd been saving. He couldn't do much to put a smile on Mina's face right now, but he could do that.

She was waiting for him in the rain, just her head poking out from the bus stop as Mina looked for his car. Christian pulled over and flashed his lights, wiping condensation off the inside of the passenger window so she could see it was him.

'Hey you,' he said, as she threw herself into the passenger seat. 'What do you want to do?'

'Could we just drive for a while?' Mina asked. 'I need to feel as if I'm moving. Everything else has stopped.'

'Sure,' he said, 'we don't even have to talk. Where are we going?'

'Take me as close as we can get to Arthur's Seat,' Mina said. 'I have to see. I want to figure out why the hell Lily did what she did.'

Christian put a cup of hot chocolate in her hands before setting off.

'Mina, are you sure about going to Arthur's Seat? I'm sure Lily would have hated the thought of you hurting yourself like this.'

'Yeah, well you never met her, so please don't tell me what she would or wouldn't have liked. Oh God, Christian, I'm so sorry. I don't know where that came from.' Mina looked away, out of the passenger window. 'I'm not sure I even know myself any more. Shit, listen, you can drop me off if you like. I'll understand if you just want to go home. And thank you for the hot chocolate. I don't deserve it. Or you.' Mina dashed an already rain-wet sleeve across her eyes.

Christian looked at her hunched shoulders, her hair that hadn't seen a shower or a brush in the two and a half days since her sister's body had been found, at her feet twisted in towards one another as if her body was literally trying to make itself disappear. He reached into the driver's door compartment and retrieved the marshmallows.

'I'm not going anywhere,' he said. 'But I am going to insist that you eat at least a dozen of these. You need sugar and you need a friend. You'll have to do more than snap at me for a second to make me desert you.' Mina turned her face back towards his and did her best to force a smile. 'If going up to Arthur's Seat is what you need, then that's what we'll do. There are no rights or wrongs when you lose someone you love. There's only getting through each day. Perhaps you will feel something. Let's find out.'

They drove for fifteen minutes, the traffic less of a problem than the driving rain, until Christian parked up on Queen's Drive as close as he could get by road to the area of Arthur's Seat that Mina had wanted to visit. It was utterly dark, even the light pollution from the city not daring to creep up the hillside. He killed the engine and sat in silence waiting for Mina to talk.

'What was Lily doing up there?' Mina whispered. 'She'd never talked about going there before. We climbed it as children, and I think she visited as part of a school trip once. But at night, in December?'

'Did you hear any more from the police?' Christian asked.

'They said we'd get the preliminary autopsy findings tomorrow. No other progress, though. No one's come forward to say they were with her. None of Lily's friends were aware who she was with.' She dunked a marshmallow in the hot chocolate, waited until it was half melted, then put it in her mouth. 'This is good,' she said. 'Thanks for coming to get me.'

'That's okay,' Christian said. 'I wanted to help. I just didn't know if you needed space or to be alone with your family.'

'I need to understand how she could leave me!' Mina blurted, pieces of marshmallow flying from her lips. She choked, leaning forward, spluttering hot chocolate across her jeans, giving up and dropping the cup into the footwell.

'Mina,' Christian said gently.

'I'm sorry, I'll clean it up,' she sobbed, both arms clutched across her stomach, hair hanging down over her face.

'Don't apologise. Just come here,' he said, sliding his left arm over her shoulders, the other hand pulling her right arm out from her body and towards him. He wrapped her in his arms, stroking her hair. 'It's okay to cry,' he whispered. 'I'm not going anywhere.'

Mina surrendered to the comfort, leaning her head against his chest, letting herself crumple. Christian rocked her gently as she cried, holding her safe, pressing his face into the top of her head, fighting the rushing tide of his own emotion. She was so fragile, and trying to absorb such an unbearably heavy blow. Minutes went by. Mina's sobbing abated, replaced with the involuntary hitching of her lungs. The more she tried to hold it in, the more wracked her body became.

'I can't do this,' she whispered, her breath raw in her throat. 'I'm never going to be able to let her go. It's like Mum has died, too. She aged right in front of me. It was like gravity distorted her face into some sort of grey mask. I can't even describe it.' Christian let her talk. He knew better than to tell her it was going to get better. He'd lost someone he loved and there was no comfort to give when it was all so new. Mina moved back to look him full in the face, pulling her knees up to her chest. 'I keep thinking, if she'd been ill would that have been better or worse. I could have said goodbye, held her hand. But I don't even know if . . . if she was scared. I mean, God, what if she wanted to die up there? Do you think it's possible that's why she went up there? How do people cope with this? It's like we've turned into a story about ourselves.' She sobbed again, her face a tortured version of the carefree girl Christian usually saw. 'They're fucking cutting her open. That's where she'll be now. Lily's lying on some metal tray somewhere, in pieces. I can't do anything to help her. I can't tell her I love her, I can't tell her not to be so stupid and selfish. I think I hate her. I hate her for leaving me. How can I hate her when she's dead? It's like everything inside me is rotting.'

Mina threw open the door and bolted, reaching a ditch before stopping to vomit. Christian ran behind, catching her in time to stop her falling forward with the spasms of her stomach. She retched twice more before her body relaxed and allowed her to stand upright.

'I should get you home,' he said. 'This isn't helping. You've got to take it a day – an hour – at a time. It'll help when the police have some answers. Come on,' he said, one arm around her shoulders as he guided her back to the car. 'I'll be here, night or day, whenever you need to talk.'

'Thank you,' Mina rasped. 'I'm so grateful to have you. Promise you won't leave me. I can't make it through this without you.'

Chapter Seven

Callanach threw his keys down and went into the kitchen, reaching instinctively for a coffee pot and fighting his desire to open the bottle of single malt he'd had in the cupboard for months. He wasn't usually much of a spirits drinker but if ever there was cause to change that, he was entitled now.

His mother, Véronique, was sitting on the couch, coat buttoned to the chin, handbag on her lap with both hands gripping the handle as if it might fly away. Callanach stared at her silhouette against the picture window of his apartment in Albany Street, just a couple of minutes' walk from the busy restaurants and bars of York Place, not that he went out much. He'd spent fifteen months making the apartment his own since beginning work with Police Scotland in Edinburgh. In all, it had been two years since his suspension from Interpol when a colleague had made the rape allegation that had stopped his career in its tracks. A few friends had stood by him, fewer colleagues, but what had hurt most was being abandoned by his mother. Even so, he still loved her. That was why he couldn't let her back into his life. It was hard enough getting over the pain she'd caused him the first time. He couldn't risk going through it all again.

He stirred the coffee, wondering if his mother still took milk in hers. She was painfully thin, that was the first thing he'd noticed. The last time he'd seen her had been in Lyon. He'd been on bail with severe restrictions on where he could go and who he could see. She'd turned up at his door with an overnight bag and a speech about how it would all turn out all right, how the allegations would vanish into thin air. Her prediction had been wrong. Even now, his world was still askew. His mother had stayed with him for two weeks, each day more tense than the one before as they'd waited for the French prosecutor to see sense, to realise it was all a vicious lie, borne of a woman's obsession with him.

His mother had withdrawn from him, in person at first, growing quieter each day, the hope draining from her almost visibly, then she'd left and he'd heard nothing more from her. Even when Astrid Borde had decided against attending court to give evidence and a not guilty verdict had been entered, his mother still had not contacted him. It was as if he was dead to her. Callanach had grieved for the loss of her from his life. Now here she was, a ghostly, diminished version of the woman he remembered, barely able to meet his eyes, even her voice a whisper of the confident, laughing person in his memories.

'Milk? Sugar?' Callanach asked her in French, translating back to English in his head as if he'd never lived in France at all.

'Neither, thank you,' his mother responded politely.

He carried two mugs into the lounge and put them on the coffee table between them, choosing the chair opposite her, keeping a barrier between them. He took his phone from his pocket and left it on the arm of the chair. He'd left Ava to brief the squad but had agreed to meet her at the city mortuary at 10pm. That gave him just one hour, not that he was concerned. Whatever his mother had to tell him after all this time could be said in the space of sixty minutes. It wasn't as if anything would change now.

'I like your apartment,' she said, sipping her coffee, holding the mug as if it were an anchor. Callanach didn't respond. Back at the police station he'd walked down the stairs from his office to reception in a daze, convinced there had been a case of mistaken identity or that it was some stupid prank by his team who had no idea what minefield they were treading in. But there she had been. Dressed in black, her dark hair still long but streaked with grey. She had been a beauty in her youth, but now dense shadows hung under her eyes, and her mouth was turned down as if pegged to her chin. She had stared at her shoes as she'd greeted him.

'Luc,' she'd said. 'Can we talk?'

'All right, Véronique,' he'd replied, holding the door to the street open for her, knowing he had to get her out of the station. She had no place in his new life. He didn't want the memory of her in his office, and he couldn't bring himself to address her as mother. She was not that any more, that had been made quite clear to him through her desertion. He had walked her to his car and they'd driven through the dwindling rush hour without sharing a word. Now here she was and he had no idea what to say to her, and no sense of what she could possibly want from him.

'Are you staying in Edinburgh?' he asked, glancing out of the window.

'At the Radisson,' she said. 'I've booked in for a week.'

'Are you in Scotland on holiday, then?' Callanach asked.

'No,' she said, finally setting her bag down on the floor. 'I'm only here to see you, Luc. I'm glad it worked out for you. Do you like Scotland?'

'I miss France,' he said. 'But I'm used to it now. It rains a lot, and it took me a year to get used to the accent.'

Véronique allowed herself a half-smile at that, reaching her right hand across her left to take hold of her wedding ring. She still wore it, in spite of the decades since his father had died. Callanach had been only four years old at the time and had no more memory of him than a large man, soft voiced, always warm, constantly laughing. It was a blur.

'When your father spoke too fast I couldn't understand his Scottish accent, even after years together. It's still hard coming back here,' she said.

'Why have you come back?' Callanach asked.

Véronique rubbed one hand across her eyes. He waited. That wasn't difficult. He'd waited so long already that a few more minutes was nothing.

'I never wanted this to happen,' she said. 'If I could take it all back, I would.'

'Is that it?' Callanach asked, his voice cold and low. 'You've come here to tell me you wish it had played out differently?'

'It was complicated,' his mother said, picking at the hem of her skirt. 'You were so closed off, you wouldn't talk to me about what was happening, then the medical evidence came out. And you didn't comment when they first interviewed you . . .'

'That didn't mean I was guilty,' he said.

'It wasn't just about you,' she said, tears forming as she reached a shaky hand into her bag to find a handkerchief.

'Who else was it about? You? Were you embarrassed of me? Exactly when was it you tried me and found me guilty? Before you even came to Lyon, or did you wait to hear my version of events before writing me off?' He was raising his voice, keeping the words slow, making sure they impacted as hard as they could. He had waited the best part of two years to have his say and he wasn't going to rush it now.

'Astrid came to see me. I never found a way to tell you,' his mother said. 'By then you seemed not to be talking to me anyway, and I couldn't find the words. So I left. Then there were those photos of her injuries. Someone put them in the post to me.'

'You spoke to Astrid and never told me? Did you arrange it with her?'

'No, no Luc, I would never have done that. She must have followed me from your apartment one day. I was going shopping and this woman stopped me in the street. She said she needed to talk to me about the case. At first I thought she was a journalist, or perhaps even someone from the prosecutor's office. I thought I might be able to speak on your behalf, make them change their minds, so we went for coffee. We were already sitting down when she told me her name. I got up to leave but she said that if I went she would make it even worse for you. I was so concerned that I sat back down and told her I'd listen.'

'I don't think I want to hear this,' Callanach said. 'How could you have been so stupid?'

'She seemed so calm. I couldn't reconcile the woman you'd described with the person talking to me. She was quiet, conservatively dressed, hair tied back, no makeup. I remember thinking this can't be her. She told me that all she wanted was to explain what had happened from her perspective, to get it out of her system. I kept thinking that maybe if I let her, she would drop the prosecution. It seemed worth ten minutes of my time.'

'After everything I'd told you about how manipulative she was? About her obsession with me?' Callanach asked, walking to the window, staring into black nothingness, trying not to watch his mother in the reflection.

'All the evidence was against you. You'd told your best friend the scratches to your neck had happened at the gym. You'd told no one about Astrid attacking you. The neighbour had heard you swearing at her before walking out of her apartment. Bit by bit, the case was building against you and nothing you said was improving the situation. I just wanted to help,' Véronique said, wrapping her arms around herself and rocking gently backwards and forwards.

'So what happened?' Callanach asked. 'Because whatever you'd intended, it certainly didn't get any better for me. Astrid didn't drop the case until the day of the trial and even then she didn't tell the truth and admit she'd invented it. I suffered through another four months of being regarded as a sexual predator.'

'I know,' Véronique stuttered. 'I know. And I'm so sorry. If I could go back . . .'

'You know what, I can't do this,' Luc said. 'I thought I could, but it's just too hard. I'm not sure what you thought would be achieved by telling me this but it certainly isn't helping me. If you came all this way to ease your own conscience, you misjudged.'

'It's not that,' Véronique said, throwing her handbag onto the couch and standing up. 'Easing my conscience, yes. I know you have no reason to forgive me. I don't think I could ever expect you to. But when I spoke to her it . . . it hurt me, Luc. She was so believable. She was like an animal that had been hit by a car, crumpled, broken. I couldn't bear to be in the middle of it. You were so aloof and angry.'

'What the hell would you expect from someone falsely accused?' he asked.

'Luc, I'm trying to explain that I'm not the best judge in those circumstances. I knew I couldn't tell you that I'd talked with her. Then the medical report came, all about the internal injuries she had, the bruises to her body. Your skin under her nails. I didn't know what to think. So I ran away. I knew I wasn't the person you needed me to be and I left. There's no good enough reason. There's nothing I can say to make it better. But I am sorry.'

'You're sorry? Supposing I accept that. Say I recognise how good an actress Astrid is, how dangerous. But after that, after you'd dropped me to face the possibility of years in prison alone, you stopped emailing. You didn't phone. When I was finally told I was free to go, I wrote to you. Even my letters were returned unopened. Was half an hour of listening to Astrid really all it took for you to abandon your child?'

'I was a mess by then. Please believe me, I wanted to speak to you. I wanted to race back, to hold you in my arms and be the mother I should always have been, but I was ashamed. I hadn't been strong enough. I'd let my own needs, my own feelings overwhelm me. I'd put myself before you and . . . how do you face your child once you've done that? I couldn't. I knew I didn't deserve you anymore.'

'You're right,' Callanach said. 'You don't. I won't let myself be dragged into this black hole again. I closed the door. To Astrid, to the nightmare of being arrested, to the disloyalty of my friends. To you. I won't relive this just so you can purge your guilt. I picked myself up, even though it was the last thing I wanted to do. I moved country, retrained, forced myself to look in the mirror, and I'm just starting a new life. Whatever you need, whatever it is you thought I could give you, I can't. We should go. I'll drop you to your hotel. I have a late conference regarding an autopsy.'

'Luc, I just need a little more time,' his mother said, picking up her bag but keeping her feet planted between the coffee table and sofa. 'This isn't easy.'

'I'm sorry but you've had all the time in the world,' Callanach said. 'I really do have to go.' He held the door open for her, checking his mobile phone messages as he waited for her to put on her coat.

Véronique looked around the apartment. 'There are no photos here,' she said.

'I had to rebuild my life without memories. There's no point staring at images of falsehoods,' he said, stepping outside into the corridor, holding the door open at a distance.

'Not even of your father?' Véronique asked. 'He would have hated this.'

'Do you mean he would have hated you?' Callanach asked.

Véronique turned away, sliding fists into her pockets and hunching her shoulders. She walked briskly past Callanach and took the stairs. He caught up with her on the pavement, opening the car door for her to get in.

'No need,' she said. 'I'll walk. That'll be easier on us both.'

'Yes,' Callanach replied. 'It certainly will.' He steeled himself and left his mother for the last time.

Chapter Eight

Ava met Callanach in the city mortuary carpark. She waited, leaning on her car, as he parked his.

'Do you want to talk about it?' Ava asked as he got out.

'No,' he said. 'How did the briefing go?'

'Everyone's still in shock. Most of the squad worked directly with the Chief at some point. I think there's a softly spoken consensus that retiring after his heart attack was what killed him. All those years in the thick of things and he ends up with golf club membership and on a diet he hated. Hardly a replacement for the adrenalin and single malt he was used to. Let's go in. Ailsa has stayed late for us.'

They walked into the mortuary, the clinical, chemical smell extending just beyond its external glass doors as if issuing an olfactory 'abandon hope' warning. Dr Ailsa Lambert was in her office, her assistant looking tired as he drew on his coat and bade them goodnight. Ava knocked.

'Ailsa,' Ava said. 'Are you ready for us?'

'Come in,' she said. 'I'd offer you both a drink only I won't allow alcohol on the premises. If ever I needed it though . . .' she stopped herself, picking up a file labelled DCI George

Begbie. 'Let's start with this. I'm entirely convinced that George's cause of death was carbon monoxide poisoning. There are no injuries or findings inconsistent with that, internal or external. The toxicology samples will be picked up from here tomorrow and sent away for analysis but I've done an alcohol test on his blood. He was sober. I don't just mean below the driving limit. I mean there was no alcohol in his blood at all. When he made the decision to take his life, he did it entirely consciously.'

'Something must have triggered it,' Ava said. 'You found no other signs of illness? Nothing that would cause him to lose hope sufficiently to believe suicide was the only way out?'

'There are no tumours, his organs – even given his heart condition – are all in reasonable order. I phoned his GP. He'd had a comprehensive check-up recently, blood tests and all. Came back clear. The notes indicate that George was in good spirits, no problems with his mood, sleeping, eating, even his cholesterol was dropping. Apparently, he was planning a surprise holiday for his wife Glynis on their anniversary. The GP has been seeing them both for years. She's as shocked as we are,' Ailsa said.

'So he drove to the coast, hooked a length of hose-pipe up to the back of his car and sat there dying, knowing Glynis was cooking dinner for him. He was stone cold sober, in spite of the empty whisky bottle in his car, with no known problems. For Christ's sake, Ailsa, it makes no sense,' Ava said.

'I'm aware of that,' Ailsa said. 'There is the matter of the markings on the inside of his left wrist.' She clicked the screen and produced a blown-up photo of the area. 'It's clearer in this photograph than to the naked eye because we've been able to filter out some of the colour. You can see here that the capital N was formed of scratches, making three separate lines. They are quite deep violations of the epidermis, consisting of multiple scratches along each line. The small c is formed of a single curve, repeated several times in the same place.' She clicked again and the c came up magnified. 'You can see here that at the top part of the curve, the scratch was so deep that it had begun to draw blood. It would have taken some effort to do that without a tool or implement.'

'Without a tool?' Callanach asked. 'You mean he . . .'

'He used his right index finger. The scratched off particles of skin were found under the nail, sufficient to see without a microscope. Obviously, we've sent that for DNA testing but there's really no doubt that he did this to himself.'

'I have no idea what the c stands for,' Ava said. 'I've seen carbon monoxide poisoning victims before, but I don't know much about the process before death. What sort of state would he have been in, once the car started to fill with gas?'

'He'd have become increasingly groggy, disoriented. Concentration would have been difficult and he'd have been feeling extremely nauseous,' Ailsa said.

'So perhaps the letter sizing was just a symptom of his confusion,' Ava said. 'Perhaps they were both supposed to be capitals.'

'You think they're initials?' Callanach asked. Ava nodded. 'Anyone spring to mind?'

'Not immediately,' Ava said. 'I'll put Tripp on it in the morning.'

'Ava,' Ailsa said quietly. 'There's no evidence of a crime here. What we have is a tragedy. A desperate event for his family to endure, but my report will say that there are no suspicious circumstances.'

'That's ridiculous,' Ava said. 'It's totally out of character and this thing on his arm . . .'

'Could have been scratched at any time in the few hours preceding his death and might be totally unrelated. Or it could be an indicator that he wasn't in his right mind at the time. It's not evidence of foul play.'

'It certainly warrants investigation,' Ava said. 'I'm not prepared to accept that this is a non-suspicious death.'

'I've been asked to copy in Detective Superintendent Overbeck,' Ailsa said. 'I have no choice. Subject to the tox screen results, my preliminary findings indicate that that body should be released for burial or cremation. George's family will suffer enough. There's no reason to keep them waiting.'

'Ailsa, you can keep this open a while. I know you can. I'm a Detective Chief Inspector. If I can't decide what to investigate and what not, then . . .'

'Ava,' Callanach said. 'You can't ask Dr Lambert to write anything other than her honest opinion. She's right about the Chief's wife. Glynis needs to be allowed to grieve. Turning this into something it's not will only make it harder for her.'

'You're right,' Ava said. She took a deep breath and exhaled slowly. 'I'm sorry, Ailsa, I didn't come here intending to pressure you. I just need to get this straight in my head. Luc, what was it that you needed to run through?' she asked, looking away.

'Lily Eustis. The young woman found dead near Arthur's Seat. Do you have an update on her?' Callanach asked, concealing his concern for Ava.

Ailsa Lambert was less concerned with how her behaviour was perceived, as ever, staring openly at Ava as Callanach spoke. 'Right, Lily, poor girl. I've spoken to her parents this evening. They're going to need more answers than I can supply, but essentially cause of death was major organ failure as a result of hypothermia. No surprise really. Out at night in December, on a hilltop in these temperatures the outcome was almost inevitable. I visited the scene, though. Someone had built a small fire. That should have kept her warm for a while.'

'She was found naked,' Callanach said. 'It would have taken some fire to have kept her warm in those circumstances.'

'The nakedness might have been a result of the hypothermia,'

Ailsa said. 'It's called paradoxical undressing. A person becomes disoriented with the increasing cold and begins discarding their clothing, thereby increasing the rapidity of heat loss.'

'So she wasn't dragged up there against her will?' Callanach asked.

'I can tell you that she was not assaulted, sexually or violently. There are no defensive injuries, no wounds. In fact she was a healthy young lady, good muscle tone, virtually no fat on her . . .' Ailsa trailed off.

'You sound hesitant,' Callanach said. 'What is it?'

'Probably nothing,' Ailsa replied, typing as she spoke. 'But for argument's sake, say I was experiencing moderate to severe stage hypothermia, enough to make me strip off my clothing and throw it down the hillside. What sort of state am I in?'

'Agitated. Probably distressed. Frantic even,' Callanach guessed.

'Exactly,' Ailsa replied, pointing to another photo on the screen. Lily Eustis lay on the ground as Callanach had first seen her, on her back, fully naked, shades of blue already darkening to black, arms out at her sides, as if she had just fallen asleep.

'What's your point, Ailsa?' Ava asked.

'She doesn't look distressed or frantic here, does she?' Ailsa asked. 'She looks as if she'd decided she was a wee bit tired and wanted to take a nap. Her body isn't folded up, twisted, scrabbling. Certainly there are no signs of terminal burrowing syndrome that can occur near death, during which she would have been curling up, seeking shelter, making herself as small as possible. There's nothing unexpected beneath her fingernails. No dirt, no skin. There is only a single mark on her skin, about two centimetres long over her abdomen, which is the imprint of a zip.'

Callanach looked down at his own notes. 'The log shows she was wearing zip-fastening jeans. We have them in the evidence vault.'

'Exactly. It's as if she was struggling with the zipper for a long time, perhaps in her confusion becoming clumsy and pressing the metal into her skin as she tried to get the jeans off. Other than that she's exceptionally clean, as if she never experienced any trauma through the whole process of losing heat and passing away.'

'You say that as if it's a bad thing,' Ava snapped. 'Are we supposed to have wanted her to be traumatised?'

'Of course we are,' Ailsa said, ignoring Ava's irritated tone. 'The human instinct is to fight death, to run from danger. They also call terminal burrowing from hypothermia hide-or-die syndrome. Her body position, the very state of her, makes no sense to me.' Ava sighed heavily. 'Lily's toxicology screen will go off tomorrow at the same time as George Begbie's specimens. Before then I wouldn't like to speculate.'

'If you're convinced Lily died of hypothermia, why run a tox screen?' Callanach asked.

'There was a slight odour to her stomach contents. Nothing I can be certain about, and it's hard to tell with the variety of food and drink available, but I thought I smelled something odd on her skin too. It was fleeting. Gone as soon as she was out of the body bag. As I said, I won't speculate now.'

'All right,' Callanach said. 'Tox screen involving what?'

'Hair, liver, bile, vitreous humour and the gastric contents, obviously. Blood and urine as standard. Some skeletal samples for good measure,' Ailsa said. 'That's as far as I can take Lily's case at the moment. Questions?'

They both shook their heads, Ava putting her coat on before Ailsa had even switched off her screen. Callanach said goodbye as Ava made her way into the corridor.

'Ava,' he called, catching up with her as she hustled out of the exit into the carpark. 'You were a bit tough on Ailsa back there.'

'I was assessing the cases,' she said.

51

'I know that, but Ailsa worked with the Chief longer than almost anyone in MIT. If she thought there was reason for suspicion, she'd be pursuing it.'

'You finished?' Ava asked. Callanach didn't bother to respond. 'Good. Now I've got work to do and you've had a difficult day. I suggest you go home. Follow up with Lily Eustis' parents tomorrow morning. Leave an update on my desk.'

'Yes, ma'am,' Callanach replied. This time Ava didn't bother to correct him as she climbed into her car and sped away.

Chapter Nine

Leaning against a pile of props backstage, he checked out the group of wannabes preening, flexing their necks and warming up their voices. It was pitiful really. So many young men and women clamouring to build a career in pretence. Acting was simply professional lying. He allowed himself a smile then checked a non-existent text on his phone to avoid conversation. The truth was that he would probably have been ideally suited for the part. Play-acting was, after all, a skill he had honed to perfection. He glanced over at Sean O'Cahill – youthful, brimming with enthusiasm, shimmering with nerves – who was next in line. Forcing himself to concentrate, he did what he was there to do. Sean's height he estimated at 5'9", and the would-be actor was slim, probably weighing no more than nine and a half stone. Those measurements were well within what he could deal with.

Taking lives was more complicated than people imagined. You didn't just blunder in unprepared. He had to know he was capable of carrying Sean. A daily work out with dumbbells ensured that would be possible, and the exercise had the added effect of keeping his body toned and desirable. He wasn't vain, but there was no point in false modesty. Good looks and taut muscles made life easier. Then there was fight or flight. Life was unpredictable. Better to imagine potential conflicts and prepare for them. He liked a fight though. Dominance. Exertion. But he knew when to run. The first lessons of his childhood – when to run, when to hide, when to remain silent. Staying in shape reduced the chances of capture.

Watching Sean warm up, he saw a man who prided himself on being jovial. There was a smile for everyone around him, one of those 'what a wonderful world' smiles too, nothing fake about it. Sean wanted to like and to be liked. That would make approaching him much easier. Manipulating him would be almost no challenge at all. A shame, really. Sean's height and weight were the key to knowing how much sedative he would need for incapacitation. He didn't want to kill him too quickly. That would give no satisfaction at all. Grief was best enjoyed slowly, a drip-drip-drip of emotion, and he wanted to be there to lick every tear from the face of Sean's best beloved. There was more to do yet. Trust to be built. A fire to kindle. That made him think of Lily. He shut his eyes, willing himself not to be distracted by the memory. He studied Sean instead. There was something vital about him. Utterly intoxicating. His hands itched to hold him.

'Sean O'Cahill?' a young man called. Sean stepped away from the mirror and waved his hand in the air. 'You're up. Good to go?'

'As I'll ever be,' Sean blustered, trying to enjoy the moment. 'No audition was ever a waste.' That was his agent's mantra. It was all one continuous learning curve. Sometimes there would be failures, less often successes, but every time you stepped onto a stage was a step closer to where you wanted to end up. Sean wasn't convinced that was right. He'd had plenty of days when stepping onto a stage was simply a short cut to rejection. Being an actor was hard. Not hard like being a surgeon or a soldier, he knew that, but the constant disappointments were an ointment that thinned the skin, and his felt worn through.

'Sean, right?' a woman called from a few rows back in the small theatre. 'Tell us a bit about yourself.'

'Sure, well I'm Northern Irish. I moved from Belfast to Edinburgh quite recently.' He remembered to smile.

'Why Edinburgh?' the woman – he assumed she was the theatre company director – interrupted.

'Obviously because I couldn't afford the air fare to Los Angeles,' Sean said. There was an immediate laugh from the group of note-takers surrounding the woman in charge, echoed from the wings where a line of other hopefuls waited to audition. 'And because I was at The Fringe last year. I saw the production your theatre company put on and decided this was the place I wanted to be. Also tartan really suits me and in Scotland I can get away with wearing what feels like a skirt when I go shopping.' Another laugh, bigger this time, more ready to engage with his style of humour. He began to relax.

'How old are you, Sean?'

'You want the age on my passport or the answer my agent tells me to give?' He grinned.

'Closest to the truth,' the director said, still laughing.

'Thirty-five if I've been drinking Flaming Pig, twenty-eight when I wake up without a hangover, and more like twenty-six when I'm in make-up.'

'Okay, we have your song choice here and a monologue. If you could start with the musical piece then run straight into the acting, that'd be great,' the director said. The pianist began to play.

'That was really good, Sean. Where did you train?' the director asked.

'Ulster University,' Sean said.

'Well, it was great. These are open auditions so we're seeing a lot of people. We won't have the call back list available until Friday but we'll be emailing the successful people and asking to see them again next week. Thank you for your time today,' she finished.

He hadn't been cut short. That was all he could think about as he left the stage. He'd finished his song, nods all round, and had actually enjoyed performing the monologue, which made a pleasant change from being wracked with nerves throughout. Reaching for his mobile, he began texting Bradley before picking up his coat, got halfway through writing the text then deleted the draft. It would jinx it, he was sure. There could be no self-congratulatory words at this stage. He'd have to play it down. Since they'd moved in together he'd lost track of how many time-wasting auditions he'd attended, but he had a good feeling about this one. If he got the call back, he'd talk to Bradley about it then. By that stage he'd be one of just a handful going for the job. It wouldn't pay much, but to be part of a company, working on a show, would be the start of something real.

He smiled at the man in the doorway, presumably awaiting his turn to audition.

'Good job out there,' the man said.

'Thank you.' Sean grinned, taking in the dirty blonde hair and open smile. 'I'm Sean.' He held out his hand.

'Jackson,' the man replied, shaking it.

'Great name, I like it. You waiting to go on?' Sean asked as he did up his coat against the sub-zero temperatures outside.

'Not sure there's much point,' the man said good-naturedly. 'Looks like you nailed it.'

'I very much doubt that,' Sean said, hoping beyond hope that the stranger was right. 'Anyway, break a leg,' Sean said, bustling past him. The man smiled once more as he left, his eyes on Sean's back as he exited. Nice guy, Sean thought.

Bradley was itching to phone his boyfriend Sean. They were both starting to give up hope that Sean would get work although neither wanted to be the first to voice such a negative opinion, but this audition played to Sean's strengths. The theatre company wanted an actor who could both sing and dance, able to 'make comedy work' was how they'd phrased the advert, and Sean could certainly do that. He didn't have film actor looks, and was never going to be cast as the hero, the hard man or the icy-stare bad guy. He was, however, good at improvising. He could deliver a killer punch line. And he was easy to be around. If he could show that off, then he should finally make it to call backs.

Bradley dialled Sean's number, cutting the call off before it could connect. He didn't want to put too much pressure on. He needed to make Sean feel good about himself, to let him know that if not this time, then one day. A decent bottle of wine, albeit within their limited budget, would be good on the way home. They could talk about the audition over dinner, brought up casually. That would be better.

Brad shut down his computer, tidied his notes and put on his coat. Life as a junior actuary was lacking the drama and thrills of the stage, but he loved it. At least it brought in a steady wage, which was nothing to be sniffed at. Sean was the sort of partner who would sit and listen to Bradley talk about his day as if it was the most important thing in the world, and for the most part Sean even managed to look convincingly interested. If there was a downside to their different careers, it was that Sean's world was so much more dynamic that occasionally Brad felt like the boring hanger-on. Every one of Sean's dance classes and physical training sessions was full of gorgeous muscled men with regular bookings under the sun lamp. Not that Sean ever deliberately made Brad feel insignificant, but as an entertainer Sean naturally drew people to him. Everyone they met remembered Sean's name immediately, social media friendship invitations came flooding in. Sometimes, just sometimes, Brad thought, it would be nice if he could be the centre of attention for a change. On his way out, he washed up his coffee mug in the work kitchen sink, chiding himself for being so ungrateful. Life with Sean was wonderful. So what if Brad sometimes felt blinded by the brightness of his lover's personality? It was a fair exchange for the moments of intimacy and sweetness. He wouldn't change what they had – not much of it, anyway – even if he could, Brad told himself as he wrapped a scarf around his neck and set off into Edinburgh's chill evening air.

Chapter Ten

A week had passed since Lily Eustis' death and Callanach was no further forward in ascertaining who she'd spent the evening with before her fateful trip to Arthur's Seat. She hadn't been seen at any of her usual haunts. Friends had been contacted, CCTV had been checked, her mobile activity and social media were blank. A few of the numbers in her mobile contacts database were dead numbers that didn't check out, but that was par for the course.

Ailsa had spoken with Lily's parents again to explain the need to hold the body until the toxicology screening results were back in case further investigations were needed. Callanach had visited them, too, intruding on their terrible grief with more questions than answers, sensing the ghost they could all still see in their house. The chair Lily used to sit in to read, the way she always took the stairs two at a time, the way she sang incomprehensibly whilst cleaning her teeth. These were the little things Lily's mother had told Callanach about. He had drunk tea, nodded, and let the words come. They might not help him resolve the questions over Lily's death, but if it helped her mother to tell him then he would listen.

Lily's sister Mina had sat listless on the couch, biting her nails and tugging at the few strands of hair that had escaped her ponytail.

'She would never have thought of going there herself,' Mina had said. 'Someone was with her.'

'We're working on that basis,' Callanach had told her. 'But no one's coming forward with any information. As the Chief Pathologist explained, there are no injuries and no evidence of any crime having been committed.'

'So that's it?' Lily's father had barked from an armchair in the corner, so shrouded in darkness with all the curtains closed that Callanach could barely see him.

'Until there's any further forensic evidence or witness testimony, yes. It's possible that the Procurator Fiscal will ask for a sudden death report, but the Major Investigation Team won't play any further role. A police liaison officer will be in touch today so you know who to contact with any questions.'

No one had said anything after that. Callanach had expected outrage, some display of frustration at the least, but the family was numb with loss. Callanach had stood up quietly, said his goodbyes and made his way out. Only Mina had followed him into the hallway as he'd put his shoes back on.

'When will we get her things back?' Mina had asked.

'I'll contact the city mortuary about that for you,' Callanach had said. 'Anything on her body or in her pockets will be in evidence, but if it's of no significance we can release it to you.'

'Thank you,' she'd whispered, opening the door for him, and closing it again before he'd had a chance to turn around and say goodbye.

Callanach had been trying to get five minutes with Ava all day. It was hard getting used to her being so elusive. The days of wandering into her office and expecting her to be available to talk theories or Police Scotland politics had disappeared with her promotion. He'd left two messages on her voicemail then been reduced to emailing her.

Eventually, late Friday afternoon, she appeared at his office door. 'You busy?' she asked.

'What's the right answer?' he replied, closing his laptop.

'Dim sum,' she said. 'I've been thinking about it most of the day. I think dim sum may be the only thing that will make this crappy week feel marginally less awful.'

'Get your coat,' Callanach said.

'I'm not sure that's how you're supposed to speak to a senior officer,' Ava said over her shoulder as she walked away. Ten minutes later they met on the street, both electing to abandon their cars for the evening in favour of alcohol. 'I've called a cab,' Ava said, 'and booked a table at the Cantonese restaurant in Abercromby Place.'

'You did all that while I was putting on my coat?' Callanach asked. The cab pulled up as they were talking.

'I might have already booked the table before I came to find you,' Ava said as she climbed in.

'Almost as if you knew I'd have no plans on a Friday night,' Callanach muttered as Ava told the driver where they were going.

'Don't be over-sensitive,' she said turning back to Callanach. 'I had a shortlist of five people I was considering inviting to dinner. I figured at least one would be free.'

'Now I wish I'd played a bit harder to get,' Callanach laughed.

'Date night is it?' the cabbie interjected. 'Me and the missus used to do that every Friday 'til I got this job. It's not the same trying to be romantic on a Tuesday evening. You two married?'

Ava looked at Callanach, opened her mouth to answer and ended up spluttering helpless laughter instead.

'Actually, the lady's my boss,' Callanach said.

'Pretty much the same as being married then,' the cabbie winked. Five minutes later, he pulled the cab over and they climbed out. 'You'd make a nice looking couple though, maybe you should think about it. You two have a nice evening,' he said, pulling away.

Ava stared after the car, hands on hips. 'Do you ever go anywhere without people telling you how good looking you are?' she asked.

'That was directed at you, too,' Callanach responded. 'Can we please go and eat now?'

'I wish I hadn't tipped him,' she said.

'You really can't just take it as a compliment?' Callanach grinned.

'What, someone thinking we're married? If I didn't need a drink before, I certainly do now. You're buying, by the way, because I know how painful the next hour's going to be with the waitresses flirting with you.'

'I have a way to deal with that,' Callanach said. 'Come on. Let's see if we can improve your mood with some saturated fat.'

'I've been waiting for a man to say those words to me all my life,' Ava said, striding past him into the restaurant, hanging her coat on a peg without waiting to be asked and taking the best table in the front window.

'Excuse me madam, that table is laid for four. I wonder if you'd mind moving to the table at the back, please?'

Callanach watched Ava's face change as she peered towards the back of the restaurant, checking out the smaller table between the kitchen door and the corridor to the toilets. Whilst Ava was usually the least pretentious woman he knew, tonight was probably not the time for anyone to mess with her. He stepped forward.

'Do you mind?' He smiled at the waitress.

She beamed at him, giving a small giggle for no particular reason. 'Yes, sir. How can I help?'

'It's mine and my wife's anniversary,' he said, motioning towards Ava. 'We really wanted this particular table. Could you accommodate us, do you think?'

'I didn't realise you were together.' The waitress moved aside and pulled a chair out for him. 'And yes, of course, as it's a special occasion. Champagne, then?' she asked.

'Naturally,' he replied, trying to ignore Ava sitting with her hands over her face. The waitress hustled away to fetch a bottle and the appropriate glasses.

'You see? No one's going to flirt with me now that I'm with my wife, celebrating – how many years is it?' he asked.

'If it wouldn't hit the press in the morning, I'd think I'd prefer you to have said I'd hired you as an escort,' Ava said, glaring at the menu. 'I really don't care what I eat. It all looks good.' The waitress put glasses on the table and began pouring the champagne. 'My husband will order for me,' Ava simpered. 'He's wonderful at that!'

'We'll take a selection of the dim sum,' Callanach said. 'Whatever the chef recommends.' As the waitress disappeared, he raised his glass. 'To lost friends,' he said gently. 'How are you doing? You've been hard to find this week. I was worried about you.'

Ava tried to paint on a tough smile, lost the battle halfway through and looked down at her lap. 'It hasn't been great. I thought it was hard losing my mum last summer. Now the Chief has gone too and I feel like a fraud sitting at his desk, hearing his voice telling me to buck my ideas up and get on with it. I spent so much time with him over the years. I suppose we don't always appreciate it, but the police force is like family. You don't like everyone, wouldn't choose half of them, but they're always there, good or bad. Begbie was one of the good ones.'

She drained her glass of champagne and Callanach refilled it.

'How's his wife getting on? I know you were close to both her and the Chief. It must be hard watching her grieve,' he said.

'Glynis is one of a kind. Married to the police force as much as to one single policeman. She's being remarkably stoic at the moment, but I'm worried how she'll cope longer term. They completed each other, if that's not too much of a cliché. The Chief was her whole world.'

'How lucky that they found each other. There are a lot of people at the station asking about the funeral. What are the plans?' Luc asked.

'Full uniform honours, but it's only open to close colleagues and friends,' Ava said. 'Glynis had another blow today. She's been told their life insurance won't pay out because it was a suicide with no suggestion of mental illness, not even depression or short-term psychological disturbance. She'll have to move in with her daughter as she can't afford the mortgage. I can't imagine what she's going through.'

'I hadn't even thought about the finances,' Callanach said. 'To have to deal with that on top of her husband's death. Isn't there anything we can do?'

'Short of finding a decent source of income for her for the next twenty years, not really,' Ava said. 'There's her share of the Chief's pension, but it's not enough for both the mortgage payments and to keep Glynis comfortable for the next twenty years. She was always a wife and mother, never had a career of her own, so she has no personal money to fall back on. Food! I'm starving.' A stack of dim sum baskets were placed in the centre of their table. 'I don't know if it's just me, but grief makes me eat constantly. I've consumed more calories in the last . . . oh, Luc, I'm so sorry. I haven't even asked. What happened with your mother? I really must be losing my mind.'

'Yup. So far you're making a pretty inattentive wife,' he said, tipping a pool of soy sauce onto his plate. 'You can stop apologising. As it happens there's not much to say. She regrets not standing by me. Apparently, Astrid got to her as well. Acted the part of victim very convincingly. My mother couldn't see through the false evidence, so she ran. That's all. These prawn things are good. Are you going to drink that entire bottle of champagne on your own?'

'Don't do that,' Ava said.

'Do what? You asked me out for dinner. I'm eating.'

'Change the subject,' Ava said. 'I know how hard this has been for you. She didn't explain any more than that? Why hasn't she responded to you since you were acquitted? All those times you tried to get in touch. She must have given some sort of explanation.'

'Not really. She kept saying it was hard for her, that she needed more time, which is bizarre in the circumstances,' Callanach said, refilling his own glass before motioning to the waitress for another bottle.

'That's it?' Ava asked. 'After all this time, why reappear now?' She took the new bottle from the waitress' hands and refilled both glasses, draining hers immediately.

'She said she wanted to explain, then she didn't. Not in a way that made sense. Can we change the subject now, please? I liked it better when I was annoying you,' Callanach said.

'No, we can't. You should talk to her again. Get to the bottom of it. If you leave it like this it'll haunt you,' Ava said.

'I'm not sure there's anything left to say. She's at the Radisson until tomorrow, then I guess she's going back to Monaco. It took me a long time to get used to the fact that she'd given up on me. I'm not sure I can turn back the clock.'

'Not sure you can or not sure you want to?' Ava asked, piling more tiny parcels of spicy prawns onto her plate. 'Take it from me, trying to repair years of misunderstandings when you're about to lose someone you love is a disaster. I should know – I couldn't have made worse decisions when my mum was dying. I'd like to stop you from making similar mistakes.'

'I'd like to think I'm able to stay rational, even when emotions are involved,' Callanach said. 'And I agree, you did make some terrible misjudgements in the past.'

'Sod off, then. I've tried to help. If you're just going to be rude, I'm going to eat in silence until I burst. This is good champagne.' Ava refilled her glass again.

'You know you've drunk a bottle of champagne in less than an hour, right?'

'Save the detective skills for solving cases. Right, all the food's gone and the alcohol supply is diminishing. I am going to the ladies' room while you settle the bill then we'll move this party along.' Ava stood up, threw her napkin onto her plate and walked off clutching her mobile.

Ten minutes later a cab pulled up outside the restaurant. Ava sighed.

'You again?' she asked, looking through the driver's window.

'Did you have a nice meal? Only it didn't take very long,' the cabbie said.

Ava ignored him. 'The booking office told you where we're headed, I take it?'

'Aye, gave me all the details. I was surprised to be seeing you both again so soon. I thought you'd be taking your time with the meal and everything. It's a nice place, that. Did you think about what I said?' He grinned at Callanach.

'I'll tip you again but only if you agree not to talk for the remainder of the journey,' Ava said.

'Fair enough,' the driver agreed. 'It'll only be five minutes. Traffic's light tonight.'

★　★　★

The taxi pulled up where the High Street met South Bridge, while Ava and Callanach were busy talking police funding.

'This isn't where I live,' Callanach said.

'I'm aware of that. It's where your mother's staying,' Ava replied.

'Not happening,' Callanach replied calmly but firmly. 'But I can walk home from here, so this'll do.' He got out, holding the door for Ava. 'It's not that I don't appreciate what you're trying to do, but there's no quick solution. If the problem between my mother and me ever resolves itself, it's going to take more than a quick chat. You can't fix everything.'

'I need to fix something,' she said. 'The Chief didn't come and talk to me about whatever was going on with him. My own mother kept her symptoms from me for months, even though she was terminally ill. I keep thinking that maybe if we'd been closer, if I'd been a better daughter, she'd have confided in me. Maybe they could have treated the cancer before it was too late.'

'You weren't at fault, and this isn't the same thing. Let me call you another cab. It's too far for you to walk to your place from here.'

'I'm cold,' Ava said. 'And I need a proper drink. At least let me buy you a single malt. The bar in here is warm and comfortable. It won't kill you to walk through the door. I'm not ready to go home yet.'

Callanach wondered if that had been the plan all along, before she'd even walked into his office and invited him to dinner. Ava was rarely taken unawares, her brain usually ten steps ahead of everyone else's. That was what made her such an impressive police officer. Even so, she was intruding on a deeply personal situation, but he wasn't ready for the emptiness of his apartment yet either. His mother had never been one for bars, rarely drinking unless they were dining with friends.

67

He wasn't even sure she was still at the hotel. Chances were that she'd left town early.

'One drink,' he said. 'Then I'm getting you home.'

'Deal,' Ava said, walking ahead of him through reception and turning right into the hotel bar.

They sat on stools. It was busy but not packed, the bulk of casual diners already finishing dessert or drinking coffee, their conversation a friendly hum in the background.

'Two Laphroaigs please,' Ava directed the barman. 'No spoiling it with water or ice.'

'You sure you wouldn't prefer it straight from the bottle?' Callanach asked.

'You can lecture me about French wine when we're in France. Never lecture a Scot about whisky. It's apt to end up with a trip to get stitches.'

'Luc?' a voice said softly from behind them.

Callanach stared at Ava.

'It's no good looking daggers at me,' Ava said. 'It's not as if you weren't aware I never take no for an answer.'

'You had no right.' He leaned across to whisper in her ear.

'I accept that,' Ava said. 'I also know that if you really hadn't wanted to stand any chance of seeing your mother you wouldn't have walked into this hotel with me. So say goodbye or hear her out, whichever suits you best. Just make a decision.' She turned around. 'Madame Callanach,' she held out her hand, 'I'm Ava Turner, we spoke on the phone earlier. I'll leave you to it. I suspect I've already done more than enough.'

'You certainly have,' Callanach replied.

Ava smiled, picked up her glass and tossed back the Laphroaig. 'Take it easy,' she told Callanach. 'Nice to have met you,' she said to Véronique, slipping her coat back on before exiting.

'I see. Your colleague didn't tell you she'd phoned me,'

Véronique said. 'I'm sorry. I didn't want to trick you into seeing me.'

'Well, I'm here now,' Callanach said. 'So if there's something else you wanted to say, now would be the time.'

'Shall we go up to my room? It's quieter there. I'm not really sure this is the place . . .'

'I'm leaving in a couple of minutes. You may not want to waste time travelling between floors. Here is fine. There's a table by the window.' He picked up his drink and walked away from the bar, silently cursing Ava's inability to restrict her meddling. They sat down. 'What was it you wanted to say?'

His mother stared out of the window. 'I don't know how to begin,' she said. 'I want to repair the damage I've done. I want my son back.'

'Is there something you need to say that I haven't already heard?' Callanach asked. 'Because I'm not here to repeat the conversation we had at my flat. You said you needed more time and I'm afraid it's run out.' He pushed his drink away across the table.

'Luc, please,' his mother said, reaching out to him. 'I can't stand the thought of losing you forever. There'll be nothing left to live for.'

'I felt like that too, when you left me. At least we have that in common. This is a waste of both of our time.' He stood up. 'Goodbye, Véronique. Safe journey home.'

'Luc, no. There's no easy way to tell you this. It was a long time ago, and I never talked about it. When Astrid accused you, her story brought it all back and I couldn't cope.' She paused, ran a shaking hand over her mouth, lowered her voice. 'I was raped, a long time ago, but it never leaves you. I had no idea what Astrid told me would affect me so badly. I'm so sorry I couldn't be there when you needed me, but it was all too much. I know I failed you. Whatever I have to do for you to forgive me, I will.'

69

Chapter Eleven

'Turner,' Ava answered her mobile.

'DS Lively here, ma'am. We've been asked to attend a road traffic accident. Your car's at the station, so I assumed you were still around.'

'I'm walking through the city trying to find a cab. Why's a car accident anything to do with MIT, Sergeant?'

'It's a bad crash, blood in and out of the vehicle, on the A702 where the road runs through the edge of the Pentland Hills Regional Park. I'm on my way there now. Only one car remaining at the scene but tyre marks indicate that a second vehicle was involved.'

'Still not hearing a reason for this telephone call . . .'

'There's no body, ma'am. No one at the scene at all,' Lively said.

'So the driver was injured and the other vehicle opted to take him to the hospital. Who's the Inspector on duty? You don't need me for this. I've been out for the evening so there's no way I can drive to a scene, no matter what's happened.'

'It has to be a DCI. The car involved in the crash is registered to a man called Louis Jones. He's known to the police but his file is marked for review by an officer of the rank of Chief Inspector or above, as directed by Chief Begbie,' Lively said. 'It can probably wait until tomorrow, but I thought that should be your call.'

'I'll be waiting at the junction of The Mile and New Street. Have a car pick me up, and make it quick, it's bloody freezing out here,' Ava said.

Coffee in hand, Ava was sitting at her desk twenty minutes later, staring at an envelope, the contents of which had yet to be reduced to the digital recesses of the cloud and trying to get her head straight. The food she'd consumed had soaked up a portion of the alcohol, but the room was still swimmy if she didn't stay focused on a single point. The sealed envelope had Begbie's confidentiality order on it, and a list of names and signatures of people who had accessed the file within the last few years. The last reader was George Begbie himself a few months earlier. Ava ran her fingers over the seal, imagining the Chief exactly where she was now, preparing to read the same sheets of paper, tapping his pen on the desk as he always did when he was impatient.

Inside was a brown cardboard file with Louis Jones' details on the front – name, date of birth, known addresses of residence and work – and it was remarkably thin. On opening it, Ava found what she had assumed she would find: a sheet of paper with the heading 'Registered police informant, initiated November 1997. Contact: George Begbie.' It was the only reason she could think of for the file being confidential. What she hadn't expected to find was her own name in the contents. She scanned that document first.

'Louis Jones – car scrapyard owner operating known car hire scheme without documentation. Utilising vehicles previously deemed scrapped, allowing or causing false number plates to be displayed on hire vehicles. Admits hiring vehicles to Dr Reginald King, denies knowledge of intended purpose. Vehicle hired from Louis Jones used in kidnap of Detective Inspector Ava Turner. Jones assisted in providing details of King's lock up on Causewayside. Interviewed by DI Callanach, supervised by DCI Begbie. No resulting prosecution.'

Ava closed her eyes. A dangerous psychopath, Reginald King, had pulled her from her car one night, taken her back to a concealed room in his house, and killed a teenaged girl in front of her. The teenager was one of three women who'd died at his hands. At trial he'd mounted a psychiatric defence and been remanded indefinitely for treatment. The hours in captivity had been the worst of Ava's life, and Louis Jones had profited from lending King a vehicle, yet neither Callanach nor Begbie had so much as mentioned the man's name to her. She turned the page, forcing herself to keep working rather than be sucked into the black mire that was her memories of what she'd witnessed. Whatever information Jones had provided to the police during his decades-old stint as Begbie's informant must have been spectacularly valuable.

The type-print was fading on the remaining pages. Ava switched on her desk lamp and settled down. The initial page was a case summary from a prosecution dating back to 1999. The prosecution's case was that defendants Dylan McGill and Ramon Trescoe, joint heads of a Glasgow based crime gang, had committed an impressive list of offences from theft and conspiracy, to fraud, blackmail and assault. Their targets had been almost entirely banks, using employees to provide confidential information about security systems and performing unlawful money transfers under threat of violence. On the few occasions that the employees had been sufficiently brave to have refused to comply, the outcome was assaults using tools best restricted to farming. The court case had been heavily covered in the press. Ava recalled it in spite of having been only sixteen at the time. A major Edinburgh crime gang had been taken out of action. The trial had been a Scottish spectator sport for the three months it had lasted.

The file contained witness statements, bank documents and the usual previous convictions, followed by a small selection of photos of the defendants and their victims. Dylan McGill was the tallest of the bunch, with a moustache that wouldn't have looked out of place on a Victorian villain, a cigarette in hand in every picture. Ramon Trescoe was dark skinned, with middle-eastern features and startling green eyes. Not someone you could mistake once you knew his identity, Ava thought. He had been photographed with several extremely attractive women, almost as if he always knew the photographer was around. There were references on file to deaths – rival gang members, henchmen who had defected, and at least one policeman – all of which were well beyond the scope of natural causes. None that had ever left a direct trail to either McGill or Trescoe though. The Procurator Fiscal had settled for putting the pair in jail for less serious offences but the result was almost as good. The sentences had been lengthy.

At the end of the file was a document signed jointly by the Procurator Fiscal and Louis Jones. Jones, Ava read, known then to his associates as Louis the Wrench, had been the provider of vehicles and other necessary hardware. Begbie, then a mere Detective Sergeant, had acquired enough information on Jones' activities to put him away for an easy decade. Instead, Begbie had approached Jones to provide information about Ramon Trescoe's activities, victims and movements. Begbie worked with Louis the Wrench for two years gathering intelligence. They must have been tense times, Ava thought, both for Jones and for Begbie. Trescoe and McGill weren't the sort of people you messed with, and no one seemed to have been beyond their reach. Begbie's relationship with Jones had ended with an agreement to keep Jones out of court under pretty much any circumstance, and landed Begbie a promotion to Detective Inspector immediately after the defendants' final appeals had failed.

Now someone driving Louis Jones' car was missing, although whether it was Jones himself or a random hirer remained to be seen. Ava noted down Jones' last known address, closed the file and returned it to the envelope, which she sealed and signed, ready to be returned to confidential documents. She picked up the phone to call Callanach then put it back down. Hopefully he was still with his mother. Interrupting them now might bring any progress to an end. Not only that, but she wasn't at all sure he would take her call at the moment anyway. She had overstepped the mark in setting him up.

Phoning DS Lively back, Ava ordered a tracker dog to the scene of the accident in case the driver had staggered away from the car dazed. Whoever it was could easily still be trekking through the parkland. If they were badly injured, the December weather was going to be the death of them. Not that Ava was sure she cared, if the driver had actually been Louis the Wrench. The thought of him breathing his last, huddled alone in the freezing cold was one she found rather satisfying. Begbie had let Jones go after a brief chat and the provision of an address for Reginald King's lock-up, knowing Ava could die, aware that other women were already dead. It hardly seemed a balancing of the scales. Whatever Jones had done to assist the police nearly two decades earlier, Ava was certain the Procurator Fiscal could have argued it was of no application to assisting a serial killer so many years later. Begbie would have had his reasons, Ava knew that. The Chief had proved his loyalty to her on more occasions than she could list, but still it stung. It felt seedy, the deal done behind a closed door with no more than a nod and a handshake. She crushed the feelings of indignation and rising anger, reminding herself how much she'd cared about the Chief, knowing it had been reciprocated. He couldn't have betrayed her.

Ava put a call through to DC Tripp who she'd seen loitering in the incident room.

'Tripp, I need you to drive me to an address. Has to be an unmarked car,' she said.

'Yes, ma'am,' Tripp replied. 'I'll be waiting outside. If you give me the address, I'll leave a note as to where we're going.'

'Not this time,' Ava said. 'I'm not sure it's even relevant to an investigation yet and the address is confidential information.'

'Okay then,' Tripp said. 'Shall I bring you a takeaway coffee?'

'No. Actually, yes. And you'll have to be a bit less enthusiastic, Detective Constable. I have a champagne and whisky hangover approaching and anyone smiling will be in the firing line.'

'In that case I'll raid the biscuit tin as well, ma'am. Nothing like a few digestives to help cure crapulence,' Tripp said.

'Let's make that no talking in the car at all,' Ava said.

Chapter Twelve

Cordelia's son, Randall Muir, set down his pride-and-joy guitar before picking up the pint of cider he'd been nursing for the last hour. He had to go easy on the alcohol if he was serious about getting up to jam with the rest of the musicians in the bar. Tonight, for the first time, he would have the confidence to go through with it. Last time he'd failed to play when nerves had got the better of him. He'd drunk far more than intended then had to perform an Olympic-style sprint to the men's toilets to lose the contents of his stomach, before staggering home with a mouth tasting like rotting apples. His mother had pretended not to notice, presenting sympathetic eyes and changing the conversation away from what he'd been up to.

The great Cordelia Muir would not judge. She wouldn't tell him off. Even asking where he went in the evenings was a habit she'd foregone in order to avoid another steaming row. Since his father had died, his mother had tried stepping into the breach with clumsy good intent, embarrassing Randall beyond anything he felt a teenage boy should have to endure. She attended football games when every other mother knew to stay away, shouting and clapping encouragement throughout.

She phoned the parents of girls at school he admitted liking and invited their families for Sunday lunch. Cordelia had even tried talking to him about porn, only to end up lecturing him about respecting women. She'd even insisted on providing packets of condoms when he went away for a weekend with his classmates, forgetting them initially, then shoving them through a car window so everyone had seen. Cordelia Muir was all things to all people. Randall just wished she would get it through her intellectually gifted brain that she would never be his father.

His older sister had cried dutifully at their father's funeral, all the time thanking God, Randall thought, that their precious mother hadn't been the one taken. What Randall knew was that life would never be as good as it had been when his father was alive. There had been boys only camping trips. There had been nights staying up late watching movies his mother would never have approved of, with a few beers sneaked in for good measure even though Randall had been well underage. There had been jokes about sex instead of talk of honour and compatibility. There had been jokes, full stop. His father knew that when he was upset, he needed to be punched on the arm and made to laugh, not to sit down and express his feelings. His father had put Randall first, before all those children in Africa with whom his mother concerned herself so absolutely. Crystal, the clean water charity his mother ran, was more her baby than Randall ever had been.

Since his father had died, Randall's guitar had become his life. His father had taught him the basic chords when he was just eight, sitting Randall on his lap and covering his son's fingers with his own. A year later he'd given Randall a guitar for his birthday. From that moment on it had been his most treasured possession. Now Randall dreamed of joining a band, touring, hearing his first record on the radio. But the bands at his school wrote navel-gazing dirges of love and longing. They sang in mournful voices with arranged harmonies – not the sort of music that got Randall out of bed in the morning to practise chords until his fingertips bled. He wanted to explode with sound, to have it thrum through him like a raging beast. The Fret was the first place he'd found where he could stand up, plug in his amp, and jam with whoever was there.

The bar was the type of place the girls at his school would hate, with enough tattoos on show to qualify the venue as a base for a motorbike gang. Randall loved it. He didn't have a tattoo, and never would if his mother had anything to do with it, but his new friend at The Fret had suggested a henna tattoo strategically positioned so his mother wouldn't see it. Tonight he was ready to show it off. He'd left home sweltering in a sensible parka jacket, a V-neck sweater, and an Oxford shirt. Round the corner from the club he'd stripped off, pulling a denim jacket over a black t-shirt then shoving his good clothes into his rucksack. Guitar over his shoulder, he'd swaggered into The Fret ready to play and was rewarded for the first time with a brief nod of recognition from the doorman. Randall felt a foot taller just walking through the door.

He identified a free table at the back, furthest from the stage, set down his rucksack and guitar then made for the bar. The girl serving didn't seem to remember him, but then Randall had never seen her smile at anyone. Her severely contracted pupils told a story of opiate abuse that Randall longed to ask her about. He wanted to know what it was like. Not from an educational pamphlet or a teacher, with their particular bias and spin, but from an actual user. Why should he be lectured on the dangers of drugs by someone who had never used them? The bar girl had a scar that ran from shoulder to her elbow, tracing a line down the back of her arm that kept Randall awake at night writing fantasies in his head.

'What do you want?' the barmaid asked.

'Um, sorry, what?' Randall said, feeling his face burning and grateful for the lack of natural light.

'I said, what do you want? Biff, turn that fuckin' amp down would you, my friggin' ear drums are already bleeding!' she yelled.

'Vodka,' Randall said. 'Double, neat.' No one had ever asked him for ID in The Fret. As long as you could pay, you were assumed to be of age. The girl slammed a full but heavily finger-marked glass down in front of him. Randall pushed his money across the bar and tried a smile, but she had already turned away. It must be tough on her, he thought, doing such a physically demanding job. The club didn't close until 3am and she would be on her feet all that time. One day, he decided, he would stay until the very end and offer to walk her home. She should have someone to look after her.

Carrying the glass back to his table, Randall checked that no one was watching as he withdrew a Coke from his rucksack and topped up the drink. Vodka made him gag if he drank it neat but this way he could tolerate it. There was no way he was going to order anything as pathetic as a vodka and Coke from the bar, though. That wasn't what real men drank. His father had favoured port after dinner, single malt whilst watching television, and cider on sunny afternoons when they'd stopped at a bar during a walk. His family had done a lot of hiking, and whilst Randall could have done without the endless lectures from his mother about birds or geographical formations, his father had made it fun with tales of youthful exploits. Randall remembered their last hike as if it were yesterday. If they could eat only one dessert for the remainder of their lives, what would it be, their father had asked each of them. They had argued for an hour, maybe more. His father had settled on lemon meringue pie, three puddings in one, he had argued. Light crispy pastry,

79

hot lemon curd, and melt in the mouth meringue. Randall had made the case for plum crumble, and his father had agreed it as a close second. A week later his father had been diagnosed with non-Hodgkin's lymphoma. Two years later they'd held a funeral that had marked the start of the end of Randall's life. He hadn't been able to eat lemon meringue pie since.

Randall spotted Christian – he of the henna tattoo suggestion – a couple of tables away, deep in conversation. He downed a large mouthful of vodka and Coke, hoping Chris would notice him without him having to do anything dorky like wave. He filled in time tuning his guitar and trying hard not to check if Chris was still there. His patience was rewarded a few minutes later.

'Hey, dude, you're here again. Good to see you,' Christian said, offering knuckles as a greeting. 'And you got the henna tat done. That's looking good, Rand.' Randall grinned and forced himself not to slip the t-shirt off his shoulder to show the hennaed Celtic knot off more fully. 'Absolutely the right way to go. I bet a lot of the guys in here wish henna had been around when they were getting their ink. Some of the designs they're wearing went out with the ark, you know?'

'Yeah.' Randall laughed. 'Hey, how was your week?' he asked. 'I mean, did you do anything cool or anything?' He was sounding too keen and it sucked to have to work this hard to fit in, but Christian threw a companionable arm around his shoulders and slid back against the sticky faux-leather sofa.

'It was kind of tough, actually. A girl I know lost her sister, hypothermia. Horrible seeing someone in pain like that. Made me appreciate how lucky I am to wake up each day and do the things I love, you know?'

'Totally,' Randall said, kicking himself for not being able to respond with something more insightful. The coolest guy he'd ever met had just shared with him, and he'd come back with a line from a spoof teen movie. He really was a dickweed, just like the other boys at school said. 'I lost my dad,' he splurted. 'A couple of years ago. At first I didn't know how to deal with it, but now I want to express myself, you know? I don't want to hide how I'm feeling any more.'

'Hey, that's rough. I had no idea. Good for you for following your dream, yeah? You going to play tonight?' Christian asked.

'If there are any songs I know well enough,' Randall said. 'What are you doing while the university is on recess?'

'Catching up on the reading. So many books, never enough time. I've got a bit of casual work to keep the rent paid over the winter. You're in luck — I just got paid. Want a drink?' Christian asked.

'Hey, no, let me. I've got plenty of . . .' Randall said.

'No way, it's my turn to buy you one,' Christian said. 'Vodka, right? Unless you want an excuse to talk to Nikki?'

Randall stared at the girl filling glasses, deciding it was easier to dream from a distance. She was so far out of his league it was painful.

'No, you're good,' he told Christian. 'Vodka would be great. Thanks, man.'

Christian sauntered towards the bar in a way Randall had tried and failed to replicate. It may be only one foot in front of the other but some men made it look like the world was there only to provide a backdrop for them. Randall picked up his guitar and strummed a few notes. Tonight's starting band was just warming up, so it was a good time to make sure his strings were tuned. It was Christian who had first persuaded him to get up and jam. Randall had been sat at his usual out-of-the-way table, and Christian had wandered over asking if he could sit down. They'd begun talking and Randall had found he could speak to Christian without feeling like a fraud. That was two months ago. Since then Christian had been at

The Fret every Thursday night, and Randall wasn't too proud to admit that he looked forward to those precious minutes of chatting before the music got too loud for it. Christian had a way of putting things that made sense – wasn't it more embarrassing to sit there with a guitar than to just get up and have a go, wanting a tattoo was natural but try henna first in case you wanted to change the design, keeping the details of your private life from your family wasn't disloyal if it meant you maintained your sense of who you were – and Randall was finally experiencing that precious event: his first adult friendship. Christian, he thought, was exactly the kind of person he wanted to grow up to be.

Chapter Thirteen

Callanach and his mother exited the hotel bar by mutual silent agreement. Privacy was required, if Callanach could find the voice to talk at all. His mother had been raped. He was sure that's what she had said, yet it had taken minutes to process those few words. He'd looked around the bar. The man next to him was laughing too loudly, mouth open wider than was decent. A woman who thought she was beyond the rules was vaping in the corner. Another man was creeping his hand sideways to touch a waitress' behind. Then he'd seen the first tear fall from his mother's eyes and his world had begun to turn at full speed again. He'd held out his hand to take her arm, and gently pulled her towards the lifts, to her room, where he could ask all the questions he did not want to ask and hear the answers that he already knew would haunt him forever.

In her room, Véronique went to stand by the window. Laughter drifted up from the Royal Mile and Christmas lights flashed dimly in the darkness, colouring his mother's face as she stared out. Callanach sat on a chair in the corner and waited. He'd been here a hundred times, waiting for a victim to find the words they needed to begin their story. It didn't help to rush them. He knew his mother was doing what every rape victim had to do before starting to talk. She was breaking down the brick wall she had built inside herself.

'How much do you want to know?' she whispered.

'All of it,' he said. 'As much as you can bear to tell me.'

Véronique nodded and wrapped her arms around herself. Her knuckles were white. She turned her back so that her face was completely hidden and began to speak.

'I was twenty-two,' she said. 'Naive, I suppose. Your father and I had been married a year. He had always been so kind, such a gentle man that it never occurred to me that I could be unsafe when I went anywhere with him. Times were not easy then. Work in Scotland was hard to find. We were struggling to pay our rent. No one seemed to want to employ a young French girl, so he was supporting us both. What do you remember about him, Luc?'

Callanach had to think for a moment. His memories from when he was four, just before his father had passed, were blurred but the vision he had was of his father's hands always held out to lift him up, or to hug him. They were strong and warm.

'Warmth,' Callanach said. 'His face is less clear as I get older, but I remember his voice. And his laugh. I think every memory is of him laughing.'

'Yes. Always laughing,' Véronique said. 'That was him. Even when things were hard for us, he never lost his joy. He was a good man who only wanted to see the good in others. I was a virgin before I got married. A lot of women still were back then. Your father was the only man I . . .'

She broke off, resting her forehead against the window, her tears mixing with a drip of condensation as she breathed against the glass.

'You don't have to do this,' Callanach said.

'Yes, I do,' Véronique said. 'You have a right to know.' She sank down to sit on the window sill. 'Your father finally got a job at Edinburgh Bespoke, a furniture-making factory. Because of his experience and his manner with the other men, his employers made him foreman very quickly. We were able to move out from rented accommodation and buy a flat. We were stretching ourselves financially but it was all right. We were young and in love, and we got by. Your father was proud of himself. He was twenty-five, had a good job and we'd begun talking about starting a family. That job meant the world to him. He made every day funny, you know? He came home with stories about his colleagues, their families, little things that went wrong. He had this photo of me, taken during our first dance at the wedding, that he kept on his desk at work. He used to tell me how the other men would say that I was beautiful, that he was lucky. It was silly, vain, but I thought it was harmless.'

She broke off on a sob, one hand at her throat. Callanach wanted to put his arms around her but couldn't. Assault victims required space, not human contact, when reliving their experiences. He knew the form, had been trained endlessly on protocols and procedures. Still, none of it had prepared him for this.

'It was the work Christmas party,' Véronique said, hardening her voice, gulping a breath. 'I was wearing a green dress. Your father had bought it for me especially. He wanted me to look my best. It had a swing skirt, just above the knee. I told your father it was too expensive but he insisted. The party was at the warehouse. It was decorated, there was a tree, they put on some music, made punch. It was nice for me to meet the people I'd heard so much about, I felt like I knew them already. I was dancing with your father. He was driving us home so he hadn't had any of the punch, but I had. Just a couple of glasses, although that was enough to make me a little dizzy. I wasn't used to spirits and I don't know what they'd put in it, but it was stronger than I'd realised.'

As if she was still there, Véronique reached out for a glass that was sitting on top of a cabinet, opened the hotel fridge and poured sparkling water. She took a long drink and sat down on the deep window sill, legs huddled up into her chest.

'There was a telephone call. One of the company lorries had broken down and it needed to be towed to a garage, but it was full of furniture that had to be delivered the next day. Someone had to take out another lorry and bring the goods back to the warehouse. Your father was one of the few people still sober who could drive the truck. I hadn't wanted him to go, but there was no real option. I remember wanting to go home, but I was persuaded to stay. Mr Jenson, one of the partners, said he would look after me. I hadn't wanted to seem antisocial.

'As soon as your father was gone, Mr Jenson offered me a tour of the warehouse. He made me feel important, talked about how much they valued my husband, did I want to see his office, and I went. I never thought for a moment . . . The music was on loudly by then, very loudly. People were singing, dancing, there was a lot of alcohol. We went up to the top floor, which was deserted. I recall wondering why he was showing me, that there wasn't anything to see. The corridors were dark and there were heavy fire doors between sections of the building. We got to the far end, as far away from the party as you could get, and Mr Jenson told me that was where his office was. He opened the door. There was another man in there, one I hadn't spoken to but I knew that it was the firm's other partner, Mr Western. He got up from the desk, came to shake my hand, complimented my dress. Although he didn't say anything wrong, I remember feeling that I shouldn't have been there. It felt strange, two men in such a small room with me.'

Callanach could picture it more clearly than he wanted. His mother – young, incredibly beautiful, too scared to put a foot wrong, to insist that she return to the party. His father's bosses – entitled, made braver by alcohol and the knowledge that no one could hear what they were about to do. It was a scene that had been replayed through history, across decades, social classes and genders. It was about the powerful and the powerless. It was just because they could.

'I told them I needed the bathroom and that I had to go back downstairs. They had a bit of a laugh about something, I can't recall what, then I saw Western nod at Jenson. I think I knew when I saw that tiny movement, just how much trouble I was in. That was all it took. The fact that they had communicated with one another, excluding me. They put a . . .' She broke off, panting hard, shoulders hunched, head down.

'Maman, don't . . .' Callanach said.

'I have to,' she replied. 'They put a bag over my head, something rough, then one of them held me while the other . . . it was fast. I thanked God for that. And it was only one of them. Then the phone rang and it was as if, I don't know, they woke up. Like they'd forgotten where they were, or who they were. I was pushed to the floor and Western pulled the bag off my head, threw it at me, told me to clean myself up. There was some bruising on my arms – I'd struggled and they'd been forceful holding me. My hair was a mess from the bag and there was makeup running down from my eyes. I was shaking and clumsy. I think it was Jenson who got annoyed, telling me to hurry up.'

Véronique stopped, studying the empty glass she was still clutching and forcing her fingers to relax so she could put it down.

'What did Dad do?' Callanach asked. He needed to move the story along. It was a selfish perspective, he realised that.

His mother had had the courage to relive the worst moment of her life and all he wanted was to scrub the image from his mind. He wanted to turn back the clock never to have heard it.

'I didn't tell him,' Véronique said. 'I found my shoes. They'd been kicked across the room when I'd struggled . . . and I wiped the tears from my face and tried to leave. Western grabbed me just as I was opening the office door. "Tell anyone," he said, "and your husband is out of a job. We'll tell him it was you who came to us. And we'll tell everyone else in this city that your husband stole from us. He'll never work again. Not so fucking high and mighty now are you, miss pretty French piece of ass?" I heard those words in my head for years. His voice. The hatred in it. I don't know if it was the picture on your father's desk that set them off, or the way I spoke and the fact that I was French. But they chose me. They knew what they were doing. They gambled on the fact that I would never be able to tell your father, and they were right. So I went to the ladies' room and I cleaned myself up. I waited outside for your father for an hour in the freezing cold. I told him I was unwell and he took me home. I vomited as soon as we got back and he must have thought it was the alcohol, so that's what I let him believe.'

'You couldn't tell him?'

'Losing his job would have been the best-case scenario, Luc. Your father adored me. He'd have killed them, both of them, for hurting me that way. The thought of losing our house didn't matter to me, we could have lived on the streets and been happy, moved to France to find work, lived with my parents. But do you think your father would have walked away? Never. He would have ended up in a prison cell and all for the sake of me needing to share my pain. I loved him too much to tell him. Worse things happen to women, Luc. That's what I told myself. It was easier to stay quiet. Easier to bear my shame quietly, alone. Better than risking it all.'

'So no one ever knew?' Callanach asked. 'You've carried that alone all this time?'

'I told my mother, after your father died when we moved back to France. Your father's death devastated me but it released me from the need to stay in this country, near those animals. I was free to take you away and start again, and I was able to stop lying to the man I loved. I'm sorry, you don't need to hear all this.'

'There are counsellors, Maman. Even now it might do you good to get some help,' Callanach said.

'I don't want to talk about it,' Véronique said, smiling gently at him. 'I don't want it to be part of my present. It's the past. I'm sorry that I didn't have the strength to tell you before. Instead, I ran. Not from you, though. From the memories.'

'I understand the trauma,' Callanach said. 'But you know me. You know I could never be capable of causing the harm those men did you.'

'I do know that. Really, I do. But there's something more,' Véronique said. 'If I don't tell you now, I never will. Eight weeks after that Christmas party I discovered that I was pregnant. Your father and I had continued having a normal relationship. I knew that if I stopped being with him, he would know immediately that something was wrong.'

'Stop,' Callanach said. 'Please stop. Are you telling me . . .'

Véronique walked over, knelt before him and took his hands in hers.

'Luc, nothing has changed. You were the only thing that mattered. The man you have always thought of as your father, was the only father who ever had any influence in your life. He loved you so much. When you were born it was as if I lost half of him to you and I never minded, not for one second.

His smile was brightest when he looked at you. He would spend hours just holding you, watching you sleep.'

Callanach stood up. 'You should have told him,' he said.

'To what end?' Véronique asked. 'If he had known the truth, he would have been blinded by my pain. But I know that he would have loved you no less, no differently, and I have always believed that you are his son.'

'No. Not when Astrid came to you with her lies. For a while, then, you believed something else. Is that the guilty burden you came to shift? That you thought, for however fleeting a moment, like father like son. You thought that my biological father was the man who had raped you, and that I had turned out the same. That's why you left me,' Callanach said, picking up his coat and shrugging it on.

'Luc, it wasn't that black and white. I was devastated by the past all over again. Nothing made sense to me. I ran because I couldn't hide the pain I was feeling and you had more than enough to deal with. This conversation we're having now, that I always knew we would have to have one day, would have been too much for you back then.'

'It's too much for me now!' Callanach shouted, reaching for the door.

Véronique threw herself in the way. 'Please, please don't go. I know how you're feeling, I want to help you.'

'I've just been told that my life may be the result of a rape, and that the man I've believed all my life was my father may not be. You have no idea how I'm feeling!'

'I shouldn't have told you,' Véronique sobbed, collapsing into the chair, head on her knees. 'I thought it was the right thing to do. I thought it would help you forgive me.'

Callanach pushed the door gently shut and sat on the edge of the bed facing his mother. 'There's nothing left to forgive,' he said. 'Go back to France. You have to give me some time now.'

He stood up, left quietly and made his way back down to the street. It looked the same as he had left it, yet he felt it should have been different. That it should have changed with him. Everything he thought he knew about himself might be a lie. The solid ground beneath his feet was gone. His mother was even more a victim than him, yet he hadn't had the strength to be the man she needed, to comfort and reassure her. Callanach turned up his collar against the icy walk home, telling himself as he went that the tears streaming down his face could be blamed on the wind in his eyes.

Chapter Fourteen

The main gates to Louis Jones' car yard were locked and bolted. Leaving DC Tripp in the car, Ava walked the perimeter of the premises looking for a way in. It turned out not to require much effort. A back gate, through which lay a short alley, had been on the receiving end of some well-applied bolt cutters, its lock on the ground in two pieces. Ava pushed the gate fully open with her elbow, pulling on gloves as she entered and switching on a torch. The lot was full of vehicles. All had seen better days, most with dents that no amount of beating would repair. The whole place was surrounded by an eight-foot-high metal fence, the inside of which had been privatised using planks of wood. Jones wouldn't have wanted anyone noting the licence plates on his vehicles, of course. Ava wondered if any of the cars there had been driven by the man who'd abducted her. She pushed the thought aside. That wasn't what she was there for, and dwelling on it was a shortcut to misery. What she needed to figure out now, was who had been driving the crashed car.

Along one edge of the lot was a brick building. There was only one door that she could see and it was sturdy, probably reinforced. The windows, however, were another matter. There were only two and both were smashed, the displaced shards reflecting streaks of torchlight. Louis Jones, by the look of it, was having a very bad day indeed. Ava put her head to the first window, darted the torch around, announced the police presence even though the premises seemed vacant, and jumped in. Someone before her had been kind enough to dash any remaining glass spikes from the lower edge of the window. To the left-hand side of the room was a desk, each drawer ripped open, the contents scattered across the floor. A landline phone lay on the floor beneath an upturned chair, and sad-looking posters of supercars that had once adorned the walls hung in tatters.

The place had been ransacked. The question was whether the intruders had caused such carnage to send a message, or whether they were searching for something specific. A rack of keys along the right-hand wall was untouched. It wasn't a vehicle they were after, then. Ava glanced around for evidence of a computer, but outfits like Jones' rarely kept their records on anything as substantial as digital files. An internal door stood ajar, nothing but blackness showing in the crack. Ava walked to it slowly, kicked it open and drew a can of pepper spray from her jacket pocket. A screech came from the back of the area and Ava ducked, sending out a jet of pepper gas, slashing the torchlight left and right across the room.

'Police, stay where you are,' she shouted. There was no reply. 'There's another officer at the front door,' Ava lied. 'If you attempt to leave the premises, you will be stopped with force.' She stood up, focusing the light and her eyes on the rear of the room. Panicked fluttering and squawking filled the air.

Ava stepped forward, conscious that the ground beneath her feet had softened. Flicking the light downwards she saw that the floor was strewn with bedding. A mattress was overturned in the corner, and clothes that had once inhabited an upturned chest of drawers were everywhere. Straightening up, she noticed a large cage in the corner containing two parrots. They were staring, making her feel oddly self-conscious.

'What sort of person keeps caged birds in this day and age?' Ava muttered. The response was further screeching as she neared the parrots. There was a huge pile of bird seed on the floor of the cage and an empty packet on the floor. 'Someone knew they weren't coming back for a while, didn't they?' she asked the birds.

Jones had obviously been living in the back rooms. A toilet and shower were situated in a side room, separated from the bedroom by a plastic curtain. In the corner, a microwave, toaster and kettle provided cooking facilities. Ava cursed quietly as she realised she would have to arrange for the SPCA to collect the birds. Making her way back through to the front office, Ava read the scrawled handwritten notes scattered across the floor. No wonder Louis Jones was reduced to living on a mattress on the floor, if that was how he did business. She picked up the landline, plugged it back in and dialled recall for the last number that had phoned in, scribbling it down before leaving. The scene would have to be secured, by which time the driver of the crashed vehicle might have been located unharmed. Unless it really had been Louis Jones, Ava thought, in which case maybe a broken limb or two wouldn't be such a tragedy.

She went back out to the car and climbed in next to DC Tripp.

'Pair of parrots need taking care of,' she said. 'Ask the SPCA to come out in the morning. They've got plenty of food to keep them going until then. Have some uniforms come and secure the premises until we've located the owner.'

'Is it a crime scene, ma'am?' Tripp asked.

'Looks like it, unless the owner decided to redecorate in a rather unconventional manner. At the moment, though, we have no burglary complainant and no grounds for doing much. I don't know what's going on yet and I'm not kicking off an investigation until I do.' She dialled DS Lively's number.

'Haven't found the driver yet,' he said. 'Do we know anything more from Jones' file?'

'Nothing I can share,' Ava said. 'Who's in charge at the scene?'

'Chief Inspector Dimitri. He's getting it all packed up now, having the car towed. The dogs have been recalled.'

Ava considered the name. 'I've met him. He was the officer in charge at the Chief's suicide; he seemed very kind. Begbie would have liked him,' Ava commented. 'Take a note of this phone number, would you?' She read out the last number that had called in to Jones' landline. 'Check it out for me. Details for my eyes only at this stage. Jones' file is still confidential. Whatever's happened to Louis Jones, given the way he lived, I very much doubt there's an innocent explanation.'

Chapter Fifteen

Cordelia Muir was feeling under the weather, which was infuriating given the meeting she was due to have that morning. A large corporation was looking for a charity to sponsor and Crystal was on the shortlist for potential recipients. Those sorts of donations were invaluable. Smaller scale fundraising was a wonderful, personal way of people changing the world, but it was the big money that made a substantial difference on the ground. She hadn't slept well now for a few days, waking up sweating and feeling nauseous although she'd stopped short of actually being sick. Things had improved slightly over the weekend, but the meeting was scheduled for 3pm and with only an hour to go, she had a headache that was proving unresponsive to painkillers.

The new volunteer, Jeremy, knocked then put his head around her door. 'I'll be off shortly,' he said. 'Is there anything I can do before I go?'

'Could you get the conference room ready for the meeting, please?' Cordelia asked weakly.

'Of course,' he said. 'Are you all right?' Cordelia was known at the office for never asking anyone else to do jobs she had time to do herself, no matter how humble.

'Thumping headache,' she said. 'I'd do it myself, only . . .'

'No w-worries,' Jeremy said. 'Happy to help.'

'Thank you. I don't suppose I could push my luck and ask for a cup of tea as well? I'm so thirsty.' Cordelia took a handkerchief from her bag and dabbed her face with it.

'Sure. Shall I have Liam cancel the meeting?' Jeremy asked.

'No! Gosh, it's too important for that. I'll be all right.' She pushed her hair back from a damp semi-circle across her forehead. 'Maybe I should try to eat.'

Jeremy disappeared off to the kettle, watching as Liam Hood got up from his seat to go and speak to Cordelia. Jeremy had decided he didn't much like Liam. He was the sort of person who listened to your conversations whilst pretending to be busy, who would read emails over your shoulder. Jeremy had only been volunteering there a week, but he could see the good the charity was doing. Since Crystal had opened its doors eight years earlier, the initiative had provided clean drinking water to vast areas of Africa, village by village. Cordelia Muir was a woman with vision and spirit. Jeremy admired her.

'I can take the meeting for you, Cordelia,' Liam was saying as Jeremy took the tea in. 'I'm from a corporate background so I understand how these people think and what they want to hear. Why don't you go home? You obviously aren't well.'

'I've prepared the conference room,' Jeremy said, putting the tea on Cordelia's desk.

'Thank you,' Liam snapped. Jeremy glared at him.

'W-would you like a biscuit?' Jeremy asked. 'Maybe some sugar w-would make you feel better?'

'Jeremy, we're busy, if you don't mind,' Liam said.

'No, that's all right. He's just trying to help. A biscuit might be a good idea. Thank you, Jeremy,' Cordelia said.

He drifted back out into the corridor, hearing Liam restart his efforts to exclude Cordelia from that afternoon's meeting.

Taking care to arrange a selection of biscuits on a china plate, Jeremy made a mental note to stay away from Liam Hood. Some people were just trouble.

Ava was on the phone with the pathologist Ailsa Lambert before even sitting down at her desk on Monday morning. It hadn't been the best of weekends. Callanach hadn't responded to her calls, save for one brief text, which had made it clear he didn't want to be contacted. The hangovers that had been so easy to shift with sugar and saturated fat during her twenties were a much more impressive foe in her thirties, and as a result she'd felt wretched right through until Sunday morning. It wasn't until Monday at 6am that she realised she'd missed a voicemail on Friday afternoon from the city mortuary.

'Ailsa,' Ava said. 'Someone from your office called me on Friday. I didn't catch the name. Do you know what it was about?'

'I asked Sally to call you with the results from George Begbie's toxicology samples. They're back quickly because there's nothing to tell you. As I suspected, there were no drugs in his system and no alcohol. Every single result is consistent with carbon monoxide poisoning. In the circumstances, and I've spoken to the Procurator Fiscal about this, there is no reason to hold an investigation into the death. I went round to see Glynis myself Friday evening. We've released the body for burial. George has already been transferred to the funeral director's.'

Ava was quiet. It wasn't that she'd expected anything else but, she realised, she'd been hoping for more. The results were in and they were absolute. The man she had looked up to her whole career, on a personal and professional basis, had simply decided not to carry on. Had his life been so empty without work, she wondered? Is that what happened to police officers when the thrill of the chase was suddenly gone? The man she'd put on a pedestal was suddenly just a selfish prick who couldn't see how blessed he was to have a devoted family and to be loved.

'Thank you for letting me know. Do you have any idea when the funeral will be?' Ava asked.

'Glynis wants it done as soon as possible. Understandable in the circumstances. There was some mention of Friday but you should confirm with her,' Ailsa said.

'I will.' Ava put the phone down. She wandered through to the incident room, disturbing DS Lively mid bawdy-joke session. 'That phone number I gave you. Did you get anything on it?'

'Aye, I got something. I looked like a proper Charlie, ma'am. I phoned the number from the scene and it got picked up over at St Leonard's police station. I asked Chief Inspector Dimitri about it while we were all still at the scene. He explained that one of his team had checked the licence plate with the DVLA who'd provided Jones' details. They were trying to ascertain if the vehicle had been stolen. I felt a right chump for not recognising one of our own station's numbers. CI Dimitri properly took the piss out of me for it,' Lively said, to much guffawing from his band of fellow officers.

'I'm sure you were more than a match for the CI, Detective Sergeant. Did you manage to remain polite with the senior officer or should I be expecting a formal complaint today?' Ava asked.

'I simply told him you'd passed me the number, ma'am, and instructed me to call it,' Lively responded.

'Nothing else?' Ava asked, sighing inwardly at the smile on Lively's face.

'He may or may not have overheard me calling him a prick as he was walking away, ma'am.'

'Bloody brilliant. Complaint then. Right, I'm going over to

see Mrs Begbie. All queries to DI Callanach in my absence. Anyone seen him today?' Ava asked.

'He's in his office. Came in early. I've not seen him since,' Tripp said.

'Aye, he was looking all dark and brooding when he appeared to get his coffee. Just the way the girls like him, isn't that right?' Lively said, earning another round of laughter.

'They're short of people on traffic duties today. If anyone has nothing to do I can order a temporary transfer out of MIT,' Ava said. The result was a sudden rush of bodies away from comedy central back to workstations.

Glynis Begbie took her time opening the door. Ava smiled apologetically. 'Glynis, hello. I was wondering if I might speak to you for a few moments.' She looked at the tear-stained face of the Chief's widow and realised it wasn't a good time, not that there would be a good time in the foreseeable future.

Glynis looked behind her into the hallway and back at Ava. 'Now?' she said.

'Is everything all right?' Ava asked. 'I'm sorry, that was crass. I know you're not all right, but has anything else happened? You don't seem . . .'

Glynis stuck a nail in her mouth and chewed as Ava stuttered through a sentence that was never destined to go smoothly. She looked unkempt, nervy, and Ava thought she could see spider webs in her hair.

'I was sleeping,' Glynis said, running a hand down her crumpled clothes.

'It'll only take a minute,' Ava said. Glynis backed away. As she stepped into the hall, closing the door behind herself, Ava felt a draught. The air was musty and the dust that speckled Glynis' clothes had made a grey/white trail down the stair carpet. 'I gather you spoke to Ailsa on Friday,' Ava said gently.

'I did,' Glynis replied. 'The funeral director was very kind. She came round Saturday and most of the arrangements are being finalised today. There's a slot at the crematorium on Friday. You'll come?'

'Of course. And a few of the squad, those who knew George the longest. It's cold in here. Is there a problem with the heating?' Ava asked.

'I'm having to watch the pennies,' Glynis said. 'Only then I . . .' She began to cry. Ava moved forward slowly and put an arm around her shoulders.

'Why don't we go and sit down?' Ava asked. 'You're covered in dust. What were you doing when I arrived?' Not sleeping, that much was obvious, Ava thought, wondering about the lie as she walked Glynis through to the lounge and sat her on the sofa.

'After my sleep, I went up in the loft. The funeral director suggested that we might have some photos of George through the decades, for people to remember him by. My old albums were still in boxes from when we moved here. I've never been up there before. George used to do that stuff.' She took a handkerchief from her sleeve, wiping tears and dust from her cheeks. 'Now that I think about it, he did almost everything. All the banking. He handled our money. Occasionally I signed a piece of paper for a mortgage or a savings account. I never even wondered where it was all coming from . . .'

'It must be hard to suddenly start looking after yourself alone. Could you ask one of the children to . . .'

'No!' Glynis said. 'I can't have them involved.' She was shaking, her face even paler than when Ava had rung the bell, looking out into the hallway as if expecting a ghost to appear.

'Perhaps I can help,' Ava said. 'Is there anything in particular worrying you?' Glynis clutched her knees, eyes on the carpet. 'Why don't I go and put the kettle on?' Ava said. 'I'm not in any hurry. You stay here.'

She walked into the kitchen, closing the lounge door as she went, making a noise with the kettle and mugs, before stepping silently back into the hallway and taking the stairs. Something had upset Glynis, only upset didn't seem to be all the story. Ava would have said it was more like fear. The loft hatch was down, a ladder extending from above and pale light shining from within. Ava glanced back down the stairs to the lounge door. It was still shut and the sound of Glynis' soft sobbing was just audible. Ava began to climb.

The loft was, as Glynis had said, full of packing boxes, some of which were still taped up and labelled and a few whose tops were breached with items poking out. There was a clear path left through the centre to the rear of the loft. Ava left her shoes at the top of the hatch to keep her footsteps quiet as she crept through the half-dark.

It was well ordered for a loft. Cobwebs were located only to the sides, and the central floor planks were dust-free. At the very back were higher piles of boxes. Ava had to skirt around them to pick up a dropped torch, banging her head on a loose board that was hanging from the inclined ceiling as she stood back up. She directed the beam of torch light to inspect the offending board, and found herself staring into a space behind it. Climbing on a box to get a better look, she saw what looked like bundles of paper amongst the insulation. Reaching her hand in, she grabbed a sample and pulled it back out, stepping down to sit on the box while she investigated. It was a package, roughly hand-sized, wrapped in brown paper. She ripped the outside, knowing that she'd gone from treading over a line in a friendship to completely violating Glynis' privacy, but something was wrong and there was no point pretending otherwise.

In Ava's hands was a bundle of fifty-pound notes, slightly crumpled, undoubtedly used. She flicked through, noting the non-consecutive serial numbers, tallying in her mind as she went. There were at least one hundred in the package. She shoved them into her pocket and stood up again, craning her neck to look further into the wall cavity. As she shifted the torch, she saw the full extent of what was hidden there. Package after package lined the eaves space, enough that she couldn't possibly count them all. She stood back, doing some mental arithmetic. If each package contained five thousand pounds, then there was a bare minimum of a quarter of a million in there.

Ava pushed the stray board back into place, then shoved boxes in front of the area she'd disturbed to return the scene to the way she'd found it, before making her way back through the loft to the ladder. Nearing the hatch, Glynis poked her head up.

'Did you find it?' Glynis asked plainly.

'I did,' Ava said.

Glynis nodded. 'I'll get us that tea, shall I?' she said, moving back down the ladder.

They sat in the kitchen, the pile of cash on the table between them.

'You've got no idea where the money's from?' Ava asked.

'None,' Glynis replied. 'The board was hanging loosely from the roof when I went to find the photograph albums. I was trying to push it back when a packet fell out. The thing is, it makes sense, and now I feel like such a fool. It's as if, looking back, maybe it was easier not to have asked the right questions. George paid for everything with cash. We lived well. I mean, he wasn't on a bad wage by the time he reached Detective Inspector, and then at DCI we were extremely comfortable. Even so, I was worried when we moved into this big house. I had no idea we'd managed to pay off so much of the old mortgage, but George said he was a good saver and that he'd put a lot of extra cash into it over the years.'

'He never gave any hint as to the origins of the cash he used? Gambling seems like the most obvious source,' Ava said, pushing the notes with her fingernail.

'Whatever it was, he had reason to hide it from me. That's if it was me he was worrying about. How could he have kept such a big secret from me?' Glynis asked. She wasn't crying now. A calm had settled over her and she was staring at the cash with unhidden loathing. 'There's no way this ends well, Ava. I know it. You might as well call in the squad and get started.'

'We don't know what this is yet,' Ava said, hoping her face wasn't giving away the despair she was feeling inside. Privately, she knew Glynis was right. There was no way cash hidden behind boards in an attic came from a legal source. 'Maybe he just lost his faith in banks, decided to keep some cash at home. Maybe he had a gambling habit he didn't want to tell you about so he hid his winnings. There are any number of possibilities.'

'You don't believe that any more than I do,' Glynis said, standing up to throw the dregs of her tea into the sink. 'Phone calls late at night, George disappearing into the spare bedroom and closing the door so I couldn't hear, declaring he didn't want to disturb me. He never gave a good answer as to who was calling, and the truth, Ava, is that I didn't push him hard for answers. An old friend from the force with an alcohol problem who needed a pal, he told me once. Another time it was someone chasing details from cold cases. None of it felt quite right to me, but it was easier not to make a big deal out of it. Now here am I, stuck with God knows how much paper money in my roof and wondering how I'm going to make the next mortgage payment. I needed the life insurance to pay off the mortgage on this place. George's pension won't cover all the bills, and once this gets out, who knows if I'll even continue to get his pension. Perhaps it's what I deserve after letting him get away with lying to me.'

'None of this is your fault, Glynis, and you're getting ahead of yourself. The police pension would only be stopped if there was a suggestion that George had been involved in criminal activity,' Ava said. There was a long pause with no eye contact. Neither of them wanted to have that conversation. 'Leave it with me and say nothing to anyone, not even your family. If you're worried about money at the moment, there's no reason you can't use some of this. As far as we're both aware, it's rightfully yours. Just, you know, keep it subtle. Maybe change some of it into smaller denominations. If you don't mind, I'll keep one of these notes for now to see if I can trace its origins. I should go.'

Glynis said nothing, following Ava to the door and hugging her hard before she left. Ava sat in her car and stared at the fifty-pound note in her hand. There were strands trying to connect in her head but they wouldn't quite complete a circuit. Perhaps she didn't really want them to, she thought. George Begbie wasn't the sort of man who didn't trust banks and was reduced to shoving money under a mattress. He'd been at pains to secure the cash in a way that neither burglars nor Glynis would chance upon it. It was his failure to discuss it with his wife that really had Ava's hair standing on end. The Chief had been disturbed enough to take his own life, after a series of late night calls and a suspect parcel on the doorstep. Now Louis Jones was missing too. Ava didn't believe in coincidences, not on this scale. There was only one thing that made the criminal world go round. From drug dealers to human traffickers, arms dealers to fencers of stolen goods, it was all about the money. This was dirty. Her instincts were as real as the note in her hand. Much as she might have wished for the Chief to have been a closet gambler, she didn't believe that for a second. If so, he wouldn't have had to hide the money for so long. He could have filtered it into his bank account and Glynis would have been none the wiser. Ava wiped a single tear from her cheek. She couldn't spend time now with pointless hypothesising about what the Chief had done. There was work to do. Finding Louis Jones and asking him a few questions would be a start. Figuring out where the cash had come from came a close second. More importantly, if George Begbie had died because of the cash that was hidden in his attic, then the money hadn't come from anything as simple as a few bribes over the years. Payoffs to look the other way while a suspect escaped out of a back door or to ignore evidence during a search were an unsavoury but relatively common thing in the police, but no one came looking to get their money back. This much cash indicated a criminal conspiracy on a grander scale, and whoever had pursued the Chief was angry. The logical conclusion, the only conclusion in fact that Ava could reach, was that someone wanted their money returned and they weren't going to stop until they had it.

Ava managed to get to her desk without being waylaid. She signed in to the Police National Computer system and accessed the database.

The computer bore the news that Ramon Trescoe, the organised crime leader Begbie and Jones had put away, had been released from HMP Glenochil five months earlier. His address was listed as The Mazophilia in Glasgow. Dylan McGill was still safely behind bars. His involvement in the stabbing of a fellow inmate had resulted in the loss of early release privileges. McGill wasn't due out for another eight months. Ava logged out of the system, folded up the paper on which she had scribbled some notes, and thrust it into her pocket.

Callanach walked in as she was looking up Chief Inspector Dimitri's number. 'I'm off to the city mortuary, ma'am. Dr

Lambert has asked me to review the Lily Eustis case with her,' he said.

'Luc, about Friday night. I know I went behind your back and I'm sorry,' Ava said.

'I'll write up a report when I get back. I expect the results of the toxicology screens are in, so I'm guessing the case will be off our list. Once that's sorted I'm intending to take a few days leave. Will that be a problem?'

'No, of course not. It's short notice but while we're not involved in anything pressing it should be fine. Could I ask what for?'

He ignored the question. 'I'll be out of contact while I'm on leave, so you'll need to make sure there's another ranking officer in my place,' Callanach responded, turning to the door.

'I see,' Ava said. 'Send your leave request through as soon as possible then.' Callanach nodded and opened her door. 'Luc, wait. I didn't mean to cause more of a problem. You know I'm here, if you need me.'

'Not necessary, ma'am,' he said.

'Fine then,' Ava replied. 'Just one question for you. You met with a man called Louis Jones whilst investigating my abduction. What was your impression of that meeting?'

Callanach paused. 'In what context?' he asked.

Ava took a breath and tried not to over-react to the hostility in the room. 'In the context of the relationship between him and the Chief. Only I note that no one thought it appropriate to bring any charges against Jones, in spite of the overwhelming evidence against him.'

'That was a decision above my rank, one I had no say in. Jones and the Chief obviously had a long-standing agreement,' he said.

'I'm aware of that. I suppose I'm really asking how Jones and the Chief seemed together,' Ava said.

Callanach thought about it before answering. 'They obviously knew one another well,' he said, 'in the sense that you can see someone for the first time in several years and fall straight back into an old pattern of communicating. Anything else I can help you with?'

'No, thank you. You should go. Ailsa doesn't like tardiness,' Ava said.

He shut the door behind him and Ava reached into her pocket to touch the fifty-pound note. Louis Jones had been burgled and was missing, possibly injured in a car crash. The Chief was dead, a huge amount of cash secreted in the loft of his house. One of the men they had put away was back on the streets. It stank, but at the same time it was largely suspicion on her part that linked events. Starting an official investigation risked dragging Begbie's name through the mud with the potential loss of his widow's pension rights. Ava picked up the phone and dialled DS Lively's extension.

'What do we know about a club in Glasgow called The Mazophilia?' she asked. Lively burst out laughing. 'Want to clue me in, Sergeant?'

'Sorry, ma'am, you might be unfamiliar with the term but it relates to a breast fetish. That's probably all you need to know about the club. I've not heard much about it personally, but I can put some feelers out if you like.'

'Thank you. Discreetly, though. This isn't one for the squad,' Ava said.

'Got it,' Lively responded. 'I'll play this one close to my chest, so to speak.'

'Oh, for fuck's sake,' Ava muttered, hanging up.

Chapter Sixteen

Callanach couldn't think about what had happened to his mother. All he could do for now, was get through the working day then go home and pack. He needed to escape. From Scotland and from his desire to find the men who had hurt his mother, and to kill them. He had never been a violent man. Irresponsible in his youth, vain undoubtedly and brash with it, but he hadn't indulged in weekend bar brawls or used his fists unnecessarily. Now, though, he could imagine the crackle of fracturing bones, smell the blood, feel the warmth of their breath as those men panted for air.

Dr Ailsa Lambert was gloving up as Callanach walked in. She handed him a suit and invited him in to where Lily Eustis' body was waiting on the autopsy table. With the sheet up to her neck, if you could ignore the seawater grey/green of her skin, she looked asleep. The world had been deprived of so much promise. Ailsa handed him a sheet of paper on which various scientific terminology was listed together with figures. One line was highlighted.

'Tetrahydrocannabinol,' Callanach said. 'Cannabis, right? Not unforeseeable, in the circumstances. You think Lily went up into the hills to party and it went wrong?'

'It was in her blood, obviously, but the strongest concentrations were in her stomach. She hadn't smoked it. It was ingested in oil form. Medical grade, Detective Inspector. We found very little physically in the stomach but what was there was incredibly pure and strong.'

'Surely that's not easy to get hold of,' Callanach said.

'If you have a rice cooker, can follow a recipe and have access to good quality cannabis buds, then it's possible to make it at home. You dry the plant in the oven, cover it with a solvent to extract the cannabinoids and filter it. The rice cooker reduces it, then you evaporate excess fluid. You're left with an incredibly potent oil. In medical terms, a portion the size of a grain of rice will alleviate pain and aid sleep for several hours. Large scale production is quite sophisticated because of its flammability,' Ailsa said.

'So we know why she fell asleep so soundly,' Callanach said. 'Mystery solved. Have you notified the family?'

'I have,' Ailsa said, 'but I did so rather carelessly, I'm afraid. Lily's parents were horrified. Not the reaction I was expecting. Lily, they said, had never taken drugs in her life. She was the sort of girl who would rather go for a jog than take paracetamol. Apparently, this young lady was a vocal anti-drugs advocate, and that included marijuana.'

'They wouldn't be the first parents to be taken in by what their child was saying as opposed to what they were doing. It's not as if eating a cannabis cookie would have been a big thing,' Callanach said.

'I agree but their reaction was extraordinary, so I waited for fuller test results that take a little longer than the basic tox screens, specifically hair and skeletal analysis.' Ailsa handed Callanach a further sheet of paper, no highlights present at all.

'What am I supposed to be looking at on here?' he asked.

'Nothing. That's the problem. Lily's parents were right. I took a hair sample complete with root and I provided the screening centre with bone samples. Either or both of those would have showed drug use going back months, and in hair the length of Lily's we can go back a couple of years. It has come back blank, for everything. I had them test for every type of drug going. Her parents were right. It looks as if she stayed completely free of even over-the-counter pain relief.'

Callanach reached one hand out to stroke Lily's hair. 'Poor kid,' he said. 'First time she tried anything, and this is what happens. Her parents must be devastated.'

'Her parents don't think she would have agreed to use anything at all, and I'm tempted to agree with them. Lily was about to start her medical training. She was a hard-working, clean living, sensible girl. It's possible she had no idea she was ingesting cannabis oil. There was also alcohol in her body – spirits – nothing excessive, but it could have masked the taste of the oil. There was food too, consumed approximately an hour before death. A hotdog and something potato based,' Ailsa said.

'Spread the cannabis oil on the hotdog, cover it with tomato sauce or mustard. You think she wouldn't have tasted it?'

'My theory is that she was completely unaware of what was in her body until it was too late,' Ailsa said, taking a bag off a trolley and writing on the label to confirm she was taking it out for inspection. 'Look at this.' She took Lily's jeans from the plastic evidence bag and held them up. 'Note the zip,' she said. 'You remember the mark we found on Lily's abdomen, where the zip of the jeans should go?' Ailsa pulled the sheet back from Lily's body and ran her gloved finger up a line of faint bruising a few inches below the girl's navel. 'We photographed it, and blew the image up. The assumption that it was caused by her jeans because she had no other injuries led us astray. Let me show you.' She beckoned Callanach over to a computer, where two large photographs sat side by side with a grid over the top. 'When you compare the detail of the zip bruising on her body with the imprint we took from Lily's jeans, you can see that the teeth on the jeans' zip are very small. The marks on the body inspected under a microscope showed a larger style of zip teeth with bigger ends than the jeans have.'

'But there are no other injuries,' Callanach said, walking back over to Lily's body and looking at the zip bruising in situ on her abdomen. 'If she was pinned down, wouldn't there be other bruising or defence wounds? What's the motive for holding a young naked woman down, when there's no other assault involved?'

'I can only tell you what the evidence shows me. The most I can be certain of is that Lily was heavily sedated. The zip bruising, without other wounds, might have occurred as part of a consensual act for example, although the lack of DNA from another person's saliva, sperm or skin makes that a strange proposition.' Ailsa packed the jeans back into the evidence bag and resealed it.

'Are you saying she was murdered, Ailsa?' Callanach asked. 'I need a clear answer.'

'That's the thing, dear boy. There is no clear answer. I suspect she was drugged, but then she was neither physically nor sexually assaulted, which makes it hard to establish a motive.'

'Accidental death, perhaps? Couple of kids get silly with some drugs, play a prank on Lily by slipping her some cannabis. It goes wrong, they run.'

'Maybe. That doesn't explain the zip bruising, though, which must have occurred when Lily was already naked or the impression wouldn't have been so clear on her skin. The cannabis oil alone wasn't enough to have killed her. The cold did that. If it's a murder, it's a clean one. If it's an accidental death, a prank as you suggest, there would have been ample time to have called an ambulance or to have got her to a hospital. Someone else was there, and they chose to abandon her. At the very least, this looks to me like culpable homicide.'

'Manslaughter, you think. What do I tell the parents?' Callanach asked.

'That you're investigating it as a possible wrongful death,' Ailsa said. 'I'll see if we can match up the detail of the zip bruising with any known items of clothing or specific brands. I'm not sure how far that'll get you, but it's all I can think to do.'

Callanach phoned Ava from his car. Her mobile was busy, so he left a message and contemplated the leave he would not now take. Lily Eustis was owed an investigation. Her family needed answers. MIT was one Detective Inspector down since Ava had been promoted and not yet replaced. Ava was still coming to terms with DCI Begbie's death, and him taking vacation time would add to the pressure she was under. Leaving now was at best reckless and at worst, selfish. He had been remarkably restrained all weekend, punishing himself for hours at the gym to keep himself busy and sane. If he couldn't serve justice on his mother's behalf, in the short term at least, he would make sure Lily Eustis' grieving family were able to lay their daughter to rest with all their questions answered.

Chapter Seventeen

Cordelia Muir's house was predictably lovely. The bulbs inside the house had an orange glow that summoned images of Christmas and family occasions, where feasts were laid out on long tables and group photographs were taken, ready to be added to albums for posterity. He stared across the street, mindful to keep his face shrouded by the shade of a doorway, telling himself he was there to plan and observe, knowing there was an element of gloating to his visit. The front door was freshly painted with not a scratch on it. No sign of a 'no cold callers' card in the window next to the door. God forbid. The great Cordelia Muir would never fail to take pity on the lowly and desperate. She would invite those trying to make a living selling cheap toiletries or watered-down cleaning products into her home, offering them tea and biscuits. Buying a selection of their low-quality wares would be a joyful event, a matter of pride for her. Would Cordelia dump her purchases directly into the bin, he wondered. No, stupid, of course not. Plenty of charity shops would be glad of the donations, or perhaps the homeless hostels. He'd resided at a few of those himself over the years. Brief respite from the cruel weather and crueler people. A few bowls of hot soup with bread the supermarkets couldn't sell at the end of the day.

He grimaced. Those were the days before he found his purpose. With purpose had come the drive to make himself fit in with the seen, accepted world. Casual work, bank notes shoved into his shoes as he slept to keep the money safe. A bedsit full of fleas, stained carpets, a smell that got worse on hot days. But he'd been able to shower. That meant more access to better paid work. And so on and so forth. Now he could pass for an ordinary man on an ordinary Edinburgh street. He was on the inside. He had a laptop, access to the internet, knowledge of people's lives that they would be horrified to see if they took the time to look. Unprotected social media sites. Addresses. He stepped further back as the lady of the house passed an upper floor window.

His car was just around the corner. It was important to make the drive from the house to the hospital in advance, to make sure he was at the right place at the right time. If Cordelia was in an ambulance, they would have the speed benefit of lights and sirens. If Cordelia's daughter or a taxi drove her, then ten minutes longer. The accuracy of the dosage was less important than the time Cordelia took the drugs. That was going to require some manipulation. He knew exactly the day when he would administer the final, massive dose, having introduced the drugs slowly in her system, breaking down her body's ability to fight the toxicity. It would be enough that by the evening medical intervention would be inevitable. He had planned it with military precision. Cordelia had to take the dosage between three and four in the afternoon. The average time for an overdose to hit the system overwhelmingly was between seven and eight hours. Exact enough for him to plan. The correct dosage, administered crushed and undetected in a drink, was three and a half grams. Less than two and a half and Cordelia might not respond acutely enough. More than four and a half grams and death might visit too promptly. He knew exactly where he would be on the evening in question. Positioned for the best possible view of the show.

One of the windows of the brown brick townhouse opened and the waterfall strains of a running bath tumbled to the street. She knew she was ill by now, of course. Cordelia would be telling herself it was a virus, perhaps stress, maybe something that needed treatment but wasn't life threatening. A stomach ulcer or a bacterial infection. There would be a lurking doubt that it was something more serious but Cordelia would be self-cautioning against fussing. That stoicism was what had given him the time he needed to embed his poison into her body. Positive thinking would kill her in the end.

He surveyed the density of the late evening traffic, checking the queues at the junctions, spotting Arthur's Seat in the far distance, a black outline against the clear dark blue of a cloudless night sky. The stars had come out to watch Lily die. It had been almost sublime, he thought. He wished she hadn't begged for her life. There was a moment when he thought Lily was going to ruin it completely, but that hadn't lasted long.

The start of the evening had been mundane. They went to a bar, had a couple of drinks, he persuaded her to eat, pleading an empty stomach that needed filling. She was too polite to let him eat alone, even though his choice of food was a far cry from her usual healthy diet. Another girl might have agreed to take the drugs willingly, seeking out the freely offered oblivion. Not Lily. That was part of her draw. She had no desire to sully herself, so he had hidden the flavour of the cannabis oil beneath onion and relish.

Alcohol had masked the effect as they'd driven to Arthur's Seat and walked the hill. He had all the necessary equipment on his back and she, little trooper, smiled all the way in spite of the climb and the cold. Setting down the wood for the fire and the double sleeping bag to huddle in together, the end was already in sight. Lily had become weary as they'd neared the top of the hill, holding out her hand for him to pull her. He wore his thick woollen gloves. How sensible, she'd proclaimed, wishing aloud that she too had dressed more appropriately for the season. 'I'll warm you up,' he'd told her. 'I'll keep you cosy all night.'

The memory faded out as a car rolled past, reverse parking on the street in front of Cordelia's house. He pulled his hood up, making sure it was far over his eyes and turning sideways to avoid the impression that he was staring at the property. Lighting a cigarette from his pocket, he took a deep drag, one eye on the woman emerging from the car. Her dark skin and extraordinary bone structure were straight from Cordelia's gene pool. This was the daughter, then. The same age as Lily had been, and just as full of promise. He liked bright women. He liked how sad they were to die, knowing all they had waiting for them in their futures. When the stakes were higher, the rewards were so much more fulfilling. The daughter all but skipped up the steps to the house, using her own key to enter, calling to her mother as she went inside. He stared up at Arthur's Seat, relaxing, in no hurry to leave the Muir house. He could almost feel the exuded domestic bliss sinking into him.

The top of that hill, he thought, was the closest he had ever come to ecstasy. He'd made a small fire as Lily had wrapped herself in the sleeping bag, taking tiny sips from the hip-flask filled with port and brandy to keep the cold at bay. Mixed with cannabis oil the alcohol made your skin feel hot even when the air was ice, spinning your head until the world was an endless merry-go-round.

'I feel funny,' Lily had said, chin drooping towards her chest. 'Cuddle me?' she'd asked.

'One more minute,' he'd told her, striking a match and dropping it onto the kindling. There had been no point taking more than one log. The fire hadn't needed to burn that long. 'Don't fall asleep,' he'd whispered. 'I want to hold you.' Not in the way she was imagining, of course, but he found language to be a conveniently imprecise tool. 'Take off your clothes,' he'd said, smiling as she blushed at his words. 'I hope you're warming that sleeping bag up for me.'

With the fire between them, he'd played at arranging a circle of rocks to keep the flames within, watching Lily do as he'd instructed. Her fingers had grown clumsy by then, he remembered, her actions slowing with each passing minute, but she had been admirably unafraid. Lily had become a woman in that moment. It would have been an exquisite maturation had she not faltered at the last. Her lingerie – white with cornflowers scattered decoratively about – remained on.

'Those too,' he'd said.

'I thought you'd do that,' she'd replied, a shiver claiming her as she spoke. He'd moved around the fire, taking a knee at her side and pulling at her knickers with his still-gloved hands, knowing he couldn't afford to transfer treacherous DNA to her skin.

'Won't you take your gloves off?' she'd asked. That was the first moment he recalled feeling frustrated with her. He wasn't proud of it, but he'd imagined it all happening a certain way, the atmosphere charged with nothing but the mournful onset of grief. It was supposed to have been beautiful.

He'd instructed her, firmly, making clear that the time for idle flirtation was over, to take off her underwear and stay where she was.

'This isn't how I'd imagined it,' she'd said. 'I feel strange. Something's not right. I need to go . . . dizzy, not good.'

To his amazement, Lily had stood up. He'd thought her well

beyond the point where she would be able to stand unaided but that was the Lily he'd spent months coming to respect. She'd wavered left, then right, hands out like a blindfolded child playing a party game, seeking an object to hold for balance. Guiding her back towards the sleeping bag in spite of her increasingly loud and annoying protests, he had briskly removed her underwear before lowering her to the floor. Her hands had fluttered uselessly, swatting him with feeble resignation as he held her down on the ground. The cold had been seeping into her by then, but still he'd needed to hold her until she could no longer fight the urge to drowse. Wrapping the sleeping bag around her body, arms and all, he'd held her still with his weight as she'd tried – and failed – to escape. It had been like wrestling a feather. When at last the cannabis oil did its job, Lily had moaned a little as she fell asleep, tears rolling golden reflections of firelight down her cheeks. He hadn't touched them. They were too beautiful to destroy.

Checking his watch, he realised he'd outstayed his welcome in the doorway opposite Cordelia's house. Sheltering in a doorway for a quick smoke was understandable. Stay forty-five minutes and canny neighbours would assume burglar or stalker. Not like the limitless time he'd had with Lily. Two hours he'd sat on the hill top, watching her puffs of breath reduce in the freezing air, letting the fire dwindle and die, allowing Lily to dwindle and die. Her death rattle was the hiss of ice water on a hotplate. Her eyes had flickered, and for one sweet moment he had imagined himself kissing those mascara tinged lashes, a proper lover's farewell. Saliva, the tiniest drop, would finish him though. The police might be fooled into believing this was an accidental death, but he wasn't about to leave them the forensic equivalent of his mobile number. He had satisfied himself with taking her hand and gently removing the ring he'd made space for in his box.

No one else would understand. They would think he'd killed for pleasure, assuming some sort of base sexual urge. The point was that Lily herself was incidental. A means to an end. Just as Cordelia was. If he'd been explaining it to that sweet little Irish actor Sean O'Cahill, he would have said they were all just props. Their corpses were a small part of a greater work, where grief was the main attraction.

He looked at his watch. Work beckoned. What was that saying about the devil and idle hands? He smiled, stole one last glimpse at Cordelia's magazine-cover home, and finalised his plans to remove her from it forever.

Chapter Eighteen

'I'm going to throw up,' Sean said, every inch the melodramatic actor, as he raised his chin for his boyfriend Bradley to adjust his collar, flattening it, then lifting it again.

'I'm not sure which looks better. I think down. An upturned collar can say tosser if you're not careful about it,' Bradley said. 'And you're not to be sick. Nothing destroys hope like the odour of vomit on a man's breath.'

'Thanks for that,' Sean said. 'I'm sorry. You should be getting back to work. I was just so nervous, I needed you.'

'Look, you got the call back. You nailed the first audition. They obviously loved you. There's no reason to believe this won't go just as well.' Bradley stepped forward, clutching Sean's hands hard as he kissed him. 'It's your break. I can feel it. If I'm wrong, you can take it out on me later.' He winked.

'How do you manage to make everything about sex?' Sean laughed. 'Right, I'm going in. Don't wish me luck.'

Bradley watched him swish through the theatre doors and disappear. He checked his watch. Thanks to an early start, he could still afford to grab some lunch. The company he worked for didn't care how many minutes you took for lunch as long as you got results, and Bradley did. His risk projections were a thing of beauty, not that anyone else understood exactly what he did.

Ten minutes later he walked through the door of Café Nom de Plume on Broughton Street. One of his favourite places, and a haven for Edinburgh's LGBT community, its facade was stylish and welcoming, the staff were fun, and the food was fabulous. More importantly, this was where he'd first met Sean. Bradley had been sitting with a group of co-workers relaxing after a long afternoon of meetings. Sean had been with a gaggle of actors who'd just received a stinking review of an experimental piece they'd performed the previous night. Before long, the two groups had become one and Bradley had found himself staring into Sean's eyes across a table crammed with cups and crumbs. Sean had been a regular back then, although he rarely went in these days, preferring the gym during the day and wine-bars at night, alternating low calorie food with alcohol. Bradley had fallen in love with the sweet tables and traditional feel, often sitting happily alone and quiet, contemplating life.

Ordering an espresso, Brad took the table in the window, noting that he'd arrived later than usual and wondering if he'd missed his new friend. Christian – they weren't on surname terms yet – had recently moved to Edinburgh and found the café courtesy of a helpful internet chatroom. Bradley assured himself that he wasn't on the lookout for anyone new, but he was aware of his soft spot for a cute face and a sad story. Christian had presented both, and over the last few weeks they'd taken to sharing a coffee at lunchtimes before disappearing back into their own lives.

A tap on the shoulder roused him from his thoughts.

'Brad, how are you?' Christian asked. 'Sorry I'm late. I'm still trying to finish my thesis. Apparently, I'm having an off day. The joys of being a mature student. Have you ordered?'

'I've got coffee coming,' Bradley replied. 'Don't worry, I was late too.'

'Really? Everything okay?' Christian asked, pouring himself a cup of tea from the pot he'd brought to the table.

'Nothing exciting,' Bradley said, feeling himself shrink with the tiny lie, more an omission really. He hadn't talked about Sean much. The day they'd met, Christian had been sitting at a table looking so forlorn that Bradley had felt compelled to ask if he was all right. Two hours later and they'd shared more than either of them could ever have anticipated. Christian was reaching the end of a difficult relationship with a fiancée who was unable to come to terms with Christian expressing a desire to see how a male partnership might feel. Discovering and then acting on your desire to try out a same-sex relationship could be traumatic, Bradley knew, but especially when you were still in a straight relationship that no longer felt right. Many of his friends had been through the same painful process, and since then he'd spent many hours counselling Christian through it. Christian's only request was total anonymity, which was fair enough given that he was still living with his fiancée. Bradley had mentioned Sean in passing when they first got to know one another but these days he felt less and less inclined to discuss him. The guilt Bradley had felt when considering the motives for that disinclination was easily outweighed by the growing enjoyment of sharing his lunch hours with Christian, and so they had fallen into a pattern. They talked about work, politics, music, about their sexuality, but not about their partners.

'So, I've set myself a date,' Christian said. 'I know I have to leave her before the end of December. I think if I don't see the new year in being true to the person I am, I'll carry this heartache over to next year.'

'You sure you're ready?' Bradley asked as his espresso arrived.

'I know I'm ready not to live half a life anymore, and that's what matters. If she'd been able to accept me as bisexual then maybe it would have worked, but she's so adamant it's a phase – I'm halfway through my twenties, who the hell starts a phase now – and I know she's never going to compromise. It's the only fair thing to do, for both our sakes.'

'So you still haven't . . .?' Bradley asked in a whisper.

'No. I wanted to go out Saturday night and try a club, but it would have meant going behind my fiancée's back and I can't do that. I need to be single first. You think it'll be weird? I've spent my whole adult life only touching women. I can't imagine what it'll be like running my hand over muscles like my own. Hey, sorry, I should stop – this was more than you were expecting over a quick coffee, wasn't it?'

Bradley closed his mouth, aware that he'd been sitting with parted lips as he pictured the scene.

'The first moves are the hardest, but they're also the most exciting. Listen, I know we agreed to keep it here but take my mobile number.' Bradley took hold of Christian's hand, turned it palm up and wrote his mobile number, thinking how big Christian's hands were, strong but soft, trying not to wonder how they would feel running over his own body. 'Call me any time if you need to talk. Any questions, even if they seem stupid to you. I wish I'd had a friend to go to when I first came out. It would have made it so much easier. Let me help, if I can.'

'You know I can't ask you to do that. It wouldn't be fair on Sean for you to be getting calls from someone he doesn't know. This means so much to me already, I don't want to jeopardise it,' Christian said.

'Text me before you call. If I can, I'll phone you back. You shouldn't go through this alone.' He held Christian's hand briefly, squeezing it before standing up. 'Now I really do have to go. There are some numbers that need crunching.' Bradley cringed at his own dull cliché.

'I'll just finish my tea,' Christian said, standing up and reaching his arms towards Bradley's shoulders, hugging him hard. 'Thanks, Brad. I don't know what I'd do without you.'

Bradley left, too aware of the rising tension in his mind and of a related rising in his groin. Christian's body was firm and wiry. He was taller than Bradley and that felt good. He tried to squash the thought before it was fully formed, but too late. It was nice to be held by someone bigger than him, stronger than him. Sean always seem so fragile and vulnerable. Christian was more alpha male, had the body of predator rather than prey. Not that he was comparing them. He was happy with Sean, he reminded himself. More than happy. They fit. They worked.

His mobile phone rang.

'Put something fizzy in the fridge,' Sean said. 'I got it! I am now a full-time member of a professional theatre group. I have the first script in my pocket. I will receive a wage, and I can stop doing crappy unpaid auditions every other day! Yes, I know, you told me so.'

'I never doubted it,' Bradley said, smiling. 'Clever you.'

'Right, love you, see you tonight. I have to get off the line and text every person I've ever met. This is going to be the most exciting year of my life. Of our lives. I can just feel it,' Sean said.

Chapter Nineteen

It wasn't until Tuesday morning that Ava finally got a call from Chief Inspector Dimitri. She waited for the complaint about DS Lively, prepared to defend him to an extent but only out of squad loyalty. The reality was that the Detective Sergeant had been given enough chances to get a grip on his insubordination. Sooner or later he was going to have to face the consequences.

'DCI Turner, sorry to bother you. I know you've a lot on your plate, only I gather you were at Louis Jones' property on the night of the car crash,' Dimitri said.

'I was,' Ava replied.

'That's no problem at all. It's just that as I'm heading up the car crash investigation I was wondering if there was something I should know? Maybe we could pool resources.'

'I didn't find anything helpful, I'm afraid,' Ava said. 'Apologies if I've crossed over into your territory.'

'Don't give that another thought. It's just that I had a report from an SPCA officer who'd been called in to rescue some caged birds. I already had Jones' details from the DVLA and sent some officers over to check out the address,' Dimitri said.

'It only ended up on my desk because of an administrative directive. We'll leave it in your hands now. Is there any news on the driver?' Ava asked.

'No, and frankly I'm not expecting any. If Jones was the driver, he seems the sort of chancer to have fled the scene. The car wasn't taxed or insured. My theory is that the other tyre tracks belonged to a friend who picked him up.'

'Yes, but the state of his premises, the way he left his birds. Do you not find that odd?' Ava mused.

'It's certainly something we're bearing in mind, although men like Louis Jones seem to attract trouble, so I don't think we'll have a shortlist of suspects for the burglary any time soon.' Dimitri laughed.

'I hear you. Jones is all yours from now on, Chief Inspector. Apologies that my squad stepped on your toes.'

Ava hung up, taking the fifty-pound note from the desk drawer where she'd stashed it overnight, then logging into the police database and typing in the note's serial number. It took a few minutes, but the result was blank. The money, or this note anyway, was not on any criminal evidence files. She was unsurprised. The bundles of money had looked well handled. If it was dirty cash, it had been laundered. It had to have been, for the Chief to have felt comfortable using it.

She checked her watch and turned on the television. Callanach was due to give a press conference about the Lily Eustis case, appealing for witnesses in an attempt to find the person or people with whom she had shared her final evening. Police Scotland was keeping its escalating concern about the suspicious nature of Lily's death under wraps for now, but they needed the public's help if the investigation was to gain ground. There was a pause as the Eustis family settled themselves at the table, then Callanach began to speak.

'We are asking for the public's co-operation in relation to

Lily's death . . .' Callanach recapped the facts as Ava tuned out. Lily's mother and father were so pale they might have been projections. Her sister was at the edge of the shot, staring off into the distance, swaying slightly. Ava hoped someone in the room was keeping an eye on her. The poor girl didn't look well. Callanach had finished speaking and was handing over to Lily's father to read out a prepared statement. Ava had already read the draft so she switched her attention back to Luc. She'd expected him to be angry after setting up the meeting with his mother but she hadn't been prepared for his coldness. Being the boss was a mixed blessing. A few months ago if he'd behaved like that she'd have had it out with him there and then. Now she had to restrain herself. He looked tough, she thought, as if he was walking into a fight. His mouth was pinched, his cheek bones standing out against his dark hair. His eyes were such a deep shade of brown they were almost black. On screen they were completely arresting. She wanted to talk to him about the Chief, about the money she'd found in Glynis Begbie's loft, but sharing this particular problem wasn't fair. Sooner or later a decision would have to be made about reporting the money, but both the Chief's reputation and his widow's financial stability were at stake. Then there was the matter of Louis Jones' disappearance. Find Jones and maybe she would get some answers, albeit possibly not the answers she really wanted. She called DC Tripp in.

'I need landline phone records for Louis Jones at the address we attended this weekend,' she said. 'Use a different reference than the road traffic accident crime number would you? I've promised CI Dimitri we won't tread on his toes.'

'Looking for anything in particular, ma'am?' Tripp asked.

'Not sure. Put together a file on the burglary of his premises as a reason to be investigating. Also, do we have any street contacts in Jones' trade? I need to know where he hung out when he wasn't at work, who his close friends were. The usual stuff.'

'DS Lively is your best bet for that. I'll ask him. At the moment everyone's waiting to see what feedback we get from the Lily Eustis press conference. What do you think, murder or a night out gone wrong?'

'Your guess is as good as mine,' Ava said. 'Either way, it's a life lost that shouldn't have been. I only hope Lily didn't die scared. That's no way to spend your final moments. I'd take pain over fear any day.'

Chapter Twenty

Lily's sister, Mina, had asked her parents to drop her at the university library after the press conference, and they hadn't argued. Mina had a notebook and pen with her, which was as much of a pretence as she could muster that she was going to the library to study. Home had become a prison of grief. Her mother spoke only in bursts of two or three words, and her father had developed a cough that seemed to never let up. She texted Christian from the library entrance and he arrived a minute later, carrying books under his arm and looking concerned.

'I saw it on the television,' Christian said, hugging her. 'How are you holding up?'

'I'm losing my mind,' Mina said. 'Can we go somewhere else? If I hear another ticking clock or person whispering, I think I might start screaming.'

'Come on,' Christian said, taking his scarf and wrapping it around her neck. 'Let's get a drink. F. Scott Fitzgerald can wait.' He put an arm around her and bundled her through the doors. 'I'm flat-sitting for a friend this weekend. Let's go there.'

★   ★   ★

The apartment was on Annandale in a brand new brown brick, smoked-glass square block opposite the carpark and bus station.

'This is expensive, so close to town,' Mina said. 'Who's the friend?'

'Someone I used to do a bit of work for,' Christian said. 'He's away on business a lot and prefers it to be occupied, so I get to look after the place. It's got two bedrooms, it's an easy enough walk from the uni, and he always leaves the bar stacked. What can I get you?'

'Vodka?' Mina asked, standing at the window and staring down into the street.

'With orange, Coke or neat?'

'Neat,' Mina said. 'Is there ice?'

'Knowing Mikey there'll be enough ice to sink a ship. Give me a second,' Christian said walking through to the kitchen. 'Should you not at least text your parents to let them know what time you'll be home?'

'They've both turned their phones off. The police agreed to make sure all contact goes through the landline. Too many concerned friends, too many requests for stories from the press. Mum threw her phone into a bin in the street then realised she still had photos of Lily on it and ran back. She had to empty out the whole thing. By the time she found it there were people standing around staring at her.'

'You said on the phone the police had found something,' Christian said. 'Do you want to talk about it? You don't have to. We can watch a movie or you can just sleep on the couch, whatever you need.'

'Could I maybe just lie down a while? I can't sleep at home. Lily's everywhere I look. I can hear her music, smell her perfume. Then there are the nightmares.'

'Come with me,' Christian said, taking her by the hand and leading her into a short corridor. 'This is my room for now.

Take my bed.' He opened the door and let Mina through, remaining in the doorframe as she kicked off her shoes.

'Stay with me?' she asked. He shook his head slightly, running a hand through his hair, and closing his eyes. 'Please?' she said, lying down. 'I can't stand to be alone anymore.'

'Just until you fall asleep then,' he said. 'But nothing can happen between us, Mina. When you look back, I can't have you feeling as if I took advantage. I care about you too much for that, and my life is kind of complicated at the moment, too.'

He lay down, slipping one arm under Mina's head so she could move closer to him, resting her forehead against his shoulder and staring up into his eyes.

'Why did they suddenly call the press conference today?' he asked, stroking hair away from her eyes.

'The lab results came back, all those tests they ran. The levels of cannabis in her body were crazy high. They think that's what made her fall asleep up there.'

'Cannabis?' Christian asked. 'You said she didn't smoke. I've never known anyone get so high on weed they didn't know they were getting hypothermia.'

'That's what the police were interested in. Apparently, she ate something with cannabis oil in, a really strong form of it. It's not fair,' Mina said, putting a hand over her eyes. 'She hated drugs. Lily was fit and healthy. She didn't even take sugar in her tea. When she realised she'd been drugged, she must have been so scared! Oh God, I'm sorry, I promised I wouldn't break down again. I just . . . I don't know how to live without her. It's like being torn apart inside. The pain is crushing. I wake up in the night and I can't breathe. I miss her so much. Do you know what this is like? Because I need someone to tell me that it gets better. If this is what it's going to be like from now on, then I don't think I want to bother waking up.'

'Where's her body now?' Christian asked. 'Will they let you see her?'

'Still at the city mortuary. Mum and Dad have been, but I can't face it. I don't want to remember Lily like that. It's not her anymore.' Mina lay shaking, her body beyond control, her head butting against Christian's chest.

'Maybe you should,' he said. 'Perhaps it'll help you come to terms with what's happened. Knowing she's gone so you don't keep hearing her at home. I know it'll be hard but I lost someone once. I tried to push it away but in the end facing it, accepting it, was the only way to stay sane. It's no bad thing to be able to say goodbye.'

'I don't think I'm brave enough. How can I look at my sister's face knowing it's the last time I'll ever see it?' Mina rolled away to face the wall. Gently, Christian pulled her back into his arms and lifted her face to his.

'I'll look after you. You don't have to tell your parents. You're an adult and a family member. You have a right to see Lily and you're braver than you know. The truth is, I don't think you can feel any worse than this. Imagining it is almost certainly worse than seeing her. She's at peace now. Whatever did or didn't happen to her, it's over. Perhaps if you see her for your-self, you can stop making up horrible scenarios in your mind and deal with the reality. I'll be there to catch you. You know that, right?'

'Don't leave me, okay? Just don't leave me and maybe I'll get through it,' Mina muttered, closing her eyes. 'If something happened to you as well, that would be the end. I know you told me right at the start that there was someone else in your life, so I understand this is all there can be between us, but I really appreciate you being here. You're a good person. The truth is you kind of remind me of my sister in that way.'

Mina let her body relax, breathing more slowly until finally her body lost its tension into sleep. Christian held her for the two hours until she awoke, watching each dreamed emotion cross her face, protecting her from the spectre of waking upset and alone. He knew too well how badly that stung.

Chapter Twenty-One

'Good afternoon.' Callanach began the briefing. 'You're all aware of the general circumstances of Lily Eustis' death. What we were unaware of, was that Lily had ingested a substantial amount of extremely potent cannabis oil such as would have prevented her from being in a fit state to have made her way safely back down the hillside. The press conference today was an appeal for witnesses city-wide who might have seen Lily out that night. We know she was not alone. Finding the person or persons she was with is the only way to establish whether Lily died as the result of a night out gone wrong or if there was a motive that might indicate murder.' He brought a map up on the screen. 'This is where the body was located. A small fire had burned out several hours before the body was found.'

'Do we know anything about what was used to start the fire?' a constable asked.

'There was nothing unusual in either the wood or the accelerant. Both could be purchased widely at petrol stations and elsewhere,' Callanach said.

'There wasn't much in the way of ashes,' Lively cut in. 'That means whoever laid the fire had no intention of letting it burn for a long period of time.'

'Or Lily passed out very early on, they couldn't revive her and ran. Maybe they never got the fire to the point they'd intended,' Callanach replied.

'They were never in the boy scouts, then, Detective Inspector. I'd have set the main log with kindling beneath it from the start, to get the underside properly dry otherwise the kindling would have burned out too fast. Looks to me as if whoever was with her made a show of lighting a fire but never really meant to get it going,' Lively finished. There were murmurs of assent around the room. Callanach considered the scene anew. It was possible that it was just a teenager who had set the fire naively, but then they had taken the time and trouble to make a stone circle to contain the flames. More likely than not they had some experience of lighting fires in the past.

'Right,' Callanach said. 'This is the drone footage that led to Lily's body being found.' He pressed play and the screen came to life. 'As it comes over the ridge, you can see the body in the distance, and it ends up directly overhead in a few seconds. Her clothing is littered randomly down the hill though we can't be sure if Lily did that herself, if someone else did it, or if the wind moved the clothes overnight. There's no particular pattern to them that we can make out.'

The screen was frozen on a close-up of the body. From the middle of the room someone muttered, 'Oh shit, I completely forgot.' Callanach looked up to where a red-faced PC Biddlecombe was chewing her knuckles.

'You forgot what?' Ava asked from the back of the room.

Biddlecombe's head shrank beneath the line of her shoulders. 'I forgot to pass on a message from yesterday,' she said. 'From Lily Eustis' sister. She couldn't get anyone from MIT on the phone and the call diverted to me. Sorry, sir,' Biddlecombe said, daring to look up for half a second and meet Callanach's eyes.

'Constable,' Callanach said. 'It might be more helpful if you told us what the message was.'

'Oh, sure. She wanted to know when she could get her sister's ring back. They had matching rings given by their parents for Christmas last year, she said. Apparently neither of them had taken them off since. I told her either we'd be keeping it as evidence or it would be with the body at the mortuary.'

'It's definitely not in the evidence logs, and we've combined our list of items seized at the scene with all the items taken from the body and clothing at the mortuary,' Tripp said.

Ava flicked to a picture of Lily's corpse in her file and stared at the hands. 'Get a team round to the Eustis' home. I want it checked for that ring. Ask her parents when they last saw her wearing it. If we can't find it . . .' her voice trailed off.

'Then it's possible someone removed it from her body before we reached her. DS Lively, head up the team and report back before the end of the day. Tripp, phone the mortuary and double-check there was nothing missing from their evidence list. Also, have them inspect Lily's fingers for indentations. If it was taken off shortly before or after death, there may still be a visible sign that she regularly wore a ring,' Callanach said.

'It's George Begbie's funeral Friday,' Ava said. 'Will you come?'

Callanach was at his desk scribbling notes from the calls he'd taken in the previous two hours since disbanding the briefing.

'I will if I can,' Callanach said. 'Lily Eustis' parents have confirmed what Mina said about the ring. Neither of the girls ever took them off. The ring can't be found in Lily's bedroom or anywhere else within the house.'

'What did the pathologist's office have to say?'

'They confirmed there's an indent on the fourth finger of Lily's right hand, which is the finger on which the parents had independently told us she wore it,' Callanach said, putting down his pen and looking at Ava.

'The combination of the drugs, the zip bruising and the missing ring puts this into a different category. Shall I warn Superintendent Overbeck we'll be upgrading it to a possible murder?' Ava asked.

'Yes. DS Lively notified the family when he was there. I'm withholding the details about the ring and the zip mark from the press, and I've requested that the family not discuss details with anyone. Finding the ring might be the only way we can put a suspect with Lily on the night in question.' He looked at Ava who was studying her feet. 'Was there anything else?'

'Not really. Actually, yes. Are you okay?' Ava asked.

'I've got a dead girl, no motive, and no forensics from a killer who almost got away with making a crime scene look like a night out gone wrong. So no, not okay,' Callanach said.

'I didn't mean this case, I meant . . .'

'I know what you meant and I'm telling you I need to get on with sorting out this murder. I'll do my best to get to the funeral on Friday. Did you make any progress regarding Louis Jones?' Callanach asked.

'That's off my desk,' Ava said. 'Chief Inspector Dimitri is following up on Jones' disappearance following a road traffic accident. Nothing for MIT to worry about.'

'That's good. You asked me before how Jones was with the Chief. I remember feeling uncomfortable not making any notes or recording the conversation. Jones was working beyond the law and the Chief was ignoring it. Whatever arrangement they had all those years ago, time hadn't reduced its importance to either of them,' Callanach said.

Ava nodded, not trusting herself to speak.

'Keep me updated,' she said, slipping out and closing the door behind her, hoping Callanach hadn't noticed how badly her hands were shaking.

Chapter Twenty-Two

Mina walked into the city mortuary alone on Wednesday morning. Christian had remained in his car over the road on Cowgate, promising to wait for her. She'd wanted him to go in with her, but only family members were allowed. She'd requested a viewing of Lily's body the day before, been told the police had to approve the request, and notified of a time to attend shortly after that. It seemed perverse, needing police consent to visit her own sister, but Christian had said it made sense. Her sister was gone. The corpse was evidence. He had texted her on and off throughout the night as she fretted about whether she was doing the right thing. In the end she had fallen asleep knowing she had to see Lily's face once more if she was ever to stand a chance of laying her to rest.

An assistant came out, sat her down and explained the procedure to her, telling her what to expect. Nothing she hadn't suspected. That Lily's face would be discoloured. That her sister might seem a barely recognisable shadow of the girl Mina loved.

'Let's go through to the viewing room,' the mortuary assistant said. 'Are you ready?'

'Yes,' Mina said, knowing she never could be, standing anyway and following.

'As the case is still active, you'll need to stay behind the glass partition. Lily is already there. Just give me a moment,' the assistant said, putting on an apron and gloves.

Mina touched the ring on her right hand. It was gold with a thin band and a knot on the top. Their parents had given the rings to her and Lily on Christmas morning the year before. As children Lily had copied everything Mina did or wore, and for years it had driven her mad. As young teenagers, she'd felt a growing sense of pride that her younger sister looked up to her so much, waiting patiently for every hand-me-down, always grateful. By the time Mina had turned eighteen, Lily was the same height and they had joked about wearing the same clothes, enjoying their bond, often choosing the same colours and styles. The rings they wore were a constant reminder of their love for one another.

Mina looked up. Lily was not as changed as she had feared. Her skin, devoid of the bloom of blood, was almost translucent, and Mina couldn't look away from her eyelashes. They laid so gently against her cheek, so familiar, long and dark. Mina had been the first person to put mascara on those lashes, transforming her little sister into a doll, laughing as she applied lipstick, landing more on her chin than her lips. Mina longed to touch those lashes, to feel their softness. The eyes beneath would never open again.

Checking there was no one else in sight, Mina took her mobile from her pocket and switched on a mobile video-conferencing app, dialling Christian where he sat across the street. He'd suggested the app the day before when they'd realised he wouldn't be able to go in with her. Holding the camera up to her own face, Mina let her tears run unchecked as Christian answered.

'I'm here,' she whispered.

'You'll be okay,' he replied. 'You look pale. Do you need to sit down?'

'No, it's weird, I don't know what I was expecting, but she's still her. Lily's still beautiful. It's almost harder being this close and not being able to touch her,' she said.

'I get it,' he said. 'Lily will always be your sister. No one can take that from you. What do you need me to do? Do you want me to see her or would that be too hard for you? It's up to you.'

'I think . . . I think I'd like that actually. I wish you'd been able to meet her when she was alive. You'd have really liked her. Do you mind if I show you?' Mina asked.

Christian paused. 'I'd be honoured. I feel like I know her so well from what you've told me. Go ahead, whenever you're ready.'

A few seconds passed with the phone camera pointing towards the floor, then it tilted and Lily's face came into view, her body covered with a sheet as she lay serene in the viewing area. After a while, the camera view changed again and Mina's face filled the screen again.

'She looks so much like you.' Christian smiled. 'Kind of makes me wish I had a brother or sister.'

'I wish I could make her come back to me,' Mina whispered. 'I'd give almost anything for one more day with her.'

'I know,' he said. 'Take your time. I'm here waiting, there's no pressure.'

'I'm coming out,' Mina said. 'I can't look at her anymore. Part of me expects to be able to wake her up and take her home. Give me five minutes.'

She turned off her phone, putting one hand to the glass and kissing the place where she could see her sister's lips.

The assistant was waiting to walk her back through the corridors. Mina left, retracing her steps towards Christian's car. He was out and opening the door before she reached him.

'Hey you,' he said, putting his arms around her shoulders and hugging her tight. 'Tell me how you're doing.'

'I shouldn't have gone,' Mina whispered. 'I think . . . I think my heart broke. It may sound stupid but it's as if I felt it. I don't know why I'm alive anymore.' Christian held her tight.

'Sir, we've got a possible sighting of Lily Eustis in a bar in Dalkeith,' Detective Constable Tripp said, putting his head around Callanach's door.

'How possible?' Callanach asked.

'The girl seemed pretty certain on the phone. We're bringing her in to make a statement and work with an artist. She'll be here in a few minutes.'

Amelia Lock was sixteen. Her mother had accompanied her to the police station, and Callanach noted the tension between them as Tripp brought tea and biscuits.

'I was out with friends,' Amelia said. 'The pub was the only warm place to go. We were going to go to my mate's place, only their dad was on a bender and we didn't want to piss him off.'

'Had you drunk much alcohol?' Callanach asked.

Amelia glanced sideways at her mother before answering. 'A bit,' she said.

'More than a bit, I'll bet,' her mother chipped in. 'Was it that Louise who bought the drinks? Dressed up to the nines, makeup so thick you could make a sandwich with it. I told you I didn't want you hanging around with her no more.'

'It's important to assess how reliable your memory is, Amelia. You're not in trouble with the police, but I need to understand the state you were in,' Callanach said.

'Two pints of cider.' Amelia paused. 'And a couple of shots of vodka. I'm sorry, Mum. I won't do it again.'

Her mother tutted. Callanach carried on before she could start a further lecture. 'What do you remember?'

'It was only when I saw you on that police thing on TV with the girl's parents. I saw the photo and I recognised her. We'd been sitting at a table in the pub together, sharing it. It was really crowded. There were a few groups out for work Christmas drinks, the music was loud, you know? Anyway, I was sitting next to the girl at the table and I remember thinking how pretty she was and how I hadn't seen her in there before. You see the same people around Dalkeith all the time. She looked so happy. I know that sounds stupid, but you don't see it very often. I suppose she just stood out.'

'Can you describe what she was wearing?' Callanach asked.

'Yeah, her top was like this red cotton shirt, nice cut. It was lovely. Probably jeans as well but I'm not so sure on that one,' Amelia said.

'Was she with anyone that you saw?'

'A man. Just the two of them as far as I was aware,' Amelia replied. 'He was quite tall, not really tall but not short and not fat. He was wearing a baseball cap, I'm not sure what colour his eyes were. The pub had loads of Christmas lights up and the main lighting was dimmed. He was white, probably in his twenties. Sorry, I didn't really look at him,' she said.

'How long were you next to them at the table?' Callanach asked.

'Not long. One drink then they left and we shoved along and had their seats. How did she die?' Amelia asked.

'I can't discuss it at the moment, I'm afraid, but you've been really helpful. We're going to ask you to work with an artist to do the best you can to remember the man she was with. Is that all right?' Amelia nodded. 'One last thing. The people you were drinking with. Do any of them remember Lily or the man with her?'

'No,' Amelia said. 'I asked, but they were all a bit drunker than me. I only really paid attention because I was the one sat

143

right next to her. I already gave the police lady my friends' names if you need them.'

'Thank you, Amelia. You've done really well,' Callanach said.

'Will this artist thing take long?' her mother asked.

'A young woman is dead,' Callanach replied quietly. 'We're very grateful for your patience.' He left, wandering in the direction of the kitchenette, heaping several teaspoons of coffee into a mug and adding boiling water. 'Lively,' he called as the detective sergeant walked past. 'Everyone in that pub with Amelia gives a statement. Any CCTV?'

'Not in the pub itself. We're checking local roads to see what we can get. Was she helpful?' Lively asked.

'She correctly identified the top Lily was wearing so we've got a positive sighting. Her description of the man wasn't clear but it establishes a timeline and Dalkeith is within reach of Arthur's Seat. I'm going to update the DCI,' Callanach said.

'I'll get off to run the interviews with the pub staff at Dalkeith. Could you give this to the boss if you're going that way? Just some local knowledge she asked me to come by.' Lively handed Callanach a crumpled piece of paper and headed away.

Sipping his coffee, Callanach leaned against the cupboards flexing his neck and shoulders. He hadn't slept in what felt like an age. Smoothing the crumples out of the paper he cast his eyes over Lively's scrawl, noting the speed with which it seemed to have been put together. It was hardly the sort of report he'd expect anyone to hand over to a Detective Chief Inspector.

'The Mazophilia – Maz – singles bar/fetish bar, Cathcart Road, Glasgow. History drug busts, suspected prostitution. Owner Joe Trescoe, brother Ramon convicted organised crime & gang ties. Convictions dishonesty/violence, not recent. Partner reported domestic violence, charges withdrawn.'

The information obviously related to an investigation, but

not one that Callanach was aware MIT was undertaking at present. He folded the paper up again, washed his mug and went to find Ava.

'Sir, there's a call for you,' a detective constable called as Callanach passed the incident room. 'Caller won't leave their name.'

'Any idea what it's about?' he asked.

'I'm guessing it's following on from the press conference about Lily. He asked for you by name,' the DC said.

'Fine, put it through to my office,' Callanach said, diverting off the corridor. He sat at his desk and waited for the red light on his phone to flash. 'This is Detective Inspector Luc Callanach. Who is this?'

'I need help, man,' a male voice rasped.

'What's your name?' Callanach asked 'Do you have information about Lily Eustis' killer?'

'What the fuck? No. You gotta get me out of here. I only ever spoke to Begbie and now he's gone. I know they're looking for me,' he said.

'Wherever you are, if you're in danger I'll send a response team to find you. Give me your name and location,' Callanach said.

'No way, just you. You're the only other one I ever met face to face. George said you could be trusted. No other polis. You don't know the stuff I know.'

'Listen, I have no idea who you are,' Callanach said, 'so you're going to have to give me something if you need my help.'

'Louis Jones, yeah? You don't tell no one you spoke to me. I was Begbie's informant. I know I still got a file. I'm out at Milton Bridge. There are some empty sheds on the west side of the golf course. Hurry up, and bring food and water. I've been hiding for days and I'm sick.'

'Mr Jones, it sounds as if I should call you an ambulance. I can have officers accompany the paramedics to the hospital to protect you,' Callanach said.

'Do that and I disappear again,' Jones said. 'It's not safe. Just get here fast.' The connection was lost. Callanach dialled Ava's internal phone and got no reply. He called a detective constable in, handed him the paper Lively had wanted forwarded to Ava, and explained that he was going out. Jones was partly responsible for Ava's abduction, which meant she shouldn't go anywhere near him, but however little sympathy he felt for Begbie's former informant, Callanach was still duty bound to help. He grabbed his car keys and ran.

Chapter Twenty-Three

Callanach parked at the roadside and used his mobile's GPS to navigate towards the western edge of the golf course. Dense trees shielded the perimeter, and he trod carefully across ice-laced leaves and twigs. Standing behind the last line of foliage, he studied the outbuildings before crossing the short stretch of grass. A trail had already been made across the field, blades crushed by earlier boots. Jones must have come this way before him.

He trod silently, keeping low as a matter of instinct rather than necessity, moving around the side of the building to an old door that was standing ajar.

'Jones?' Callanach shouted, taking a torch from his coat pocket and flashing it into the darkness of the shed. The windows had long since been blackened by dirt and cobwebs, any remaining light blocked by the old furniture that was balanced precariously in every space. 'This is DI Callanach. Louis Jones, can you hear me?' He crept forward, raising a hand to cover his mouth. The shed was musty and stale, but worse than that was the odour of decay. Something had died in here. Probably more than one something, and they had lain down and rotted.

The wind picked up, rattling the side of the shed and sending the outer door crashing inwards. Callanach stumbled into a pile of chairs that collapsed to the floor in a splintered heap. 'Louis, come out with your hands raised.'

He got up, brushing spiders from his head, pointing the torch back towards the rear of the hut. Pushing between a couple of old ale barrels, he tried not to breathe in the foul air, wishing he'd ignored Jones' request and brought backup. As he avoided an old badger trap, his foot landed on something that managed to be both soft and crunchy at once. He shone the light downwards as he stepped back. The fingers on which he'd trodden curled inwards. Callanach knelt down, shining the light up and down the torso, knowing that it was too late. The bodies of the living didn't generally smell like this. Jones has lost control of his bowels, bladder too from the looks of the floor. Laying down the torch and taking a knife from his pocket, he cut through the gaffer tape that had been sealed around Jones' neck and removed a bag from the head.

'Louis?' Callanach said, tapping his cheek lightly. Something felt wrong. Jones' face, whilst warm, wasn't moving the way he expected it to. The lower half was stiff and inflexible. Holding the torch in his mouth, Callanach got a better look. As he slid one hand beneath Jones' head, his fingers plunged into a warm wet mess, stringy to touch with boney splinters in the mix. 'Fuck!' He pulled his hand back out, watching the grey red mixture slide off his fingertips. Louis Jones was dead, and no amount of resuscitation was going to make any difference. His brains were currently decorating a wide section of the floor, the entrance wound a neat black hole on his forehead. Flashing the light slightly downwards, Callanach took a closer look at Jones' mouth. His bottom lip had been pulled upwards over the top lip and a nail gun had been used to send an industrial pin into his upper palate.

148

Callanach lowered the head gently back to the floor. Whoever had killed Jones was gone. There simply wasn't enough space in the shed for them to be hiding. He phoned for backup and a forensics team, then reversed out of the shed disturbing as little as he could, waiting at the door until the Scenes of Crime team arrived. They established a cordon several metres around the edge of the shed and processed Callanach standing on an evidence sheet to catch any traces he might have displaced on the bottom of his shoes. Ailsa Lambert arrived soon afterwards, suiting up and entering with a photographer, exiting soon after looking sickened.

'What are your thoughts?' Callanach asked the pathologist as he was handed temporary clothes so that his own could be tested.

'I can tell you this. That nail was put through his mouth before he was shot dead. Given the amount of nerves in the area between the mouth and nose, through the roots of the upper teeth, it would have been beyond excruciating. It's a form of torture I cannot even contemplate. The only good news is that he would have passed out so quickly that I suspect he was unconscious when he was shot, relieving the terror at the very end. It's strange though, I haven't seen anything like that since . . .' Ailsa stopped mid-sentence, lost in a recollection. Ava wandered up behind them both.

'Since when, Ailsa?' she asked. 'Nail-gunning is a new one on me, so it must be a while back.'

Ailsa stripped off her gloves and deposited them directly into a clinical debris bin. 'There were a couple of these oh, I'd say, two decades ago. It's the act of silencing. Not because he was about to be shot. For that, the killer just needed a cloth to put in his mouth and some duct tape.'

'It's symbolic,' Ava said.

'A warning to others, I'd say. There were a few organised

149

crime killings in the eighties and nineties with similar wounds,' Ailsa replied. 'Your Mr Jones has not been dead very long at all. I think if you'd arrived ten minutes earlier, Luc, you might've bumped into the murderer exiting the hut. I'll perform the autopsy tonight and get you a preliminary report tomorrow, but cause of death was cessation of brain function from the gunshot. He also has severe bruising to his chest but that's older, and a leg wound that must have bled a great deal when it first happened. He'd made a reasonable effort to bind it himself.'

'Would those injuries be consistent with a car accident, specifically if he'd been driving?' Ava asked.

'I'd need to check the damage to the car to give you a precise answer, but in principle, yes. I have to go back in with the photographer now. Speak tomorrow.' Ailsa left.

Callanach accepted the offer of a coat from a passing constable, cold in the thin SOCO suit without his own jacket.

'Do you want to explain what you were doing here?' Ava asked when they were alone.

'Do you want to tell me why you were asking about Louis Jones a few days ago, and here he is less than alive? What is this?' Callanach countered.

'You're going to have to forgive me pulling rank but I'm not here to answer questions,' Ava said, keeping her voice low, moving closer to Callanach. 'You were here without backup and without my authority. No one even knew where you were. It's a miracle you're not lying on that floor with Jones right now. Get home for some clean clothes then get back to the station. We need to talk. Don't say a word to anyone else in the meantime.'

An hour later Callanach carried two cups of coffee in to Ava's office.

'Peace offering,' he said, setting a mug down on her desk.

'Too little too late,' Ava said. 'You could have been killed. Explain in very simple language how it came to pass that you were in a shed on a golf course with a dead missing person who was a former police informant.'

'Jones phoned me,' Callanach said. 'I agreed to meet him. He sounded scared, panicky, said he was sick. He asked me not to talk to anyone else . . .'

'You realise that procedure takes precedence over the requests of people who were instrumental in getting me abducted in the past.'

'That's exactly why I didn't tell you,' Callanach said. 'That and the fact that you weren't around and I had to move fast. I offered him an ambulance or uniformed officers. He refused both.'

'And that wasn't a warning sign to you that something was going on that you should have informed me about? Jesus, Luc, you're not a bloody cowboy. Chain of command, remember? Also, don't pull that paternalistic bullshit on me, keeping me out of it for my own good.' Callanach sat back and sipped his coffee. 'I want a statement on my desk in an hour and I want every single word Jones said to you, as close to verbatim as you can recall it.'

Ava's phone rang. She glared at it then picked it up.

'Yes, Chief Inspector Dimitri,' she said. Callanach stood up to leave. She waved him back into his chair. 'That's right, Jones is confirmed dead. Uh huh, Dr Lambert confirmed that some of his injuries were consistent with a road traffic accident. No, those injuries were not the cause of death and MIT will be handling the case from here.' There was a pause. 'Of course, I agree you should have been notified when we had a location for him,' Ava said. She raised her eyebrows at Callanach. 'Not at all. I was fully aware of the fact that my DI was en route to meet him. I made the decision to send a detective first and bring Jones in. The plan was for you to interview him later on.' She took a swig of coffee as Dimitri answered. 'Sure. I'll see to it that you have access to my DI's statement as soon as it's available, probably in a few days given how busy we are with the Lily Eustis murder.' There was more muffled talk from within the receiver. 'I very much appreciate your offer of assistance. Goodbye Chief Inspector.' She hung up.

'You shouldn't have done that,' Callanach said. 'You want to talk about being paternalistic? I don't need you lying to cover my back. I didn't follow procedure, I had a good reason for my decision and I'm prepared to defend myself.'

'I wasn't defending you. I was defending . . . forget it. It's done. Your statement should make it clear I authorised you to go to Louis Jones. I'll write one up that says I considered the risks and that we had no way of knowing he might be in danger. Organise some officers to make the usual enquiries in the golf club area. And have someone approach CI Dimitri's team for access to the car Jones was driving on the night of the accident. Ailsa will need her forensics team to examine it now that it might be relevant to the murder enquiry.'

'Am I handling this investigation?' Callanach asked.

'Of course you are. You were the person Jones reached out to. You found his body. Doesn't make sense to hand it over to anyone else,' Ava said.

'Then what are you not telling me?' Callanach asked.

Ava glanced at him, then tapped a couple of computer keys as she stared at her laptop screen. 'Nothing. He was an informant, though, and that means we have to keep the investigation into his death quiet until we know what we can and can't release. That means you report only to me. No statements go out of MIT's hands.'

'He hasn't been a police informant for a very long time. Nothing we find now is going to jeopardise an ongoing investigation. Ava, you were asking me about Jones before. Did you know something was going to happen?'

'No,' she replied, focusing on her screen. 'I need that statement as soon as possible. You should put Lively on the Jones investigation. He has the right sort of contacts.'

Ava waited until Callanach had left then looked up Glynis Begbie's phone number. She had tried to persuade herself that her instincts were wrong or that she was over-reacting, but each time the facts boiled down to this. George Begbie – the least likely suicide candidate imaginable – had killed himself leaving no note and for no apparent reason. Louis Jones had fled his car injured after his premises had been searched. He, too, had ended up dead. Together they had worked on one of the most prominent Scottish organised crime cases imaginable. One of the men they had helped put away was now out of prison and George Begbie's loft was stuffed full of unaccounted-for cash.

No she thought, she wasn't imagining the danger. If Louis Jones' killers were after the money, George Begbie's house was the last place they had left to search. She phoned Glynis, telling her to pack a bag and get her daughter to pick her up. After that, Ava clock-watched until the bulk of her squad had left the office, then went home to pack. Half an hour later she was at the Chief's house, waving Glynis goodbye.

She unrolled her sleeping bag in the guest room, not that sleep seemed a likely outcome. Her head was buzzing and there was a battle, if not a war, raging in her conscience. Perhaps if she had talked to Chief Inspector Dimitri about her concerns for Jones he wouldn't be lying on Ailsa's table waiting to be cut apart now. If only she had shared her suspicions rather than trying to protect the Chief's memory, and for what? But she knew the answer to that. The Chief would turn in his grave if he knew his widow would be left unable to pay the bills. As for the money secreted in the roof, that would require better information. It seemed likely that Begbie had killed himself rather than face up to what he'd done. The thought that she was covering up what might well have been criminal activity sat heavily with her, but what good would it do to start a formal investigation? Glynis Begbie would lose everything. George Begbie's name would be ruined and perhaps he deserved that, but Ava couldn't bear the thought of condemning him when he wasn't around to explain what he'd done and why he'd done it.

The nail through Jones' lips had been the final nail in the coffin of Ava believing that there might be some innocent explanation for the cash in the attic. The gangland crime bosses Trescoe and McGill were undoubtedly involved, and that meant they believed something of theirs had been taken. How George Begbie had come by it was anyone's guess, Ava thought, but it wasn't a chance finding. Either the Chief and Louis Jones had banded together to steal the cash, or when Trescoe and McGill got sent down, Jones and Begbie had found a way to profit from the existing organised crime rackets. Either way, it had been a death sentence. You could never really clean dirty money, no matter how much time passed. The problem was that if Louis Jones had talked before he died, then Glynis' house was the inevitable next stop for whoever had killed him. There was no way Ava was going to risk Glynis being there when they arrived. She understood how those men operated and it was brutal. They'd obviously been instructed to find Jones and make him talk. Whether he did or didn't, he'd been a dead man walking. They wouldn't stop until they found what they were looking for, and that, she had no doubt, was currently providing additional loft insulation above her head. Louis Jones' killers wouldn't want to go back to their boss empty handed. They would act as soon as they could, and that meant tonight. Ava heated up the curry she'd ordered from the takeaway, forcing herself to eat for energy in spite of her lack of appetite, then checked that all the doors were locked and made sure her taser was charged.

Chapter Twenty-Four

'It's just a bug. Probably norovirus,' Cordelia Muir told Jeremy as he fussed around her. 'Honestly, don't worry about me. Just don't get too close. Wouldn't want you catching anything!'

Jeremy handed her a box of tissues and glared at busybody Liam Hood through the glass partition, as he nosed through the fridge. With a last reassuring pat on Cordelia's shoulders, Jeremy went to confront him.

'W-what are you doing?' he asked.

'None of your business. Shouldn't you be washing up or something?' Liam said.

'I'm not here to w-wash up. I help Cordelia now,' Jeremy responded, checking on his boss through the glass. She was clutching her stomach, her head bent nearly to the desk. 'W-was she like this yesterday?' he asked.

'You're very interested. Worried it might be contagious, are you?' Liam asked.

'No, I w-was . . .'

'Yeah, whatever, I was being sarcastic. There's some filing on the side needs doing. Perhaps you should concern yourself more with volunteering and less with everyone else's private lives,'

Liam said, slamming the fridge door shut and returning to his desk. Jeremy walked to the kettle, throwing the switch and waiting for it to boil. He didn't like Liam. Liam talked about other people behind their backs and was disrespectful to Cordelia. He was mean.

Jeremy took a cup of green tea to Cordelia and opened a window to let some fresh air in. There was an undercurrent of sweat and vomit that Cordelia would hate if she was aware of it.

'You should go to the doctor,' Jeremy said. 'Liam said you've been ill all week.'

'I know. The truth is that I'm too busy. You know how full the diary is. There's nothing they can do for stomach bugs anyway. I'll just end up spreading it to other patients who already have weakened immune systems. I swear doctors' offices are the most unhealthy places in the modern world.'

'I could phone for you. Make an appointment. I'm sorry to sound rude but you really don't look w-well,' he said.

'Maybe you're right,' Cordelia said. 'The number's on my phone. Could you do that?' She picked up a handful of tissues and ran for the toilet again. Jeremy picked up her mobile, wrote down the number for her general practitioner and went to his desk with Liam still glaring.

'I told you to get on with the filing,' Liam said.

'I'm phoning the doctor for Cordelia,' Jeremy replied.

'Maybe you should let me do that.' Liam bent over to grab the paper from Jeremy's hand. He ducked, swivelled on his chair, and moved away.

'I need to make sure she gets an appointment,' Jeremy said. 'I'll do it from her desk.' He shut the partition door to keep Liam away and called the surgery. By the time Cordelia returned, grey in the face and shivering through a sheen of perspiration, he was writing down a time and date. 'They were busy until

Monday, that's five days away but there's some virus going around and the receptionist said they're swamped. I've made you an appointment with Dr Marylewski and put it in your diary. You mustn't forget to go.'

'Probably the same virus I've caught, which is rather reassuring if it's doing the rounds. I won't forget and Monday is fine. Chances are I'll be right as rain by then. Thanks for doing that,' Cordelia said sliding down into her chair. 'Are you okay? You look worried about something?'

'It's not important. It's just that Liam . . .' Jeremy muttered.

'Liam what? You can tell me, Jeremy. Don't be nervous,' Cordelia said, taking a tentative sip of the green tea and putting it straight back down.

'I don't think he w-wants me here,' Jeremy said. 'I must have done something wrong.'

'You haven't, I promise,' Cordelia said. 'Sometimes people get used to a working environment and a new face throws things out. Give it time. He'll come around.'

Callanach finally arrived home at 11.30pm. The artist's impression of the man seen at the pub with Lily Eustis was useless. Not only would no one ever recognise a suspect by it, but Amelia had declared it looked nothing like the man only she couldn't say why. On top of that, it turned out that the car Louis Jones was driving had already been crushed. It was uninsured, untaxed, and Chief Inspector Dimitri's team had no way of knowing a murder was about to happen. As a result, the car had been shipped off to the wreckers and turned into a cube of mangled metal the day before. So much for Ailsa being able to compare Jones' injuries with the damage to the car. He decided to wait until the next morning to break that one to Ava.

After a long shower he climbed into bed with his laptop

trying to shed the images of the day. He could still feel Louis Jones' brains on his fingertips and that was as good a repellant for sleep as he could imagine. He picked up his mobile, wondering if Ava was still awake, too aware of the stress between them to allow himself to dial her number. Instead, he opted for an entry on his contacts list he'd been intending to call for weeks, work and time never allowing, and dialled the only journalist he'd ever completely trusted.

'Lance,' he said, when the mobile was answered. 'It's Callanach.'

'I'm going to skip the part where I tell you it's midnight and that I haven't heard from you for three months. Instead I'm going to explain for, I don't know, maybe the tenth time, that whilst you may be a police officer you do have a first name. Traditionally when people become friends that's how they address one another. Are you phoning to tell me how much you've missed me, or to give me the scoop of the year? Preferably both,' Lance said.

Callanach smiled. 'You want me to start again and introduce myself properly?' he asked.

'No, the accent was enough of a giveaway. How are you doing?' Lance continued without waiting for a reply. 'And thank you for asking. I've fully recovered from the police brutality last time you dragged me into one of your cases.' Six months earlier Lance had provided some off-the-record assistance to MIT in tracking down two psychopathic killers. It was an unfortunate coincidence that another investigation had overlapped, leaving Callanach and Lance Proudfoot operating at the far edges of the law. Lance had been the one caught in the crossfire.

'I can't believe you're still moaning about that. So a senior officer from Scotland Yard dislocated your ankle. Big deal. You're a journalist. You're supposed to be prepared to put yourself in harm's way to get a story. I'd have thought the knowledge that you were morally in the right would have been enough reward in itself. Did you want me to send flowers?' Callanach asked.

'A bottle of single malt might have been nice. Even journalists have feelings, you know. I couldn't ride my motorbike for weeks. Maybe I should have sued. Is that why you're phoning? Am I being offered some compensation?' Lance laughed.

'Actually I need some help,' Callanach said.

'The sort of help that might lead to something I can print or . . .'

'The sort of help that if you printed it, it would get us both arrested, or alternatively badly beaten, maybe worse. It's best you know the reality up front,' Callanach said.

'Did your mother never teach you to talk to a girl nicely before asking if she fancied parking up?' Lance laughed. The silence on Callanach's end of the line was enough to stop his joviality in its tracks. 'All right, spill the beans. What is it this time?'

'Local knowledge,' Callanach said. 'The sort the police don't often hear when people are too scared to chat. A man called Louis Jones is dead. He ran an underground car hire business for customers who might not want to leave a paper trail for one reason or another. Have you heard anything about him?'

'Not a mention. I'll ask around though, see what I can dig up,' Lance said.

'No, listen, don't do that. If Edinburgh's most well-informed journalist hasn't heard anything, then there's a good reason. Forget I asked, Lance. This one's too hot at the moment.'

'If you're sure, it's not as if I have people knocking down my door to give me exclusives. How about that dinner we never got around to organising instead? It'd be good to catch up.'

'It would,' Callanach agreed. 'Can I call you another time to set a date? Things at work are . . . you know.'

160

'I get the picture. Don't be a stranger, though, you hear? I may moan about the ankle, but the truth is I haven't had that much fun since, well, I can't remember when.'

Callanach rang off. He was short of friends in Edinburgh, and Lance – journalist or not – was one of the kindest, most genuine people he'd met since his arrival. That was exactly why he'd changed his mind mid-call. Whatever Louis Jones had been mixed up in was too risky for anyone he cared about. That went for Ava, too, only Callanach had the feeling there was an awful lot she wasn't telling him.

Chapter Twenty-Five

It was 3.30am when Ava heard noises from the kitchen. The metallic clunking and squealing was the unmistakable hallmark of a lock being worked. She'd deliberately left the key in the door to make life harder for them. They couldn't break the double-glazed panel above the handle without alerting the entire neighbourhood so they had to come up with something more impressive than that. It was the first indication that she was dealing with professionals. Ava stood, glad she'd remained fully dressed, sliding her feet quickly into trainers and stepping behind the curtains she'd left half drawn.

There were whispered voices, soft enough that the sound wouldn't have woken her from deep sleep, but it confirmed that there were at least two of them. She knew this was the point when she should be phoning for backup, but the same arguments that had stopped her from reporting the bundles of cash stopped her again now. They weren't expecting her, which was one thing in her favour. More problematic was the fact that if these were the men who had shot Louis Jones earlier, then they were likely armed with guns. She stayed where she was, pressing back against the window, keeping her breathing calm and quiet.

They weren't ransacking the place, but they were searching. Louis Jones might have told them that Begbie had the cash, but they obviously didn't know precisely where it was stashed if that was what they were looking for. It took several minutes before the men were ready to try upstairs but soon enough their footsteps murmured over the carpet.

The door squeaked slightly as it opened. Ava held her breath. She was more used to entering other people's properties at night than being the one practising avoidance. She felt out of control, and the adrenalin was making it hard to stay still.

Someone went through the drawers, the wardrobe, pulled the bed away from the wall and slid their hands under the mattress before moving on to the next bedroom. All Ava wanted was a glance at their faces, preferably without being seen. She sneaked forward through the room towards the doorway, keeping low.

The door swung open smacking her in the face, not hard but the shock was enough to make her cry out. Scrabbling backwards she noticed the torch forgotten by one of the searchers on the floor. She had time, as a man rugby-tackled her legs, to think what a rookie mistake she'd made. He must have been as shaken as her, coming back for his torch, finding some woman sneaking up on him.

Her reaction was instantaneous and instinctive. She rolled to the left raising her right elbow to smash it into her assailant's face, at the same time as drawing her right knee to her chest then kicking hard downwards, connecting with his upper thigh. His gloved hands reached for her neck as she tried to sit up. Ava let him come, one hand exploring behind her for a weapon, extending her free hand to thrust her fingertips into the soft area at the base of his throat. He backed off fast, breaking the pressure of her fingers. As he moved away, her hand closed on the only loose object beneath the bed, and she swung a shoe viciously towards his eyes.

A booted foot stamped on her arm, pinning her to the floor. She felt the bones in her forearm grind against one another as the second man kicked her head like a football. It had bounced off the floorboards before she could control it. By then the second man was standing over the top of her, one foot still on her forearm, the other pressing into her shoulder.

'What's this then? That's not very ladylike, fighting dirty like that,' he said.

'Please don't hurt me,' Ava whispered, making her upper body go limp, playing nice.

'Ah, you see, that's not going to work. It might have worked had you been in your pjs or a wee nightie, but you're fully dressed. That's a sleeping bag, I see. Who exactly were you waiting for?' he said. Ava stared up at him. He was at least 6'4", big built, with shoulders that could have passed as padding on an American football player.

'I'm house-sitting for my friend,' she said. 'She's in hospital for an operation and has to stay overnight. I didn't want to put her out washing bedding so I brought a sleeping bag. Fell asleep reading,' Ava said. 'Take anything you want. I don't want any trouble.'

'Yet you fight as if trouble was your middle name.' He reached a huge hand down and gripped her cheeks, pushing them together, making her teeth ache. 'I'm going to need you to answer some questions. You should be aware before I ask them that my friend here has a knife. You're quite pretty at the moment. Do you like being pretty?'

Ava nodded her head, no acting required for tears to form in her eyes as she fought the rising pressure in her head.

'That's good. Now, we have reason to believe there's some money in this house. Money that doesn't belong here. It needs to be given back. I think you can help show me where that money is. Don't try to speak. Either nod or shake.' Ava shook her head and the hand gripping her face began to tighten further. 'I'm going to let you have that one. We'll pretend you misunderstood me. Last chance. Are you going to show us where the fuckin' cash is?' Ava began drumming her feet on the floor, struggling to speak but emitting only gargling sounds. The big man leaned down close into her face. 'Well, I'm disappointed but my friend is probably getting quite excited right now. He's known as something of an artist in face-carving circles. What do you think, Knuckles, can you turn this face into a living nightmare to make sure she never forgets us?' He stood up, releasing Ava's face, keeping his legs either side of her body, her left arm still pinned to the floor. He faced his mate who was still catching his breath in the doorway.

'How much time do we have?' the smaller man asked laughing.

'Oh, I'd say we're good for an hour or . . .'

Ava pulled the taser from her hoodie pocket with her right hand, finally able to stop the drumming with her feet she'd used to mask the noise of switching it on. Aiming as best she could, Ava shot up the big man's legs towards his testicles. He had time to looked horrified before his entire body flew backwards and smashed into the wall. Ava had never heard a man scream quite that high or that loudly, and she'd seen men get shot. Then again, tasering a man in the testicles at half a metre away was not approved police procedure. The big man was down and still screaming, but Knuckles was lumbering over. Ava dropped the taser and jumped up. It was no lie about the blade. Knuckles brought it down towards Ava's face with clumsy force. She made a cross with her lower arms several inches in front of her chest, catching his striking arm in the junction of her two wrists. Grabbing his wrist with her right hand and twisting it hard, she brought Knuckles' upper body down to where she could smash her knee into his nose. The sound it made was all the confirmation she needed that it was broken.

Ava grabbed the knife, wrestling it from Knuckles' hands and holding out both knife and the taser towards the two men on the floor.

'The money's gone,' Ava said. 'It's become a generous donation to a local charity, anonymous obviously. You're too late. I'm leaving, and I'm giving you two minutes to get out after me. After that the police will be waiting outside to escort you from the premises. Come back here again and it'll be your final resting place.'

She ran down the stairs, unwilling to test her theory as to how slowly both men would now be moving. Taking her coat from the kitchen, she disappeared through the back door, hiding behind bushes in a garden opposite and waiting for them to appear. They took longer than she'd hoped but that was probably because they appeared to have been rummaging through Glynis' freezer for a bag of peas, which the big man was clutching to his groin as he hobbled away. Knuckles' face and shirt were a mess of blood, and he too was unsteady. Ava watched them climb into a car with a licence plate so muddy she couldn't make it out, and drive away. She left it five more minutes before exiting the garden, returning to the house only to lock Glynis' door before going to her car.

Her right hand was warm and sticky, the pain just beginning to register. There was a substantial cut running along the palm, splitting the skin between thumb and forefinger. It was deep, throbbing and no amount of positive thought was going to persuade her that she could avoid getting professional help. She checked the time. It was close to 4am. Accident and Emergency was what she needed, only someone there would recognise her and this was such an obvious knife wound that questions would be asked. She wrapped her hand in the towel she kept stuffed in her gym bag on the back seat and began to drive.

Dr Ailsa Lambert lived on Belford Park not far from the Scottish National Gallery of Modern Art, an institution of which she was a prominent member. Ava knew that because her own mother had worked with Ailsa on the board, just one of many ways in which their paths had crossed before her mother's death in the summer. The pathologist had been a fixture in her life well before Ava joined the police force. Ailsa was never given to dramatics, never pre-judged a situation, yet was always the first to deliver painful truths. And she was a master of discretion. Ava hoped that was an attribute she could rely on now. She rang the doorbell.

The dogs barked first. Ailsa had three King Charles spaniels. They kept her company, Ava supposed. Ailsa's husband had left her after five years of marriage and she'd never bothered to find another partner, remaining childless and making a maternal commitment instead to her career. After a few seconds an upstairs light came on, then the hallway light and finally the door of the grand old, double-fronted house was opened.

'Ava Turner, that towel had better be clean,' Ailsa said. 'Get in here right now and let me see what you've been up to.'

Ava walked straight through to a kitchen where she'd eaten more than her fair share of cakes and drunk hot chocolate when she and her mother had visited. 'It's not as bad as it looks,' she said. 'I just need to get cleaned up.'

'I am not given to swearing, young lady, but if I were I'd be turning the air blue by now. How much are you going to tell me?'

'Not much,' Ava said. 'Could I have a glass of water, please?' She sank down onto a chair and closed her eyes.

Ailsa peeled the bloody towel away over a bowl as the kettle boiled. 'You're going to have to offer me some sort of explanation. I need to know what I'm dealing with. Take your coat off, we're going to be a while.' She held Ava's hand up to the light, wiping the blood away with antiseptic wipes. 'You're fortunate the cut hasn't gone through any tendons. It's deep. You've lost a fair bit of blood and you'll have scarring for life.'

'I take it my career options as a hand model are limited then,' Ava said.

'Joke with me after 6am when I might be prepared to listen. You're obviously here because you can't go to the hospital so we'll dispense with needless evasion. How did this happen and how long ago? More to the point, is your tetanus up to date?'

'I got stabbed by an angry man as I was disarming him about twenty minutes ago and yes, it is. Does that cover everything?' Ava replied as Ailsa first handed her a glass of cold water, then poured hot water into a bowl and took a pack of cotton wool down from a cupboard.

'Hardly. I take it you haven't registered the damage to your left arm yet.' Ava looked to where Ailsa was staring. Her left forearm had blackened already, the tread of a boot visible in relief on the skin. 'Close your fist,' Ailsa instructed. Ava tried, making her hand close halfway before giving up. 'You ought to get an x-ray. I take it that's not going to happen.'

'Correct again,' Ava said. 'Thanks, Ailsa. I didn't know where else to go.'

Ailsa sat down to riffle through a medical bag. 'I still keep everything needed for the living but you'll remember I've only stitched corpses for thirty years now. Just in case I do a bad job and you consider suing me.' She smiled as she took a needle and surgical thread from the bag. 'It's a clean wound. I can give you some topical anaesthetic but you really need an injection to numb your hand before I start stitching and that's something I don't have here.'

'Glass of brandy, then?' Ava joked.

'Good idea,' Ailsa said, walking into the lounge and clinking bottles. 'Have you given Luc my address? I don't mind him coming here. I won't be getting back to sleep now in any event.'

'I haven't called him and I'm not going to. This is my problem. No one else can know.'

Ailsa put a large tumbler of brandy on the table in front of Ava, followed by a smaller measure for herself. 'It's your problem, is it? If the wound had been to your inner thigh or your neck, you'd be dead. What address would I have been called to for the purposes of examining your corpse, may I ask?'

'You can't. In fact, you can't ask anything, Ailsa. The men who did this to me, the people they work for, they're dangerous. At the moment they don't know who I am and that's the way I want to keep it,' Ava said. Ailsa picked up the needle and Ava braced herself, looking away. She had no particular fear of needles but it seemed wise not to actually watch this one going into her skin.

'So you didn't tell them you were a police officer. Whoever you're protecting, are you sure they're worth it? I'm sorry, there's no way round it, this is going to hurt a great deal.' She began stitching.

'They're worth it, and I'm not in any immediate danger. Jesus, Ailsa, that's painful,' Ava said.

'You won't take the Lord's name in vain in my house, I don't care what rank you are these days. Finish your brandy. You'll not be fit to drive for a few hours in any event.'

'Thank you,' Ava said, reaching out her undamaged hand to rest on Ailsa's arm. 'I could use some sleep.'

'That's the first time since I've known you that you've taken advice without arguing. I'm not easily scared, Ava, but you've put the frighteners on me. Ignore my advice, you usually do, but you should speak to Luc about this. He's your friend. I trust him. I know you do too,' Ailsa said.

'He is my friend. That's why I'm keeping him away from this. If I'm going to commit professional suicide then I'm not dragging anyone else down with me.'

Ailsa cleaned up and put gauze over the wound. 'Is there anything I can do to help? I may be old and decrepit but my brain is still functioning properly.'

Ava thought about it. There was a lot left she didn't know for sure, like the identities of the men at Glynis' house and what the Chief had done to create such a horrible mess that he'd killed himself, although a picture was forming more clearly in her head. The Chief and Jones had profited in grand terms from Trescoe and McGill's imprisonment, exacerbated by being part of the team that had landed the crime bosses in prison. It was hard to quantify the level of vitriol that must have spawned, festering within the confines of a cell over a period of many years. Whatever the exact mechanics of how Begbie and Jones had ended up in possession of the proceeds of organised crime, it had proved to be a life-shortening decision. It left more than just a bad taste in Ava's mouth. Her concern, now though, was Glynis Begbie. Ava's grief over the Chief's death was becoming a poisonous cocktail of anger, disappointment and fear. Whoever had rammed Louis Jones' car then nail-gunned his mouth shut, the same week the Chief had killed himself and left his family devastated, had some questions to answer.

'You have an alarm and a CCTV system, right?' Ava asked her.

'I do, top quality. I put a lot of people in prison with my testimony over the years. No point taking chances,' Ailsa said, cleaning up the post-operative debris.

'Would you invite Glynis Begbie to stay? She shouldn't be at her house, not for a while after the funeral. It's important that she has company,' Ava said.

'I see,' Ailsa responded. 'Does Glynis understand that it might be better for her not to go home?'

'She does. I know she'd be glad of the invitation to stay with you. You'll keep your alarm on though, right?'

'Of course,' Ailsa said. 'Now go to bed. Some healing is required.'

'The alarm, Ailsa. I need to know you won't forget. Promise me,' Ava said.

'All right, I promise. But you're not doing anything to reassure me that whatever's happening is in hand.'

'It is,' Ava said. 'It will be.' She corrected herself, hiding the lie by turning her head away from Ailsa as she spoke. Someone had murdered Louis Jones in cold blood. If they were capable of that, they were capable of anything.

Chapter Twenty-Six

Randall had been itching to get out of the house to go to The Fret. He'd spent the week practising 'Stairway to Heaven' and had been considering getting up to do a solo. A month ago he'd never have contemplated such an overwhelming feat of bravery but the world lately had seemed a better place. His mother, Cordelia, had been increasingly distracted, the fortunate consequence of which had been her failure to ask to check his homework and talk through the minutiae of his college day. That left more time for the guitar, shopping, and for broadening his range of henna tattoos. He still hadn't quite got the nerve to get a real one. That would also require fake ID, which he had no idea how to obtain. He was pretty sure Christian would have the answer to that one, although he might be cautious about it. Christian was great, but there were times when he made a bit too free with the words of wisdom.

This evening his mother hadn't even asked where he was going when he went to the door. True, she would assume he was headed for the library, which was his fall-back excuse, but not having to actually lie was a weight off his shoulders. She'd been lying down since getting home from work, blaming over-tiredness and a poor night's sleep. Randall knew she hadn't been well. He'd heard her vomiting a few times in the past week, followed by the furious cleaning of her en suite. She was paranoid about passing germs around; her own worst enemy, never relaxing properly, never just having fun. No wonder she was ill.

He sauntered into The Fret, aiming a sullen 'S'up' at the doorman, who looked as bored as ever, but who managed to raise an eyebrow at him. This was the first time he'd arrived later than Chris, which pleased him. Chris was standing at the bar, chatting with a couple of regulars, texting as he spoke, oblivious to how the world was such an easy place for him. If Randall tried to do that, he would end up dropping his phone or losing the thread of the conversation, or laughing at the wrong time. Randall took the last free table and stowed his guitar beneath it, clutching a handful of pound coins for a drink. He wished he'd remembered to ask his mother to change the coins for a note. It looked so babyish going to the bar and counting out his money. Still, he had to have a drink in front of him, and he needed the alcohol if he was going to risk a solo.

Christian finally noticed him, raised a hand and continued his conversation. Randall gave a broad smile and waited for him to come over, as he tuned his guitar. It didn't really need it. He'd sat in a bus stop for half an hour fiddling with it while he waited for enough time to pass so he wouldn't get to The Fret early. He kept Christian in his peripheral vision as he strummed, realising that if he didn't go and grab a spare chair, there would be nowhere for Christian to sit, and then he might not come over at all. Not that he needed the company. He was fine on his own. But it was better to look like he had a friend. The problem now was that Christian would see him getting the chair and that was definitely not cool. He should have got there earlier.

His phone rang. It was his sister, probably wanting to talk about what they should get Mum for Christmas, or worse, to have a go at him for not playing the dutiful son and telling their mother where he was going. She was such a creep. He couldn't recall her going out once when she lived at home before uni. It was always studying with her. The house had been constantly quiet because she needed to concentrate. Well, he was his own man. He hit the end button without answering the call, propping the guitar against his chair and heading to the bar. His phone began to ring again as he was waiting to be served. He sighed, killed the call, and waved a clinking bundle of coins towards the barman. No sign of his favourite barmaid tonight. Typical. Just as he was about to play solo. He'd dreamed about how she would look at him and wondered if tonight might be the time to stay late and offer to walk her home. He even had a fold-up umbrella tucked away in his backpack. He wouldn't get it out until they were alone, but she'd appreciate it. They might even hold the handle together.

When his phone began to ring for a third time, he made a point of swearing loudly, knowing he could ignore two calls but probably not three without someone getting suspicious of his whereabouts and sending out a search party. It was his sister again. He sauntered to a quiet corner, abandoning his place in the bar queue and trying to look nonchalant.

'Yep,' he said, holding a hand over the mouthpiece in an attempt to dampen the noise. No doubt his sister would be reporting back to his mother.

'Where are you?' his sister screeched.

'I'm out,' Randall said. 'I don't answer to you. Tell Mum I'll be back in a couple of hours. I've got to go.'

'No, you have to get a taxi to the Royal Infirmary. Mum collapsed. She's in an ambulance.'

'That's ridiculous. I only left home a while ago. She can't be that ill. I'm in the middle of something,' Randall said.

'Randall, you stop whatever you're doing right now. I know

you're not at the library because the library doesn't sound like that. Mum might be prepared to put up with your bullshit, but I'm not. Just do what I've told you,' his sister said. He heard the squeal of brakes from her end of the line. When she spoke again her voice was softer. 'Randy, Mum's really not well. You have to come. The paramedics were worried. Her . . . her vital signs weren't good. I'm not sure . . .' her voice trailed off.

'You're not sure what?' he asked, feeling a sickness snake up from his stomach towards his throat.

'Just get to the hospital fast, okay? We'll be in Accident and Emergency. Text me when you arrive and I'll find you.' She rang off. Randall stared at his mobile, wondering if he'd imagined the urgency in his sister's voice, trying not to fill in the blank at the end of the sentence. A lurch of guilt unbalanced him, the knowledge that his mother had been ill when he'd left home. He hadn't even bothered going in to check on her. It had been such a relief to get out of the house without the usual interrogation that he'd thought only of the evening ahead. Perhaps if he'd checked on her, he'd have known she needed a doctor. He reeled, clutching the wall for support, then Christian was at his side, a steadying hand on his arm.

'Hey, man, you look pale. You need some fresh air? Nerves got the better of you?'

'I . . . I need to get to the hospital,' Randall said.

'You feeling that bad? Should I call an ambulance?' Chris asked.

'Not me. It's my mum. She's ill. I have to get there really fast but I don't have enough money for a cab. Could you, maybe . . .' Randall said.

'Hey, no problem. I'll drive you there myself. Wait for me by the door.'

'This is really embarrassing. I'm sorry,' Randall muttered.

'It's your mum. You're supposed to go running. Don't let all the bullshit going on in here make you less than you really are. Every person in this room is terrified that they'll make a fool of themselves. Don't get sucked into it. Appreciate what you have and protect it. I told you about my friend who lost her sister recently, yeah? What she wouldn't do to turn back the clock. Let's get going,' Christian said, putting a gentle hand on Randall's shoulder and pushing him in the direction of the door.

The nurses were kind as they walked Randall to the cubicle where his mother was being fussed over by a team of medics. A fan was chugging away at his mother's face. His sister was standing in a corner conferring intensely with a nurse. Randall stood outside the circle, wondering why it felt as if he didn't exist. Christian had hugged him as he'd dropped him off. A proper hug, hard, brief, but it had meant the world. In every other aspect of his life, he was a troublesome child. Some days it felt as if that was all he would ever be.

'Sorry, we need to clear the room,' a doctor said.

'What's happening?' his sister asked.

'We're preparing your mother to perform a lumbar puncture to get a better idea of what's attacking her system. At the moment we don't know if it's a bacterial infection, a virus or something else. I can't be sure we're treating it effectively until we've narrowed down the possibilities.' He turned away, handing several vials of blood to a waiting nurse. 'Walk these down to the lab for immediate testing. Do we have a urine sample?' he asked another nurse. She nodded. 'Right, priorities, get Mrs Muir's temperature down and work on a diagnosis. Keep up rehydration. Antibiotics via drip.'

'Randall,' his sister said, finally noticing him. 'You shouldn't be in here.'

'You told me to come,' he said, watching the saline dripping into his mother's arm and wondering how that helped.

'I told you to phone me when you got to the hospital. Come on,' she walked over and slid an arm around his shoulders. They left the cubicle together. 'Are you okay, Rand?'

He tried to answer, croaked, gave up and pushed his face into his sister's shoulder. They stood like that, hugging one another, until a nurse offered to walk them to a private area.

'Why is she unconscious?' Randall asked. 'She wasn't that ill when I went out.' He hadn't meant to make his guilt quite so plain, but it was there, branded on him.

'She's badly dehydrated. The doctor says her body is trying to cope with whatever is attacking it, so it's shutting down the systems it doesn't need at the moment. They're doing all they can,' the sister said, clutching his hand.

A porter wheeled his mother out as a man appeared, thrusting papers and a pen towards his sister. Randall abandoned the waiting room and consent forms, to follow his mother along the corridor, wondering at how her beautiful black skin could suddenly shrivel into a dull, lifeless shell as if every cell was deflated. She looked, he thought, as if she had already given up. The hospital gown was almost completely flat over the top of her body. How had he failed to notice how much weight she had suddenly lost? Even her hair, perhaps the only source of vanity in his mother's life, looked thinner and dried out. And there had been a strange smell when he'd first entered the cubicle. Sweat, only not like you'd find in a changing room. That smell was of exertion and vigour. This was something acidic and chemical.

A door closed in front of him, forbidding access to all but hospital staff. He touched the glass, peeking through to where his mother was being wheeled into another room and he caught a brief glimpse of gowned, gloved figures. His mother was tough, Randall told himself. He had never seen her give in to anything. There was no reason to believe she would start now. She would survive. She had to.

177

Chapter Twenty-Seven

Being in uniform wasn't an aspect of the job Ava enjoyed, but it was necessary at formal occasions. The Chief's funeral was one such event and even though it was to be a small affair, traditions had to be upheld. Superintendent Overbeck would be there, as would other senior brass and a few retired officers. The ceremony would be simple and quick. No one wanted to linger at the side of a hole in the earth.

Ava had recovered enough yesterday to make it into the station mid-morning. Glynis Begbie had accepted Ailsa's invitation to stay with her after a brief update from Ava about the unwanted guests at her home. The only frustrating part of the day had been finding out that Louis Jones' car had been destroyed before it could be examined to relate Jones' injuries to the crash. Ava proofread Callanach's statement about Jones' death as she did up her tunic buttons with one hand and held a cup of coffee in the other. The statement was about as bland as it could have been in the circumstances, the language kept formal.

'Having obtained DCI Turner's permission to meet with Mr Jones, I used my own vehicle to approach the scene, parking on the roadside within a short walk of the western side of the golf course. I approached cautiously. No other persons were within my line of sight. No disturbance was audible as I approached the shed. No . . .' Ava's phoned buzzed. She jerked her hand, spilling coffee over the statement.

'Bloody typical,' she muttered, grabbing a handful of tissues and mopping the sleeve of her uniform. Paying her respects reeking of coffee and looking like she'd been doing the washing up in her uniform wasn't what she'd planned, and she needed to get a copy of Callanach's statement over to Dimitri before she set off. She sprayed a few puffs of Chanel No. 5 over the sleeve and went back to reading.

'No disturbance was audible as I approached the shed . . .' The next word was splattered. All she could read of the word she remembered as 'No' was the N and half of the o, rendering the remainder unreadable.

'N, c,' she said. Ava looked at her watch. 'Fuck, fuck, fuck.' She snatched up her mobile and dialled the emergency line for the forensic pathologist, knowing Ailsa wouldn't be answering her private mobile this morning with Glynis Begbie at her house. 'Pick up. Damn it, Ailsa, pick up the . . . oh thank God, listen, I need you to meet me at the funeral parlour where the Chief's body is.'

'Ava,' Ailsa whispered. Feet echoed rapidly along a corridor and a door banged shut. 'I was with Glynis. What on earth can we possibly do there now?'

'No time,' Ava said. 'I need you with a . . . I don't know . . . a magnifying glass or whatever you use to pick up minute disturbances on the skin. Right now, Ailsa. I'll see you there and whatever you do, don't let anyone move his body.'

Fifteen minutes later the pathologist was mid-discussion with a funeral director when Ava walked in. He glared at Ava as he unsealed the coffin lid and left them alone, gritting his teeth as he closed the door, shouting orders at his team regarding the delay.

'If my department gets a complaint, I'm blaming Police Scotland. This is extremely close to the line as far as proper procedure goes. The body's been released for burial. Technically speaking a court order's required without the family's written consent to reopen the coffin. What can possibly need investigating at this stage?' Ailsa asked.

'The scratched letters N and c,' Ava said. 'I don't think they stand for anything. I believe it was a message to us, only the Chief didn't finish. If you can get a closer look at his left wrist, I'll show you what I mean.'

Ailsa took a bottle of luminous yellow dye from her bag and swabbed Begbie's skin with it, gently washing off the residue and drying the area. Shining a bright light on the wrist, she positioned a high-powered lens over the area. Ava looked down at it and traced the arc of a curve, the mirror image of the c, which would have completed the circle.

'You can only just see it,' Ava said, 'but the dye has collected on another scratch. He was trying to make the letter o, Ailsa. He just didn't have time to complete it.' She stood back to let Ailsa get a better look.

It took thirty seconds before Ailsa picked up a camera and began to snap the image. 'It's difficult to discern, but I'll concede you may be right.'

'He couldn't have made the letter o on his wrist in a single move. The nail he was using to scratch with would have turned the wrong direction. It was the last shape he needed to make, and I'm guessing he lost consciousness or realised he was being watched and had to stop.'

'Why would anyone be watching and fail to stop him committing suicide?' Ailsa asked. 'What you're suggesting doesn't make sense.'

'That's because it wasn't really suicide. I think it was sit and breathe in carbon monoxide or take a bullet in the head, possibly something nastier and more prolonged. I'm guessing he wanted to spare Glynis that. Given the choice, Louis Jones might have chosen this way out as well,' Ava said bending back over the lens for a last look. 'The Chief wanted us to find it. I think the thought of everyone believing he'd committed suicide was appalling to him.' She looked up. Ailsa was staring at her, arms crossed, an expression of thunder on her face. Ava took a breath. In all the years she'd known Ailsa, she'd never seen her so angry.

'Louis Jones? The man who was executed with the use of a nail gun, shortly before you attended my house needing medical attention? Ava Turner, I care about you enough to go above your head. You've already proved to me that you're in danger. You asked for my discretion and I gave it, but if there's some link between George Begbie's death, Jones' facial muti-lation and the injury to your hand then all bets are off. Do you hear me?'

'Go over my head and you'll destroy the Chief's reputation and obliterate Glynis Begbie financially. You have to stay out of it, Ailsa. For your own sake more than mine,' Ava said.

'It seems to me I'm already in it. You've upgraded a suicide to a murder while the body should be in transit to the grave-yard. How are we going to explain that to the waiting family? Not to mention the fact that the upper echelons of Police Scotland are probably saving us seats right now, wondering where we are.'

'We're not stopping the funeral. This goes down as a tragic suicide. The Chief gets buried with as little controversy as possible. Any other course of action waves a big red flag. We're only here now because of a spilt cup of coffee, anyway. It doesn't really change anything,' Ava said. She walked to the internal door and opened it, shouting through to the funeral director. 'You can close the coffin. Thank you.' Ailsa repacked her kit and put on her coat.

Together they walked to their cars. 'So that's the end of it?' Ailsa asked. 'Now you know George didn't give in, that he wouldn't have left us voluntarily, you can find peace?'

Ava leaned against her car and closed her eyes in the watery December sunlight. 'You'll know if I lie to you, won't you?' she asked.

'I will,' Ailsa said.

Ava reached out and gently squeezed Ailsa's arm, not quite meeting her eyes, then climbed into her car and drove away.

Taking a seat in the second row at the graveside, Ava was aware of Ailsa a few chairs along, still fuming. The vicar was reciting some familiar lines. Glynis Begbie was dignified and quiet. Callanach was standing in the group of mourners beyond the scope of family and closest friends, next to DS Lively. It was perhaps the only time Ava had seen the two of them next to one another without any abuse breaking out. There were a few faces Ava didn't know, but not many. The police had been George Begbie's life. Hard, then, to imagine he had gone so far astray, but large amounts of money could tempt anyone, particularly when the pay was low at the start of a police career, with long hours and a family to support. Perhaps it had just been impossible to watch the bad guys reaping the rewards when everyone else was saving the pennies. Whatever the case, Ava had her answer. The Chief had, with his ebbing strength, made it clear that his staged suicide was something else, the marking on his arm the very opposite of a suicide note. What was she supposed to do now? The mourners stood as a prayer was read and the coffin was lowered into the grave. People were crying, men and women, at the loss of a friend, the end of an era but it was all Ava could do to keep the anger from bursting out of her. The Chief had not only been deprived of his life, he'd been deprived of justice, no doubt hoping his sacrifice would keep his wife safe, but Knuckles and his partner in crime had still come for the cash. What were the chances that they'd fallen for her ruse about the money being donated to charity? Not great, she thought. These were people who wore suspicion closer than their underwear.

A movement in the crowd distracted her. DC Tripp had stepped forward, shaking Callanach by the arm and motioning for him to move. Within seconds Callanach had disappeared altogether. Ava stayed in her place as the ceremony drew to a close. Glynis finally broke, sobbing on her daughter's shoulder, her legs giving way as she tried to walk to the car, leaving a beloved husband in the mud. That was the second Ava admitted to herself what Ailsa already knew. That she couldn't, wouldn't, leave it. That whatever crimes the Chief had committed, he'd deserved better than to end his life in a car full of poisonous gas. The only caveat was that Ava had to ensure Glynis Begbie was no longer a target for the thugs looking for the Chief's cash, and for that she needed a plausible explanation as to where it had all gone.

'Ailsa,' she said, catching up with her. 'I think I have a way that I can get Glynis safely back into her house. You're still on the board of that charity offering grief counselling, right?'

'I am,' Ailsa said.

'Could you make an announcement, today if possible, that the charity has received a substantial anonymous donation in cash? Express your gratitude for it, say you understand why the donor might not want to be named, but that grief affects us all at some point. Something like that. I'll find a way of making sure the story gets in the press.' At least then, Ava thought, the thugs who broke into Glynis' house might half-believe her story that the cash had been donated to charity. Callanach had a contact who could help her with the media coverage.

'I can do that,' Ailsa said.

'Thank you,' Ava said. 'I know I've no right to ask so much of you.'

'It comes at a price. Check in with me, twice a day. Morning and evening, 8 o'clock. I want to know you're safe. I owe your mother that much.'

'It's a deal,' Ava said. 'Although my mother was well aware that I couldn't be stopped once I'd made my mind up about something.'

'Eight o'clock,' Ailsa reminded her. 'Starting tonight.'

Chapter Twenty-Eight

Callanach walked into the Royal Infirmary and asked the receptionist to page the doctor whose name DC Tripp had given him. Tripp had disappeared off to interview the family members, and Lively was visiting the deceased's house where a cleaner had been told to allow him access. The doctor appeared as Callanach was checking his watch for the ninth time.

'Could I see your identification please?' the doctor asked. Callanach handed it over. 'Thank you. I don't mean to be rude but you'd be amazed how many unstable individuals hospitals attract.'

'That's fine. What can you tell me?'

'Walk with me,' she said. 'I'll show you the body. I think the family has finished their goodbye visit now. I'm Selina Vega. I was the Accident and Emergency Senior Registrar who dealt with Mrs Muir when she was first brought in.'

'When was that?' Callanach asked.

'Last night. Her daughter called an ambulance when she found her mother barely conscious on the bathroom floor. Extremely high temperature, stomach cramps, severe dehydration following a protracted period of sickness. That was the information provided by the paramedics. By the time she arrived here, she had lost consciousness and didn't regain it before her death, which was at 11.09 this morning.'

'All right,' Callanach said, scribbling notes.'So why am I here?'

'We ran tests to identify the cause of the illness. What we found in Mrs Muir's bloodstream was very high levels of a chemical known as DNP. Dinitrophenol. It's commonly used in unlicensed, non-prescription dieting tablets. You can buy them on the internet easily, but too high a dose can be lethal. She's in here,' Dr Vega said, opening a door.

Callanach checked the tag on the wrist of the corpse before him. Cordelia Muir. Her eyes were sunken, with what must have been eye-catching cheekbones prominent at each side of her face. Her skin was cold but her muscles still soft. She had no spare flesh on her.

'So you want to report it as a criminal offence because of the unlicensed drug?' Callanach asked the doctor. 'I appreciate the sentiment, but there's no way of ascertaining where the drugs came from.'

'Actually, it's not that,' Dr Vega said. 'It was her daughter's reaction when I told her what we'd found. Apparently Mrs Muir was a paragon of good health and responsible eating. Decaffeinated tea and coffee, obsessive about eating enough vegetables, clean proteins only. Sugar was a dirty word. She attended a gym regularly, and I can confirm that her overall muscle tone, although wasted after her illness, is impressive.'

'So the diet tablets?' Callanach said.

'Don't fit,' Dr Vega finished for him. 'Not at all. The daughter says she's been feeling ill but not for more than three weeks. There was no reason for her to lose weight. If it was something more psychological, like bulimia or anorexia, then she has no other signs. Her teeth are fine, so the vomiting hasn't eroded the enamel yet, confirming it's not been a long-term situation.'

'No other possible cause of the sudden weight loss?' Callanach asked.

'No indication of cancer in the blood-work, although it was the first thing that crossed my mind. The high temperature was the giveaway. I've worked in well-woman clinics, and illicit diet tablets are notorious for it. We had a fan on her when she first came in, as she was burning up. If she was taking those tablets voluntarily, then she was taking many more than she'd have been recommended and she doesn't fit any of the usual types. Her age is wrong, her weight is wrong, I gather there's no history of depression or self-harm.'

'The body will need to be transferred to the Edinburgh City Morgue,' Callanach said. 'I'll make sure the pathologist is aware of the circumstances. In the meantime, I'll need you to give a statement to an officer. How did the family seem?'

'Distressed, obviously,' Dr Vega said. 'Oh, I see what you're asking. I'd say they were shocked. I think they were expecting Mrs Muir to pull through, and as for the revelation that she had high levels of DNP in her body, all of their reactions seemed genuine. Is that what you were after?'

Callanach raised his eyebrows. He hadn't realised he'd been so transparent, but then family were always the first suspects in murder cases. 'Sorry, I wasn't trying to trick you into betraying a grieving relative. It's just that first impressions count for a lot, before people have a chance to fix their masks securely.'

'That's okay. I understand how hard your job can be, balancing kindness against the need for answers. It's often the same for me,' she said. 'You're French, right? Do you ever find it hard trying to read people's emotions through a second language? When I first moved to England from Spain I struggled with that. Not the words or their definitions, but the things my patients and their families weren't telling me.'

'Have you been here long?' Callanach asked.

'Ten years,' she replied. 'I still can't get used to the cold. It's one thing when you're skiing. It's not quite the same when you're just trying to buy groceries.'

Callanach smiled. 'I sympathise,' he said. 'I should go and talk to the family now. Could you show me the way? Unless you're rushing off somewhere.'

'I'm off duty. I was just waiting to talk to you before heading home. Come on, I'd be happy to take you. I need to say goodbye to them anyway.'

★ ★ ★

Spreading his palms wide on the door to the hospital mortuary suite, he breathed in slowly and deeply.

'I'm here, Cordelia,' he said. 'Thank you.'

He imagined her body covered by a sheet, and wondered why anyone bothered to hide corpses from the world. Was it that the living feared staring into the eyes of death or that the dead shouldn't be bothered by the still beating hearts going about their business around them? More likely, he thought, that it was all too easy to imagine the dead as monstrous. He knew monsters. He understood them. None of the ones he'd met had ever been dead. They had promised him safety in their foster homes. They had smiled and lied, talked about him above his head in legal speak, acted as if they cared. The dead were harmless enough.

A nurse rounded the corner, head down, studying a brown folder thick with patient notes. He stepped back to let her pass. Cordelia was gone. He regretted not having been there within sight of her at the end, but he couldn't have it all his own way. Imagining her death, knowing the symptoms she would have suffered, was enough and he hoped it was not too painful a passing. He was capable of empathy, no matter what the experts said about sociopaths. His priority now was to make the most of Cordelia's death. To wring every tiny emotion from it. Dying for nothing would be the ultimate insult, after all. He slid his right hand into his trouser pocket and ran his fingers along the length of the beautiful ink-pen he had yet to add to his box of treasures.

Then there was the budding West End star, Sean, to think of. Life was complicated at the moment. So many people to please. So much need for him. All the time, he had to remember who he was, cover his tracks, avoid, plan, prepare. There were times, he admitted, when he doubted it was worth it. But then there was the grief. The outpouring. That was his reward. The love he gave and received. Pulling up his hood, he opened the photo gallery of Sean on his mobile, and blew Cordelia a final kiss goodbye towards the door. Each death only made him long for the next all the sooner.

Chapter Twenty-Nine

'We seized Mrs Muir's handbag and all its contents, sir,' a detective constable said, handing Callanach an updated evidence schedule through the incident room chaos. 'The tablets were found in a zipped pocket inside the bag, set in the inner lining along with some sanitary products.'

'Where are the pills now?' Callanach asked.

'Sent to the lab, but we've found similar pills online. I'm willing to bet that's what she was taking,' the detective constable replied.

'We use victims' names, not pronouns,' Callanach snapped. 'How soon do we get the lab results?'

'Tomorrow,' Lively joined in. 'Only one of the tablets went to the lab for chemical profiling. The rest went for general forensic testing. It looks as if they came from a tub of pills Mrs Muir kept in her desk at work. They were shoved right to the back of the bottom drawer.'

'No markings on the pills themselves?' Callanach asked.

'None,' Lively confirmed. 'Not unusual for internet purchases of unregulated medicines. Prevents tracing them back to a particular provider in the event of an incident like this.'

'So it looks as if the daughter may be wrong about her mother not knowingly taking diet pills,' Callanach said. 'Check Mrs Muir's internet history and emails for references to diet supplements and weight loss. See if we can find out where she bought them.' A buzz from his pocket was a message from Lance Proudfoot suggesting a place to meet. 'Let me know as soon as the preliminary autopsy report is in. I'll need to review it with DCI Turner.'

Lance and Callanach met in a coffee shop just off Middle Meadow Walk, usually full of students for its proximity to the university, but the December holidays had thinned out its usual clientele.

'God, there was me looking forward to seeing you, and I find you with a face like the innards of a haggis. Surely it can't be that bad, man!' Lance bellowed. He wrapped Callanach in a brisk hug as he stood to greet him, slapping him hard on the back. Callanach had no choice but to smile back. It was impossible to feel sorry for yourself around Lance.

'I ordered you espresso, none of that ridiculous latte you philistines like so much,' Callanach said. 'It's good to see you, Lance. Sorry I left it so long.'

'Ach, don't sweat it. My son graduated in September and promptly decided to move back in with me, much to my horror. I seem to spend all my time either shopping, cooking or cleaning. I'd forgotten what it was like to have another person around the place. I tried to persuade him to move in with his mother but apparently my ex-wife recently found God. Rather restrictive to a lad in his early twenties, apparently,' Lance said, taking a swig of the espresso and grimacing. 'How do you drink this stuff without single malt in it?'

'Lance, forgive me. I'm going to have to be quick. Thanks for agreeing to help. Another officer has asked for a story to be put out and I wondered if you could assist,' he said. He didn't use Ava's name. Her instructions had been to keep any police link to the story completely hidden.

'What details can you give me?' Lance asked.

'Here,' Callanach said, sliding a piece over paper across the table. 'It's straight forward. A large anonymous donation has been made in cash to a charity. The details are all there with a statement from Edinburgh's Chief Pathologist about it. Can you run it on your news blog?'

'The real question is why you need me to run it,' Lance said.

'It's urgent. Other news channels might not be interested. It needs to be prominent,' Callanach pleaded.

'I'd ask what the backstory is, only I can see from your face that I might as well ask the Queen what Prince Philip's like in bed. Have you got time to eat? I'm starving,' Lance said.

'Sorry, I don't, but I'll buy you a sandwich if that makes it up to you,' Callanach said.

'Never mind, I'm supposed to be watching this svelte, dreamboat figure. Is it a charity fraud case? Forget it, I'll stop asking,' Lance said. Callanach shook his head. It wasn't even that he didn't want to answer Lance's questions. The truth was that he didn't have any answers to give him. Ava had contacted him with the details and asked him to get it done. End of story.

'But you can't blame a journalist for trying. Will you come to my place for dinner soon, when you don't have to rush away? I'll make sure my boy is at his mother's for the weekend so we can talk without listening to his music through the wall.'

'I'd like that, thanks Lance. I'll be in touch.'

Christian was waiting in the carpark for Randall Muir. He'd called an hour earlier, asking to be collected from the hospital and driven home. The boy's head was bowed as he walked between the cars, looking for Christian through the drizzle. He flashed his headlights and waved a hand out of the driver's window.

'Hey, Rand, what's happening? Haven't you been home since last night?' Christian asked.

'No,' Randall said. 'I—she—we couldn't leave.' He rubbed a hand across his eyes, determined not to cry in front of Christian. He'd been so sure he could make it home without blubbing and they hadn't even left the carpark yet.

'Randall,' Christian said softly. 'What happened?'

'Mum's dead,' he said. 'Some sort of pills, they reckon. I couldn't understand most of what they said. My sister is still there dealing with the police.'

'Oh, no. I'm so sorry. You should have called me. I'd have come and just, I don't know, been there with you,' Christian said.

'It's okay,' Randall said.

'It isn't okay. Not at all.' Christian put an arm around his shoulders, pulling him close and gripping him tightly for a few seconds. 'I wish I hadn't encouraged you to spend your time at The Fret. You should have been at home with your mum, not listening to a load of losers showing off.'

'No,' Randall said pulling away from him. 'I wanted to be there. I needed to be there. You don't know how much it meant.' His cheeks coloured and he turned to the window before Christian could see his embarrassment.

'What can I do to help?' Christian asked. 'Shall I take you home?'

'Yes, please,' Randall said. 'My sister's going to her house to get some clothes, then she's coming over. Maybe you could come in and meet her? We could call out for pizza or something. Mum used to do all the cooking.'

'I don't think she'll want anyone else there right now, but thank you. I have another friend I need to see tonight. God

193

knows how this could have happened to two of you. It's like I'm a jinx.' He started the car engine. 'You said the police were there. Why was that?' he asked, filling the silence.

'The doctor said my mum had taken non-prescription drugs, the sort you get off the internet for losing weight. I don't think they're legal in this country so the police were brought in.'

'That's awful. The people who make that crap should be shot. Did you even know she was taking them?' Chris asked.

'No. She didn't need to lose weight. I reckon they've got it wrong. I knew she wasn't feeling well but I never guessed. You know what the worst thing is? When I left last night, I never even said goodbye to her. I was so worried about getting out of the house, and' – he dashed tears from his eyes – 'and I was pleased she was ill so she didn't give me any hassle. Feels like it's all my fault.'

'That's not true. Your mum knew exactly how much you loved her. It's not your fault, Randall. This is going to be tough, I've been there. I lost my mum, too. Blaming yourself won't bring her back and it won't help. If you'd known what she was going through, you'd have stayed, wouldn't you?'

'Yeah, of course.' Randall sniffed.

'There you go. That's what you have to keep hold of. Even if you had been there, chances are it was too late for you to have changed anything. Which house is it?' he asked.

'That one,' Randall said, pointing across the road. Christian pulled up. 'Thanks. I'm sorry to have called you.'

'I'm glad you did,' Christian said. 'Make sure you eat and get some sleep. No one wants you getting ill as well. Call me if you need me. It's no trouble.'

Randall climbed out of the car, giving a quick wave and running inside. Watching Randall made Christian think of Mina. He hadn't answered the message she'd left him earlier. He picked up his phone and dialled.

'Hey,' Mina answered the phone softly. 'I'm in the library. I had to get out of the house. Are you nearby?' she asked.

'No, I've just dropped off a friend and I think he might need me later so I won't make any plans, if that's okay,' Christian said.

'Yeah, fine,' Mina said. 'I understand. How about meeting up tomorrow instead?'

'I've got some work. Holiday stuff, but I've got to take it. Next term's fees aren't going to pay themselves. As soon as I've got a free day, I'll call you. Are you going to be okay?'

'It seems harder now that it's getting closer to Christmas. I keep wondering what to buy Lily then remembering I don't need to this year. The police are coming up blank. My parents have completely stopped going out,' she said.

'It's early days. Wait until the new year. It'll be easier to move forward. I'd better go. I need to keep my phone free,' Christian said.

'Sure, sorry. Your friend, is he okay? You sound worried,' Mina said.

'A bit. His mother just . . . you know what, you've got enough on your plate,' he said.

'It's good for me to think about other people. Can you tell me what happened?' she asked.

'He lost his mother. They think she died from taking some unlicensed diet pills. It's so sad. His father had already passed. Now it's just him and his sister,' Christian said.

'That's so unfair,' Mina said. 'Poor him. Is there anything I can do to help?'

'No, it's very raw. He needs time with his family to come to terms with their loss. It's weird though. First you lose Lily then this happens to someone else I know. I feel like I'm spreading bad luck around. I know that's stupid, and that it's nothing to do with me, but it's uncomfortable. As if whenever I walk into someone's life, I ruin things for them.'

'Don't say that,' Mina said. 'If you hadn't been around, I'm not sure I'd have coped. You've been so strong for me. I'm sure you'll do the same for your other friend, too.'

'Listen to you, making me feel better. I've got to go, but I'll make it up to you. We'll do something together in a couple of days, okay?'

'That sounds good,' she said. 'Christian, thanks for everything.'

'I'm glad I could be there when you needed me,' he replied. 'It was a privilege.'

Chapter Thirty

Ava hadn't slept. The thought that Glynis Begbie had been robbed of a husband by men who were confident they wouldn't be prosecuted for it was driving her to distraction. Then there was Louis Jones. That death she could do something about. The problem was where to start.

Ava picked up Jones' phone records and ran through them. The last call was from a phone in St Leonard's police station, so it was the previous few numbers she was interested in. Ava ran three numbers through the computer. One was from India. The search engine listed it as a popular complaints number, which looked like a standard computer virus scam. The next incoming call was from Glasgow. Ava blocked her mobile number from being identified, and dialled it.

A female picked up, shouting about music and noise. 'The Maz,' the voice said. 'Geordie, shut the fuck up, I can't hear a frigging thing. Who is it?' the woman shouted.

Ava ended the call. It made sense, as did the fact that the big man and Knuckles had Glaswegian accents. The Maz was the address Ramon Trescoe had given on his release from prison. The phone call was also the first firm link between Trescoe and Louis Jones. She studied the remaining calls on the log before Jones had disappeared into the night and headlong into a nasty car accident. Jones had phoned someone straight after he'd taken the call from The Mazophilia. Was he asking for help, she wondered. She dialled the number on the log. A recorded message provided details of a ferry company operating out of Cairnryan Port, running the service over to Belfast. That explained both the route Jones was taking out of Edinburgh and the speed at which he'd left his premises. More importantly, it was an indication of the nature of the call from Glasgow beforehand.

Ava wished she could turn back time and get a look inside Louis Jones' car. What did a man on the run take with him? Was he carrying bundles of used notes, similar to those Begbie had stashed in his house, or had he given up on that and decided his life was all that mattered? She made one more call.

'Chief Inspector Dimitri?' Ava said, tucking her phone between ear and shoulder as she opened a notebook. 'This is DCI Turner. Could you email me the evidence log for Louis Jones' car? I can't find a copy of it in our investigative records.'

'I'll send it, of course, but to my knowledge the car was empty. Some food cartons. No weapons, no drugs, nothing of note,' Dimitri said. 'What is it you're looking for?'

'Anything about where he was going or why he was leaving Edinburgh,' Ava said.

'I'll have someone send over the paperwork. No other leads then?' he asked.

'It's early days,' Ava said. 'Tell me, the other car involved in the crash, presumably you have tyre marks or paint flecks.'

'A forensic road traffic accident investigator attended the scene. I haven't reviewed his report as it didn't become available until after Jones was dead and by then it had become your case. I'll do whatever I can to help, though,' Dimitri said.

'Not necessary,' Ava replied. 'I'll chase the accident investigator's report myself. It would have been more helpful if we'd been made aware of which officers had attended the scene in the first place.' She was trying not to snap. Playing blame tennis between departments was unprofessional, and Dimitri had been nothing other than courteous and helpful.

'Sorry, I'd asked one of my constables to pass you the information but she's pregnant at the moment and frankly I'm finding my commands go in one ear and out the other. She's about as useful as a kitten in a dog-fight these days,' he said.

'What's her name?' Ava asked.

'I beg your pardon?' Dimitri said.

'I said, what's her name? Your pregnant PC?'

'Janet Monroe. I'll be sure to chase the matter up with her.' He rang off. Ava unclenched her jaws and strode through to the incident room. In her frustration, she'd just made matters worse for some poor constable who was already, no doubt, feeling as if pregnancy was a step down on the career ladder. It wasn't what she'd intended at all.

'DC Tripp,' she said, 'I need to know which road traffic accident investigator attended the scene of Louis Jones' crash. Then I'll need contact details for a PC Janet Monroe who's on Chief Inspector Dimitri's squad. Is the preliminary pathologist's report on Cordelia Muir in yet?'

'Only to confirm that death was caused by the high levels of DNP in Mrs Muir's blood. Other than that, no injuries, no defensive wounds, no self-harm, no illness apparent but they're waiting for the full tox screen,' Tripp said. 'Detective Superintendent Overbeck's chasing you. She phoned earlier but the call got diverted as your line was busy.'

'Bollocks,' Ava muttered. Appeasing Overbeck was the last thing she felt like doing, but it was best dealt with swiftly, like lancing a boil. Back at her desk she put the call through to

Overbeck's secretary, half-hoping the Superintendent would now be engaged with some other task. No such luck.

'Progress report, Turner,' Overbeck demanded.

Ava slumped. When Overbeck was in one of those moods nothing was going to pacify her. 'Cordelia Muir died of poisoning from a high level of DNP. We're chasing the drug trail. She had pills both in her handbag and her desk, so we need to identify the vendor. There's not much change in the status of the Lily Eustis investigation. We know where she was drinking before her trip to Arthur's Seat but her male companion has still neither come forward nor been identified. The murder of Louis Jones is in preliminary stages. Cause of death was the injury from the gunshot to the head.'

'Did you figure that one out yourself or did the pathologist have to confirm it?' Overbeck asked. Ava didn't bother to answer. It was better to allow Overbeck her moment of sarcasm then move on. Engaging her was destructive. 'Jones' known enemies? Any forward movement there?'

'He's on the periphery of criminal activity in the area through his vehicle hire business. DS Lively is conducting those enquiries, ma'am,' Ava said.

'So, to summarise, you have three dead bodies and no one in custody to account for any of them. The explanation for that is? I mean one I can give to the board. Not the usual babble about evidence and forensics.'

'In the Muir case, the drugs may have come from abroad and might prove impossible to trace. As far as Lily Eustis goes, there was a delay before we considered it a murder and there is very little to go on evidentially. Regarding Louis Jones, I'm waiting for forensics reports,' Ava said.

'You're still talking and yet I'm hearing nothing of substance. Look under some rocks, Ava, that's my advice. If it's not obvious which ones are relevant, kick a lot of them until something nasty crawls out, then put a bloody glass over it and get it in a cell. You're aware I have a limited amount of patience? Update me within forty-eight hours.'

As unwelcome as one of Overbeck's lectures was, this time she'd made a fair point. Sitting around waiting for useful information about Louis Jones' killer to appear was no strategy at all. Ava had the address of The Maz club and two suspects to follow up. There was little point wasting any more time.

Courtesy of roadworks, Ava's journey from Edinburgh city centre to Glasgow took an hour and forty-five minutes, by which time the sun was getting low. The Mazophilia Club, home to the Trescoe family, was on Cathcart Road in the Govanhill area to the south of the city centre, a small mercy that meant she bypassed the worst of the Glasgow traffic. The downside was that the area itself wasn't the place she wanted to be as the sun went down.

She found the club eventually, not that the signage was hugely helpful as the main door was in a side-alley. The facade was black with scratched up gold lettering, and a smokey grey outline of a woman with the sort of curves rarely seen in real life. Ava silenced her screaming inner-feminist, bought a packet of cigarettes and a lighter from a nearby shop, turned up her collar and put on the woolly hat and gloves she kept in the car for winter visits to scenes of crime. Walking slowly around the block towards the club's entrance, she lit a cigarette, smoking without inhaling. When the law had changed to make smoking in pubs and clubs illegal, it had inadvertently provided a perfectly plausible excuse to hang around outside in the middle of winter. The main problem was trying not to cough.

The club was windowless, although two other doors provided fire exits. At the back of the property was a further door, but this had a number attached and there were windows on the first and second floors. In the upper of those were curtains. This was separate from the club then, presumably providing living accommodation. Behind that, was a pedestrian walkway through to a parking area.

A door slammed in the main alleyway. Ava leaned against a wall, lighting a new cigarette.

'I've told you, I'm not going to work there if you let them touch me. The deal was they can look but that's it. I don't want people grabbing ma fuckin' boobs. They want to do that, they're going to have to fork out a lot more than they're paying to get through the door.' The accent was all Glasgow but the face, as Ava peered round for a look, was more Asian. She was pretty. Too pretty to need to work in such a dive, Ava thought, but then people got trapped by their own lives. The man she was with put a hand on her shoulder.

'It's not such a big deal, is it? You're here to entertain. If anyone gets really out of hand, one of us'll show 'em the door. It's as safe as houses. Take it as a compliment and smile,' he said.

'How much of a compliment would it be if I grab your ball-sack?' the girl responded.

'I think I'd be fairly pleased with myself,' the man said.

'Yeah, well what if it was one of those sweaty pigs in there? Honest to God, most of the time I can smell them before I can see them. We should make them take a frigging shower before they come through the door.'

'That's Mr Trescoe's customers you're talking about. You don't want to let the boss hear you talking like that. I'll ask the bouncers to keep a closer eye on you tonight, okay? Anyone gets frisky, they'll sort it, but no more mouthing off. You're eye-candy. That's not so effective with a face like you've just been pissed on.'

'Yeah, well, if it happens again, I'm complaining to Joe Trescoe myself,' the girl said.

'If you talk to Mr Trescoe like you just spoke to me, you'll end up being escorted home by Knuckles. You want that?' There was silence. 'Didn't think so. Now let's get you a drink, loosen you up before the place gets busy. No more moaning, right?'

The girl, face still thunderous, threw her cigarette on the ground and walked inside, the man's arm around her shoulders. Ava edged out of the shadows. Joe Trescoe, the club's owner, was Ramon Trescoe's brother. No doubt, now that he was out of prison, Ramon wasn't wasting any time inserting himself back into Glasgow's less than honest money-making schemes. Short of loitering for the next twenty-four hours, though, there was little hope of seeing Ramon himself. The one positive was hearing Knuckles' name mentioned. What Ava needed now was to put all the pieces together. She stamped her feet. It was time to go home. There was no point risking being noticed, especially when one of the men inside was still sporting some burn marks on his testicles from her taser. Next time she was there, she'd be better prepared. Next time, she'd be dressed to kill and perfectly happy to do so.

Chapter Thirty-One

Callanach sat with the forensics report in front of him. The lab results on the tablet from Cordelia Muir's handbag verified the presence of the so-called weight loss drug dinitrophenol. He had already contacted the Food Standards Agency who had responded with a sense of exhaustion, commenting only that stopping the flow of such drugs into the country was about as likely as persuading a teenager not to use social media. The report also confirmed that Cordelia Muir's DNA had been found on the tablets in her handbag, and that the pills in her desk also matched the chemical makeup of the drug in her body. It was conclusive, and it made Cordelia's death illegal, but with no emails or texts showing where she'd purchased the drugs, there was no case for MIT to follow up. All that remained was for Callanach to prepare a file for the Procurator Fiscal. The other task was to break the news to Mrs Muir's family.

A constable wandered into his office, left a note on his desk then disappeared again. Callanach stopped typing to read it.

'Telephone call from Dr Selina Vega re Cordelia Muir,' it read, followed by a mobile number.

'This is Detective Inspector Callanach,' he said, as she answered his call.

'That was quick. I was wondering how the investigation is going into Mrs Muir's death. Do you have an autopsy report yet?' the hospital registrar who had treated Cordelia asked.

'I have,' Callanach said. 'Generally the report doesn't . . .'

'Over coffee, if you've got time? Then I can have a proper look at it. I'm off duty today if you're free to meet up.'

'That's fine, if you'd prefer to talk in person. Did you want to come into the station?' Callanach asked.

'I'd prefer somewhere with sofas and Danish pastries.' Dr Vega laughed. 'There's a little Spanish place tucked away on Niddry if you'll promise never to take anyone else there. I don't want it getting too popular as it's my regular hangout.'

'I think I can promise that,' Callanach said. 'An hour from now?'

Esencia looked tiny from the outside, but the café extended back through the building on Niddry Street, its ancient walls darkened over centuries. Upon opening the door, Callanach had been overwhelmed by the mingling aromas of coffee, spiced wines and cured meats. For a second he was far away in sunshine, enjoying the fresh air. It could have been Portugal, Greece or Spain. He held on to the sensation as long as he could before bringing himself back to reality and looking around for Dr Selina Vega.

He found her with a book on her lap in a corner, her long hair twisted up on her head, wearing a pale denim shirt and brown suede jeans. She smiled as he approached.

'You found me,' she said. 'I've ordered us coffee, deep-fried calamari and patatas bravas. That okay?'

'I wasn't expecting you to do that, Dr Vega. I hope you'll let me get the bill,' Callanach said.

'It's the least I can do. I felt a bit guilty forcing you out of your office. It's just so nice to be able to meet up with a fellow immigrant. And please call me Selina,' she said. Callanach hung his coat on the back on the chair and made himself comfortable. Selina Vega was beautiful. Tall, slim, with dark brown eyes and a wide smile. He'd not registered that she might have been interested in anything other than a professional context but the meeting suddenly felt more like a date. He took out a paper copy of the autopsy report and put it on the table without opening it.

'I'm Luc,' he said. 'If you miss Spain that much, why not go back, if I'm not prying.'

'I had a boyfriend here, we lived together for a few years, it went wrong. Now I'm on a career path and the hospital is excellent. I go back regularly to stock up on sunshine and trips to the beach. Scotland doesn't have the ideal climate for surfing. What about you?'

'My father was Scottish,' he said. That much, at least, was certain to be true whatever he found out about his biological roots. It was also the easiest way to answer the question without lying. 'I haven't been surfing for such a long time. Years, in fact. I used to go down to Les Cavaliers regularly in my early twenties. It's funny how work distracts us from the things we love.'

'Tell me about it. My dream was to travel the world scuba diving. As a teenager, I used to carry around a list of wrecks and reefs I wanted to see. I managed a few of them, then it was all revision and research. There's always a sacrifice, but it's worth it. Those times when I long for the ocean, I remind myself of the good I'm doing.'

'Speaking of which' – Callanach took the opportunity to open the report and hand it to her – 'here's the preliminary report. We're waiting for the full tox screen but basically it confirms your initial diagnosis.' The coffee and food arrived. Callanach served as Selina read.

'That's a high level of DNP, more than the dosage would recommend even with illegal tablets. I've read up about her. She was a bright woman. She'd have known she was taking too much,' Selina said.

'We don't understand what her motivation was yet,' Callanach said. 'Her children are terribly shocked, much the same as when you saw them at the hospital, but we found pills in her desk at work and in her handbag, too.'

'I see that,' Selina said. 'They do the best fried calamari, don't they?' she commented through a mouthful. 'What was the DNA source on the tablets in her handbag?'

Callanach took the report back from her, turned a page and read from the relevant paragraph.

'Skin cells, hair fibres. Looks like plenty of DNA on the loose tablets,' Callanach said. 'The same goes for the bottle of pills in the bottom drawer of her desk.'

'Which you'd expect. It's her handbag. She'd have had makeup, tissues, pens, a hairbrush – every cross-contaminant you can think of. Her desk would be full of other items she touches regularly. But none of the DNA on the pills comes from fingerprints that I can see,' Selina said.

'True, but we don't find fingerprints on everything. Objects get wiped or wet,' Callanach said.

'I handle tablets regularly. They have smooth, dry surfaces. The oil from my fingers or palms would inevitably leave some sort of print, but especially if I tipped them from a bottle into my hand, then manoeuvred them into a zipped section of my handbag. That's why at the hospital we use gloves or pots to hand over tablets. If those pills had been handled by Mrs Muir, I find it impossible to believe they wouldn't have partial prints on them.' She picked up her coffee. 'Oh damn,' she said. 'Now you have a look on your face that tells me you're itching to get away. I shouldn't have said anything.'

'Is your mind always so clear?' Callanach asked.

'Not when I'm near the sea. Then I can hear nothing but the waves and see only the light playing on the water. I wish there were two of me. One to work and the other to spend my time building campfires on beaches and staring at the stars. Will you at least finish your coffee?' Selina asked.

'I will,' he replied. 'Any other insights?'

'Only this,' she said. 'I never spoke to Mrs Muir, but I met her daughter and that's usually a good gauge for the maternal figure. She was immaculately dressed, prim, even. Precise in her questions, clean, short nails – I'm a bore for noticing these things. I suspect her mother was the same. I have trouble imagining her tipping loose pills into her handbag. If she wanted to take a few out of the bottle, it seems more likely she'd have put them into another container or at least a small plastic bag. Women know their handbags get full of dust and fluff. You wouldn't want to swallow anything that had been loose, even from a side pocket.'

Callanach finished his coffee and took a last mouthful of the patatas bravas. 'The food here is excellent. Thank you for suggesting it. I'm sorry that I have to leave so abruptly.'

'Next time I'm going to refuse to talk shop with you if this is what happens,' she said. Callanach stood up and put on his coat. She rose with him, slipped a gentle hand onto his shoulder and kissed his cheek. She smelled of vanilla and cinnamon, Callanach thought. 'If you decide to keep hold of my mobile number and maybe call to ask me out for a drink next week, it might be easier if you know in advance that I'll say yes.'

By the time Callanach arrived back at the station he couldn't even recall how he'd responded to Selina Vega's final statement. She was neither arrogant nor presumptuous, just filled with an easy confidence and good humour. Given her combination of intellect, personality and looks, Callanach couldn't imagine that any man had ever turned her down. The issue was that he was in no state to be inviting a woman on a date. That would create an impression of a future he would be unable to fulfil. It was better not to open doors at all, rather than scrabbling for excuses to close them later. He was impotent. Useless in a relationship. The irony of possibly having been conceived through rape, and left impotent as a result of a similar accusation was almost intolerable. Selina Vega didn't know it, but she was better off without a phone call from him. Nothing but disappointment could follow.

He headed for Crystal's offices. DC Tripp was due to meet him there with an employee who would open the premises for them. An MIT squad had visited Cordelia Muir's offices briefly before but it wasn't a crime scene and hadn't been cordoned off.

'You're the polis, are you?' a woman asked at Cordelia's office front door. 'You don't look like I'd expected. I'm Sian,' she said.

'DI Callanach,' he responded. 'Is there an alarm on the premises?'

'Don't need one. There's no cash here, no products. I suppose you might fancy burgling the place if you had a crush on multi-coloured packs of post-it notes. Is there news? Do you know what happened to Cordelia?' she asked.

'That's still confidential, I'm afraid. I appreciate you letting us in,' Callanach said, looking around for Tripp. 'I'll go on inside, but my colleague will arrive shortly. Sorry to ask, but would you mind waiting out here? We need to minimise disturbance.'

She didn't bother to answer him, continuing the conversation where she'd left off. 'None of us knows what'll happen to our jobs. I hate to sound mercenary but Cordelia was a bit of a one-woman marvel. We managed the day-to-day, but she was the driving force behind all the large-scale fundraising and the international relations, as well as handling all the legal stuff. We haven't been told anything. I don't even know who'll approve our wages this month. I may work for a charity but that doesn't make me one,' Sian said.

'I'll be as quick as I can,' Callanach replied, avoiding the questions and walking in.

It was obvious that no one had been inside since Cordelia's death. All the lights were off and it was colder than a populated office would have been. The space was about as standard as could be. There were several desks in rows in the front area, with a larger office separated by glass at the rear end. To one side there were toilets and a small kitchen area with a sink, a cabinet for crockery, cutlery and cleaning essentials, and a fridge. At the far side was a conference room.

Callanach pulled on a pair of gloves and took out his phone, photographing each section of the office, being careful not to move anything. He went into Cordelia's private office, moving her chair out of the way with his foot and opening the drawers of her desk. The contents were carefully arranged. Not obsessively so, but her ink-pen box was positioned next to a pot of ink and sat on blotting paper. Mrs Muir had liked everything just so. There was no rubbish around, nor crumpled papers or loose receipts. Another drawer contained a file entitled sponsorship queries, the next had stationery supplies, and the bottom one held letters and to-do lists. That was where the bottle of pills had been found, right at the back lodged behind the paperwork.

On the top of her desk, family photos were neatly framed and arranged. Odds and ends were in a desk-tidy. Selina was right. This wasn't a woman likely to have emptied loose pills into her handbag. Her life was orderly and clean. There wasn't a speck of dust in sight. Callanach had the uncomfortable sense that he was still missing something. Cordelia's daughter had never believed her mother would take diet pills. MIT's investigations had revealed nothing except admiration for the deceased. She was regularly invited to speak at charity events and widely liked. Cordelia had no known enemies, although he knew from experience that anyone could attract unwanted attention. The issue, if a crime had been committed against her, was how.

He opened the fridge, photographed the contents, then inspected each item individually. In the door were cartons of milk, one opened, two unopened. On the shelves were plastic tubs with varying degrees of food remaining inside. Two were blank, and of the remaining six, two were labelled Cordelia's. Callanach took them out, pulled evidence bags from his pockets, filled in the time, date and place of seizure for the log and sealed the tubs inside. As an afterthought, he took out all the remaining tubs and put each one in an evidence bag.

'Sir?' a voice said from behind him. 'Do you need me to do that?' DC Tripp asked.

'Get gloves on. I'm looking for a source of contamination with DNP. All food and drink to be seized. All drawers and cabinets to be checked for pills,' he said. 'We'll need to return clean items to the owners. The staff are already getting frustrated about the lack of communication. The last thing we need is them moaning to the press because we haven't returned the mug their boyfriend bought them.'

'How will we identify the people whose belongings we're removing?' Tripp asked.

'There are personnel files in Mrs Muir's office. Go through them, get the name of each person on payroll here. Speak to the lady outside for details of any cleaners. If someone planted those pills in her drawer, they had to have access to her desk,' Callanach said.

'I don't understand the motive, sir,' Tripp said.

'It could be a disgruntled employee. It could be racially motivated. Could even be someone on the payroll of a foreign government who didn't appreciate Mrs Muir's charitable work in their country. There were no fingerprints on the bottle of pills. If you think about all the people who must have handled the packaging, including Mrs Muir, that's rather unlikely, isn't it?'

'Almost impossible,' Tripp agreed.

'Someone wiped the bottle. They were careful about it, which means they had a motive to do so. I can't think of one single reason why Cordelia Muir might have done that herself.'

Chapter Thirty-Two

Bradley was waiting at the Café Nom de Plume. He'd arranged to meet Christian there, walking a tightrope between innocence and deceit, and treading it heavily. Sean was full of scripts, rehearsals and the new fabulous people in his life, exciting opportunities so blinding he had hardly noticed Bradley's distractedness. It was Brad who was struggling to fake it. At night he closed his eyes and saw Christian's face. In the mornings he walked to work past the door of the Nom de Plume and imagined seeing his new friend's face at the window seat that had become 'their table'. Lately he had taken to wondering how it might feel to be the first man Christian ever kissed, which was why the fact that Christian was late, very late, stung. Bradley was finishing his coffee and preparing to return to work when the door finally opened.

Christian looked different. His hair was flopping over his face, his skin had lost its usual lustre, his slow smile absent. He lowered himself into the chair next to Bradley and shook his head.

'I'm sorry. I hate keeping you waiting.' He said it so quietly Bradley had to lean in to hear.

'What happened?' Bradley asked.

'My fiancée left,' Christian said. 'The last few weeks have been rough. Two people I know have lost loved ones. I asked my partner to be patient, to share me, let me be where people needed me most. But she couldn't. Then I told her about you.'

Bradley pulled his chair closer to Christian's. 'Has she gone for good?' he asked.

Christian nodded, putting his head in his hands, elbows resting on the table. Bradley slid a tentative hand across the back of Christian's shoulders, feeling the tension in his muscles, trying to concentrate on what his friend needed from him.

'Am I going to make you late back to work?' Christian asked. 'It's just that my girlfriend was so upset, and I was trying to leave it on good terms. I know it's the right thing for both of us that she's gone, but I didn't want it to end like this. Do you believe in curses, Brad? Do you think your past can follow you?'

Bradley put his hand back on his coffee mug, hoping Sean wouldn't call as he often did about that time. He slid his hand into his pocket and turned down the ringtone volume. Christian needed him right now.

'I think we're more aware of events that remind us of our past,' Bradley said. 'If it's something bad that we haven't come to terms with, then perhaps we expect the past to repeat itself.'

Christian crept one hand slowly along the table, reaching out for Bradley's fingers, grasping them in his shaking palm. 'I mess everything up in my own life but I'm good at finding people who need me. I'm good at being a friend, I think. I see people in pain and most of the time I can help. It's as if I help other people as a way of coming to terms with my issues. Does that make sense?'

'A lot,' Bradley said, wanting to understand, hesitant to interrupt Christian while he was opening up.

'When I told her about you, she asked if I'd been thinking

about you as more than just as a friend. I wanted to reassure her. I believe in being faithful, emotionally and physically, but I couldn't lie to her anymore,' Christian said.

Bradley flushed. 'What answer did you give her?' he asked.

'I told her I wanted to get to know you better. I didn't need to say anything more than that. She knew all the ways I meant it,' Chris replied. 'I hope you don't mind. You and I have been spending so much time together. These few minutes at lunchtime have been the only moments of peace for me. I've been propping up Mina and Randall, then going home to . . . it's been draining. It seems so presumptuous now. Can you forgive me?'

'As if there was anything to forgive,' Bradley said. 'If it helps, I've been thinking about you, too. I don't want there to be any pressure between us, though. I like being around you, just talking. I've felt, I don't know, listened to for the first time in a while.'

'Maybe I could come over to yours one evening this week?' Christian asked. 'Do you think it's time we moved on from sharing coffee and work stories?' He smiled and Bradley felt a surge of adrenalin usually reserved for first kisses and running from bullies.

'Perhaps not my place,' Bradley said. 'Things are complicated. I could come to yours?'

'Too soon. A lot of her stuff is still there and I'll see her face every time I turn around for a few months yet.'

'Of course, how insensitive of me,' Bradley said.

'Let's find a quiet bar and go for a drink then. Neutral territory. I'll text you when and where. Say next Friday?' Christian asked.

'That sounds good.' Brad smiled.

'You'd better go. I called in sick today but your boss will be expecting you back.' He reached his arms out to Bradley for a hug, holding him close. Bradley was aware of the warmth of Christian's body and the flatness of his stomach. He made himself remember Sean's smile, his humour and gentleness. The attempted diversion didn't last long.

Once Bradley had left, Christian took out his phone and called Randall. He knew the family had been busy organising Cordelia's funeral but he'd expected Randall to have been in touch. He was worried that he was internalising his grief. That was a disaster.

'Chris, hold on. I'll go upstairs,' Randall said. Christian could hear him running, then the sound of breathlessness before he began to talk again. 'Thanks for phoning. I wanted to call you but I was worried I might annoy you. I don't want you to think I'm a pain.'

'That's the last thing I would ever think,' Christian said. 'I won't ask how you are. I know the answer to that already. I just phoned to see if there was anything I could do for you.'

'I don't think so. My sister won't let me out of her sight. The police are still investigating. It's like they want to find something,' Randall said.

'They're just doing their job,' Christian said. 'It'll calm down. When I lost my mother, I surrounded myself with her. I got out every photo I could, her personal possessions, clothes, everything. I sort of made myself a nest. It helped. Sometimes you have to give in to grief, embrace it. My friend went to see her sister's body. It hurt, but I think it's helping her to move on.'

'Maybe when they let me out of the house we could go somewhere, listen to some music or whatever,' Randall said.

'Yeah, of course. Just keep in touch, all right? No one gets through this stuff alone. I've got to go, lots to do at home, but I'll keep my phone on.'

'Thanks, Chris. It's good having you there.' Randall ended the call.

* * *

216

Since Cordelia's death, the Muir family home had taken on the atmosphere of a grand library, filled with a heavy, hushed air. Randall wandered through to his mother's rooms. She had the largest bedroom with a dressing area, a bathroom and a study. He hadn't been into her bedroom since she'd died. It felt as if she could see him. He tried to sit on the bed but the pillow retained a dip where her head usually lay. Instead he went to her dressing table, opened the top drawer and reached his hand in slowly. Her jewellery was in there, each piece in its original box, nothing out of place. At the back though, something rattled roughly. He pulled the drawer open as far as it would go, leaning down to look inside. Carefully he pulled out the object rammed right to the back. It was pasta, old and beginning to crumble, but still on the string in a line just as it had been when he'd given it to her so proudly, what, twelve years ago? He remembered making it in his reception year at school. Each pasta tube had been coloured with crayon scribbles, now too faded to make out the shades, but the red wool he'd used as a string hadn't snapped with the passing years. It was extraordinary that she'd kept it so long without him knowing. He put the necklace into his pocket, closed the drawer, reopened it to take out her favourite pair of earrings, and closed it again.

The wardrobe housed aspects of her he had less love for. The suits, the crisp work shirts, the tailoring that had removed her from him to an office and a world with which he had been unable to compete. Those long days when he had wanted her to do puzzles with him, or bake cakes, when she had endless piles of paperwork, showing love to so many who weren't him. He hadn't understood then. It seemed easier now with her gone. Pride had swelled, pushing anger out of its way. He longed to take back the harsh words he'd said, the declarations of her love he hadn't returned. Not that his lack of response had in any way diminished her insistence on telling him. Every

217

morning as he'd left for school, mantra-like, she would tell him she loved him as he left the house. And every morning, all he'd replied was a variation on the theme of see you later.

He took the one thing of hers that he had always loved to see her in, not that he would ever have admitted it to her face. His mother's dressing-gown was towelling, tea rose pink, and soft from countless washes. He pushed his face into it, smelling soap, perfume and – he knew he was imagining this – books. That was what he'd been missing. Her favourite books. In her study, he took down *Pride and Prejudice*, *To Kill a Mocking Bird* and *The Scarlet Letter*. It wasn't enough. It didn't adequately sum up the depth of her. He added *The Help* and *The Great Gatsby*, using her dressing-gown like a sack and taking them back to his own bedroom.

A nest, that was what Christian had suggested he build. This wasn't enough for that. Not even close. He went back to his mother's bedroom and pulled the duvet off her bed, grabbing her pillows as an afterthought. Another trip. From the bathroom cabinet he took her favourite perfume, the lipstick that she wore every day, her hand cream. Back to her study to take the cushion from her reading chair. He went through the drawers of her desk, taking photos, letters, a diary. In his room he arranged them, using her duvet as a base, scattering pillows and cushions around himself, spreading out his treasures, spraying perfume into the air, rubbing the hand cream into his own palms as he arranged photos like charms to keep away the darkness of her loss. He pulled Cordelia's dressing-gown over himself, clutched her diary and settled down to read. Christian had been right. This was the closest Randall had been to his mother for longer than he could remember. It was like soaking her up. If he closed his eyes and drowned out the world, perhaps he could believe she was right there with him. Perhaps then the pain would go away.

Chapter Thirty-Three

Ava handed in her mobile phone and keys at the desk of HMP Glenochil, signing in and waiting while her identity badge was checked. Dylan McGill – Ramon Trescoe's former partner in crime – had agreed to see her. McGill had no idea why Ava wanted to talk, of course, but that was the thing about serving a long sentence. Any break from the norm was as good as a holiday. Any movement out of your cell was like a month-long cruise when your normal day consisted of a twenty-two hour lock in. The approach had been made through formal channels. Ava might have been investigating Begbie's death under the radar but she was on the clock for Louis Jones. She'd even got McGill's former solicitors' details from the court record and notified them that she intended to visit their client. McGill, however, had declined the offer of a lawyer to accompany him. Presumably he thought the visit would be more fun without legal advice. That was fine with Ava. No independent record of their conversation gave her greater flexibility.

She was body-checked before walking through to a visitation room where she contemplated the sense or otherwise of her actions as McGill was brought from his cell. There would be a guard outside the door within easy screaming distance, not that it would help if McGill had secreted a shiv up his sleeve, but his business partner was out in the real world with access to women, alcohol and deep-fried food. McGill would want to join Ramon Trescoe as soon as he possibly could. Knifing a police officer hardly seemed like a smart move for a man who wanted a change of address that desperately. Not that Ava intended to allow McGill's relationship with Ramon Trescoe to remain as trusting as it had been for the previous few decades. It was amazing how the slightest hint that a co-conspirator had talked to the police could undo a lifetime of friendship, and information flowed through prisons like money through a gambler's hands. It wouldn't take much for Ramon to get entirely the wrong end of the stick about the little chat she was about to have with McGill, and she had a few cards to play that would ensure he fell foul of the suspicion of having ratted on his best mate. Of course, if Ramon Trescoe had nothing to hide, he would have no reason to worry about Ava's visit to his business partner.

Dylan McGill was shorter than she'd expected from the description in his file, and a shadow of the man she'd seen in various photographs. Incarceration had physically shrunk him, not that she felt a shred of sympathy. McGill and Trescoe had been violent thugs when they were convicted, and they remained the same men now. He looked Ava up and down as the guard sat him in a chair and indicated to Ava where he would be should she need assistance.

'A Detective Chief Inspector coming to visit. You look like my first wife. She turned out to be a right bitch,' McGill said. 'Do you have any smokes?'

'I don't, and you know I'm not allowed to pass you anything, so let's drop the preliminaries. Do you remember a man called Louis Jones?' she asked.

He sniffed. 'The thing is, I've met a lot of people in here over the years. Can't remember all their names. Better with faces myself.'

'All right,' Ava said, pulling out a photo of Jones. 'Here you are then. You might remember him better as Louis the Wrench.'

McGill picked up the photo and took a long look at it. 'Nope, still nothing coming back to me. Why are you asking?'

'He was involved in a car accident and now he's missing. I'm trying to locate him. Information in your file has him down as a former associate. Did you keep in touch with him after you were convicted?' Ava asked.

'An associate? Is that what my file said? Louis the Wrench was no friend of mine. I'm guessing your information also noted that when me and Ramon got sent to our various fuckin' government holiday camps, Jones miraculously escaped the attention of the Fiscal.'

'I was wondering about that,' Ava said. 'How did that happen?'

McGill leaned forward and lowered his voice. 'You wearing a wire, DCI Turner?'

'No,' she said opening her jacket. 'Wouldn't do me any good, as I'm sure you're aware. You're not under caution. I'm not taking notes, you haven't got a lawyer, there's no video or audio recording happening.'

'So what little dance is it we're doing? Louis Jones, the prison grapevine tells me, is keeping a slab warm and won't be doing any more talking. I'm guessing you know that already, girl,' McGill said. 'Caskill, you got a light?' The prison guard walked in, lit the roll-up McGill pulled from his pocket, and left again.

'And why would that information, about a man you claimed not to remember, have reached your ears, Mr McGill? Was it you who ordered the hit?' Ava asked.

'I'm in lock-up. High security at that. I have neither the contacts nor the cash to organise such things, if it even was a hit. I rather like the concept that overcome by remorse at being a filthy fuckin' rat, he nail-gunned his own mouth shut then put a bullet through his brain. Why don't you try investigating that scenario, love?'

'Your bosom buddy, Ramon Trescoe, has the contacts. No doubt there are a few people who have the cash and owe you two favours. You boys didn't drag anyone else down with you at the trial, code of honour and all that. I'm sure enough of your former associates still exist to make your homecoming reasonably pleasant,' Ava said.

'What are you here for?' McGill asked.

'I want to know who killed Jones,' Ava said.

'Bollocks, do you. If this was on the record there'd be another officer with you, I'd have been forewarned and my brief would be here telling me to go no comment. But since we're not on the record, and because I'm in a better mood than usual, I'll help you out. Take your face while it's in one piece, and get it out of my business. That goes for Ramon's too. He's served his time and as far as I know he wants to watch the satellite channels and eat takeaway. If Jones is dead, he had it coming. You don't want to get mixed up in the big boy stuff.'

'I thought you'd say that,' Ava said. 'I'm disappointed, obviously, but it's not unexpected.'

'Then why come?' McGill asked.

'Oh, I don't know. I saw your file, thought you looked like an interesting chap and decided I just couldn't stay away. Sorry to have disturbed you. Next time I come I'll be sure to bring cigarettes.' She called in the prison officer. 'Mr McGill and I have had a really useful chat. He's one of the good ones. Wish they were all like him.'

Caskill raised his eyebrows and pulled McGill to his feet.

'Do you want to tell me what the fuck you're playing at, lady?' McGill asked.

'You know how this works, Mr McGill. You scratched my back, now I'll scratch yours. I'll have a chat with the Governor, see if I can't get you some increased privileges as a thank-you.'

'She's fuckin' crazy,' McGill said to the prison officer. 'Get me out of here. I'm missing lunch as it is.'

Ava walked back to the processing centre to pick up her belongings. The actual content of her conversation with McGill had been irrelevant, although it wouldn't do any harm if he repeated Louis Jones' name to a few fellow inmates. Just the fact that McGill had sat in a cell with her – unaccompanied to boot – would be enough to make Ramon Trescoe twitchy, especially if McGill suddenly found himself on the receiving end of some unexplainably favourable treatment.

The Governor was waiting for her in reception. 'DCI Turner,' he said. 'We haven't met but I've heard a lot about you. Did you get what you wanted today?'

'I did,' Ava said, 'but I need your help with a couple of things.'

'Of course,' the Governor said. 'Whatever I can do to assist.'

An hour and a half later Ava was home, stripping off her suit and going through her wardrobe for something that would help her blend in that evening. She applied makeup more heavily than she could ever remember having done in her life, the only possible exception was aged eight and raiding her mother's makeup case. With smokey eyelids and dramatic liner, she put a dark foundation on, adding blusher and finishing with cherry red lipstick. After that, she opened the packing on the hair straighteners she'd bought that day, took every curl out of her hair and pinned some of it up on top of her head. The effect was to make herself almost unrecognisable.

When the doorbell went Ava was still staring in the mirror, trying to talk herself out of what she was about to do. She peered through the spy-hole.

'Could you open up?' Callanach said. 'It's freezing out here.'

Ava opened the door a crack. 'I'm just going out,' she said. Callanach didn't respond. His open mouth said it all. 'You need me right now?' Ava asked, rolling her eyes. She closed the door to disengage the chain, then draped a jacket over her injured hand to cover the bandage before opening up to let him in.

'Anywhere nice?' Callanach asked, still staring.

'It's a hen party. Themed. You know the sort of thing. What was it you had to talk to me about that required the use of communication other than by mobile phone?' Ava asked.

'Cordelia Muir,' Callanach said. 'I think she was poisoned.'

'We've established that,' Ava said. 'All DNP deaths are categorised as poisoning. There's no legal form of tablets containing dinitrophenol.'

'No, I mean it looks increasingly likely that she had no idea she was ingesting them. I've been back to her offices and removed several items for testing,' Callanach said as Ava disappeared into her bedroom, leaving him talking from the lounge. 'Where exactly are you going?'

Ava returned with a long raincoat over high-heeled boots, one hand in her pocket, bouncing keys up and down in the other. 'Some club in town,' Ava said. 'You're suggesting this is murder. Premeditated murder.'

'I'm saying I need to investigate it with that possibility in mind. I'll need to go through her house in the same way I have the office. The children aren't obvious suspects but I need to rule out the possibility that the poisoning was happening there. I think the daughter will let me have access voluntarily but I wanted you to be aware of what I'm planning.'

'All right. If you have grounds then go ahead, but if it's one of the children they'll have had ample time to get rid of any evidence by now. Listen, I've got to go. We'll talk tomorrow. Briefing in the morning, okay?'

'Sure,' Callanach said, stepping out through the front door she was holding for him. 'Whose hen party?'

Ava fumbled with her keys as she secured the door.

'A girl from my old riding club. I'm only going out of politeness. I'll probably fake a headache and escape in an hour.' She climbed into her car, throwing her handbag onto the passenger seat. Callanach opened the passenger door and leaned his head in. 'Try not to get arrested,' he said, slamming the door, noting the pepper spray amongst the contents of her bag.

'Least of my problems,' Ava muttered, spinning her tyres on the wet tarmac.

Callanach stared after her, hating himself for not believing a word she'd said, but it wasn't just her explanation that had made him doubt her. Ava had looked scared. Not just nervous, but deeply unsettled. He couldn't help but wonder why.

Chapter Thirty-Four

Back at the station, Callanach cursed the rain that had turned to sleet, and the additional traffic from late-night shoppers. It had taken half an hour to travel across the city, and a further half-hour to update his team and establish that Cordelia Muir's daughter was happy to accommodate a new search. Even Detective Superintendent Overbeck had drifted through en route to an event, reminding Callanach of Ava's out-of-character night out. Wherever Ava was going, it certainly wasn't to a high-class dinner with the rest of Police Scotland's brass.

'You're going to Mrs Muir's house tonight?' Overbeck asked Callanach.

'Yes, ma'am,' he replied. 'DCI Turner signed off on it. I'm briefing her in the morning.'

'If she's not still crying off sick. I had planned to sit her next to the Lord Lieutenant's mother. Dreadful bore. Talks about her children incessantly. No wonder Turner decided to get a convenient bloody migraine. Now I'll end up next to her. While I've got your attention, Detective Inspector, this doesn't turn into a murder enquiry unless you are absolutely damned sure that's what it is. I can do without another statistic showing how badly we're failing, thank you.' Overbeck clacked away on killer high heels, checking her lipstick in the reflections of the glass as she went. Callanach watched her go, quite willing to accept that Ava might have told a lie to get out of a stuffy dinner with her superiors, but less convinced that she wouldn't be equally happy to have repeated the lie to avoid a fancy-dress hen party.

By the time Callanach arrived at Cordelia Muir's house, a body of officers was bagging and labelling various items, placing most in cold boxes for transfer to the lab. Lively was logging the items as they were processed, and Cordelia's daughter was sitting on the couch, holding an open book but staring at the wall. Callanach had explained the police presence only in terms of ascertaining the source of any tablets that might have been overlooked at home. As he reassured the young woman that Police Scotland was putting its full investigative resources into the case, a thumping echoed from upstairs, followed by the slam of a door and the heavy scrape of dragged furniture.

'Sir,' DC Tripp called down the stairs. 'There's a bit of a, um, thing. Could you . . .?'

Callanach excused himself from his conversation and went up. Three officers were stood between one bedroom door, which stood open, and another, which was closed.

'I'm afraid Mrs Muir's bedroom has been disturbed,' Tripp whispered. Callanach looked through the doorway. The bed sheets were hanging off, all the drawers and cupboard doors were open, their contents scattered. A trail of objects wound across the carpet towards the ensuite and back out to the hallway.

'What's happening in there?' Callanach asked, motioning towards the closed door.

'That's the son's bedroom, Randall. He's locked himself in and won't respond verbally. We're hearing what sounds like sobbing and he's barred the entrance with something heavy,' Lively said.

'Randall, this is Luc Callanach. We met briefly at the hospital. I would like to speak with you, to make sure you're all right. I know this is difficult and the last thing I want is to invade your space. If you could open the door just an inch so I can see your face and talk, then I'll ask my squad to give us some privacy.'

'Leave me alone,' Randall called, his words hitching with his breath.

'I understand,' Callanach said, 'and that's what we want to do. But I cannot leave someone who might be a danger to themselves without establishing first-hand contact. Would you rather talk to your sister?'

'No!' Randall shouted. 'Fine, I'll open it. But then I want to be left, okay?'

'Okay,' Callanach said, motioning for the other officers to step away from the door. There was heaving, some heavy breathing, then the door opened a crack. 'Hello, Randall. Thank you for doing that.'

'You've seen me, now get lost,' Randall said, starting to push the door shut again.

Callanach forced his foot forward just enough to prevent it from closing. 'Absolutely, in just one moment. The thing is, we're in what is now your house, so I need to explain what we're doing here. I need to check your mother's things for any tablets or other medicines, to confirm what she was taking. Do you understand?'

'Yeah,' Randall said.

'Great, that's good. A few things in your mother's room have moved recently by the looks of it, and it's important that we go through all of her personal items. Do you have anything of hers in there?'

Randall cast an eye back over his shoulder, letting the door fall open another inch. Callanach caught a blast of perfumed air from the curtained gloom and took the opportunity to step closer to the doorway.

'A couple of things, but they're private. There were no tablets. I didn't do anything wrong,' Randall said.

'Of course you didn't. You had no idea we were coming, or what we'd need to do. But if you have items of hers in there, we will need to take a quick look to ensure that we're being thorough. Is that okay?'

Lively was calling additional men up the stairs.

'No, it's not okay. You're not touching any more of my mother's stuff. It's mine now. You'll ruin it all. You'll mess it up,' Randall shouted.

'We'll be very careful not to touch anything we don't need to. You can stay there and watch us, tell us where everything came from.' Callanach pushed the door gently, allowing more light from the hallway to penetrate the darkness, showing a mass of clothes, bedding and effects covering the floor.

'No!' Randall screamed. 'I don't want you here. You're not coming in. No one's coming in.'

'Randy? What's going on? Why won't you let them in?' His sister appeared at the top of the stairs.

'You never wanted me to be close to her,' Randall shouted. 'Now you're sending them in to take everything of Mum's from me. Well, you can't. You can't take her away again. I won't let you.'

Callanach looked at Randall's sister, pointing towards the door and gesturing to open it up. The sister nodded, stepping away, head slumped. He wedged his foot more firmly in the door as Randall tried to shove it closed. Callanach used his shoulder, dropping his weight to get better leverage. The door flew open and Randall dived backwards, scrabbling away. Tripp switched on the light and the squad readied themselves to deal with whatever was happening inside.

Randall was curled in the middle of a chaotic mass of clothing, bedding, jewellery, books and papers. He was rocking himself, sobbing quietly, reaching out to stroke each object in turn, pulling an old dressing-gown over his head as he babbled.

'I'll call a doctor,' his sister said quietly.

Callanach oversaw the initial stages of retrieving items from what Randall was calling his nest, then left the Muir family doctor trying to administer a sedative. His mobile rang at 10pm just as he was preparing to leave.

'Luc, this is Ailsa Lambert. Do you have a moment?'

'I do,' Luc said, stepping into the deserted kitchen. 'Is it about the Louis Jones autopsy?'

'No, that's all finished. Actually, I was wondering if Ava was with you,' she said.

'She's gone out for the evening. Is it urgent?' Callanach asked. There was an extended silence from Ailsa's end of the phone, until Callanach heard tutting. 'Ailsa, what's wrong?'

'She was supposed to phone me this evening but I haven't heard from her. I was concerned,' she said, her voice vague and unsure, not at all like the Dr Lambert he was used to. 'I still am concerned.'

'I saw her earlier this evening, so I shouldn't be too worried. She was dressed up to go out,' Callanach said.

'Did she say where?' Ailsa asked.

'She said it was a hen party,' Callanach replied. 'Some girl she knew from her old riding club has got her dressing up like a French courtesan, and that's putting it politely.'

'A hen party?' Ailsa said. 'We're talking about the same Ava Turner, are we? Have you ever known that girl to do big crowds of women, particularly ones given to mass silliness and costumes?'

'Why was she supposed to call you, Ailsa?' Callanach asked. 'And why would she have agreed to call if she'd arranged to go out? I don't understand.'

A long sigh issued from Ailsa's end of the phone. 'I've been worried about her. Ava was attacked and her hand was badly injured. She agreed to keep in regular contact to stop me from over-reacting. Her phoning me at regular intervals was part of the bargain, only now she's not answering her mobile.'

'Do you have any idea at all where Ava might be right now?' Callanach asked.

'I'm afraid I don't, but if it's at a hen party I'll book her in for a psych evaluation. Find her for me, Luc. I should never have agreed to stay quiet, and I won't forgive myself if anything else happens to her.'

Chapter Thirty-Five

Ava proffered a twenty-pound note, only to have it waved away by The Maz's reception staff. Apparently only the male guests had to barter their way in with cash. She checked in her coat but kept her bag, self-conscious in the lacy basque until she realised how much more she was wearing on top than most of the girls in the club. Her first stop was the ladies' toilet, adding more eye-liner and redoing her lipstick. The drive to Glasgow had been peppered by thoughts of what could happen if Knuckles or the big man recognised her, but now that she was inside it was the last thing on her mind. She'd almost failed to recognise herself as she'd appeared in the mirror. Little chance of anyone else guessing who she was.

Making her way to the bar, Ava ignored the looks she was getting from both men and women, glad of the low light and thick makeup that covered her embarrassment. Her only previous visits to clubs like this had been for drug busts or trafficking operations. This was less fun. With a gin and tonic in hand, she wandered slowly around seeking out the best place to sit and watch the comings and goings.

'You want something in that drink?' a man walked in front

of her, barring her way. He was big but it was excess weight rather than muscle, not that she could afford to get into a confrontation.

'No thanks, I'm fine,' she said, dropping her English public school accent and adopting her best Glaswegian, moving to one side and waiting until he let her pass.

'Here alone?' he asked, ignoring or oblivious to her hint.

Ava sighed. 'I'm meeting someone shortly. Could I get past, please?'

'I have good pills,' the man said. 'They loosen you up, yes? You prickly.' He was 6'4", closing on sixteen stone, Ava estimated. Not someone she wanted to have a fall out with so early, although later on she might feel differently. For now, she had to excuse herself without getting into a row.

'I'm just coming down from something else,' she said. 'I'll find you later though, yeah? Get a pick-me-up.'

'No charge for you. I haven't seen you here before. Your name?' he asked.

'Pixie,' Ava said, wondering where the hell that had come from. 'I've only just moved into this part of the city. Thought I'd check out the scene.'

'You tell barman, Domo said free drink tonight. I look after what you need,' he said.

'Thanks, Domo,' Ava said, moving past while he was being nice. 'I'll remember that.' She located a booth and parked herself in it, wishing she'd thought to buy two drinks to indicate that someone else was coming. Domo was obviously on the payroll here, providing drugs and who knew what else. The music cranked up a notch, and the upper balcony brightened to reveal girls stepping into dance cages. The lighting changed shade, leaving the club bathed in swirling red and gold hues. She checked her watch. It was nearly 11pm. Another male wandered towards her and Ava shook her head immediately, grateful that one was easier to dissuade. Two women walked past, one supporting the other as she swayed and lost control of her stiletto heels. Whatever Domo was persuading women to put into their drinks, she didn't want it in hers. Taking a pretend sip, she pulled out her mobile and made a show of texting. It was getting busier now with the pubs tipping out. There were maybe one hundred and fifty people spread over two floors, not that she had any intention of taking the full tour tonight.

It was another half-hour before Ava saw the club's owner, Joe Trescoe. He swaggered in, wearing a shirt that should never have made it out of the sixties, with Levis that would have looked better on a man with a lesser beer gut. His hair was thinning and slicked back over his head showing his age, but his eyes were as alert as a young snake. Ava watched him watching his employees – checking who was smiling, who was working fast, who was cruising – and knew he missed nothing. He wasn't interested in the women who walked passed him topless. Joe Trescoe's gaze didn't stray for a second from his business interests. He greeted a few people as he walked the floor and to his side, half a step behind like a monarch's spouse, was the man Ava had seen outside the club persuading the dancing girl not to make a fuss about being touched. They strolled towards the VIP area, a bouncer moving red cords aside, and stepping out of the boss' way.

The curtain behind the ropes was pulled back to facilitate Joe Trescoe's entrance, and Ava caught her first glimpse of Knuckles since their disagreement at Glynis Begbie's house. A four-fingered brass duster on his right hand shone as it caught the light, a warning to everyone not to approach without permission. She noted with some pleasure the bruising that dappled his face, presumably from their encounter, but given the nature of his work she guessed there were plenty of people who might throw a punch in his direction over the course of a normal week.

'Your friend not coming?' Domo asked, appearing in her booth.

Ava shifted her gaze away from Knuckles, smiling politely. 'He's just running late. Do you need a ticket to get into the VIP area? It looks nice.'

'Invitation only and must be member. You pretty though. Good body. Maybe you get membership cheap,' Domo said.

'That's . . . kind of you,' Ava said. 'But I don't need membership. I usually work late so I won't be able to get here that often.'

'Maria,' Domo shouted. 'Bring glass prosecco for lady.'

Ava considered refusing the free drink and realised she couldn't. It was one thing making excuses but she had to stay in character. She accepted the glass the girl brought over gracefully, pretending to take a sip. 'Thank you,' she said, waiting to see if Domo was going to leave her in peace. Apparently he wasn't. 'So how long have you worked here?' she asked, her heart sinking as he sat down next to her.

'Year and half,' he said. 'Hey, Perry. Get some girls upstairs. Many men with nothing to look at.' Ava looked round to the man Domo was shouting at, tensing as the big man whose testicles she'd fried sauntered towards them. She picked up her glass and held it to her lips, obscuring at least part of her face and giving her something to focus on.

'I've just sent two more girls up there. That enough?' Perry asked.

'One more,' Domo added.

'D'you want me to take her up?' Perry motioned towards Ava.

'Idiot. This is customer. Apologies,' Domo said, waving Perry away with the back of a hand. Perry turned to go, glanced back over his shoulder and faltered. Ava averted her head and held her breath, wondering just how close Perry had come to recognising her. By the time she risked another look around, he was walking up the staircase with a slope-shouldered woman trudging behind him.

'I heard Joe Trescoe owns this place. Is that right?' Ava asked between sips.

Domo stiffened, looking at her more sharply, his eyes darting towards the VIP area.

'Why you ask about Mr Trescoe?' he said. His voice was soft enough but there was no mistaking the drop in temperature. Ramon Trescoe's brother obviously valued his privacy.

'My dad used to talk about him, back in the day. Said they used to party together when they were in their twenties. I guess Glasgow was a bit different back then. Nowhere like this around for a start,' Ava said.

Domo responded by pulling out a mobile and snapping a photo of her before she could object. 'Mr Trescoe like to know who in his club. What you say your name is?' he asked.

Joe Trescoe was obviously more paranoid than Ava had anticipated. She smiled obligingly. 'Pixie MacDonald. He won't know me though. My dad moved away from Glasgow and spent the last few years of his life behind bars courtesy of the fuckin' polis. It's just nice to know that dad's friends are still around. It would've made him happy, his mates having made it out of the dirt.'

'Father dead now?' Domo asked.

'Couple of years ago,' Ava said, wondering just how far she was going to have to spin the lie. 'Heart attack. If that man ever ate anything not deep fried then I didn't witness it.'

Knuckles appeared from behind the VIP curtain and waved in Domo's direction.

'Must work,' Domo said. 'We talk later.'

Ava smiled, masking her relief. Domo's English skills might be limited, but he wasn't stupid. No doubt that was why he'd

236

been chosen to control the floor. A noisy gang entered and Ava was able to relax as they filled the remaining ground-floor space. Braving the bar, she bought a second drink and put it in her booth untouched. A girl passed her by, then back-tracked to talk to her.

'You alone, hen?' she asked.

'Waiting for someone,' Ava said, trying to figure out where to look. The young woman was topless, wearing a skirt that had no business pretending to be more than a handkerchief and heels that could double as an offensive weapon. Ava guessed her age somewhere between twenty and thirty but with the layers of makeup it was hard to be precise.

'Right. I like your basque. That's a gorgeous shade of red. Auditioning today, are you? I'm Sugar,' she said, sitting down in the booth and sliding along next to Ava.

'Auditioning?' Ava asked.

'Job interview. I saw you with Domo. All the girls have to do an evening to see how they get on with the punters before they get taken on. You're a bit older than Joey usually likes his girls but you've got nice tits so that'll make up for it.' Ava opened her mouth to comment, decided she was better off just smiling, and closed it again. 'You should get up and move around a bit. We're supposed to socialise rather than just waiting for men to come over. Get 'em swinging, if you know what I mean,' Sugar winked.

'Thanks,' Ava said. 'So you like working here?'

'Pays the bills. Some of the guys are creeps but ain't that just the way of things? It's warm. The drinks are free, although there's a limit to how much you're allowed. They want us friendly but not pished. That's some good muscle definition you've got there. Go to the gym, do you? That'll help when they get a bit frisky.'

'Occasionally,' Ava said, looking at Sugar's arms which were pale and dimpled, her skin a testament to the perils of unhealthy living. 'Is that who runs the place then, Joey?'

'Joey and his brother, Ramon.' Sugar leaned her head in and dropped her voice. 'He only got out of clink recently and Joey's been in a mean fuckin' mood since Ramon came back. So much for brotherly love. What did you say your name was?'

'Pixie,' Ava said, cringing as she said it aloud again.

'Pixie, I like that. Suits you. You can hang around with me if you want. The regulars like a new face. I bet between us we could chalk us some serious tips. Might help if you undid a couple more buttons on the basque. The harder these boys are in the trouser department, the freer they are with their wallets.'

'Maybe in a while. I'm still a bit nervous,' Ava said. 'So Joey's brother. What's he like?'

'Bloody gorgeous,' Sugar said. 'Doesn't talk much. He's got those smokey eyes and these really long fingers. For an older bloke, he's quite sexy. He watches, all the time. Doesn't join in with the bullshit. Some of the girls think he's scary, but I reckon he just got used to his own company when he was inside.'

A man appeared at their table with a stupid grin on his face and a ten-pound note in his fist. 'Sugar, you wanna dance with me?' he slurred.

'I'd love that.' She smiled sweetly, getting up and keeping her back to the drunk as she mouthed 'fuckwad' at Ava. 'See you later, pet.'

Ava got up when Sugar was ensconced on the dance floor in the arms of the drunk, and moved to a table with a better view through the curtains into the VIP area. A few other people were making their way in now, each ushered through by Knuckles, with Domo loitering nearby to make sure plenty of drinks were being handed around. The music grew louder and slower, the lighting more intimate and new girls appeared. Then Ava saw him. Ramon Trescoe walked down the stairs as if he were on a film set instead of what was simply a new take on a strip joint. His left hand touched the balustrade only lightly, and he moved with an ease that was extraordinary to watch. More notable on him than his brother, were the effects of his Middle Eastern heritage. A cigarette in his right hand in spite of the smoking ban, he was wearing an impeccably laundered white shirt, only a few flecks of grey showing in his black hair.

Ramon paused a few steps from the bottom to survey the scene. Ava kept still, wanting him to notice her, rather than drawing attention to herself. He did, his eyes ceasing their arc of the room to rest on her face, although he didn't look her up and down as she'd expected. Ava broke eye contact first, diverting her attention towards her drink. Ramon continued down the stairs and entered the VIP area as Ava kept her head turned to the side. It was one thing getting his attention. It was another being too obvious about it. She risked a glance towards the VIP section to see Ramon watching her. He smiled and Ava felt a sickly rush of adrenalin, shifting uneasily in her seat as she decided whether to commit to her plan of making direct contact with Ramon Trescoe, or get out while she still could. Getting close to Ramon was the fastest method of confirming her theory about Begbie's death, but Ava was taking an unquantifiable risk and she knew it. It wasn't as if she'd never done undercover work before. She was familiar with the procedure. There were no credit cards or identification documents in her handbag, she'd rehearsed her cover story in her head and even removed every piece of paper from her car in case anyone got that far. Even her mobile was locked, with both fingerprint and coded security systems.

Ava made light of Ramon's interest, raising her glass casually in his direction. In reply he tilted his head to one side and crushed out his cigarette before taking Knuckles by the arm and whispering to him, as he glanced back in Ava's direction.

She pushed the pepper spray deep into her bag, making sure it was fully covered by a scattering of makeup, her purse and mobile. By the time she looked up, Knuckles was pushing through the now crowded dance floor in her direction. That was it, then. Ramon Trescoe was inviting her into his den. She swallowed her nerves, thought of George Begbie dead in his car, of Glynis who would face old age alone, and steeled herself to avenge the Chief's murder.

'*Qu'est-ce que tu fais*? What the fuck are you playing at?' a voice cut across her thoughts. Callanach was striding towards her. She held up a hand to stop him before he got too close. Knuckles was halfway across the dance floor. If Callanach said her real name out loud they would both be in serious trouble, and any chance she had of getting close to Ramon Trescoe would be lost.

Heads turned as Callanach walked through. Absolutely bloody typical, was all Ava had time to think. Her detective inspector had a face that was difficult to forget, and he'd given plenty of televised press conferences on behalf of Police Scotland. She moved towards him and further from Knuckles.

'Don't say another goddamn word,' she told him. 'Not one.'

'Hey, you,' Knuckles called out. 'Mr Trescoe has invited you into the VIP area. You're keeping him waiting.'

'She's busy now,' Callanach said, stepping up.

Ava pushed in front of him, keeping her own body between Callanach and Knuckles. 'Could you tell Mr Trescoe thank you. My friend here was just leaving. I'll see him out then I'll be over.'

'I can see him out for you,' Knuckles said. Ava didn't need to worry about him recognising her face. The man couldn't get his eyes more than half an inch above her cleavage. 'You can go straight over. Mr Trescoe won't mind me helping you out.'

'I'll only be a minute,' Ava said. 'Would you be a love and tell him Pixie said thank you. I won't be long.'

'Aye, well, clock's ticking. That invitation won't last all evening. Best be quick,' Knuckles said.

Ava hustled Callanach towards the reception area. 'You've got to go,' she said. 'You're about to ruin everything.'

'That's fine, I'm leaving and you're coming with me,' Callanach said. 'I don't know what the hell you're trying to achieve, but you've scared Ailsa and that's something I thought I'd never witness.'

Ava pulled Callanach towards her, ran a hand around the back of his neck and pushed her mouth forwards onto his cheek, millimetres from his mouth. Keeping her fingers wound through his hair, pressing her body against his, she pulled them together into the shadow of a wall.

'Ava,' Callanach said softly. 'What's going on?'

'Stop talking and keep your face shielding mine. This place is more of a scum magnet than I'd realised. We have to get out of here now. Some members of Edinburgh's least desirable drug dealing crew have just walked in and whilst they won't recognise me like this, they'll sure as hell recognise you. Keep your face down and let's get out of here.' They made for the door, walking slowly at first then hurrying towards the corner of the street and away from The Maz.

Ava pointed at her car. 'Get in,' she said, opening her own door then slamming it hard. 'Could you explain what the fuck you're doing here? Do you have any idea how much danger you put us both in back there? Those are not the sort of people you screw around with. At least two of the bouncers were carrying weapons. Are you really so moronic, you can't figure out that when I've gone to so much effort to be unrecognisable, you are the very last person I should be seen with?'

'Have you finished?' Callanach asked.

Ava stared upwards, counted to five in her head, then leaned forward to rest her forehead on the steering wheel. 'I'm your superior officer. If I'd wanted backup, I'd have arranged it. If I'd wanted you to know where I was going, I'd have told you. You had no right.'

'You are unbelievable,' Callanach said, tugging a pack of Gauloises cigarettes from his pocket and sticking one in his mouth, the desire to actually light it stronger than he'd felt at any time in the last year. 'I'm here because you had an agreement with Ailsa. Do you remember telling her you'd phone every twelve hours? Eight o'clock was your deadline.'

'Bollocks,' Ava said quietly. 'I forgot.'

'Yeah, you forgot. I didn't follow you here. I was back in Edinburgh doing my job. I knew you'd lied to me about the hen party and I let it go, but then Ailsa called me. You'd requested information from Lively about this club. Given how you were dressed when I called round earlier, it didn't take much to find you.'

'How much do you know?' Ava asked quietly.

'I know that if this was about Louis Jones you'd have done it on the record and with backup. I also know you are the least believable person to have a name like Pixie, so perhaps more realistic preparation wouldn't have gone amiss. You might be my superior officer but still, you should have come to me,' Callanach said.

'I couldn't. I still can't,' Ava said.

'I thought you trusted me,' Callanach replied.

'Trusting you and feeling entitled to drag you into a potentially criminal conspiracy are worlds apart. I'm going to drive you to your car and I expect you to go home. We can't talk about it anymore. Promise you'll let it go.'

'Fine,' Callanach said. 'My car's in Hollybrook Street.'

'That's it?' Ava asked.

'I think we should get back to Edinburgh, don't you?' Callanach asked.

'I think we need to establish when you've crossed a line,' Ava said, starting her car.

'Convince me you're not in any danger, that I've misconstrued the whole thing, and I'll gladly play the humble fool,' Callanach said. 'But given the fact that you're still shaking, I guess I'm not going to be apologising any time soon.'

Chapter Thirty-Six

'My sister called a doctor out,' Randall slurred down the phone to Christian. 'He offered me a sedative and I said no, but my sister told me it was that or they were going to send me somewhere I wouldn't have any choice about taking medication.'

'She's just looking out for you,' Christian said. 'The sedative will help you rest. Where are you now?'

'In the guest room. They won't let me back in mine until they've cleared it all up. They say I made a mess, but it was just my nest, Chris, like you suggested. It was helping me remember her.'

'Shit, man,' Christian said. 'I never imagined it would cause trouble. Was it bad?'

'The police were here. They kind of busted into my room. My sister says I have to see a counsellor. It's like they want someone to officially confirm that I'm a screw up. You're the only person who listens rather than lecturing me. I mean, not that I don't have any other friends, you know, but they're younger than you. I don't mean that you're old. Fuck, I'm such a dick. Nothing I say comes out right.'

'Hey, Rand, it's cool. I know what you mean. How about you get some sleep. I'll check on you tomorrow.'

Christian hung up. Randall stared at the phone, wondering if he could call back so they could carry on talking. Of course he couldn't. His sister was running him a bath and it would be ready in a few moments. He'd had to agree to leave the bathroom door open, though. Couldn't have him falling asleep in the water with so much sedative in his system. His sister had insisted on the bath before he was allowed to get into bed when she realised he'd lost control of his bladder as the police had pulled him from his nest. He hadn't even felt it go. The expression on her face virtually screamed that she believed it was all just some juvenile attention-seeking stunt.

He climbed slowly into his dressing-gown, keeping his back to the doorway where every few minutes his sister would check on him. As if he needed to piss himself to get attention. If he was that desperate he could do a hundred more impressive things. Walking out of the front door, for a start. Going missing for forty-eight hours might be a good idea. All his sister saw when she looked at him was a problem that needed solving. Handling. Perhaps he should save her the effort and handle himself. He wandered into the bathroom, waiting until his sister had finally left the room before removing his dressing-gown. She would be back in a few minutes.

He slid open a bathroom drawer and searched the contents. The top layer was the usual bathroom debris – tweezers, cotton buds, plasters. Below that were random items of makeup, lip salve, dental floss. At the bottom were the sharps. Nail scissors, a splinter needle, a packet of razor blades. They'd belonged to his mother who had always wet-shaved her legs. It seemed as if those were her final gift to him. Everything else had been taken or tainted by the police and his sister, but these were his.

He freed a blade from the pack, picked up a bar of soap and

a flannel, then stepped dreamily into the bath. Sinking down he rubbed his left inner arm with the soap, softening the skin. He could hear his mother's footsteps on the stairs. No, stupid, not his mother. That was his sister, coming back to check on him. He slid the blade inside the flannel, folding it over and balancing it on the side of the bath. She put her head round the door.

'Oh good, you're in. Ten minutes, okay? The doctor said the sedative would kick in soon. Make sure you're cleaned up and I'll be back to help you out. You need some sleep. We all do. I'll make you some warm milk, like Mum used to. Just hang in there, Randall.' He wondered how to respond, what the appropriate answer was to being told to hang in there. What was he supposed to hang on for? His mother wouldn't reappear. She had gone to join his father in some distant place he didn't even believe in. He had no desire to attend her funeral, full of well-intentioned, well-dressed gentry. Why hang in there to be told he had to go and live with his sister, watching his every move and rationing his pocket money.

Taking the razor blade from the flannel, he ran it gently along the skin of his arm, tracing the path of the vein from wrist to elbow. He knew how to do it properly. Not across the wrist. That was for idiots who were issuing pathetic and stop-pable cries for help. He had to open the vein lengthways, several inches, to ensure it would bleed fast enough to leave him beyond help. The metal was slippery in his fingers. He lost it twice into the bath water before figuring out that gripping it through the flannel was easier.

This was what he was fated for. It was obvious now. Everyone at school would be horrified. They would wonder if they could have done more to befriend him. They would talk about him in hushed tones, huddled in corners. Teachers would check their form rooms for signs that others might follow his lead.

These events caused suicide clusters. He'd read about them online. Perhaps they would put his photo up on the wall at The Fret. Perhaps the barmaid — Nikki — would look back and wish she'd got to know him. It was his one regret, never getting round to walking her home. That, and the feeling that he was letting Christian down. But Christian understood him. He might be the one person who would mourn the loss of Randall's potential.

With the blade gripped firmly through the flannel in his right hand, Randall held out his left arm, closed his eyes, and prepared to cut.

* * *

He lay on his bed, reading the multitude of Cordelia Muir obituaries, scanning online for any police update on Lily Eustis' death. The reality was that the media had a short attention span. The second a new, juicier, story came in, the recently dead became nothing more than worm food. Except to him. For him, their passing was a gift. The first time he'd seen Lily she'd been at a restaurant with her family. Sitting between her mother and her sister, she'd been giggling at a joke their father was telling. He'd been working the bar, casual labour for minimum wage. What he recalled was the girls' hands. They could have been aged five and three, their hands clasped, fingers laced between one another's, the sister playing with the beads on Lily's bracelet. At one point Lily had leaned her head on her sister's shoulder, staring up with adoring eyes. They were both so beautiful. Their love was pure. Only family did that for you. Girlfriends, boyfriends, even husbands and wives, came and went. Lily and her sister were contented and blissfully unaware of the vicissitudes of life. He had loved them, both of them, on sight. Loitering behind them, delivering drinks, listening to their conversation, it had been easy to overhear their names and figure out that the sister – Mina – was studying engineering at Edinburgh University. From there on, finding Lily had been child's play and killing her had been sublime. For a brief, heavenly moment he'd felt truly alive. Still, it wasn't enough. He was grateful he had another planned already, something to look forward to. This time he would be even closer to it. He could watch it happen, stand in the middle of the action, not spectate from the sidelines, witnessing only the collateral damage. It would take a greater degree of planning than before, not to mention a more polished performance, but the trap was already laid.

He unwrapped the package he had just picked up. The heroin contained in the clear plastic wraps looked harmless enough. To the unsuspecting eye it might resemble light brown icing sugar. To novice users it was rapture. To an addict it was the only thing between staying alive and juddering into an early grave. He calculated the amount he needed. This was science. He was getting to the stage when he could write a book on it: How to subdue people until you're ready to kill them. It would have a limited audience, he recognised that, but to the few who required the information it would prove invaluable. This time he needed his prey to remain upright. Too heavy to carry far, if he was unconscious it would result in an ambulance being called, and that was unthinkable. His moment – his pay-off – would be ruined.

He opened a slim plastic case, withdrawing a plastic syringe, running the tip of one finger down the shaft of the needle, careful not to prick himself. Not that there was any danger of infection. This beauty was unused, still waiting to find purpose.

Replacing it in the case, he shut his eyes tight. Another needle had started all of this. His mother wasting away in a chair that would soak up the fluids she would lose as she wallowed in her own death. She'd beckoned to him, or perhaps that had been her death twitch, a final hurrah from muscles she could no longer control. As mesmerising as it had been, he'd found he could not go to her. The thought of touching her was intolerable. She had begun to rot long before the moment that had sealed her fate. This next event would be his homage to that day. Not long to wait now.

Chapter Thirty-Seven

Ava parked her car, regretting spending the previous few hours in stilettos. Walking towards her front door, she caught the outline of a man in the shadows to one side of her porch. She thrust one hand into her bag, withdrawing pepper spray as she braced for an attack.

'*Vraiment*?' Callanach said. 'Really?'

'You scared the pants off me, you moron,' Ava said, striding to her door and unlocking it.

'Are you sure? Given the length of that skirt I was wondering if you'd bothered wearing any tonight,' he said.

'Not funny. I thought we'd finished this discussion in Glasgow. Did something happen between there and here?' Ava asked. Callanach side-stepped her and walked into the hallway.

'You thought we'd finished the conversation? I'm not sure if your promotion has had an adverse effect on your intellect or if all the makeup you're wearing has left you rather thick-skinned, but we hadn't finished the conversation. It just wasn't safe to continue it two blocks from the club you were staking out with no backup and no warrant. I'll put the kettle on, shall I?' He walked into her kitchen as Ava disappeared into the bedroom, reappearing two minutes later wearing a sweat shirt and jeans.

'Say what you want to say, let's get this over with then I'm going to bed,' Ava said.

'We're off the clock, so you can stop giving orders now,' Callanach said. 'Given that everything you've done this evening was without police authority, I should also caution you against reminding me of your rank.'

'Actually, it's the fact that you're in my house that gives me the right to call the shots, but you can keep polishing that chip on your shoulder if you think it'll look better shiny.' Ava sat down and picked up the cup of coffee Callanach had made her.

'Can we start again?' Callanach asked, sitting next to her. 'I was worried about you, that's why I turned up in the club. How's the hand?' he asked, reaching out and turning over her palm to inspect Ailsa's handiwork.

'Sore,' Ava said. 'But it gave me a reason to taser a man in the balls.'

'Anyone I know?' Callanach asked.

'Probably the man who killed Louis Jones,' Ava said. 'Does that help?'

Callanach sat back and thought about it for a moment. 'You've identified the suspect in a murder case for which I'm responsible, and you didn't tell me? A man who's also guilty of assaulting you. A man who Ailsa believes is part of an organised crime setup given the style of execution they employed with Jones, and you went after him on your own. You want to know if that helps? I'm trying hard not to shout at you, Ava, but you're not making it easy this evening.'

'There's the door.' She pointed.

'All right. Let's do this in policing terms. If I had a name for one of Louis Jones' killers, I could work the case backwards then present the evidence to the Procurator Fiscal in the correct order. No one would ever need to know. Perhaps it would solve your problem, whatever that may be, at the same time. We both get our man,' he said.

'It's not him I'm after,' Ava said. 'You're right about Jones being executed. I want the people who ordered it, rather than the trigger man.'

'That'll be impossible. There won't be a record of a conversation, nor any witnesses. The only way you'll prove something like that is if you flip the killer, and they'll still be looking at a life sentence so nothing to gain,' Callanach said. 'Do you have any wine because your instant coffee hasn't improved since I was last here.'

'Bottle of Lagavulin in the cupboard next to the TV,' Ava said. 'Get two glasses.' Callanach brought the bottle to the table, breathing in the scorched earth scent and pouring generously into each glass. Ava took hers, closing her eyes as she leaned back. 'I know I won't get anyone to give evidence against the men who ordered Jones' killing. I was planning on handling it differently. That, believe it or not, is why I was dressed like something out of a bad vampire movie and hanging around a place dedicated to the love of breasts.'

'Want to let me in on the plan?' Callanach asked.

'Nope. Do you want to tell me what happened with your mother, because you've had a face on you ever since,' Ava replied. Callanach emptied his glass and poured another. Ava did the same. 'You see? We both have secrets. Now is about the time you're supposed to climb down off that ridiculously high horse you've been riding for the last hour.'

'A secret is a different thing from a death wish. You can hate me if you like, but if I have to have you followed every day until this thing is over, I will. The people who ordered Louis Jones' death will have no scruples about ordering yours. If you've already been injured by one of their thugs then you're marked. Come on, Ava. You're brighter than this. Nothing is worth playing those sorts of stakes.'

'Suppose Louis Jones wasn't the only hit that was ordered. Suppose there was someone else involved. Someone who Jones had dealings with in the past.'

'Is this about the Chief's relationship with Louis Jones?' Callanach stared at her. 'You don't really think Begbie's death is tied up in all of this? Ailsa signed it off as a suicide. No one challenged the findings,' Callanach said.

'I couldn't. I still can't. Glynis Begbie will be devastated if I go official with what I know, and she's been through enough already. Officially the Chief sat in a car and waited for it to fill with carbon monoxide, but I don't believe he did so of his own free will. I won't tell you more than that. I meant what I said about there being a line between giving you information and the two of us entering a criminal conspiracy. We're standing on that line right now, and I'm not taking you over it, so don't ask.' She put her glass on the table and rested her head on her drawn-up knees.

'Ava . . .'

'No. I've made up my mind. You wanted me to trust you, and I have. That's as far as I'm prepared to go. If you don't back off, you and I will find working together very difficult indeed.'

'So give me the information that relates to Jones. Maybe if I know who I'm looking for it'll help,' Callanach said.

'All right,' Ava said. 'Tomorrow, though. I can't think straight now. My office at 8am.'

'Fine,' Callanach said. 'But you have to promise never to set foot in that club again. Non-negotiable.'

'My pleasure. The music was terrible anyway,' Ava said, standing to walk Callanach to the door.

He leaned against the doorframe as he did up his coat. 'You're sure it wasn't all just a ruse to get me to kiss you at the club?' he asked.

'We didn't kiss. That would have required mouth to mouth contact. And if I ever lose my mind sufficiently that I decide to kiss you, I'm not the kind of woman who needs to make up an excuse,' Ava said.

'Still, that not-kissing-thing we did' – Callanach smiled as he stepped away from her door – 'It lasted a while.'

'There were a lot of people to avoid. You'd best go home and let your ego get some sleep. It'll have another arduous day of imagining being admired to deal with tomorrow.'

Chapter Thirty-Eight

Ava was at her desk by 7am in spite of the amount of single malt she'd consumed the night before. She skimmed the update on the Louis Jones' case that had been left for her to review, although there was so little evidence that studying it was pointless. No relevant phone records. No car left to inspect. No witnesses at the scene. Ava scanned a note from Tripp who'd been chasing the road traffic investigator for her. There was a name and email address, but still no report on file. That would need chasing straight away. Below that was a post-it bearing the name Janet Monroe with a mobile number. Ava frowned. It rang a bell but she couldn't place the name immediately. She was emailing the road traffic accident investigator for an update, when Callanach walked in.

'You couldn't sleep either?' he asked.

Ava shook her head. 'I'm back to square one with the forensics on Louis Jones. Sounds like we're not the only ones in early,' she commented as the sound of smashing crockery echoed up the corridor. 'Did you call a briefing?'

'Tripp and Lively are here putting together the evidence from Cordelia Muir's office and house. They're in voluntarily

255

so if it's overtime you're worried about, there's no need,' Callanach said.

'I'll leave the money worries to Superintendent Overbeck,' Ava said. 'Shut the door, would you? Anything I tell you has to stay between us.' Callanach did so then sat down with a notepad.

'Two men. I suspect both live in the Glasgow area. The smaller one is known as Knuckles. The larger is called Perry, although I don't know if that's a first name or a surname. I've written out descriptions of them for you.' She handed over a scrap of paper. 'Rewrite the descriptions in your own hand-writing then destroy my note. The car I saw them driving was a black Audi. I didn't get the registration number. We need to know if there is any evidence of that car having been involved in the accident with Louis Jones. I've just emailed the crash investigator although obviously I can't ask any specific questions.'

'Was there was any damage to the Audi that you saw?' Callanach asked.

'I didn't get a close enough look and it was under fairly stressful circumstances. I was hiding in a hedgerow at the time.'

'If it was superficial they could have had it repaired by now anyway,' Callanach said. 'But we may also be able to place the vehicle near the scene of Jones' killing later. I'll get Tripp to check the CCTV in the area of the golf club at the time of the murder for similar vehicles.' There was a knock at the door and Tripp appeared. 'God almighty, Tripp, do you have special powers?' Callanach asked.

'I can touch the end of my nose with the tip of my tongue,' Tripp said, sounding confused.

'Not quite what I was thinking,' Callanach said. 'Was there anything specific you wanted me for?'

'Just to say I've made a list of all the Crystal staff members.

I'm off to visit each one this morning and take a statement regarding access to Cordelia's office drawers, food and drink,' Tripp said.

'Good. There's some CCTV I need looked at when you're back so, I'll leave a note on your desk about that,' Callanach said.

'Well done, Tripp. Make sure you get a feeling for any grudges Cordelia's staff might have held. Work disputes, disciplinary notes, working conditions – the usual,' Ava said. 'But out of courtesy, and so I don't have to grovel to the Superintendent again this week, perhaps don't start knocking on doors until after 9am, Detective Constable.' Tripp reddened and checked his watch. 'I meant to ask about your notes on the Louis Jones case. You left me contact details for someone called Janet Monroe. Did you speak to her?'

'I did, ma'am. She's in Chief Inspector Dimitri's squad although she's off on early maternity leave now,' Tripp said.

'Yes, that was her. The kitten in the dog fight,' Ava said. 'She must hate me.'

'Sir, gentleman at the desk to see you. Says he's been trying your mobile but you're not picking up,' PC Biddlecombe mumbled down the phone line through a mouthful of food. Callanach held his desk phone further from his ear to dampen the sound of chewing.

'I don't suppose you managed to take a name, did you?' he asked.

'Half a mo,' she spluttered. 'He's asking for your name.'

'I thought he might want that. Lance Proudfoot. I'm a journalist. Tell him I've a gift for him,' Lance said.

'Right you are. Sir, it's . . .'

'*Dieu, aide-moi*,' Callanach whispered. God help me. PC Biddlecombe was a kind soul but she was about as sharp as a marrow. 'I heard, Constable. You were holding the phone as he was talking, remember?'

'Super. I'll sign him in then, shall I?' Biddlecombe asked.

'Well done. He can come up to my office unaccompanied. Lance knows where to find me.' Callanach put the phone down, aware that Lance was laughing in the background. He made a few notes to get some preliminaries going on the Glasgow suspects until Lance arrived at his door.

'Happy Christmas,' Lance said, putting a brown paper bag down on Callanach's desk.

'It's not Christmas. I'm pretty sure I remember what date that falls on,' Callanach said, peering inside the bag at a white box.

'It's a present, anyway. There's no gift receipt, so you'll just have to trust my judgement.' Callanach pulled a bottle of Châteauneuf-du-Pape from the bag, noting the year and whistling appreciatively.

'That's very thoughtful, not to mention generous. Is there a story attached?' Callanach said.

'On my news blog you'll find an article, fully researched and extremely well written if I say so myself. It explores the growing trend in anonymous donations to charity. Why donors don't want recognition, the good the money does, and the psychological effect of making a difference without public reward. I've had rather a good response to it, been asked to produce some follow-up pieces for a couple of Nationals. Proper money on offer, too. Thought I'd repay the creative prompt.'

'You didn't need to,' Callanach said. 'Although I'm certainly not doing anything as foolish as handing back the wine.'

'I thought we might get brunch. It's a Saturday after all. Even detective inspectors are allowed to eat at the weekend.' Lance smiled.

'Another time?' Callanach asked. 'I've got a lot to do . . .'

'And not enough time to do it,' Lance finished for him.

'More that I'm trying to figure out how to do it,' Callanach said.

Lance sat down. 'You could always try asking for help,' he said. 'You managed it a couple of times before, although I get the impression it might not be your strongest skill.'

'I can't, Lance. You've done enough already. Last time. I dragged you into a case you ended up with a dislocated ankle, as you like to remind me. You have writing to be getting on with,' Callanach replied.

'Strangely my experiences with you have made writing a somewhat dull pleasure compared to running the gauntlet of criminal investigations. Will you not throw an old dog a bone? It's obviously something you can't figure out through normal channels or it wouldn't be testing you so hard,' Lance said. 'God, will you make me beg, man? I can write article after article, but the days are trickling through my hands. I want to help, Luc. Not for you, but for myself.'

'These are bad people,' Callanach said.

'If I thought I was helping fit up good people, I'd be worried.' Lance smiled.

'The dangerous kind of bad. You're not to go near them. It's just additional information I need. Do you have any contacts in Glasgow who'll keep their mouths shut for you?'

'As a young man I played in a Glaswegian rugby team. When you share showers with a man, you soon find out if he can keep secrets or not,' Lance said.

'Now we're definitely not going out for brunch,' Callanach said. He dashed some notes on a piece of paper and handed it across his desk. 'Two names, local thugs I think, but you don't want to be on their radar. Anything you can get. Addresses, vehicles, known associates.'

'Can you tell me what it is they've done?' Lance asked.

'Safer to say the list of things they're not prepared to do might be very short indeed. Call me the second you have anything, then stop. No following up, no day trips to Glasgow. If you want to keep all your limbs attached don't mention Louis Jones' name. I want your word.'

'I thought the French were supposed to be charming,' Lance said. Callanach stared at him. 'All right, you have my word.' He walked to the door.

'Lance?' Callanach said. 'Stay safe.' He watched as Lance disappeared out of view. He reminded Callanach of the father he'd spent his life imagining. He wondered about the sense of letting Lance getting involved, shaking off his disquiet. His friend was an old-school journalist. In the past, he'd chased stories more dangerous than this one all over the world. He'd know if he was getting out of his depth, Callanach told himself. Lance would be fine.

Chapter Thirty-Nine

Detective Constable Tripp was knocking on the front door of Crystal's second staff member by 9.15am. His first interview had been cut short by a coughing bout from a woman's three-year-old son that had required him to exit quickly, hoping he hadn't caught anything that would end with a sick day. It was December and he hadn't missed a single hour of work all year.

Eventually, a window next to the front door opened and a man stuck his head out.

'What?' he asked.

'Sorry to disturb you, sir.' He held up his police identification. 'I'm Detective Constable Max Tripp with the Major Investigation Team. Would you be Mr Liam Hood?'

'It's not even ten o'clock,' he said. 'Could you not have phoned ahead?'

'It's an ongoing investigation. Sometimes things crop up. I apologise for the inconvenience. Could you spare a few minutes? It's just routine,' Tripp said. The window slammed shut and the front door opened seconds later.

'Come on then. It's bloody freezing air you're letting in.' Liam Hood was in his fifties, greying, with a map of blood vessels across his nose that depicted a journey through many bottles of alcohol. The carpet was threadbare and a dull lightbulb hung from a fitting devoid of such frills as a lampshade.

'My wife left me. I haven't decorated since. A light's a light,' Hood said. 'I suppose you'll want to sit down.' He indicated a wooden chair that Tripp took without staring anywhere else in the room. Liam Hood was as perceptive as he was gruff, but he didn't stand out as the ideal candidate to be working for a charity. 'Hurry up and talk,' Hood said as Tripp took out his notes.

'You worked with Cordelia Muir's charity for more than three years, I gather,' Tripp began.

'Are we going through it week by week because I had plans tomorrow,' Hood said.

Tripp did his best to look amused. 'What was your relationship like with Mrs Muir?' he asked.

'Cordelia was my boss. She told me what to do, controlled what I earned and gave me the grand total of twenty-four days off a year. How well do you get on with your boss?' Hood growled.

'Actually, my boss is a great bloke. Sometimes people don't really get him, but to me he's—'

'I didn't want you to actually answer that. Could you explain what you're doing here? This isn't routine. We were told Cordelia died from complications with medication. Why all the questions suddenly?' Hood asked.

'We're following up all possible investigative routes at this point. What was it like working for Mrs Muir?' Tripp responded.

'She was too lenient. Bit of a soft touch if you ask me. Someone's kid had a school sports day, no question about it, they were straight off to watch the egg and spoon race. Slight temperature? Couple of days in bed, get well soon cards all round. I kept telling her she needed to toughen up but she always spouted some quote about paying it forward or whatever.'

'Was anyone taking advantage of her, in your opinion?' Tripp asked, keeping his eyes on his notebook.

Hood took his time before answering. 'You're on a dirt-digging mission.'

'It might be easier if you would just answer the questions. This is for completeness. We have no specific target in mind,' Tripp said.

'Everyone in that office was gutted when she died, that's the truth. They might be a bit lazy sometimes, take the piss with the sick days once in a while, but no one wanted her gone. I told her to get herself to the doctor, but she was happy to wait for an appointment rather than making a fuss and insisting on being seen early. Bloody typical. All those hypochondriacs clogging up the system with their ingrowing toenails. If she'd been seen earlier . . . sod it. Can't turn back the clock, can you?'

Tripp was writing furiously. 'Sorry, you know she had a doctor's appointment booked how?'

'We talked about it at the office. Cordelia was really suffering, looked like a bad case of flu. She was sweaty, pale. We all knew she'd been sick a few times but it wasn't in her to go home ill. Eventually she agreed to get an appointment. The next thing we knew, she was dead.'

'And who in the office had access to her desk?' Tripp asked.

'Everyone. No one was precious about that stuff. If you needed to borrow a notebook or a calculator you went to someone else's desk. Even Cordelia's, except for her ink-pen. Her husband gave her that. It was the one thing we all knew not to touch.'

Tripp closed his notebook and stood up. 'Thank you, Mr Hood. I appreciate your time. I'll leave you to your weekend.'

From his car, Tripp called the station to get confirmation of

Cordelia Muir's doctor's appointment. The tragedy was all the more poignant if it might have been avoided. Most of all, it confirmed what they had assumed to date: Mrs Muir had no idea why she was sick. Twenty minutes later he was standing on the next doorstep when a call came through from the station.

'DC Tripp. We've had confirmation that Mrs Muir did have an appointment booked to see a Dr Marylewski. The receptionist recalls the booking.'

'Thanks, confirms what I've been told this morning. I can't believe the receptionist remembered it. Whenever I call the doctor's surgery, the receptionist can't remember my name from one minute to the next,' Tripp said, knocking on the door.

'To be fair, it only rang a bell because she'd offered an earlier appointment, which was turned down. She said that when she heard Mrs Muir had died, she was devastated to think it might have been different if she'd been available on the earlier date.'

The door opened. 'Yes?' A woman stood in a tracksuit, chewing a bacon sandwich.

'I'm so sorry, one minute,' Tripp said to her, holding up his badge and stepping off the doorstep to talk privately. 'Did the receptionist say why Mrs Muir turned down the earlier appointment?'

'It wasn't Mrs Muir she spoke to. Apparently, it was a young man, although she didn't catch his name. Said he worked with Mrs Muir and had been asked to phone on her behalf.'

Tripp frowned at the pavement. Cordelia Muir had been sick for a while by then. According to Liam Hood she'd finally given in and accepted the need to see a doctor. It must have been a fairly important matter to have taken priority in her diary over getting medical attention.

'I'll be back later,' he muttered to the figure on the doorstep.

'Apologies for having bothered you.' The door was shut before he made it off the front step.

Fifteen minutes later he was back at the station accessing Cordelia Muir's online diary, and cross-referencing it with the weekly planner she kept in her handbag. The doctor's appointment was in there, but there was nothing else that appeared to be of major importance booked in for the preceding days. No cogent reason for turning down an earlier appointment. Tripp phoned Cordelia's Muir's daughter who confirmed her mother's intention to get checked out with a doctor, then he called Cordelia's assistant, Liam Hood.

'Mr Hood, this is DC Tripp. We spoke earlier today,' he began.

'Did I strike you as suffering some form of dementia? Only I remember you being here perfectly well. What is it you want this time?' Hood snarled.

'The doctor's appointment. I traced it, but the receptionist said it was made by a young man from the office. I can't seem to identify who that would have been from the staff details I have here,' Tripp said.

'It must have been that little git, Jeremy,' Hood said.

'I don't have anyone called Jeremy on the staff logs,' Tripp said. 'He's not on the payroll or mentioned in your human resources file.'

'That's because he's a volunteer. Comes in a couple of days a week and he's not on payroll. Reckons he's doing it to put something back, whatever the hell that means. As he's not an employee he wouldn't have had the sort of files we create for a new staff member. He filled in an application form though. Not sure where it'll be.'

'I don't suppose you'd be prepared to meet me at the office and help locate that document, would you?' Tripp asked quietly.

'Oh, for Pete's sake. I have no idea if my job still exists, it's the weekend, and you want me to drive into the office and help you find a piece of paper?' Hood asked.

'I appreciate it's a lot to—'

'Half an hour,' Hood muttered before hanging up.

Tripp said a soft thank-you into the air and put his coat on again, sticking his head around Callanach's door. 'Sir,' he said. 'There's something I think you should know.'

Chapter Forty

Ava needed some way of ascertaining, beyond any doubt, Ramon Trescoe's part in Louis Jones' death. If he'd killed Jones, he was responsible for the Chief's suicide too. Callanach had ruined her chance of getting close to him when he'd hauled her out of The Maz, so an alternative plan was required. Thankfully, a phone call to the Glasgow branch of Police Scotland opened up a possibility. Sandy Peterson, better known to Glasgow's beat officers as Sugar who Ava had met at The Maz, had numerous previous convictions for public solicitation and had served time in HMP Cornton Vale for a string of thefts and a drug deal gone wrong. The photo Ava brought up on the computer screen matched Ava's memory of Sugar from the club, even if there were more lines around the girl's eyes these days. Sugar also had an active Facebook page. Not wise, Ava thought, given the sort of men she attracted during her working hours. The social media page, with the sort of non-existent security settings that would have the parents of a teenager in meltdown, led to a mobile number, and that was all Ava needed.

She couldn't send an anonymous message, that would be too

obvious, but Sugar wasn't one for good organisation, that much was clear from what she posted. People who were poorly organised lost track of friends, phone numbers and contact details all the time. Ava put on her coat and went shopping. An hour later she was back at her desk taking a new pay-as-you-go mobile from her pocket. No contract. Untraceable. Just what she needed.

Typing in Sugar's mobile number, she formulated a message. 'Hey Sugar. Long time no see babes. I was up at Glenochil holiday camp yesterday visiting Jimmy. They're all talking about The Maz. That's where you work, dontcha? Haven't seen you for ages so sending hugs. Loadsa love xxx.' Ava added some suitable emoticons as an afterthought and put the mobile down, as her desk phone began to ring.

'I'm at Cordelia Muir's office,' Callanach said. 'I think you should come over. There's something you need to see.'

Ava's new mobile buzzed as she was walking to her car. She opened the text as she fumbled in her handbag for keys.

'OMG soz. Not sure who this is lol. Never remember to put names in. Who was talking about The Maz?'

Ava typed a reply as she put on her seatbelt. 'Lol. It's Debs. Been a while since Cornton right? The boys at Glenochil was saying Dylan McGill's got a nice new cell all to himself. They're right jealous. When they was talking about The Maz I thought I'd say hi. Looking for work myself, if anything's going? Let me know. Gotta be better than the street. Must go babes. Ask about that work for me yeah?'

There was no way Sugar would want anyone from her prison days turning up to work at The Maz so the lie was as safe as Ava could make it. Given Sugar's frequent trips in and out of Cornton Vale there had to have been at least one Debs in there with her. Chances were that Sugar was using at the same time she was dealing drugs. She'd have forgotten more people than she remembered from those days, Ava thought.

By the time Ava pulled up outside Cordelia Muir's office, Callanach was standing in the doorway looking up and down the road.

'Waiting for me?' she asked.

'Checking for security cameras that might have a focus on this part of the road,' he said.

'What's going on, and can we talk about it inside? It's minus two out here.' Ava walked past him and perched on a radiator inside the office, quickly abandoning the position when she realised it wasn't working.

'Tripp went out interviewing Crystal's staff,' Callanach said quietly, mindful of Liam Hood who was huddled over a kettle at the rear of the office. Tripp was on his mobile, making notes. 'Cordelia Muir had a doctor's appointment planned, made for her by a staff member, only we had no record of him. Turns out he's an unpaid volunteer – recently taken on – so not on payroll and no formal HR records were prepared.'

'And?' Ava asked.

'Cordelia only became ill after that volunteer started working here. She asked him to phone the GP on her behalf, only he turned down the offer of an early appointment with her doctor, and accepted one several days later.'

'You think that was a deliberate delay to prevent her GP from diagnosing the problem?'

'I can't find any other explanation for it,' Callanach said.

'It's leaving a lot to chance,' Ava said. 'What if Cordelia had just picked up the phone and called the doctor herself?'

'Tripp spoke to Cordelia's daughter about that. Cordelia was known to be stoic to the point of stubbornness. Almost never visited the doctor, came to work whether she was fit to or not.

Hated making a fuss. Wouldn't have taken much probing to have found out she was unlikely to have bothered the doctor with the symptoms until she was at breaking point. If it was a risk, it was a calculated one. Mr Hood, the gentleman back there, has been through the filing cabinet and found an application form for the volunteer who organised the doctor's appointment.' He handed the form to Ava.

'Jeremy Dolour. What do we know about him?' Ava asked.

'We know that the National Insurance number he gave was either wrong or false. No one with that name and date of birth has any public records we can find. No driving licence. No NHS number. Tripp is on the line to a uniformed officer who's checking the given address for us.'

'Did Jeremy have access to Cordelia's desk?' Ava asked softly.

'Her desk, and the fridge where Cordelia kept her meals in plastic containers. He made her drinks regularly too,' Callanach said.

'And he was a horrible little creep, did you tell her that yet?' Liam Hood shouted from the far end of the room.

'Let me introduce Mr Hood,' Callanach said, raising his eyebrows briefly at Ava. 'He's worked here with Cordelia for three years. Apparently, Jeremy came in unexpectedly and offered to volunteer. Cordelia felt sorry for him and invited him to come in one day a week, unpaid, to do general administration and office assistant work. Soon after that he was in two days a week.'

'He was too keen. Always there offering to help, following Cordelia around like a lap dog. No one else ever bothered going near her when he was in. I told her something was up with him and I wasn't the only who felt it either. That wasn't Cordelia's way though. The more you tried to persuade her that someone was no good, the harder she'd fight for them,' Hood said.

'Would you work with one of our artists, Mr Hood? If we

don't have a photo of Jeremy you might be able to give us a likeness,' Ava said.

'That'll take another few hours, I suppose. Not that I've got anything else to do on a Saturday. Every day's a weekend until we're told what's happening to this place,' Hood muttered.

'We'll have you driven to the station and make sure you're bought hot food to keep you going if that helps,' Ava said.

'Sorry, ma'am,' Tripp intervened.

'That'll be my cue to get lost then,' Hood said, as he wandered back in the direction of the kettle.

'The address Jeremy Dolour gave does exist, but when officers knocked on the door it was opened by a young woman and her husband. They're on honeymoon in Edinburgh and have rented the place through Airbnb.'

'Airbnb?' Callanach asked.

'Houses and apartments to rent if you don't fancy a hotel. You can register your address and let your property through the website. We're making further enquiries, although it looks as if all the information Jeremy gave was false,' Tripp said.

'Cordelia Muir obviously didn't know him or suspect him. Where's the motive?' There was silence. 'All right. Get officers out interviewing the remaining staff members about Jeremy. Maybe he let something slip that'll lead us to him. A girlfriend, hobbies, a vehicle. Do we have his fingerprints?'

'Hard to be sure. We can eliminate current staff members, but other people who've worked in this office previously are in the mix, cleaners were from an agency so different people each week, tradesmen, visitors. It'll be almost impossible to ascertain which are his without a comparison,' Tripp said. 'Mr Hood describes him as having a pronounced stutter on words beginning with w. Jeremy's in his mid to late twenties, wore glasses, didn't really speak to anyone except Cordelia.'

'I'll have to talk to the Muir family,' Ava said. 'If it gets out that we're investigating a specific suspect, they'll be devastated. Keep this quiet for now, would you?'

'They may be too busy to talk at the moment, ma'am,' Tripp said. 'Cordelia's son, Randall, was disturbed attempting suicide a couple of days ago. They found him quickly enough that he wasn't badly injured, but as a result he's had to be committed. Also, and this may be nothing, but Cordelia's ink-pen is missing from the box she kept it in on her desk. Apparently, all the staff knew never to touch it, as it was a gift from her deceased husband. I checked, and it hasn't been located anywhere else that I can find from the evidence logs.'

'Usual lines of enquiry,' Ava said. 'Cameras that might have caught him coming to or leaving these premises. Check with Cordelia's daughter to see if she recognises the artist's impression as soon as that's completed. Luc, make sure there's a briefing pack and get the whole squad together first thing tomorrow morning. The rest of the weekend is officially cancelled. I'm going back to my office to call the Superintendent. I'll see you both there.'

In her car, Ava sat back and closed her eyes. Cordelia Muir had over-ridden Liam Hood's instincts about Jeremy. It was so often the way. Some people judged quickly, acted on their instincts and protected themselves effectively. The Cordelia Muirs of this world fought the desire to judge. They made themselves more kind to the dislikeable, not less. They opened their arms to those society rejected, then they became victims. There was no right answer, no litmus test for danger, but Jeremy Dolour had approached the charity offering help and Cordelia hadn't had the heart to turn him away. If he was responsible for her death, it was a callous act facilitated by her goodness. The phone in her pocket buzzed.

'You've started a bloody storm here Debs!' the text read. 'My boss called a screw at Glenochil who says a lady copper visited McGill. Does your Jimmy know anything about it?'

'Ain't got much credit left. Will call when been to shop,' Ava wrote, turning off the phone and opening her car door. She took out the sim card, crushed it beneath her heel, and dropped it with the phone into the bottom of a rain-filled bin, covering it with other rubbish. Her conscience pricked for a few seconds. The Governor at Glenochil had been good enough to comply with her request to move Dylan McGill into a cell on his own with full privileges restored. Ramon Trescoe had contacts amongst the prison guards. After the length of time he'd spent there, it was inconceivable that he wouldn't. Now, though, Ava had crossed a line. She'd put McGill's life at risk. If Ramon Trescoe believed his partner McGill had talked to the police, there'd be a price on his head already. Ava had signed in using her proper identification, knowing that the prison guards had access to the visitors' log. Once they had her name and found a photo of her on the internet, Knuckles and Perry would know straight away it had been her at Glynis Begbie's house. Of course, if Ramon Trescoe hadn't been involved in Begbie's death, he wouldn't make the connection between the two events. But if he went after McGill, it was as good as a signed confession. Ava was banking on the latter.

Back at her desk, feeling cold in spite of the blasting heating, Ava had already telephoned Glenochil's Governor and requested a secure watch on Dylan McGill. The Governor had known better than to ask too many questions and in any event, Ava suspected her voice had said it all. Still, she was playing games with a man's life and as hard as she tried to ignore it, she felt as if she'd stooped to a low that was the opposite of all the reasons she'd become a police officer. For a few furious moments she cursed George Begbie for landing her in the middle of such a mess. He'd profited from whatever he'd done and now others were suffering. Even so, her loyalty to her former boss wouldn't let her drop it. If she didn't close the case, it would plague her forever.

Steeling herself, she flipped open the file on Louis Jones and forced herself to keep busy. The note with a phone number for the poor woman from Dimitri's team who'd had been scapegoated for failing to pass on the forensics report was at the top of the pile of papers. Ava was dialling before she'd really thought through what she was doing. Anything to take her mind off the danger she'd put Dylan McGill in.

'Janet Monroe,' a tired voice said.

'PC Monroe, this is DCI Turner with MIT. Is this a good time to talk?' Ava asked.

'I'm at home doing nothing, ma'am. I've been let go early on maternity leave, supposedly for my own good. How can I help you?' Janet sounded like Ava felt.

'I was phoning about the forensics report on the Louis Jones car crash. CI Dimitri said you'd—'

'I apologise, ma'am. CI Dimitri said he'd asked me to chase that for you. I must have missed it. That's why he let me go early, on full pay, mind you, so I suppose I shouldn't be complaining.'

'I didn't call you for an apology, Janet. I called because I was concerned that I might have exacerbated the problem with CI Dimitri. I'd like to help,' Ava said.

There was a long pause.

'Chief Inspector Dimitri was clear that whilst on leave I wasn't permitted to discuss his team's ongoing investigations. I probably shouldn't be talking to you,' Janet said.

Ava bit her lower lip. She'd battled enough sexism during her early days in the police that it stung when she came across junior female officers still having to tolerate it.

'How long before you're officially on maternity leave?' Ava asked.

'Another eight weeks,' Janet said.

274

'And you're fit for work? No concerns from your doctor or midwife?' Ava checked.

'No. My GP told me to relax and enjoy. I think he actually muttered the words "lucky girl" when I said I'd been released from duty early. He probably doesn't know what I was thinking when he said it, or he might have backed out of the room rather sharpish,' Janet said.

Ava laughed. 'I have a bit of a situation here. We have the Louis Jones murder, an unresolved situation with the Lily Eustis case, and what appeared to be an unlawful killing by illegal drugs may just have been upgraded to murder. As a result I'm short-handed. Just so you know, I'm offering you office duties assisting in the investigations. No field work.'

'Sorry ma'am, I don't understand,' Janet said.

'I'm asking you to help out in MIT, providing additional cover until you're due to go on maternity leave. I'll clear it with the Superintendent. You could start tomorrow,' Ava said, knowing she'd have to grovel to Detective Superintendent Overbeck, but it was worth the humiliation for the sense of doing something right.

'Gosh, I didn't think . . . yes. Of course. I'd love to have a placement within MIT even if it's temporary. But CI Dimitri?'

'Technically Chief Inspector Dimitri has released you from his squad and I'm sure he'll be understanding. Listen, I know it'll be a Sunday but we're briefing tomorrow at 8.30am on the Cordelia Muir death. No uniform. See you here. Bring your own mug.'

Ava ended the call feeling better. She'd made it a policy to help other women on the way up the career ladder, just as Begbie had helped her. It didn't take much to extend the hand of friendship. Between Lily Eustis, Cordelia Muir and Louis Jones, MIT needed every pair of hands they could get. Ava couldn't escape the feeling that her squad was getting nowhere fast.

Chapter Forty-One

Mina Eustis sat with her phone in her lap. She'd lost count of the number of texts she'd sent. Christian had replied to a few, but he was still busy. It wasn't clear if he was out of town or not, but there was some crisis, which meant that whilst he was thinking of her, he couldn't be at her side.

In a multitude of ways life was harder now than when Lily had first died. No more escape into the numbness of shock and disbelief. No more police visits, or flowers from well-wishers. Even the press had deserted them. The area outside their front door was a barren and harsh egress into a world that would never be what it once was. Her parents had slipped from grief into a chilled depression. If it was possible for human beings to become a season, they were winter. Mina had been angry at them for a bitter moment, then almost every emotion she had ever felt had left her. She could rationalise. Her parents should never have had to lose a child. No parent should suffer that fate. The loss had rendered them little more than walking corpses. They needed time. The world had continued to spin. Mina had missed so many classes and course-work assignments that the university had regretfully but formally written to confirm that her place was closed. They had at least urged her to restart the following year. She'd thrown the letter in the bin without her parents even seeing it. Mina knew it was the right thing to slip away quietly from her past life. Her friends needed to carry on living. They needed to laugh, study, watch films and get drunk. They had been sympathetic to a fault, but she couldn't expect them to understand what it was like for her. She couldn't keep burdening them with it. The universe could not fold in on itself for one family's grief. Mina understood. She was alone.

Christian getting bored of her should have been predictable, too. Who did she think she was kidding? Lily had been the beautiful, outgoing one. Lily who could have had any man she wanted but who had simply smiled kindly at the stupid boys who threw themselves at her so regularly. She was, her sister had always declared, waiting for someone special. Mina wasn't destined to have men like Christian around her, and when she did it was always with that just-good-friends limitation.

Lily had been with a man the night she died. It must have been a date for Lily to have hidden it from them all. If she'd been going out with a mere friend there'd have been no need for secrecy. Mina could understand it. There was always the sense that by talking about things you jinxed them, and it was nice to have secrets. Mina just wished Lily had shared that one with her. They'd always been friends. Yes, there had been the usual childish squabbles, but in truth they'd grown up without much sibling rivalry. If Lily was alive now, Mina would be lying on her sister's bed, talking about Christian, explaining how one day he'd appeared in the library, asking if she had change for the drinks machine, saying how much he liked the band whose retro t-shirt she was wearing. Funny that she couldn't even remember which t-shirt it was now. After that they'd formed the habit of sitting near one another in the library to study, and there he always was. Until now.

She wanted Lily to walk in, hug her and tell her she was being silly – to reassure Mina that Christian wouldn't have deserted her. He alone amongst her friends had known what to say and how to say it, never treading on egg-shells the way everyone else had. Perhaps it was because he was that bit older, but Christian was unafraid to talk about death. Surely he wouldn't just drop her because he was busy with other people. He knew how badly she needed him. He was the only one she had let see the full extent of her pain. Mina hit the call button she had promised herself she would leave alone. She had stopped leaving him voicemail messages, mainly because she could no longer stand the neediness in her own voice when she spoke. But now there was no prerecorded message to greet her. Christian had switched his voicemail off. That was it then. As clear a message as he could have sent.

Mina walked to the kitchen cupboard where her mother kept the alcohol. It was kept better stocked these days than it had been in past years. She took a bottle of vodka from a shelf, considered taking orange juice from the fridge as a mixer but the effort was too much. Instead, she plodded back up the stairs, letting her mobile slip from her fingers to the floor as she opened Lily's door. Closing the curtains gently – Lily had chosen them – she loosened the bottle cap and turned off the light. The bed was comfortable. The pillow still smelled of Lily's favourite perfume. The sheets remained slightly crumpled where Lily's feet had kicked around each night. If there was a sanctuary where Mina could find oblivion, then that was surely it.

Christian turned his phone off. The calls from Mina had been incessant, and now Randall was asking him to visit. The last contact from Randall had come from a number his phone hadn't identified, although given the contents of the message the reason for that was clear. It appeared that Randall's mobile had been taken away when he was admitted as an inpatient to a secure facility where he was, from the sound of it, being very heavily medicated indeed. Presumably he'd been able to find a landline to call from. Christian shook his head at the inevitability of it all. Randall had reeked of weakness from the outset. His inability to deal with his mother's death had been so foreseeable that it was almost boring. There had been a blade involved though, which had been a surprise. Christian had anticipated something easier – a softer exit – sleeping tablets, perhaps. The grief Randall had been feeling must have been absolutely overwhelming for him to have attempted such an immediate and unpleasant escape from it. Christian allowed himself the luxury of imagining the scene for a few moments.

Right now, though, Bradley was the one who needed him most. Sweet Bradley with his soft hands and beseeching eyes, slowly coming to understand that Sean wasn't really right for him at all.

Christian had been looking for someone like this. Someone who wanted to listen to him as much as they wanted to be listened to. Chris had his own story to tell. He too had burdens and struggles. With Bradley, he could let some of that out. There was Sean, of course, between them like some invisible reminder that all new friendships bore the guilt of stealing time from existing ones, but things would change.

Speaking of Sean, his career seemed to be going from strength to strength. The theatre company he'd recently joined had commissioned a black comedy from a local playwright and rehearsals were getting a lot of press attention, Bradley was telling him.

'Sounds wonderful,' Christian murmured over his coffee. 'I'd love to see it.'

'God, yes,' Brad said, bringing the sentence to a short close and losing his smile. 'You know I'd love that but I . . . I still haven't really talked about you to Sean. And now that I haven't talked about you for so long, I feel kind of weird explaining how we know each other so well. Not that well, obviously. I think I probably should have mentioned you to him before now, that's all.'

'Don't stress. I completely get it,' Christian said, reaching out a hand to Bradley's knee. 'We try to protect the people we love, and then before we realise it our very attempts to make things simple have grown into a new form of threat.'

'How do you always know exactly what to say?' Bradley grinned. 'That's precisely what's happened, even if I couldn't have put it into words. So, what about you? What's been happening in your life this week?'

'The boy I told you about who lost his mum – he attempted suicide,' Christian said.

'Oh no, you should have called me. Are you okay? That must have been a terrible shock. What's happened to him?' Bradley leaned forward, taking the hand Christian had put on his knee and gripping it between both of his.

'He's being looked after at a hospital. I feel kind of responsible. I know that's stupid but maybe I wasn't there when he needed me or I gave him bad advice. I don't know,' Christian said.

'I don't believe that for a second. All you did was offer him a shoulder. I bet he'd say you were a true friend.' Bradley sighed. 'You've had a tough time of it recently, what with your break-up as well. You know I'm just a phone call away if you ever need to talk. Don't worry about the Sean thing. I've decided it's time to talk to him about you anyway. I don't want to pretend you don't exist anymore.'

'Not yet,' Christian said. 'It'll sound crazy but this time we have, that no one else in the world knows about but us, it's all that's been keeping me going. I've had so many people relying on me so to find you, in this perfect place, I'm not ready to burst the bubble yet.'

'I'm in your hands,' Bradley said, flushing slightly as the words came from his mouth. Christian leaned forward, slid one hand round the back of Bradley's neck and rested his forehead against Brad's shoulder. He stayed like that for a minute, eyes closed, listening to Brad's pounding heartbeat. Finally, satisfied, he sat back up.

'I'll meet Sean soon. We'll put all of this right. There won't be any awkwardness or competition. Trust me,' Christian whispered. 'I'd never do anything to hurt you.'

Chapter Forty-Two

The incident room was full. Every new photograph and evidential detail had been pinned to the board alongside the details of Cordelia Muir's death, and in the centre of it all hung the artist's impression of Jeremy Dolour.

'The employees put hair colour between light brown and dark blonde,' DS Lively told the room. 'Jeremy is, they estimate, in his late twenties, which reflects the date of birth given on his volunteer application form. At present there's no substantiated link between him and Cordelia Muir's death, so the official line is to interview him as a witness. However, none of the information he provided to Mrs Muir was correct and we can find no record of anyone of that name and approximate age. You should assume he took steps to conceal his true identity. His motives for that, if they are innocent, are unknown.'

'Where are we supposed to look for him then, sir? Seems we haven't got much to go on,' an officer shouted from the rear of the room.

'In case you hadn't noticed, son, we are the police. It is our job to find people. Sometimes those people don't want to be found, which makes things more difficult, but if you expected the bad guys to be standing around waving flags then you'd best change careers,' Lively replied.

Ava intervened.

'We're struggling to find any CCTV footage on which we can positively identify Jeremy. Too many hoods up and umbrellas at this time of year, and the low light doesn't help. We'll need most of you chasing former employees, donors to the charity, going back through diaries to see who has been in the office in the last six months and obtaining their fingerprints for exclusion. Jeremy's DNA will be in that office somewhere, as will his prints. Any other ideas?'

'The interior of the fridge, ma'am,' a voice said from the corner. Everyone turned around. Eventually chair legs scraped the floor and a young woman stood up. She was Hispanic, delicate, and absolutely tiny except for her belly, which she was holding protectively as she spoke. 'I looked at the photos of the office earlier. One of the witnesses, Mr Hood I think, said that Jeremy had regular access to the fridge. If that's right, you can expect the visitors not to have touched it. The outside will have been wiped down by cleaners occasionally. The inside, though, will be a discrete area, cleaned less often. It'll cut down the enquiries we need to make to eliminate people.'

'PC Monroe?' Ava asked. The woman nodded. 'Let me introduce you. This is Janet Monroe who is helping swell our numbers for the next few weeks and who will provide backup from here. Thank you, Constable. That's a good start.'

Callanach's mind drifted as tasks were assigned and a timetable agreed. He and Ava had run through those details prior to the briefing. It was Tripp he was interested in. The Detective Constable was facing the opposite direction from the remainder of the team. In the time Callanach had been with MIT in Edinburgh he had never once witnessed Max Tripp less than one hundred per cent focused on a briefing, usually taking notes, with his hand constantly raised to ask questions. Today his head was elsewhere. He was staring at the board where the paperwork containing details of Lily Eustis' death were starting to curl slightly at the edges. There had been frustratingly little progress. It wouldn't be long before Superintendent Overbeck ordered the allocated squad to be reduced.

The conference broke up. Men and women scattered, collecting equipment, claiming computers and desks, forming smaller groups to talk through what their day would entail. Tripp stayed where he was, staring at Lily Eustis' face.

'Tripp,' Callanach said. Nothing. He walked over and put a hand on his shoulder. 'Max, are you all right?'

Tripp looked at him.

'Too many coincidences, sir. It's the same killer.'

'In my office, Tripp,' Callanach said. 'Coffee first.' They walked together to the tiny kitchen where not enough value was placed on hygiene. Callanach and Tripp opted for throw-away cups rather than the lottery of bacteria-laden mugs. Tripp walked half a pace behind Callanach as they made their way to his office.

'Sit down,' Callanach said. 'Tell me what's going on.'

'This mysterious man walks into these women's lives. No one knew who Lily Eustis was with that night. There's no CCTV, no DNA. More importantly Lily didn't see anything dangerous coming or there's no way she'd have been outside in December. She was sedated with easy to obtain drugs. He established a relationship of trust, then he sat back and watched Lily die. With Cordelia Muir, it's the same. This time he showed his face publicly, but he gave false details. Jeremy is in the sort of age group that would have appealed to Lily. The description from the workers in Muir's office say he was physically attractive. Not stand out, or stunning, but a good-looking man. Slim, 5'11", blondish.'

'What about the stutter?' Callanach asked. 'Why would a murderer with such a specific and recognisable trait put themselves in the public view before killing, especially if he was at pains to hide himself so well when it came to Lily.'

'Because we're assuming the stutter is real,' Tripp said. 'I had a boyfriend with a stutter once. When he tried to talk to people at parties, they'd look away, find someone else to chat with. They literally didn't meet his eyes, couldn't bear the embarrassment of attempting to communicate with him. Worn carefully, the most outrageous outfit becomes a disguise. I wonder how many of Jeremy's co-workers spent time actually talking to him. My guess is that it was easier not to.'

'You're saying the stutter was a performance?' Callanach asked.

'I'm saying it may have helped him avoid people, which is what he wanted. It may also have had the effect of making Cordelia more prone to taking him under her wing. Think about it, he goes into the office, is struggling to talk easily to the first person he meets, so Cordelia intervenes. He doesn't need to pour out his heart or tell a sob story. Mrs Muir is already feeling protective, empathising. That's the kind of woman she was. If she was a pre-planned target, he'd have known that.'

'Tripp, you're not just describing an organised killer but one with a high IQ, stunning impulse control and perfect planning. Not to mention his acting ability. It's hard to imagine that no one would have been suspicious of him,' Callanach said.

'Liam Hood was. He didn't know why, but his instinct was that he didn't like Jeremy and didn't trust him. Other members of staff discuss the same lack of ease when he was in the office,' Tripp said.

'If that was the case, why didn't they raise it with Cordelia?' Callanach mused.

'Would you want to be the one pointing the finger at a man

volunteering his time for free to help a charity? A man with a speech impediment, who Cordelia had already decided should be given a chance. Do you think she'd have listened? It would have taken a brave person to have made a complaint based only on gut feelings of dislike.'

Callanach sat back in his chair. 'It would have taken a reasonable knowledge of pharmaceuticals to have killed both women. Lily and Cordelia must each have trusted whoever got close enough to kill them, so a high-functioning sociopath ticks the boxes in terms of having the social skills required. The general physical description, vague though it is in Lily Eustis' case, is an approximate fit. We're still without a motive for either killing, though. There's no discernible link between Cordelia and Lily. So, what is it, the joy of ending a life? If that was it, wouldn't he abduct them, watch them die, knowing he had the ultimate power over them? We're not sure if he hung around long enough to witness Lily's final breath, but he must have known he wouldn't be there to see Cordelia pass. It doesn't fit any known profile, no established pattern. There just isn't the sort of pay-off psychopaths need from their offending.'

Tripp folded his hands together in his lap. 'Lily's ring's missing, an object deeply meaningful to her family. We haven't properly explored the issue of Cordelia's missing pen, but it's another object with far-reaching emotional ties. The list of coincidences keeps getting longer. I don't know why this killer is taking these lives,' Tripp said. 'But if I'm right, the second killing was much more audacious than the first. So far he's got away with it, which means he'll kill again. He'll be planning it already.'

'I'll talk to DCI Turner,' Callanach said. 'Your theory has to stay quiet for now.'

'Understood,' Tripp said, standing up and leaving quietly.

Something about his exit felt wrong. It took a few minutes before Callanach realised why. It was the first time Tripp had ever left his office without his last word being 'sir'.

Callanach walked into Ava's office without knocking, a move that earned him a hard stare from Ava and a questioning look from PC Janet Monroe.

'I take it you need me urgently, DI Callanach,' Ava said.

'I'll go,' Monroe muttered.

'Constable Monroe, this is Detective Inspector Luc Callanach. Janet has joined us from CI Dimitri's squad,' Ava said.

'Right,' Callanach said. 'Your team handled the Louis Jones car crash. Perhaps you could review the papers for me. I still don't seem to have all the forensics back. I need the results to compare with the murder scene evidence. Speak to DS Lively about it, would you? You can't miss him. He'll be eating biscuits and talking more loudly than anyone else.' Callanach smiled. Monroe excused herself to start work as Callanach sat down. 'You've borrowed a uniformed officer from another squad? What prompted that?'

'When I chased the Louis Jones crash report, Dimitri disciplined Monroe for not getting it to me and sent her off on early maternity leave as a thinly veiled reprimand. I felt bad and we could use her. So, no progress on the Louis Jones case then?'

'I have someone making enquiries,' Callanach said, adding, 'and it's better you know nothing about it. Plausible deniability, is that the phrase?'

'I think we're both past denying anything,' Ava said. 'Do you have an update on the man currently known as Jeremy?'

'No but I have an update about DC Tripp,' Callanach said. 'He's convinced that Lily Eustis' killer and Cordelia Muir's killer are the same man. For what it's worth, I'm starting to agree with him.'

'Oh fuck,' Ava let the words float out on her breath. 'Sum it up for me.'

'Two deaths, unexplained, unexpected. Both pharmaceutically facilitated. Short time span. Key witnesses failing to come forward. Males from each case we are interested in are the same age, gender, race, rough description. Close geography. Planned and well-executed avoidance of a forensic trail. Both victims missing personal items, which might have been taken as trophies. Could be two separate killers but really, what are the odds of that?'

'What you're not saying, is that you're here because I need to notify the Superintendent about it. Wonderful. I can drop that bombshell during the phone call when I'm explaining that there's no case progress for Louis Jones,' Ava said.

'*Qui court deux lièvres à la fois, n'en prend aucun,*' Callanach said. Ava tipped her head to one side and looked unimpressed. 'It's an old French saying. It translates as, he who chases two hares at once, catches none. Leave Louis Jones and the Glasgow trouble to me. Take control of the Muir and Eustis murders. If both women were killed by the same man . . .'

'Then he'll kill again soon,' Ava said. 'That's exactly what I was thinking.'

Chapter Forty-Three

Ava's conversation with Superintendent Overbeck had been brief and brutal. More than one threat had been issued and some swear words used that Ava had never heard before. She hadn't thought that possible after several years of providing police cell bed and breakfast to some of Scotland's most accomplished drunk and disorderlies, but Overbeck was the queen of profane hyperbole.

'That's all you've got,' Overbeck had cut in to the middle of Ava's explanation.

'There are too many coincidental similarities between the Eustis and Muir cases to ignore the possibility that it might be a series of murders, ma'am,' Ava had replied.

Overbeck had laughed, reminding Ava of nails being dragged along on a chalkboard.

'You're asking Police Scotland to fund a case based on the fact that, in the absence of positive evidence, you can see a lot of coincidences. Goodness me, we must be hard up for work to do. I tell you what. Why don't you see if we can't find a few other cases where there are dead bodies and we'll lump them into the same investigation.'

'It's a bit more than that, if you don't mind my saying, ma'am,' Ava had responded quietly.

'I do fucking well mind you saying, actually. The victims are from different races, different ages, were sedated with different drugs, and came from different areas of the city. You have to be out of your tiny, apparently underused mind!' Overbeck had snapped.

'If it's the same killer and there's a further victim, given the similarities, Police Scotland will be sued. In those circumstances I would feel obliged to explain that I had put forward the case for these being serial murders,' Ava said, cringing as she issued the half-threat, knowing her relationship with Overbeck was at an all time low, and was sinking to depths she'd believe already plumbed.

'Why you facetious little . . .' Overbeck had ranted for a while. Ava had shifted the receiver away from her ear until it was over. 'Damage limitation, Turner. Keep it out of the bastard press until you have actual evidence. If you're struggling to understand what that is, buying a frigging dictionary. And when this particular shit-storm starts blowing in the air, my boot, Detective Chief Inspector, will be firmly winging its way towards your arse. Got it?'

'Got it, ma'am. Many thanks for your help.' Ava had ended the call before the Detective Superintendent could respond to that one.

Now Ava was sitting outside the Eustis' house, waiting to reveal yet more awful news to Lily's parents. The day had begun badly, was about to get worse, and was due to end with a lecture from Ailsa Lambert cleverly disguised as dinner.

Ava pulled a file from her bag and walked up the path. Mr Eustis opened it before she could knock. He raised a hand to usher her through to the lounge where Mrs Eustis was already waiting. They sat.

'Thank you for seeing me and apologies for disturbing you on a Sunday. I'm here because I need to ask if you recognise this man.' Ava raised the artist's impression of Jeremy from the file. Mr Eustis took it first, then handed it to his wife. Her hands shook so badly that he reached out to steady it for her.

'Who is he?' Lily's father asked.

'A volunteer who worked for a charity called Crystal, based in Edinburgh. The charity's founder, Cordelia Muir, also passed away recently,' Ava said.

'I don't understand the relevance, I'm afraid,' Mr Eustis said. 'I've never seen this young man before and he looks a few years older than Lily. You darling?'

Mrs Eustis shook her head and looked away.

'We've checked Lily's social media pages and her phone, but there's no photographic or video evidence that she knew this man. Did Lily have anything to do with Crystal, or perhaps get involved in any charity volunteering?' Ava asked.

'She was too busy studying for that,' her father said. 'You could try asking her friends. It might be that one of them introduced her to this man. Did he . . . do you think he had something to do with her death?'

'At the moment we're after a positive identification to eliminate him from another investigation. He's proving rather hard to trace. You should be aware, as you may hear more about it in the next few days, that Cordelia Muir's death is also being treated as non-accidental.'

'Was there cannabis oil involved in Ms Muir's death, too? Only I'm struggling to connect her with our daughter,' Mr Muir said.

'That was a different type of drug,' Ava said, 'I know I don't need to ask you not to speak to the press, but there is another family involved so I'm sure I can count on your discretion until we're in a position to move forward publicly. It may be that this young man had nothing to do with Lily. We're just covering all bases.'

A door slammed above them, feet pattered along a hallway, and the unmistakable sound of retching could be heard even with the bathroom door closed. Ava looked to Mr and Mrs Eustis. Neither made to go upstairs and see what was happening. It was an ongoing situation, then.

'Is that Lily's sister upstairs?' Ava asked. Mr Eustis nodded. 'Do you mind if I go and conduct one more search of Lily's room? I'd like to check there's nothing that connects her with this man. A photo, a name on a piece of paper, that sort of thing.'

'I'll put the kettle on,' was Mr Eustis' response, which Ava took as consent. She made her way up the stairs and kept Lily's door fully open, watching the bathroom from the end of the bed where she sat flicking through one of Lily's books. Ava was staring into the pages when the bathroom door finally opened and a girl tiptoed past. 'Are you okay?' Ava called softly. There was a moment of stillness, silence. The girl was deciding on her options. She could pretend she hadn't heard and keep walking or come back. In the end, either good manners or curiosity won.

'I'm all right, thank you,' she said. Her voice was hoarse and she was thinner than any twenty-something should be, with lank hair matted across her brow and sallow skin.

'I'm DCI Turner. We met briefly when this all started although I don't expect you to remember.' Ava stayed on the bed, keeping Lily's book on her lap. She held out her hand to shake the girl's. Next to her on the bed was the sketch of Jeremy. The girl walked forward.

'Mina,' she said, holding out her hand out to take Ava's. There was a pause so brief it was more of a micro-hiccup in the flow of the girl's steps, then she was shaking hands. Her grip was weak and hesitant. Ava didn't blame her. Who wanted to make physical contact with the woman investigating their sister's death? That was too much reality for anyone. 'Who's that?' Mina asked, motioning down to the sketch with her free hand.

Ava let Mina's hand go and picked up the picture. 'Someone we're looking for in relation to another investigation. Do you recognise him?'

Mina gave a quick shake of her head. 'Why him?' she asked.

'He disappeared quite suddenly, and may have given false details. He fits the vague description given of the man in the pub with Lily. He also has a stutter. Did Lily ever talk about someone who fitted this description? Or ever show you a photo of a man who could have been him?'

'No,' Mina said. 'I feel ill again. Sorry, I have to go.' She took a step away and Ava stood up.

'Mina, can I call a doctor for you, or a counsellor? Your parents are trapped in their own grief, quite understandably, but you need some help to get through this. I can see you're not well.'

'I've been drinking,' Mina said, grinning too broadly.

'No one would blame you for that. Think about it, would you? There are people I can contact who will help. Whenever you're ready.' Ava reached into her pocket, pulled out a card, and left it on Lily's bed. 'I'll leave this for you as well, just in case any of Lily's friends come over. It would help if you'd show them the picture and ask if they recognise him.'

Ava returned to the lounge doing up her coat. Mr Eustis was handing his wife a glass of water and opening a bottle of painkillers.

'I'll be off now. Thank you for your time. I'll call if we have anything else to report,' Ava said.

'You didn't tell us his name,' Mrs Eustis called out as she went towards the front door. It was the first time she'd spoken, Ava realised, her voice a scratch on a record, making Ava wonder how many days it had been since Mrs Eustis had said anything at all.

'Jeremy Dolour,' Ava said, turning around and heading back into the lounge.

Mrs Eustis began to laugh. The water she held started to spill as her stomach spasmed. Her husband stumbled backwards, his face a picture of horror.

'Stop! Stop it,' he said. 'Stop laughing. There's nothing funny about any of this. I'm so sorry,' he directed towards Ava. 'She's not herself. The doctor said she needs time to work through it.' He bent down and took the glass from his wife's hand.

'Dolour,' Mrs Eustis said. 'You don't get it, do you? What do they teach you people at college these days?'

'Mrs Eustis,' Ava said, bending down and taking Lily's mother's shaking hands in her own. 'What don't I get?'

'It means grief. He's having a laugh at your expense, I'm afraid. Perhaps at ours, too, by the look on your face.' She stopped laughing abruptly and stared at her husband, her eyes widening, as if waking from a nightmare. 'I think I'd like to lie down now,' she said.

Chapter Forty-Four

Lance Proudfoot, Callanach's go-to journalist friend, headed for Bridgeton, to the east of Glasgow city, guiding his bike through the traffic into James Street. The area wasn't bad but it was the retailers that told the story. Funeral directors, charity shops, solicitors, gambling outfits. Businesses whose doors stayed open when others failed. The Jupiter was a decent enough bar if you were of an age that appreciated the music playing a little lower, and that life without Wi-Fi could still be meaningful. Serving James Street customers for thirty years, the bar was more of an institution than a local. The sign outside hadn't changed and Lance suspected the menu might well offer the same fare it had back in the day, but the man leaning against the inside of the cherrywood bar looked as if he'd suffered more than one lifetime of hardships.

'What'll you have?' he asked as Lance walked in.

'Will you still serve me if I ask for coffee?' Lance asked. The man turned to clatter a cup and saucer, muttering to himself. 'Now is that any way to greet an auld friend, Grogs?'

The barman turned round, taking a bent pair of glasses from his pocket and thrusting them against his face.

'Well, I'll be feathered and tarred! Sir Lancelot, is that you? We all assumed you'd been killed by that posh lot over in Edinburgh for not pronouncing your vowels properly.' He held out a hand and took Lance's in his, shaking it hard. 'How long's it been? I hope I don't look as old as you, no offence pal.'

'You're all right, Grogsy, you've got some road to tread until you've my wrinkles. So, do I get a coffee or is that not allowed in here?'

'Aye, you great blouse, I'll fetch you a coffee. Don't expect me to join you though. Some of us have traditions to uphold,' he said, pouring himself a double whisky and slamming it onto the bar. Lance watched his mate's hands tremble and knew it wasn't tradition that had him drinking at eleven in the morning.

They raised their drinks to one another, caught up on old friends, running through the time-honoured checklist that had slipped into Lance's life since his fiftieth birthday – deaths first, divorces second, illnesses third, good news last as there always seemed so little of it.

'Come on then, you can't kid a kidder. You didn't just happen to walk into my bar. What is it you need?' Grogs asked.

'The ancient currency of a man who owns a bar. I need information. A pal of mine owes some money. I won't go into details, but there's a rumour his debt might have been bought by some people best avoided. I said I'd take a trip, see if I can't sort it out,' Lance said.

'Forewarned is forearmed, is that it?' Grogs asked. Lance nodded. 'Who does he owe?'

'I don't know who's grinding the organ, but the monkeys are called Knuckles and Perry. Govanhill lot, I gather.'

Grogsy stopped fiddling with bottles and leaned over the bar. 'This mate, that wouldn't be you, would it? Because those are not men with reputations for gentleness.'

'No, no, not me. The most trouble I get in these days is

when I misspell names. It's a friend of a friend, nothing personal, but it gave me an excuse for a day out on the bike.' Lance smiled.

'All right then, but it's bad news. I've never met Knuckles, he's an enforcer. Rumour has it he's done several stretches, most notably for death by dangerous driving. Started off as a murder charge, mind, but by the trial there was a distinct lack of witnesses as to the words exchanged between Knuckles and the man he killed. Story goes it was a blackmail racket where the funds had dried up. Knuckles' first name is Ed. Don't know the surname. Brian Perry I've met a handful of times, lives out west in Pollok. Used to see him at the dog track over in Rutherglen. Wasn't a bad sort until he got mixed up with a particular crowd. These boys, Lance, they're not lightweight. Whatever trouble your mate's in, the debt'll have to be paid. I've lived in this city fifty-six years, there's not much going on I don't hear about sooner or later. What's your friend's name? Maybe I can find out just how deep in the creek water he is.'

'Don't go bothering yourself, I don't want to put you out. So, whereabouts do these lads hang out? I could do with knowing where my mate should avoid,' Lance said.

'There's a club, The Maz. Girls don't have to pay to get in, men do, that sort of place. But you can't talk to these ones, Lance. Not even you have sufficient charm to worm your friend out of this. Steer clear is my advice.'

'Fair enough. You've been a pal. I'd best be heading home, then. Look after yourself, Grogsy. I like what you've done with the place,' Lance said, tucking his helmet under one arm and getting a twenty out of his pocket.

'Ach, away with you. You're seriously trying to pay me for a damned coffee, are you?'

Lance left it on the bar. 'I'm paying you so as next time I visit, you'll have bought some better coffee than that.'

'Cheeky git,' Grogsy said, sliding the note off the bar and into his pocket, raising an arm in farewell.

It took Lance ten minutes to reach The Maz, then another ten to find somewhere secure to park the bike. It wasn't exactly worth a fortune but it was precious to him, not least because without it he'd be struggling to get home. Satisfied he'd left it safe, he wandered through Govanhill's back streets to get the lay of the land. Keeping his camera in his backpack, he hung a sensible distance from the rear entrance to The Maz. The club was everything Lance disliked. He'd found enough information on the internet in sixty seconds to know that it involved young women parading their bodies in front of men who could afford to pay for a look, and those men weren't going to be well-mannered, romantic types. He could understand that times were changing, but what self-respecting bloke wanted to be gawking at a woman's breasts the same time as a couple of hundred other men? His marriage might have ended in divorce, but it wasn't because he'd ever behaved disrespectfully. The ex-wife had been heading for her fortieth birthday and begun declaring that she felt trapped, hadn't seen enough of the world. Sure enough, she'd ended up moving all the way to the other side of Edinburgh and taking annual trips to the Costa Del Sol with a bunch of girlfriends who had a remarkable ability to remain tanned all year round. On their final day residing in the same house, Lance had asked her why she felt the need to leave him. To see more of the world? He could understand that, but why not do it together? Her reply had involved the words boring and dull. After that Lance had switched off. There were some conversations it was better not to be able to recall accurately. Whilst he didn't want to admit that one motivation for assisting Callanach was throwing off the spectre of his wife's parting words, he was aware that since she'd left he'd begun taking risks previously not in his nature. Grogsy's warning hadn't exactly been water off a duck's back, but it was the middle of the day. Knuckles and Perry were hardly likely to be roaming around outside with shotguns.

He located the car he was looking for at the rear of The Maz quite easily. The owner hadn't made any attempt to conceal it, parked as it was in the row of spaces at the rear of the club. The patch-up job on the front passenger side had been done well, but the pristine nature of the patch spoke volumes. The headlight was a new unit, compared with the rust-speckled driver's side, and it had been fitted very recently indeed. The paint work was a perfect match, although lacking the usual fine lines that an older car would have accumulated. It was, however, a tiny remnant of tape from where the paint had been sprayed that gave the work away. The devil was always in the details. Lance checked that no one was watching from any nearby windows or loitering on street corners from where he could be seen, then he took out his camera and clicked off a series of photos, ensuring he got the number plate and both headlights for comparison. Short of knocking the club door and asking to speak with the owner, that was all he could do. He slid his camera into his pack, checked again that no one was watching and made his way back to the bike. From the upper corner of the building, a black lens on a black background, hidden in the shade of the guttering, moved sideways in time with Lance's progress out of the car parking area. Less then a minute later, a tall, elegant figure slipped out of the club's backdoor.

Lance was just putting his rucksack into a pannier when a man stopped him, holding out a sheet of paper.

'Excuse me, sir? I think you dropped this,' the man said, taking hold of Lance by the shoulder as he was putting on his helmet. Lance started, instinctively pulling away, moving out of the man's reach. 'Are you all right?' the man asked.

'Yes, fine, apologies,' Lance said, settling down as the man smiled gently at him, leaving the piece of paper in his hands. He was good looking, a similar age to Lance, with the distinctive skin and hair colour that denoted eastern European forefathers in spite of the Glaswegian accent. 'I wasn't aware I'd dropped anything.'

'My mistake,' the man said. 'You have a good day.' He walked away, leaving Lance holding the paper, still breathing hard. When the hand had landed on his shoulder, he'd been convinced he would turn round to see either Knuckles or his side-kick Perry. It had all seemed like some harmless adventure until then. Now Lance wasn't so sure.

He opened up the sheet of paper to check it hadn't fallen from his rucksack.

'Happy Hour – Monday to Thursday, 7pm to 10pm. Membership rates available,' it read. 'The Mazophilia Club welcomes you.'

Chapter Forty-Five

Ava took the stairs in the station two at a time. 'Tripp!' she shouted. 'Where the hell's DC Tripp?' she yelled into the incident room.

'He's with Cordelia Muir's daughter at their house, ma'am,' someone replied.

'God-frigging-dammit,' Ava said, storming towards her office and firing up her laptop. She bit her lip until a search engine page appeared, typing in 'Dolour, meaning,' and waiting for a circle to spin irritatingly around. 'A state of great sorrow or distress,' came the result. 'Origin – Middle English via Old French from Latin; pain, grief.'

'Cocky little bastard,' Ava said.

'You mean DI Callanach, ma'am?' a voice said from the doorway.

'Bad timing for jokes, DS Lively,' Ava said. 'The man we've been calling Jeremy Dolour made his intentions very clear when he filled in his application form to volunteer at Cordelia Muir's charity. Tripp's convinced it's the same man who left Lily Eustis to die. What does your gut say?'

'Tripp's a pain in the arse, ma'am. He's the kid in class who knows the answer to every question. He'll volunteer to clean out the paint tray, and he won't even dirty his jumper in the process. He doesn't fit in, to be honest, and he's going to struggle to lead because the rest of the team perceive him as weak. The truth is though that if Tripp is certain it's the same killer, then it probably is. The boy has good instincts. Doesn't miss a trick. Worst taste in music I've ever been subjected to in a moving vehicle, but otherwise he's as good an officer as any I've worked with.'

'I think so too,' Ava said. 'Which means that moving on from Lily, where the killer wore gloves, left no DNA, kept his relationship with her secret from everybody, in one leap he inserted himself into a working situation with Cordelia Muir. That's not a normal escalation pattern, even for a psychopath.'

'He scored a victory. Lily Eustis' body was, forensically speaking, an almost unprovable murder. If he hadn't left the zip mark on her skin, we'd never have suspected anything. He's good, and once he'd worked that out, he was able to move on to something much more risky,' Lively said.

'Perhaps,' Ava said. 'Or maybe he needed a bigger thrill. Maybe he needed more contact with the world, more of a buzz. Which means that whatever he's moving onto next will be—'

'Worse,' Lively finished for her. 'There's still nothing linking the two murders, though. That's what we need if we're going to find him.'

'I got distracted when I left the Eustis' house,' Ava said. 'It was Mrs Eustis who told me what the word dolour meant, but Lily's sister Mina was there. I went upstairs to check on her. She saw the artist's impression of Jeremy and she said something strange. I can't quite remember the words she used.'

'What question did you ask her?' Lively said.

'I asked her if she recognised him,' Ava said. 'That's it. She responded with, "Why him?" I didn't think about it at the time. I assumed she meant why did we suspect that one particular person, but that wasn't it. It was more like she was asking herself. When I tried to engage her to talk about him, she said she felt ill. She even offered the information that she'd been drinking.'

'Do you want me to go back there? We can pick the sister up and bring her here if it'll help focus her mind. Maybe she doesn't want to talk around her parents,' Lively said.

'No, don't do that. She's broken. Really, deeply grieving, still in shock I think. I need someone she'll open up to.'

'How about your wee officer you've brought in from Dimitri's team? She's the size of a church mouse and maybe the pregnancy thing will work in our favour,' Lively suggested.

'That's not a bad idea. PC Monroe is working with DI Callanach at the moment, but I'll explain that we need to borrow her. Could you brief her and drive her over there. Keep the parents talking while Monroe works with Mina.' Lively stood up. 'And DS Lively, it's generally considered sexist to call a woman constable "a wee officer". Best not repeat that one.'

'Yes, ma'am,' Lively said.

'Also don't call DC Tripp a pain in the arse to me again or I'll promote him over your head, understand?' Ava said.

'Do I at least have your permission to continue being disrespectful to DI Callanach, ma'am? Only without that I can't see the point of continuing to work in MIT?'

'Get out, Lively,' Ava said, turning her attention back to her laptop. Her phone began to ring as he closed the door. 'Turner,' Ava said.

'DCI Turner, this is the Governor from Glenochil prison. I thought you should know there was an attempt on Dylan McGill's life earlier today.'

Ava put down the coffee that had been halfway to her mouth. The milk in it suddenly smelled sour.

'What state is he in?' Ava asked.

'Alive and being cared for in our hospital wing currently although I've put a transfer to a different prison in progress. There's been a substantial amount of disturbance here since it happened. I thought I should notify you.'

'Thank you,' Ava said. 'How badly is he injured?'

'He's received a total of forty-four stitches across his face. It's a nasty wound. The doctor says the nerves were likely cut. He won't be able to move certain muscles in the future. Speech therapy will be required.'

'I see,' Ava said quietly. 'Did you catch the man responsible?'

'The man we believe is responsible was found dead on the floor of the shower block less than ten minutes later. It appears someone ordered the hit on Mr McGill then decided to silence the attacker to prevent him from talking. Given that you were Mr McGill's most recent visitor, and that you seemed to have some intuition that his life might be in danger, I was wondering if you could shed any light on why Mr McGill suddenly found himself a target,' the Governor said.

'As far as the attempt on his life went, that was just a hunch. I'm afraid I can't give you any names. Believe me, if I could, I would. I was interviewing him about the recent death of a man called Louis Jones. He was a known associate of McGill's before his conviction. There are court records if you'd like to take a look,' Ava said.

'I see,' the Governor replied. 'Well, perhaps Mr McGill will be able to tell us more if he ever regains his speech.'

'Let's hope so,' Ava murmured. She put down the phone, doubled over, and forced her stomach to disobey the desire it felt to empty itself into her waste bin, wondering how she was going to live with what she'd done.

Chapter Forty-Six

PC Janet Monroe was sharp. Callanach realised that within five minutes of discussing the Louis Jones murder with her. The last time he'd been responsible for a pregnant officer, though, she'd ended up losing her baby, and nearly losing her own life too. He still hadn't forgiven himself for not taking better care of her.

'So there's no doubt that Louis Jones' car was hit by another vehicle,' Monroe was saying. 'There was recent damage to the rear of Jones' car, and forensics removed paint flecks while I was at the scene that were sent to the lab for processing.'

'I still haven't seen those results,' Callanach said. 'Presumably they will at least give us a colour, possibly even the make of vehicle involved.'

'If it's the original paint. Some manufacturers have very specific chemical footprints that we can trace,' Monroe said. 'I'm waiting for a call back from the lab to find out what stage they're at.'

Callanach looked at his phone. Lance had texted through details about Knuckles, Perry and a licence plate from an Audi with recent repairs to its front passenger headlight area. The plate had come back as registered to a Joseph Trescoe, the address was The Maz. All he needed now was to tie the paint from Jones' car to the Audi and he'd have a credible motive for researching all the relevant cars in the area. It was thin, but it was enough to start an investigation.

Ava knocked his door as he was responding to Lance's text. Monroe was on the phone so Callanach stepped into the corridor to talk.

'There's been an attempt on Dylan McGill's life in Glenochil prison,' Ava said. 'The timing is such that Trescoe must have ordered the attack. It was soon after I'd visited McGill.'

'You think Trescoe put two and two together and came up with more than four?' Callanach asked.

'I made sure he did,' Ava said. 'Knuckles and Perry realised I was no ordinary member of the public the first time I tangled with them, then a female officer visited McGill in prison. They must have assumed McGill gave me information in return for favourable treatment inside and they'll have my name from the prison visitors log by now. I'm certain Ramon Trescoe is responsible for both Begbie's and Jones' deaths. You're going to have to come up with something fast.'

'If I can tie Joe Trescoe's car to the Louis Jones accident, we can tail the vehicle until either Knuckles or Perry is driving it, then bring them in for questioning,' Callanach said. 'Hopefully we can play them off against one another.'

'They'll never spill who ordered the hit,' Ava said.

'They used Joe Trescoe's car so at the very least we can work on a conspiracy charge,' Callanach said.

'Sir' – Janet Monroe opened the office door – 'I've just heard from the forensics lab. There was a mix-up with the paint samples sent by the road traffic investigator. The evidence log shows that paint flecks were identified and bagged but between the crime scene and the lab they were misplaced or mixed-up. They can't be located.'

'That can't be right,' Ava said. 'Did you check with the road traffic investigator?'

'I did,' Monroe said. 'I've worked with him on several cases before and he's usually very thorough. He recalls taking the paint flecks. Proper procedures were followed to ensure non-contamination with other evidence. It's all in his statement.'

'So now we have literally no way of proving what type of vehicle was involved in that crash. When the hell are we going to get a break?' DS Lively headed up the corridor towards them. 'I'm sorry, Luc,' Ava murmured. 'I need to borrow PC Monroe for a couple of hours, to go with DS Lively and talk to Lily Eustis' sister. I know it's bad timing.'

'That's fine,' Callanach said. 'Looks like I'm starting all over again with Louis Jones. I'll be at Jones' business premises if you need me.'

Louis Jones' car lot-cum-home/office had yet to be cleaned up or claimed by a family member, not that anyone was likely to take it on as a going concern. Callanach forced his way into the office, leaving the door open. The lights weren't working, presumably as a result of an overdue electricity bill. The place was a mess. He played the scenario in his head. Jones knew he was on borrowed time. He'd have taken a few clothes and his wallet. Knuckles and Perry must have turned up soon after Jones fled, leaving wreckage in their wake as they searched for their boss' missing money. Ava had arrived next, not for long, but she too had trodden across the strewn debris. Dimitri's squad after that, checking for signs of Jones after the car crash. Then Callanach had sent the forensics team in when Jones' body had been found. Right now it resembled a war zone more than a business, and still no one had found anything that could help solve Jones' murder. The difference was that Callanach knew who was responsible. What he had to do was draw a line from A to B that was provable in a court of law.

He picked up the chair that had been tipped onto its side and set it behind the desk, sitting down and facing the door. One barred window looked into the car lot, the other smaller one had a view into the street. Callanach thought back to his first meeting with Jones. He was undoubtedly a man used to dealing with the tougher end of society. In his younger days he'd run with one of Scotland's most notorious organised crime gangs. It beggared belief that he wasn't ready to put up a fight when necessary. Callanach searched the desk drawers but they'd been scoured before, and it was too obvious a hiding place anyway. He ran his hands under the desk, checking for a strap or the remnants of tape. Still nothing. The floor was concrete, the ceiling missing the sort of panels that would have allowed Jones to hide anything there.

He pushed the chair back and stood up, turning slowly around. The skirting board was scuffed, the paintwork heavily worn just behind the chair. Callanach squatted down to look. The wall above the skirting had boot marks running down it. Standing up again, he set his back against the wall and ran his heel hard down onto the skirting. A long section fell away, leaving a dark cavity beyond. Callanach put his hand in, reaching his fingers around a bundle of cloth inside and pulling. Drawing on gloves, he unwrapped the bundle on Jones' desk, just as Jones himself must have done on more than a few occasions. Inside was a Glock combat pistol, modern but definitely used, and still loaded with spare ammunition alongside it. There was also a wad of notes, a mixture of tens and twenties, totalling close to one thousand pounds.

Something had made Jones leave in a hurry. So fast, in fact, that he hadn't even stopped to pick up a weapon or his stash of emergency cash. Why bother packing clothes when the gun would have been so much more useful in his predicament? And he'd found the time to feed his birds, albeit carelessly. Callanach put the gun, ammunition and cash in evidence bags then photographed the loose skirting board section and returned to his car. Nothing Jones had done made any sense. He was a man used to defending himself. He wouldn't have been scared to pull the trigger if he'd been in a corner, especially given what he knew about the men who were coming for him. There was no innocent explanation, Callanach knew that. The case was about as dirty as they got, and Ava Turner had put herself squarely in the firing line.

Chapter Forty-Seven

Mina was home alone. Mr Eustis had driven his wife to pick up a repeat prescription from a twenty-four-hour chemist. Judging by the amount of empty bottles in the kitchen, Lively thought they might also be stopping to reload on a different kind of tranquilliser. He didn't blame them. Lively had lost enough colleagues and friends over the years that the concept of losing a child was a horror he couldn't bear to imagine. He'd let Janet Monroe go upstairs to speak with Mina in her bedroom where she'd said she would feel most comfortable, but only after he'd checked the place out. Mina had gone through the motions of making them a cup of tea in the kitchen whilst Lively had slid his hands under her pillow and duvet, checking her drawers and under the bed for concealed weapons. Desperate times turned people wild, that was what he knew. Six months earlier DC Salter lay bleeding in his arms, the baby inside her already dead. He wasn't going to leave another officer to the same fate. PC Janet Monroe was an interesting one. She hadn't bothered to make conversation during the drive, taking on board only the information needed to conduct the interview. Lively liked that. Leaving Mina and Monroe to settle in one another's company for a few minutes, he crept up the stairs to sit where he could hear the conversation.

'Listen, Mina, we really need to speak with this man. It's about a lady called Cordelia Muir. She died not long after Lily. You won't have heard about it on the news because it looked like the death was accidental from consuming diet pills with a poisonous ingredient. But now it seems more suspicious and this man may be implicated.' Monroe held up the poster of Jeremy, making sure Mina directed her eyes towards it.

'The other police woman asked me earlier. I told her I don't know him,' Mina said.

'I think DCI Turner left a copy of the poster with you. Do you have it?' Monroe asked.

'Yes,' Mina said.

'Could I see it?' Monroe asked.

'Why? You've got a copy in your hands. Won't they be exactly the same?' Mina didn't move. Janet Monroe looked around the bedroom.

'We've done a couple of different versions,' Monroe lied. 'I just want to make sure the one left with you earlier is the most recent, you know, in case you're able to ask any of Lily's friends about it.'

'I'm not sure what I did with it,' Mina said, her voice dropping a few tones, eyes darting nervously to the side.

'I can help you look. My bedroom's always messy. I have no idea how I'm going to cope with a baby.' Monroe stood up and looked through the pile of papers and books on Mina's desk, keeping her back to the girl but watching her in the mirror. Mina made a play of looking on her bedside table but the tell-tale side movement of her hips was a kicking action, no question about it. Monroe went to where Mina was standing, and lifted the bedcovers to check the floor. 'There, found it. I knew it couldn't have gone far.' She pulled the A4 sheet of paper from under the bed. 'Let's sit down again, shall we?'

'Actually, I'm not feeling all that good,' Mina said faintly.

'So you told DCI Turner earlier. You really should think about trying to eat regularly, even though it's the last thing you'll feel like right now. Your body needs fuel. You can't let yourself be destroyed by grief.'

'Could you go now, please?' Mina asked.

'Very soon,' Monroe said. 'I just need to check this picture is the right one.' She held it up, checking around the edges. Here and there the paper was shabby, and in places the ink was blurred. The grubby marks across it relayed a story Mina would never have been willing to tell voluntarily. 'This has been handled, a lot. All that since DCI Turner left a couple of hours ago? Given that you don't recognise the man, that's a lot of interest in this picture.'

'I don't know him,' Mina insisted.

'What if your sister did?' Monroe asked.

'She didn't. She couldn't have,' Mina said, wiping away tears with the back of her hand.

'Why couldn't she have known him, Mina? How can you be so sure, unless he's someone you've had contact with?' Monroe let the words sit. Mina's tears became sobs, and the sobs became a howl. 'When DCI Turner asked you about this man, you said, "Why him?" Is he important to you, Mina? Someone you think is special?'

'He doesn't wear glasses, so that's not him. The other police woman said he had a stutter or a lisp or whatever. I know it's not him. Why are you pushing me? I don't want to do this. I don't want you in the house anymore. My parents will be back in a minute and when they see me this upset, they'll make a complaint, so you really should leave straight away!' By the time Mina had finished, her voice was at shouting pitch. Lively went to stand in the doorway.

312

'It's all right,' Monroe told him. 'Mina just needs some time, don't you?'

Mina looked at Lively leaning against her doorframe, and nodded. 'Yes,' she said. Lively went back to his place on the stairs.

'So this isn't your friend, right? There are obvious differences between the man we're looking for and the person you're concerned about. I understand that. The good news is that we have the fingerprints of the man we're looking for. We got them from the fridge in Cordelia Muir's office where he volunteered for a while. That means your friend can't be wrongly accused. We'll be able to eliminate him from our enquiries quickly and easily. He won't be in any trouble at all and I'm sure he'll be pleased to help. We have no interest in catching the wrong man, Mina. The sooner we talk to your friend, the sooner we can cross his name off the list and get on with finding Cordelia Muir's real murderer.'

'My friend's not a murderer,' Mina whispered.

'Exactly my point,' Monroe said. 'So actually, by not giving us his details, you're doing more harm than good. You said he doesn't wear glasses?'

'No,' Mina said.

'Where did you first meet him?' Monroe asked.

'At the university. He's studying for a Masters degree in American literature, so there's no way he was volunteering at some charity. I used to see him in the library all the time,' she said.

'That's great, Mina. Really helpful. Could you give me his name?'

Mina hesitated. 'Do I have to?' she asked.

'I think you know the answer to that already,' Monroe said.

★　★　★

313

DS Lively was downstairs radioing the information through to the incident room, while Janet Monroe continued to speak gently to the girl sobbing on her bed. 'The man's name is Christian Cadogan,' Lively said. 'He fits the description of our sketch of Jeremy albeit that Mina reports he does not wear glasses and has no stutter. Apparently, he's a mature student at Edinburgh Uni. She believes him to be twenty-seven years of age, and she's given us a temporary address in the city for him. Have uniforms check it out immediately. Ask DC Tripp to contact me, would you?'

Half an hour later, after a conversation with Mr and Mrs Eustis, they climbed back in their car. 'Shall we go straight to Cadogan's address?' Monroe asked. 'I know you want to.'

'You're on desk duties,' Lively said. 'I'm not taking you anywhere there's a disturbance likely to occur.'

'I've just been on field duties interviewing a witness, so I think we can view the rules as moveable depending on what's required,' Monroe replied.

'Argue all you like. I'm your superior and my decision is final,' Lively said.

'I'll stay in the car. We're not far away. It's a waste not to go there yourself. You have a feel for the case already. The uniforms who attend won't have your sense for what's going on,' Monroe said.

'Are you always like this?' Lively asked.

'You mean logical and honest?' Monroe answered.

By the time they arrived in Annandale Street, uniformed officers had tried the door and got no answer.

'That's not cheap,' Lively said.

'Hardly student digs,' Monroe replied. 'Mina said Christian is currently house-sitting for a friend. She was there with him a while ago, so he definitely has the keys.'

'What do we know about the place?' Lively asked the sergeant in charge of making enquiries.

'We've just spoken to a neighbour,' the sergeant replied. 'Not all of these flats are occupied yet, they're still so new. The neighbour was under the impression that the flat we're looking at is rented out for short-term lets. Holiday makers, businessmen in Edinburgh for a week at a time.'

Lively put his hands on his hips. 'There's a website, right? One where you can book these sorts of places. I can never remember the names of these things.'

'Airbnb,' Monroe said.

'Is that what the neighbour was talking about?' Lively asked. The sergeant checked his notebook and nodded. 'Clever bastard,' he said. 'He gave a different address on the Cordelia Muir application form, but that property was rented through the same website.'

'They'll have credit card details on file,' Monroe said. 'If he had the keys to this place, then he had to pay for it somehow. Let's find him.'

Chapter Forty-Eight

The briefing room was overflowing. Callanach watched Ava talking to PC Monroe and DS Lively. Her arms were wrapped around her waist, her shoulders huddled up towards her neck as if she were standing outside with no coat on. Across the room, Tripp was studiously ignoring the noise from the crowd and tapping away on his computer, eyes scrunched as he typed and clicked. An alert buzz from his mobile reminded Callanach that Lance had left him a voicemail earlier that he had yet to play. He stepped into the corridor for some quiet.

'Luc, it's Lance. I've emailed you photos of the damage to the car that hit Louis Jones', with the licence plate showing. My source confirmed the link between the thugs you were asking about – Knuckles and Brian Perry – and The Maz club. The two lads are well known in certain parts of Glasgow and they're not people you'd want to mess with. I'll fill you in properly when I get back to Edinburgh. There was one other thing, although it's probably unrelated. As I was . . .'

Ava called the briefing room to order. Callanach paused the voicemail replay and went to take a seat. Lively began by summarising the information provided by Mina about her friend

Christian Cadogan, and finished with a description of the Airbnb accommodation. Tripp stood up.

'We've done an all agencies records search and identified nine men known as Christian Cadogan over the age of eighteen in Scotland. None of them have previous convictions for anything other than driving offences, petty theft, benefits fraud or breaches of the peace, so we need to narrow down the field. More importantly, we still do not have a firm evidential link tying Cadogan to Lily Eustis' death. All we have at the moment is Mina Eustis positively identifying the artist's impression of the man who worked in Cordelia Muir's office as someone who had befriended her shortly before her sister's death. It's a link, a strong one, and he is our main person of interest, but we do not yet have a case we could take to court. Even if we find the Christian Cadogan we're looking for, currently he'll take advice from a lawyer and immediately claim coincidence. Cordelia Muir's daughter does not recognise the man we now believe to be Cadogan. She is currently picking up her seven-teen-year-old brother, Randall, from the hospital he was admitted to following a suicide attempt. DCI Turner and I will speak with Randall immediately after this briefing to ascertain if he has had any contact with Cadogan. We're still trying to make sense of this case, and where all the pieces fit. If located, remember that Cadogan may be dangerous.'

Ava stood up. 'Alarming the public by announcing that there may be a repeat killer on the loose is not an avenue we want to go down before we're sure of the facts. However, we should all be setting our minds to what Cadogan might be planning next. The Cordelia Muir killing was substantially more audacious than Lily Eustis', so either Cadogan was just finding his feet or the buzz wasn't enough the first time. That means he might do something even more reckless this time, possibly more violent or extreme. The priority is to locate him before that happens.

I'm pulling everyone off the Louis Jones investigation except PC Monroe and DI Callanach until we have Cadogan in custody. I need the university library's CCTV footage checked to see if we can identify Cadogan on the occasions when he met Mina Eustis there. What do we know about library security?'

'Students and staff have swipe cards,' a uniformed officer read from a notebook. 'But you can access the library as a visitor. You get a day pass, although you have to produce some ID.'

'We already know Cadogan's not a mature student as he claimed to Mina Eustis. He's not on the American literature course or any other, certainly not under the name Christian Cadogan,' Monroe said. 'There are cameras around the campus, some inside the library, but it's going to take a lot of checking. We have officers on their way to the university now to liaise with security.'

Callanach fetched the strongest coffee he could stomach and went back to his room. Janet Monroe was already waiting for him.

'You did well with Mina Eustis,' Callanach said. 'I'm afraid there's not much to work with as far as Louis Jones' murder goes. I found a handgun and a stack of used notes left in a concealed space in his office. Makes me wonder if he was really running at all. Maybe we got it wrong.'

'Jones had time to take the gun, but didn't? Maybe he underestimated the threat,' Monroe said, 'although he left his precious birds with a month's supply of seed dumped in their cage.'

'How did he know that he needed to leave?' Callanach asked. 'Someone either warned him or scared him, in person or by telephone.'

'I'll go back through the phone logs,' Monroe said. 'Presumably someone looked at the last incoming call?'

'That won't help. The final inward call logged was from St Leonard's police station, chasing the owner of the vehicle after the crash had been reported,' Callanach said.

'The call before that then,' Monroe said, opening the file and running her finger down the call log column. 'There's nothing before Dimitri's call for an hour, in which case Jones would have had plenty of time to have left and he'd have been well away from the outskirts of Edinburgh before the crash took place. Doesn't make sense. Someone must have tipped him off in person.' Monroe grabbed a pen and began scribbling notes. 'There's something wrong with the timings.' She tipped her head to one side.

'How do you know?' Callanach asked.

'The times are wrong between Jones' crash and the call log. Maybe it's a software glitch,' Monroe said.

'Can't be. It's all centrally logged by the telecoms provider. The time is never manually controlled. What's the problem?' Callanach asked. She didn't answer. 'Monroe?'

'The call from St Leonard's went through twenty-seven minutes before the crash was called in,' Monroe said. 'Which isn't possible. I know the crash time was recorded properly because I was one of the first on the scene. So the call log must be wrong.'

Callanach looked over her shoulder. 'How did Ava miss that?' he asked.

'DCI Turner wouldn't have had access to the road traffic accident case file at that time. She wouldn't have been able to put the timeline together accurately,' Monroe said. 'I'll contact the telecoms provider and let them know there's a fault on their system before any other investigations are compromised.'

'Monroe,' Callanach said quietly, 'what if it's not a fault and the log is right?'

'I'd have realised. I'm always careful about accurate case timelines. I was responsible for putting the file together for the Procurator Fiscal,' Monroe said.

'You'd only have been looking at the timeline on the crash, not cross-referencing it with a possible burglary.'

'But Jones' address would have been checked in any event to see if he was there. Eventually he'd have been logged as a missing person. Sooner or later the burglary would have come to my attention too.' Monroe frowned, flicking back and forwards between the files. 'Give me a minute would you, sir?' she muttered, picking up the phone. There were a few minutes of redirection of calls before she spoke again. 'Jock,' she said eventually. 'It's Monroe. Listen, I've checked out a number from an investigation log and it comes back to your extension. You know the evening we attended the Louis Jones car crash, were you at your desk when we got asked to attend that incident?' There was another pause. 'So, if you didn't call out during that period, do you have any idea who did?' Monroe's face froze briefly then went slack as her colleague answered, resting a hand over her eyes. 'Cheers Jock. No, not an issue. Just tying up the loose ends for my statement. Want to finish up all my outstanding paperwork before the baby, you know how it is. Give my love to the wife.'

She rang off, opening the call logs one last time before meeting Callanach's eyes.

'What?' he asked.

'Makes even less sense now,' Monroe said. 'A little while before we were sent over to the Louis Jones crash, my colleague was away from his desk. Returned to find CI Dimitri just ending a call. Dimitri explained that his own landline had been playing up.' Callanach thrust his hands into his pockets and stared out of the window. 'Sir, if you're thinking the Chief Inspector had anything to do with this, there's no way I wouldn't

320

have realised there was something wrong sooner or later.'

'Not if you left on early maternity leave, Callanach said. 'That left him free to finalise the prosecution papers himself,' Callanach said.

Monroe closed her notebook and looked at the floor. She stayed that way for more than a minute. 'The missing paint flecks,' she said. 'You suspect that someone made sure they went missing.'

'Not only that. There was also the speed with which Louis Jones' car was demolished. Destroying it immediately for lack of tax and insurance seems a bit hasty, especially given the fact that it had been in an unresolved accident,' Callanach added.

'This is ridiculous,' Monroe said. 'If we report these suspicions, I'll be branded a bitter employee who didn't like being told to take time off. Chief Inspector Dimitri has no motive for interfering in your investigation. None of it makes sense.'

'Louis Jones didn't take his gun with him,' Callanach said. 'If he did speak with CI Dimitri just before he fled his offices, maybe he thought he'd be safer unarmed. A man with a gun is liable to have serious, possibly lethal, force used against him by the police, and no one would have questioned it. Jones knew that perfectly well.'

'What are you going to do?' Monroe asked.

'Nothing until I can establish a motive,' Callanach said. 'Get DCI Turner on the phone and tell her I need immediate access to the case file involving Ramon Trescoe, Dylan McGill and Louis Jones. Everything that's happening now seems to be linked to that. If there's evidence to be found, it'll be in those documents. I'll be in records waiting for her to authorise their release. Make sure she knows there's not a minute to lose.'

Chapter Forty-Nine

Ava signed off release of the Trescoe case to Callanach, though what use it might be she couldn't imagine. She and Tripp were waiting in Cordelia Muir's living room when Randall arrived home. His sister had been appointed his guardian, and contact had been made with Randall's psychiatrist to ensure he was fit to be questioned about the artist's impression of the man they were now calling Christian Cadogan. Even so, it felt like an intrusion. The poor boy had just lost his only surviving parent. Life was cruel, and rarely in small doses. A part of Randall would, Ava knew, always be seventeen years old, forever stuck in that moment when his mother had been ripped from him. The things that happened during such formative years were a constant trap waiting to ensnare you at every low point throughout your life. Ava hoped his sister was up to the task of meeting Randall's needs as she dealt with her own grief.

Randall walked in looking more self-assured than Ava had expected. He'd been in shock when he'd attempted to take his own life, but the young man who held his head high as he entered the lounge seemed quite composed.

'I'm DCI Turner,' Ava said, holding out her hand to him. He took it, shaking hers with a firm grip. 'I'm sorry to meet you under these circumstances, especially when I'm sure you simply want to be left alone to settle back home.'

'That's okay,' Randall said. 'I was told you had some questions for me.'

'I do,' Ava said, opening her file. 'Would you sit down a moment? I won't keep you long.'

Randall sat, reaching a tremulous hand for the arm of the chair before lowering himself in. His composure was at least partly acted then, Ava thought, aware that she should detain him for as short a time as possible.

'I'll fetch tea,' Randall's sister said, leaving Tripp and Ava to maintain the polite facade. Randall's eyes caught the light from the miniature chandelier that hung centrally in the room, and Ava saw their glaze. His pupils were dilated, and an oily sheen decorated his skin that she suspected was more to do with medication than the pitfalls of teenage life. She had a five-minute window, no more.

'Randall,' Ava said. 'There was a man who worked for your mother, a volunteer. He called himself Jeremy. Did your mother ever mention him to you?'

'No,' Randall said. 'I didn't really ask her about the people at work. Was that wrong?'

'Not at all, I can't imagine any teenager being interested in what their parent's day in the office was like. That's not why I was asking. I just wondered if you had any information about him. Where he came from, why he was volunteering, even if it didn't seem important.'

'She never mentioned him at all. I think . . . I think we mainly talked about me and my day,' Randall said blandly. 'I don't recall ever asking about hers.'

'We've had an artist draw a likeness of him that we're circulating.

323

Would you mind taking a look? It's possible that he might have gone by a different name,' Ava said. She turned over the sketch she'd been keeping on her lap, watching Randall's face as he stared at the image. The corners of his mouth rose slightly. He held out his fingertips to gently brush the page.

'It's the wrong picture,' Randall said.

'What do you mean?' Tripp asked.

'That isn't Jeremy. You've got the wrong picture,' Randall insisted.

'Sorry about that,' Tripp said. 'Perhaps there was a mix-up at the police station. Sometimes people put things in the wrong file.'

'Yes, that must be it,' Randall murmured.

'Who is it then?' Tripp asked.

'It's my friend.' Randall smiled. 'I met him at The Fret, the club where I play.'

'Play?' Tripp asked.

'Guitar. It's what I want to do. I'm going to go professional. Everyone else thinks it's a joke but I know I can do it.'

'What's your friend's name?' Tripp asked.

'Why?' Randall said, looking up from the sketch suddenly.

'We'll need to speak to him anyway. It looks as if there's been a mix-up,' Ava said.

'What are you trying to do?' Randall asked, his voice raising a pitch.

'Randall,' Ava said softly. 'The man in this picture was also friends with a girl called Mina Eustis. Her sister, Lily, died in tragic circumstances up at Arthur's Seat. Maybe you heard about it. She was given a high dose of cannabis oil, lost consciousness and was left alone to die in the cold. Your friend is the link between the two cases.'

'It's all a mistake,' Randall muttered.

'Maybe, but it's only fair that we give your friend a chance to put the record straight, don't you think?' Tripp said.

'It's not him,' Randall repeated, his voice a low whine that made Ava's heart ache. It was as if the boy was pleading with himself, so similar to Mina's disbelief when she'd first seen the likeness of the man who'd befriended her. Cadogan was a master manipulator, able to cloak himself in different personalities, become whatever his victims needed most.

'Mina's friend's name is Christian Cadogan. That's the man in this photo. The people your mother worked with provided us with his description. We have to find him, Randall. Other people may be in danger. I know you want to protect your friend and I think that's admirable, but the best thing you can do is to tell us what you know,' Ava said.

'You think he killed my mother, don't you?' Randall said.

'I think he needs to answer some questions about why he was volunteering in your mother's office and why he gave a false name and address. It's important that we establish what his relationship was with Lily Eustis. Can you help us, Randall? You may be the only one who can,' Ava said.

'I'll help. Of course. Whatever you need,' Randall said. 'Will you give me a moment? I need to use the bathroom. Then I'll tell you everything I know.'

'Thank you,' Ava said, leaning forward and taking his hands between hers. 'I know this is terribly hard. Losing a parent is devastating. I can't even start to imagine how you feel, but I want you to know that you're not responsible for any of this. Whoever is guilty of your mother's death, you couldn't have foreseen it and you couldn't have stopped it.'

'That's a very gracious speech, DCI Turner,' Randall said, adopting the language he'd heard his mother use so often.

Ava flinched. The boy's words had been kind and softly spoken, but buried within them was a steel she hadn't expected.

His sister entered with a tea tray and began handing out cups and saucers as Randall, humming a lullaby, began to ascend the stairs.

Lance Proudfoot became aware of the car parked next to his garage only once he'd lifted the door to wheel his beloved and ancient motorbike inside. He'd spent the afternoon at his office updating his news website, not that having access to one of Edinburgh's senior police officers was winning him any exclusives. He was reduced to just feeding through whatever Police Scotland chose to tell the press, as and when it suited them. The trip to Glasgow had been fun, though, woken him up. He should look up a few more of his mates from the days before his knees got too creaky to play rugby and his bank balance got too low to go drinking every weekend. He still hadn't heard back from the voicemail he'd left Luc Callanach, but nothing new there. Getting him to return calls had been an uphill struggle since the day they'd met.

Closing the garage door, he clocked the fact that there were two men sitting inside the vehicle. A window was open issuing smoke and a radio was emitting sounds best reserved for personal headphones. Lance was making a mental note of the licence plate – you could never be too careful, there were plenty of burglaries in the area – when the driver's door opened suddenly.

'Are you Mr Proudfoot?' the driver asked.

'Why would you be looking for him?' Lance replied. The man asking the questions wasn't all that physically imposing but he had a face that suggested an uncanny ability to find trouble and maximise its outcome.

The second door opened. The man who climbed out of that one was a giant. That was Lance's first thought. The second was that they had his address. They didn't just happen to be sitting outside the correct row of garages by chance. And if they had his address, it was just a short walk to his front door and to his son who was sitting, oblivious, probably playing a computer game inside.

'That's a nice motorbike,' the man mountain said. It was a Glasgow accent, no question. 'Taken any fun trips on it lately?'

'I don't want any trouble,' Lance said.

'What sort of trouble were you anticipating?' the driver asked.

Lance tightened his fist around his keys, keeping one key poking out between his fingers ready to strike a blow that might give him enough time to run away screaming for help. He was tough and he wasn't anybody's fool, but this was a quiet back-alley. The line of garages covered the view to one side, walls at the rear of the apartment blocks to the left and right provided cover from overlooking windows. Unless someone else drove in right now, no one would ever know what had happened to him. He was prepared to fight, but he was no match for two men at once. Perhaps in his twenties he had been, at a stretch in his thirties. At this age, these lads would just laugh at him.

'The problem with you holding your keys like that is that it makes me nervous,' the big one said, walking to stand behind him whilst the driver stood in front. 'When I'm nervous I get a bit twitchy.'

'If you just tell me what you need to know, I'm sure this can be resolved easily,' Lance said, trying to figure out which pocket of his motorcycle jacket he'd zipped his mobile into.

'Oh, okay, that's fine then. What we want to know is why you were nosing around the back of The Maz taking photos. What our boss wants to know is what type of food you like?'

Knuckles and Perry, Lance thought. I am most royally fucked.

'What type of food I like? Why would your boss care about that?' Lance asked, wondering how fast he could run with his adrenalin boosting him, and whether or not his heart would pack in before they caught up.

The cosh connected with the back of Lance's head before he had time to finish the risk assessment. 'Because you're coming for dinner at ours,' Knuckles laughed, tucking the stick under his arm as he and Perry took a leg each and dragged Lance the few metres to the back seat of their car and the waiting roll of gaffer tape.

Chapter Fifty

Randall fixed a smile on his face and began to ascend the domestic mountain before him. He reminded himself to grip the handrail, and how his leg muscles needed to relax then tense to mount each step. He nodded at the photograph of his mother and father that watched his progress from the adjacent wall.

'Goodnight, Mum. Goodnight, Dad,' he said quietly as he passed them.

From the lounge below came the clinking of cups and saucers, the tinkle of tea spoons making their progress around the cups. It was strange. He'd never been so aware of sound before. Or of the knife-edge shadows the lights cast just below the rim of each stair. The scent of furniture polish drifted from the bannister as he ran his hand along it, courtesy of his sister who had embraced cleaning to scour the grief from her skin. He drank it all in. It tasted of loss.

In the time it took him to arrive at the top of the stairs he had been able to conjure Christian's face in his mind, his real face, not the flat, loveless monstrosity the police had recreated. Why they had him wearing glasses in the sketch was curious, unless he needed them for reading. That might explain why Randall had never seen him wearing them. And the police had missed the inch long, pale scar to the left of his mouth, so faint he could understand why they'd failed to see it. The scar had made him more human, less difficult for Randall to like. It had made the blonde hair and strong jaw easier to take. Christian's eyes were deeper set than the sketch portrayed. How had his mother's employees spent so much time with him and seen so little, when Randall had been deprived of those hours, having the most cursory glimpse into Christian's world and yet had noticed so much.

His mother's bathroom was pristine. The drawers through which he had rummaged had been carefully rearranged. Fresh flowers adorned a vase. Taps shone as if no fingerprints had ever marred their surfaces. His sister needed counselling, Randall thought, for when she ran out of things to clean and simply had to sit and mourn.

The mirror called; there was only so long you could stand in a bathroom without looking at yourself. Randall had lost weight. His cheekbones were a cruel slash across his face. His hair had grown longer, and it suited him. Perhaps that was what Nikki from The Fret might have found attractive. The version of Randall that was more wild, more edgy. Oddly enough, he thought, it was a version that better resembled Christian. How long had he known him? A few months, he guessed. Longer than the time his friend had allegedly – that was silly, why lie to himself now? – longer than his friend had been volunteering at his mother's charity.

Therein lay the problem. Randall could ride the magic carpet of medication and float above the almost certain knowledge that Christian had been involved in his mother's death. He could wipe away the tears he'd shed when his friend had stopped returning his calls after the hospital admission. But he couldn't ignore the facts. Randall opened a drawer and let his fingers drift across the vanity detritus within. Christian had found him, befriended him. Christian had even listened to him moaning about his home, life, about the restrictions his mother had imposed on him.

Randall found what he'd been looking for. He undid his trousers, let them fall to his ankles and sat down on the toilet seat, making himself properly comfortable.

Christian had bromanced him, that's how social media would report it. He had made Randall feel understood, buddied up, cool, been exactly what Randall had needed just when he'd needed it most. He laughed. There was a song in there somewhere, from a generation ago.

The pain that medication had not dulled – that no amount of pills would ever be able to diminish – was that Randall had felt the truth from the second he had seen Christian's face on the police woman's lap. Randall had all but sent Christian to his mother. His weakness and neediness, those things he had so ridiculously thought Christian had somehow been sent to assuage, were what Christian had been looking for. In pouring out his heart, Randall might as well have poisoned his mother himself.

There were different types of pain. He hadn't appreciated that before, but now he could write a paper on the subject. There was the pain of loss. There was shocked pain, where every word was a physical blow. There was the slow, dull ache of reality as it leaked inside every time you made the mistake of waking up, followed by that mewling baby, self-pity. Then there was a gulf. Randall thought he'd fallen into it once, but even that had been a false sense of security. He was finally at the bottom and it wasn't as dark as he'd hoped. Sadly, he could still see the faces of his mother and father staring down at him from the top, disappointed half-smiles on their faces. He might

331

have been stupid before but now he was gifted with the most outstanding clarity. This feeling, this self-loathing, would never leave him. Not for one single second. And still it played second fiddle to his guilt.

He took the razor blade in his hand. His sister had hidden them well, but not that well.

The worst of it all, the bullet wound in his soul, was that Randall still missed Christian. Where there should have been hatred, vitriol, rage, there was only the sad knowledge that his friend would never sit with him again, never slap him on the back. The low, vile creature he was still craved Christian's attention. He did not deserve one single additional breath.

Randall looked downwards, careful to ensure that his inner thigh was positioned fully over the toilet bowl. It hardly seemed fair on his obsessed sister to leave mess where she had created order. With the blade between his fingers, he slashed hard and deep across the inside of his thigh, careful to ensure that he worked his way through both skin and muscle to expose the artery. This, surprisingly, was not painful at all. The life flowed from him without drama. No one could label it a cry for help. No one would worry about his future care. Christian could mourn his loss, or not. It didn't matter now. Randall had been told it would only take a minute or so if he did it right. That was the ridiculous benefit of being committed with other similarly-minded teenagers. There was plenty of good advice on hand for those with tough enough constitutions.

Randall hoped his sister would be able to forgive him. He had failed at existing as his family had wanted him to. He had failed at protecting the mother he had not known was the centre of his world until he was without her. He had even failed at making a friend.

The sob that had been threatening to leave his mouth became

a croak. Randall closed his eyes and recalled the last time his mother had hugged him. She had kissed his temple and put her love into clean, clear, beautiful words.

The water beneath him bloomed red. He collapsed.

Chapter Fifty-One

Ava was on her feet first, as if she'd been expecting it, only that was hindsight speaking. She sprinted up the stairs, hammering her shoulder into the locked bathroom door. Down in the lounge a woman was shrieking. They had all known, the second they'd heard the thud of Randall's collapsing body. There was no mistaking some sounds, even if you'd never heard them before and never would again.

She kicked the lock, splintering wood and sending a shard of pain from foot to knee. The sensation dulled when she saw Randall. There were few recently dead bodies she would not have attempted to revive, but Randall had emptied himself of life by a method that was utterly irrevocable. The toilet bowl spoke a story she wished she had never served in the police long enough to see. He had been strong and brave, holding himself in place until almost all was spilled. There was a puddle on the tiled floor, but new grouting would fix that. All in all, there was remarkably little to see for a scene shot through with so much horror.

She raised a hand to Tripp who was sprinting upwards towards her.

'Keep everyone downstairs,' she said. 'Call Ailsa.'

'No ambulance?' Tripp tried, the desperation clear in his voice.

'Too late,' Ava said, kneeling down and checking hopelessly for a pulse, for something to do. 'Christian Cadogan, you fucking bastard,' Ava muttered to herself.

Tripp was silent for the journey back to the station. Ava kept herself busy listening to the radio, but the noise in her head was louder. Randall Muir's death was their fault. The psychiatrist may have declared Randall fit to be questioned, but Ava had known better when she'd seen his blank eyes. In her need to achieve a resolution, she had caused another death. A seventeen-year-old boy had been pushed too far. That's what the inevitable investigation would conclude. And rightly bloody so.

'That was nothing to do with you, Tripp,' she said, pulling up to park.

'Ma'am, you can't take responsibility,' Tripp said.

'That's exactly what I have to do, Detective Constable,' Ava said. 'I need you to type up the notes of our meeting with Randall. Then I need you to make a statement because there's going to be an enquiry into how I handled it. You are not to soft-soap, minimise or deflect. Do you understand me?'

'Ma'am, I . . .' Tripp tried again.

'I'll take that as a yes,' Ava said, climbing out of the car and walking away.

Ava made it to her office before fury took her. The mug a college mate had bought her years ago proclaiming her to be the world's best friend flew to a corner of the room, raining pottery shards across the floor, stagnating coffee showering her desk with droplets. The chair on which visitors sat became a weapon, destroying the already dying yucca plant, fracturing its pot, and leaving a jumble of debris in its wake. The photo of Ava taken the day she had been promoted to Detective Chief Inspector proved the ideal place for her fist to vent its wrath. Callanach approached from behind, kicking the door closed as he strode across to grab her, wrapping his arms around hers, lifting her feet off the ground as she fought him.

'Ava,' he said softly. 'Ava, Tripp told me. Let me help.'

He lowered her to the floor, sitting with her, holding her tight against his chest until the shaking subsided.

'Nothing you say will make any difference,' Ava said. 'That boy bled out above my head while I drank tea and made small talk about biscuits. If I'd been vigilant, I'd have known he wasn't in a fit state. Randall Muir would still be alive now.'

'You're trying to solve two murders,' Callanach said, 'and prevent another, maybe more than one, from taking place. You know enough about killers with this profile to know Christian won't stop until he's caught. What were you supposed to do? Wait a week, even just a day, to ask Randall Muir what he knew? You'd have been swapping one dead body for another.'

Ava pulled away from him. 'I'm not up to this, Luc. I don't want to do it anymore. It's too hard. Now I know why Begbie always looked so exhausted, why he ate too much crap and hid a bottle of whisky in his desk. When the pressure's on it's like quicksand. I thought I could make a difference, but all I've done since I was promoted is lose the people I'm supposed to protect.'

Callanach stretched out, lying full on the floor, staring at the ceiling. 'It's not just you, Ava. The buck doesn't stop at your door. Every woman and man in MIT, the uniformed officers who provide backup, the forensics teams, the civilian administrators. All one team, working for a single cause. You think you're responsible because you're emotionally invested in these cases? If you weren't, there would be something very wrong with you.'

'Wrong like Overbeck?' Ava asked, wiping her eyes with her sleeve and brushing her hair back from her face.

'Exactly like our beloved Detective Superintendent,' Callanach said. 'But you're not her. So don't quit now. There's too much at stake.'

Ava let her body roll backwards onto the floor, lying at Callanach's side and putting one hand beneath her head. 'I feel like shit,' she said. 'Tell me what to do.'

'*Respirez juste une minute,*' he said, twisting onto his side to look at her. 'Just breathe for one minute. All these problems will still be here sixty seconds from now, and you'll be ready to deal with them.'

Ava closed her eyes, forced her body to relax, and made her mind blank. She had been lurching from crime scene to crime scene, crisis to crisis, without stopping to take control of it all. Police work was in large measure about being reactive. At this point she needed to be proactive, to out-think, out-manoeuvre Christian Cadogan. By the time she opened her eyes, Callanach was sitting up and leaning against her desk. She stood.

'I'm better,' she said. 'Thank you.'

'I see that,' he replied, 'but you're allowed to crumble from time to time, Ava. Having emotions is what separates us from the sociopaths.' He walked towards the door.

'Hey, you asked for permission to read the original Louis Jones case file. Did you find anything?' she asked.

Callanach shook his head. 'Just being thorough,' he said. 'Nothing for you to worry about.'

It had been well hidden, no doubt about it. The casual observer would never have found it. But Callanach had known what he was looking for in the file and, sure enough, tucked away in the police officers' notebooks, in the list of materials deemed unnecessary to prove the case, was what he'd been searching for. In the previous investigations of Ramon Trescoe, one Police Constable Dimitri had been first to the scene. Searching Ramon's premises, PC Dimitri, then just twenty-one years of age, had found no relevant evidence. Interviewing Dylan McGill, PC Dimitri had – in his naivety or so it had appeared – failed to properly caution the suspect and the evidence was thrown out at trial. Only when Begbie began working with Louis Jones had a case been put together that did not fail. There was no doubt that Chief Inspector Dimitri had been on the gang's payroll for decades. While they'd been away, he'd risen through the ranks, and now Dimitri was everything Trescoe and McGill could ever have dreamed he would be.

Ava didn't need to know. She was in enough danger. Messing with Trescoe's boys, trying to investigate Begbie's death under the radar, protecting his widow against retribution and financial ruin. A line had already been crossed. Callanach had to fix it without involving her. He put his head around the incident room door.

'DS Lively,' he said, 'I'm swapping PC Monroe back onto the Eustis and Muir murders. I'll need some help with the Louis Jones case though. You're with me.'

'Does Monroe not make your coffee quite how you like it, sir?' Lively asked, to a round of laughter.

'I don't need anyone with such a high IQ on my investigation,' Callanach said. 'Thought you'd do perfectly. My office, two minutes.'

Lively appeared ten minutes later.

'I'm more use out there. That bastard's going to strike again. Monroe is desk-bound anyway and the Jones case is a dead end . . .'

'Sit down and keep your voice down,' Callanach said. For once Lively did as he was told without question or comment. 'There's a corrupt police officer helping cover up the Jones murder. Just how much crap will rain down on MIT if we expose him?'

'Well, that's going to start a shit-storm of a magnitude no amount of umbrellas will protect us from. Who knows?' Lively asked.

'Me, you, Monroe.'

'You're certain about this, are you?' Lively checked.

'I don't have any tape recordings of him making a drunken confession to a prostitute, if that's what you had in mind. Do I doubt my judgement? No. I believe it goes back many years,' Callanach said.

'So, what's stopping you from reporting it?' Lively asked.

'I want to convict Louis Jones' murderers first. If they figure out we know who's helping them, they'll disappear. Also, the police officer involved outranks me. We're going to need to prove more than a series of evidential blunders and a telephone call that happened earlier than it should have done.'

Lively leaned forward in his chair. 'Please do not tell me you are about to take down a chief fucking inspector. That'll be career suicide for everyone involved. As I recall, you've some experience with that from Interpol, so maybe think again about giving it a second bash, no?'

'It's organised crime. The main players have been off the streets for a long time, but they're out of retirement and gearing up to get back in the game. More people will die, Sergeant. They need to be stopped, Dimitri included. What do you know about him?'

Lively gave a quick, wry smile. Callanach got the impression the Detective Sergeant wasn't all that surprised to hear Dimitri's name. 'He's popular with a small band of the old type and some of the younger ones who're willing to do anything to get convictions,' Lively said. 'The brass like him because he gets things done. Personally, I wouldn't trust him as far as I could throw him, but that won't help. You'll need to incriminate him in the middle of something big. No half measures or we'll all be wondering what's going to happen to our pensions.'

'I'm giving you the chance to walk away from this. If you don't want to run the risk with your career, then fair enough. You decide,' Callanach said.

'It's not like I can leave a former aftershave model to handle it on his own, is it? You might break a nail. Besides which it's almost impossible to understand anything you say with that accent. You could accuse Dimitri of assassinating JFK and no one would have a clue what you were talking about. My personal feelings about you aside, sir, a team's a team. You're in Scotland now. This is how we do things.'

Chapter Fifty-Two

Tripp, Monroe and three other officers paraded into Ava's room carrying nine files between them. They sat down.

'What do we know?' Ava asked.

'Of all the Christian Cadogans we can find, two have military backgrounds,' Tripp said. 'One served time abroad in active war zones, the other was a flight instructor. Neither has a disciplinary record and we have good background checks on them.'

'Any chance the one who saw active service is suffering post-traumatic stress disorder, making him delusional and dangerous?' Ava asked.

'If that's the case, it's not indicated in his medical records. Left the army with commendations. Currently works in private security,' Tripp said. 'Of the nine men with the same name, we can exclude three on an age basis, and two who aren't caucasian. Leaves us with four.'

'We've been through the DVLA records and cross-checked against the passport office. There are photographs of all the possible candidates. None is a visual match,' Monroe said.

'People can change their hair colour, wear contact lenses, use prosthetics. The photos could be a lie, or his current look could be a disguise. The name too, for that matter, but it's all we've got for now. I want the outstanding four interviewed, and I mean today. Contact the relevant police authorities. I'll speak with the brass and get the enquiry extended. What else do we know?' Ava asked.

'Randall talked about playing guitar. His sister told me about a club he'd been attending. His family knew all about it, apparently, although his mother didn't let on as she wanted Randall to feel he was pushing boundaries in a controlled way,' Tripp said. 'It's called The Fret. I just had a call from the officers who circulated the artist's impression of Christian Cadogan there for verification. Staff have confirmed the likeness and say they saw him with Randall on more than one occasion. The manager also said there were rumours a barmaid had a one-night stand with Cadogan. I'm waiting for the address, then we'll be straight round to see her. What's interesting is the timescale. Randall and Cadogan have been going to the club for months. That means Cadogan met Randall before he started volunteering at Cordelia Muir's charity.'

'You think he targeted Cordelia because of Randall? How does that fit with Lily and Mina?' Ava asked.

'I'm not sure. The sisters were close, on everyone's account. Their parents, Mina herself, friends, even their social media posts were full of nothing but love for each other,' Tripp said.

'Jeremy, aka Christian, gave his surname as Dolour,' Monroe interjected. 'Grief. That's what he's achieved. It's almost as if the murders were incidental. He befriended two young people, identified their primary source of love, and took it from them.'

'Which would explain why he didn't care about being present for the actual deaths,' Ava said. 'The killings weren't the point. He wanted to experience Mina and Randall's grief first-hand, close-up.'

'Sick piece of shite,' one of the other officers muttered.

'Sick and dangerous,' Ava said. 'DC Tripp, go ahead and release the artist's impression to the public. Keep the name quiet for now. Anyone suspecting they've seen him should contact us. If we make him run without catching him, he'll just cross a border and start killing again under a new name. Get hold of that barmaid, see what she knows. Report straight back to me as soon as we've checked every Christian Cadogan in person. Timer's running out of sand. No one goes home until we've made some progress.'

'Hey, how's it going? I'm sorry, you won't remember me. We met at the auditions for that theatre group. I'm Jackson, and you're Sean, right?' The man held out his hand.

Sean shook it. 'Wow, great memory. That was a crazy day, it's all a bit of a blur to me now. Are you having lunch? This is a great bar, although almost too close to the theatre. I have to force myself to walk past and buy a sandwich instead most days. Not enough willpower for that today, obviously!'

'Yeah, I was supposed to meet a friend here for a drink but she got caught in traffic. I guess this is really close to the theatre. I hadn't thought about it. What are you rehearsing at the moment?' Jackson perched on the edge of a chair as Sean swallowed a mouthful of sandwich before answering.

'The Arts Council commissioned this great new play about the death of one generation giving birth to the next, from the perspective of the ghosts of the forefathers. It's about loss, regret, hope and change. Beautiful writing. You should come and see it,' Sean said. 'What about you? Are you working at the moment?'

'Filling in, bit of this, bit of that. An actor's life, you know how it is.'

Sean laughed. 'Do I ever? Would you like to join me? I'm just grabbing a bite of lunch before I get back to it, but I'm not waiting for anyone.'

'Just for a minute then,' Jackson said. 'I'm out shopping, not that I can afford it at the moment, but I've got a free pass for a night club tomorrow night. The Lost Boys, do you know it?'

'I do. I quite often end up there myself on Friday nights. Who're you going with?' Sean asked.

'It's a Billy No Mates night out. I'm quite new to the scene here. Thought I'd see if I could meet some new people,' Jackson said. 'I never know what to wear the first time at a club. Somehow I always end up sticking out like a sore thumb.'

'It's a mostly denim kind of place,' Sean said. 'Definitely dress down rather than to impress. Listen, do you want me to meet you there? I know tons of people. I can introduce you, help you out. I know how it feels to start in a new city. If I hadn't met my partner, Brad, I'd probably have given up and gone back to Belfast.'

'I don't want to put you out,' Jackson said.

'Don't talk daft. We'd have ended up there anyway after a few glasses of wine, we always do. Ten o'clock, okay? I'll meet you outside,' Sean said.

'I won't say no,' Jackson said, standing up, 'but you have to let me get the drinks. Looks like I have some new jeans to buy. See you tomorrow.'

Christian waited until he'd diverted into a new street before texting Bradley.

'Can't wait any longer. I know it was the right thing to break up with my fiancée. You're all I can think about. Can we talk tomorrow tonight? I'm busy earlier on, but we could meet somewhere at about 10.30pm.' He pressed send.

It was five minutes before Bradley replied. 'Sean out clubbing tomorrow night. I've made my excuses. If you fancy coming here we'll have the flat to ourselves.'

'Only if you're sure. Be nice to have some privacy. Text me the address. Can't wait,' Christian replied before putting his phone away. He really did have shopping to do, although not the kind that could be accomplished in the high street. An appointment had been made with the sort of man who went by a single name, usually regarded as a noun. He couldn't quite recall what it was. Wolf? Coyote? Something canine, ridiculous and a clear signal to the authorities that he would neither pay taxes nor park legally. Then Christian would need to rest. He could function when tired, but his memory wouldn't be as sharp, the enjoyment not quite so acute. Bradley wanted him but was still in love with dear, insignificant Sean. It would make for an odd combination of loss and guilt, not dissimilar to what Randall had experienced. Apparently, the boy had committed suicide. It had been inevitable, Christian had known that from the second he met him. There was so much about Randall that had been pathetic. So convinced that he hated his mother, when all he'd ever really expressed was his dependence on her, and entrenched love of her. The only other female Christian had ever heard him long for was that slut of a barmaid – Nikki – and he'd made sure she wouldn't bother looking in Randall's direction. A few beers, a sympathetic ear and one night in her bed had accomplished that. He couldn't have the boy turning to anyone other than him in his hour of need. That would have defeated the object. Just like Bradley. Christian would be there when he was needed.

Chapter Fifty-Three

Nikki Breakwater, The Fret's much admired barmaid, opened the door to her Craighouse Terrace bedsit wearing an inside out t-shirt and pyjama bottoms. 'What?' she said, looking Tripp up and down. 'You're polis. I paid that fine.'

'You're not in any trouble, Miss Breakwater. Can I come in so we can talk?' Tripp asked.

'About?' she asked.

'This man,' Tripp said, holding up the sketch of Christian Cadogan. 'Your manager at The Fret thought you might be able to tell us a bit about him.'

'Five minutes,' Nikki sighed. She backed into the sparse room, leaving Tripp to follow as she threw herself onto the bed, lighting a cigarette.

'Do you mind if I open a window?' Tripp asked.

'Do you mind changing the season from winter to summer first, or agreeing to pay my heating bill?' Nikki replied. Tripp stood as far away from the smoke as he could manage. 'What is it you want to know?'

'What name did he go by in The Fret?' Tripp asked.

'I only ever called him Chris, but I think it was something posher than that,' Nikki said. 'What's he done?'

'We need to eliminate him from our enquiries in a serious matter, so any information that helps us find him will be very important. We can treat anything you tell us in confidence if that makes you feel easier,' Tripp said.

'Oh my God, that was proper policeman spiel, that was. How much do you know?' she asked.

'We understand that you and Chris may have become intimately acquainted. Sorry to ask you such private questions, but it's an important matter,' Tripp said.

'We screwed once, about three weeks ago, if that's what you're asking,' she said. Tripp winced. 'Fucktard never phoned, didn't show up to The Fret again afterwards and left me with dirty sheets. Whatever he's done, I never want to see him again.'

Tripp looked at the bed she was slouched across. The sheets were hanging out from beneath a grubby blanket, grey at the edges, the pillow case shining yellow with grease.

'Um, Nikki, this may be a bit personal. Please don't be offended. I was wondering if you'd washed your sheets since your evening with Chris?'

'Are you judging me?' Nikki asked. 'There's no bloody washing machine here, pal. I'm not even on minimum wage. I work 'til three in the morning. Do you think I want to spend my day at the launderette? How often do you wash your sheets anyway?'

'I'm not judging at all. I can't even start to imagine how hard things are. You should be proud that you have a job. Many people wouldn't bother. But if you haven't washed your bedding then Chris' DNA will still be on it. If we can find him soon, you might be helping us save lives. I need to put that sheet and the pillowcase in a bag and take it away. You won't get it back, as it'll be evidence. What I can do is give you £20 to buy new bedding instead. You'll just need to give a statement about Chris and tell us who else's DNA might be on there, so we can exclude them.'

'Just mine, you cheeky scrote. You think because I'm a barmaid that I pass myself around?'

'Not at all, but I had to ask. Could I get you to stand up so I can strip the bed, please?' Tripp took a twenty-pound note from his wallet and handed it over as he took an evidence bag from his other pocket. Ten minutes later he was racing towards the forensics lab, blues and twos flashing and wailing as he radioed the news in to the control room.

'Just do the frigging press conference already,' Detective Superintendent Overbeck told Ava. 'I'm not standing up there to do it for you. This bizarre balls-up of an unproven serial killer case is not having my face attached to it. And don't give it to one of your underlings. Take responsibility, Turner. It comes with the pay grade.'

'I understand that ma'am, but the press liaison office can read out a prepared statement with the artist's impression. There's no need for me to be involved personally,' Ava said.

'Unless you count the fact that I'm telling you to. In case you're interested, I am in the process of explaining the death of a seventeen-year-old boy to the board, no less than the son of a murder victim, that occurred when you and DC Tripp were on the premises having just interviewed him. So my recommendation is that you follow orders and don't add to my currently excruciating list of MIT fuck-ups. How about that?' Overbeck said.

'I think that's clear,' Ava said. 'I'll have my report on Randall Muir's death on your desk tomorrow.'

'You'll email it to me before midnight tonight. I'm in front of the board tomorrow trying to save your arse and present a vaguely believable answer to the question of why I thought you were qualified for the post of Detective Chief Inspector. If it helps, you might just be able to keep your job if you can stop the people of Edinburgh from being terrified in their beds at the thought of a serial poisoner roaming the streets unchecked and befriending their precious children.' Overbeck hung up. Ava stared into the receiver. As harsh as it felt, Overbeck was only dishing out what Ava knew she deserved. Avoiding the press conference had been a long shot, and it was for one reason only. If Knuckles and Perry hadn't identified her yet, they sure as hell would after her face had been splashed all over the press. Too late now. And Overbeck was right. Ava had to make amends for Randall Muir's death.

She phoned the press liaison office. 'Press conference, one hour. Get as many outlets there as you can. Make it clear it's a big story. We want maximum air time and column space. Online press as well.'

The press liaison office went into action. The deadline wasn't a problem. Stories like those guaranteed viewers and newspaper sales. The media would be all over it. In an hour's time the phones would start ringing and they wouldn't stop all night. They began making calls, television first and the larger news outlets after that. Finally, they reached out to the online press, using mobile numbers to ensure attendance rather than simply emailing.

Nearing the bottom of their list, a press officer dialled Lance Proudfoot's number. It went to voicemail. The officer cut off the message and tried dialling a second time. That time the call was cut off in the middle of ringing without passing through to voicemail. The press liaison officer gave up and moved on to the next name, at exactly the same moment as Lance's mobile was put out of action forever.

Chapter Fifty-Four

Pollok wasn't Glasgow's finest area – that was how Lively had described it to Callanach – and it seemed a fair assessment as they drove through looking for Brian Perry, The Maz's hired muscle. The housing had a lifeless air. December might have been to blame, but people walked with hoods up, avoiding eye contact, and there was little sense of community spirit. DS Lively had let slip to a few of Dimitri's known police associates that MIT had a firm lead on one of Louis Jones' killers, and that a raid was planned to facilitate an arrest at 3am when the suspect would hopefully be asleep and taken unawares. That was why they were approaching Perry's flat at 3pm. A quick check of his local authority information confirmed that Perry lived alone, which was why they had chosen his address over father of three, Knuckles. It was going to be a long day but Callanach's senses were telling him that the excruciating hours of piss-taking from Lively would all be worth it in the end.

He let Lively knock on the door while he waited round a corner. That had been Lively's idea. In the Detective Sergeant's words, Perry was no way going to open the door to a man who looked like a ladies' underwear salesman. Callanach admitted that whilst Lively could have been less insulting about it, he had a point.

Lively hammered on the inset glass pane a few times. A huge figure appeared in blurred outline a couple of minutes later.

'Yeah, what?' Perry bellowed.

'I've got some info that my boss wants sending on to your boss. Too much heat to go straight to The Maz at the moment. We think there might be surveillance,' Lively said.

'How did you find me? Knuckles usually deals with this stuff,' Perry shouted.

'We're polis, you numpty. Finding people's what we do. Dimitri said you'd help. Now let me in before the entire population of Pollok knows you've a cop on your doorstep having a cosy wee chat.'

'Load of fuckin' bollocks this is,' Perry mumbled as he opened the door. 'I'm not even working at the moment. Supposed to be able to have a lie in. I was at the club until 2am this morning. Don't you shites ever rest? Come on then, get inside.'

Lively stepped into the kitchen and drew his taser, pointing it directly at Perry's bare chest. 'Take my advice, don't try and run. This hurts like a bugger on bare skin.' Callanach entered behind him, closing and locking the door.

Perry was all bulging eyes and jitters. 'Aw no way, man, I've had enough of friggin' tasers to last me a lifetime. Dimitri can't do this. He doesn't want to fall out with Ramon. Have you lost your minds?'

'Calm down, Mr Perry,' Callanach said. 'You don't need to worry about anything. As long as you do as we ask, you won't be harmed. Do you have any coffee?'

'Who are you?' Perry shouted. 'Who the fuck's he?' he directed at Lively, pointing to Callanach. 'I've met Dimitri's men. I sure as hell never met him before. I'd remember that one.'

'We only wheel the pretty cops out for very special customers,' Lively said. 'Now, would you be more comfortable sitting here in the kitchen or going through to the lounge? If you ask nicely we might let you put a jumper on, only those armpits are level with my nose, and they're not making me feel very welcome.'

'You don't work for Dimitri,' Perry mumbled, casting his eyes backwards over his shoulder as he trudged into the lounge.

Lively smiled. 'I've been on the force three decades, man. You think I can't tell when someone's about to try and bust out on me? I'd hoped it would be more civilised than this, but however you want it. On the floor, son.'

'I'm co-operating,' Perry said.

'I'm delighted. Now lie on the floor on your stomach with your fingers laced on the back of your head.' Lively extended the taser until it was no more than inches from Perry's neck. 'You should see the burns these things leave. If you're really out of shape it can give you a heart attack. I hope you don't mind my saying but a little more vitamin D and giving the chips a miss might be an idea.'

Perry hit the taser away and made a dash for the hallway. Callanach followed, kicking him hard in the back of one of his knees and sending the big man crashing to the floor. The sound of Perry's knee caps hitting tiles made Lively wince.

'Oh come on, I told you not to. I'll be amazed if one of those knees isn't broken.' Lively kicked Perry in the side. He rolled over clutching his knees to his chest. 'Now I've got no choice but to tie you up and I won't be able to hand you a nice cup of tea.'

Callanach picked up a chair, grabbed Perry under the arms and hauled him up, securing his wrists with handcuffs.

'Don't touch my legs,' Perry screamed. 'My right knee's broken, I swear it is. I need to get to the hospital. You bastards!

First that fucking police woman tasers me in the balls, now you've broken my leg. Aw, Christ that hurts!'

'Which police woman would he be talking about?' Lively asked Callanach.

'Probably best not to ask too many questions,' Callanach said. 'Is he secure?'

'He's going nowhere,' Lively replied. 'If you're making coffee, though, I strongly recommend rinsing those cups with boiling water. My instinct is that Mr Perry here is unfamiliar with proper housekeeping traditions.'

Callanach smiled. 'Sugar?' he asked.

'Two, thank you. Very kind of you, sir,' Lively said. He had a policy of enjoying every cup of tea he drank. The way Lively figured it, you never knew which brew might turn out to be your last.

Chapter Fifty-Five

Ava was reviewing the reports on the various men in the UK known as Christian Cadogan. It was useless. Every one of them could be excluded. Responses from the press conference were starting to flood in, but the problem was following up the reports. A couple of additional positive identifications from The Fret's regular crowd had been noted, and another from the newsagents near Cordelia Muir's offices, but nothing advancing the enquiry.

DC Tripp was still at the lab waiting for the DNA from the sheet to be analysed. Some things couldn't be rushed, but Ava had ordered him to remain there until the results were in.

'So if we work on the assumption that Christian Cadogan is not his real name, then it's either random in which case he's played a blinder wasting our time, or it has some particular meaning to him,' Monroe said.

'Such as?' Ava asked, closing the files on her desk.

'I don't know, something literary, a cult figure, maybe someone musical as he targeted The Fret. Could be anything,' Monroe said.

'All right. Not much else left to check, see what you can

find. Have you heard from DS Lively? He's not answering his phone,' Ava said.

'He went off with DI Callanach as soon as they transferred me back on to the Cadogan case. Hasn't been in the incident room since. I can check with the control room if you like, see if they've reported in?' Monroe offered.

'No need. I'll call DI Callanach myself,' Ava said as Monroe left her office.

There was no response from Callanach either and no one had a trace on them. It looked as if they'd taken one of their own cars rather than a pool vehicle, wherever they were. Ava quelled a sense of unease and reminded herself that Callanach could look after himself. They had agreed to split the investigations. She needed to focus on her end.

Her landline rang. She snatched up the receiver.

'Turner,' she said.

'Tripp, ma'am. The DNA results are in. We're currently running it through the database to check for matches. Any progress there?'

Monroe walked in without knocking.

'Hold on, Tripp,' Ava said. 'What is it?' she asked Monroe.

'We've found an interesting alternative Christian Cadogan,' Monroe said.

'Putting you on speaker, Tripp,' Ava said. 'Do we have an address?'

'Not exactly,' Monroe replied. 'Unless you count Seafield Cemetery.'

'This Christian Cadogan is dead?' Tripp asked. 'Then I don't see how it helps.'

'Bear with me,' Monroe replied. 'There's a case file. I'll read you the summary. We've got photos too, and I'm rarely squeamish but I've had to shove them to the back of the file. Christian Cadogan died in police custody. He was arrested following an enquiry when a primary school notified social services that a child had failed to attend for several weeks and that the mother couldn't be contacted. The boy in question was only five years old at the time, had just started school and wasn't well known to the teachers. There's a report on that aspect available from social services. The attending officers' statements are grim. Let me read directly from the first police officer who entered the flat. "I attended at 12.30pm after a call from social services requesting police follow up. I could hear a child crying within the flat so I rang the doorbell and knocked repeatedly. There was no response at the door. I lifted the letter box and proceeded to look through the opening. The smell from the property was overwhelming. There was plainly something wrong. At that stage I could not see any movement or evidence of inhabitants. The flat was on the ground floor, so I proceeded to the side of the property checking for open windows. At that point I could hear the child crying more clearly and began knocking windows to establish contact with whoever was inside. I also called for backup and was informed that other officers were on their way to assist." There's a plan showing the layout of the property,' Monroe said, handing a document over to Ava. 'These photos show the external state of the place.'

Ava flicked through them. The windows were dirty to an extreme, preventing any view into the flat. Externally, the place told its own story of decay and isolation. A smashed glass pane that had been boarded rather than replaced, peeling paintwork on window frames that would have done nothing to keep out the freezing air, grime running down the outside walls from gutters above that might not have been cleared for years.

Monroe went on. 'The officer continues after backup arrives. "Having consulted, we made the decision based on intelligence from the school and social services, that we should force entry to immediately secure the well-being of the minor.

Using a baton, we broke the glass in the back door to the flat, although the key was not inserted in the lock to enable entry. At that stage we kicked the door to break the lock and entry was made. Initially we had no choice but to remain outside and cover our faces. The odour of rotting from within the property was so strong my eyes were watering. I called out to announce the police presence and requested anyone inside to present themselves immediately. At that stage, we could no longer hear the child crying.

'"I entered the property first, followed by PCs Hutchins and Delaware. We went through the kitchen where tables and chairs had been overturned. There were large amounts of towels in the sink covered in what we believed to be human faeces. We heard movement from the lounge, announced our presence again and our intent to enter the property fully. I drew my baton and positioned myself ready to defend myself or disarm attackers. There was no verbal response to our announcement." These are the photos of the kitchen, ma'am,' Monroe said, handing over a pile of faded photographs. Ava scanned them and dropped them onto her desk almost immediately.

'Carry on,' Ava said quietly.

'The police officer continues,' Monroe coughed, frowned and carried on, 'he continues, "In the lounge we found a man holding a boy whom I estimated at that stage to be between four and five years old. The man was huddled into the corner of a settee, clutching the boy to his chest. The boy was crying quietly but clinging to the man and shaking visibly. The child was naked and extremely dirty. At that moment, the cause of the smell also became apparent. The decomposing corpse of a woman was in an armchair in the room, also naked. My fellow officers entered behind me. The smell was so strong that PC Hutchins was forced to exit so as not to vomit in the crime scene." Do you want me to carry on?' Monroe asked.

'Oh God,' Tripp said.

'Get it over with,' Ava added.

'Right, "I asked the man to hand over the boy but he did not immediately comply. I tried to engage him in conversation but his words were incomprehensible and I formed the impression that he was under the influence of either alcohol, drugs or both. I put down my baton, stepping forward with my hands raised. At that point the man slid his hands into the space between two sofa cushions and withdrew a gun. He pointed the weapon at me first of all, then at his own head, and finally at the boy's head. At this point I backed away rapidly. The boy started crying again as the man began to rant. He was twitching and becoming increasingly erratic. By then we had withdrawn slightly towards the kitchen to calm the situation and avoid an escalating conflict scenario. The child's screams were becoming louder and more desperate. The male began shouting repeatedly at the child to shut up. I attempted to engage the man in conversation. This approach was unsuccessful. He pushed the gun hard into the child's forehead and pulled the trigger. At that point, the gun failed to fire. Myself and PC Delaware immediately tackled the man. He dropped the boy and resisted arrest but we were able to restrain and immobilise him. He was handcuffed and removed from the property." I'll read the forensics evidence now as that has the more relevant sections,' Monroe said.

'The pathologist's report states, "The victim was female, aged between twenty-two and twenty-five years. She had been dead for approximately two weeks. Decomposition was well underway. The material of the chair beneath and surrounding the body was soaked with leaked fluids, although it is possible that contents of both bladder and bowel were emptied whilst the victim was still alive. Cause of death was respiratory failure following opioid use. Extremely high levels of opioids were found in blood and tissue samples. Needle marks on arms suggest long-term drug use prior to the massive dosage that rendered her unconscious and stopped her from breathing. Brain function would have ceased thereafter. One particularly marked, poorly administered needle puncture wound into her left outer thigh leaves unresolved questions. It is unlikely that this was self-administered. Evidence suggests that the deceased was right-handed and thus self-injecting the outer left thigh was unlikely. The puncture wound was large at the surface, suggesting severe force and movement when it was administered, unlike normal regular drug user entry marks. A 4cm scratch below the puncture wound suggests carelessness or roughness with the needle point on exit. Bruising around the puncture wound is consistent with extreme force in inserting the needle. The puncture wound goes directly in at 90 degrees to the outer surface of the leg, unlike usual drug needle entries. This is the only needle puncture wound on her legs, and there is no scarring on this area of her body. Additionally, she had lacerations and bruising to her face suggesting a fight some time prior to death. She had unset ageing fractures, and a new fracture to her cheek bone that had not begun to heal." That's the main thrust of it,' Monroe said.

'But Cadogan died in police custody,' Ava said. 'What was the cause of death?'

'Apparently he hung himself with a sheet. This happened twenty years ago. No CCTV in the cells. No one saw it, no one was ever charged,' Monroe said.

'What do we know about Cadogan?' Tripp asked.

'Long list of previous, starting with petty offending as a teenager, mainly drug offences in his twenties, possession of weapons, the usual violence and arrests that you find with drug dealing. Never got convicted for anything major, but was known by police to be a dealer. Aged thirty-eight at death. The state paid for cremation and distribution of ashes at the cemetery.

No family could be found. Autopsy showed that he was also a long-term drug user. Homeless at the time of the incident after which he died.'

'And the link to our Cadogan?' Tripp asked. 'Is this a relative seeking late justice for the death in custody?'

'I don't think so,' Monroe said. 'It's the little boy who's interesting. The records show he didn't speak for weeks, not a word, so in an effort to reassure him social workers told him that Cadogan was dead. Apparently, he broke down. The social worker wasn't expecting that. They assumed he'd be delighted, but he became violent and distraught. After two days of rocking and biting himself, he described some of what had happened. There's a transcript. He said, "The man came to give Mummy something to help her sleep. She told me to stay in the kitchen. I didn't want to. I wanted to see the man before I went to school. Mummy started screaming at me to go back in the kitchen but the man laughed and said he wanted to give me a hug. Mummy said no and hit him. She was shouting at him. That made him laugh even more. Mummy hit him and he got cross. He wouldn't leave, so Mummy started screaming at him. There was a fight and he hit Mummy then she fell asleep. I tried to wake her up. She wouldn't wake up though and the man didn't leave. He said I didn't have to go to school. He said he didn't have a house so he would live with me now. I tried each day to wake Mummy up. He said I could have him as a daddy as I didn't have a mummy anymore." That's all they got out of him. He was sent to foster carers and referred for the usual medical and psychiatric follow-ups, but we don't have very much more on him.'

'The child watched his mother get murdered, then spent the next couple of weeks with the man who killed her, caring for him, calling himself daddy. How the hell does this stuff slip through the net?' Tripp asked.

'More easily than you'd think,' Ava said.

'Where's the boy now?' Tripp asked.

'We don't know. His name was Jason Elms. Neighbours said his mother always called him J. He was five at the time, but appeared younger to the police officers attending because he was so underweight and small for his age, probably a result of poor diet. He had some contact with the police during his teenage years, mainly street scuffles, then went off the radar. He doesn't claim any benefits, no known address, nothing,' Monroe said.

'J,' Ava said, opening the Lily Eustis file on her desk and flicking through the mobile call logs. 'Lily had a contact called Joe in her phone but the number didn't work. No other details, any texts they'd sent one another had been deleted.'

'That could be anyone,' Monroe said.

'Right, but then we have Jeremy, another pseudonym. We know that one was false,' Ava said. 'Do we have DNA from Jason Elms' offending?' Ava asked Monroe.

'Yes, and a photo, although it's ten years out of date and I reckon he's changed his appearance substantially. The DNA is on file from an ABH charge although he was only given a community sentence due to his age,' Monroe said.

'Tripp, check the DNA you have against Jason Elms' file. Monroe, work with the artist on ageing Jason's custody photo to see if it matches the current Christian Cadogan sketch,' Ava said.

'Anything else, ma'am?' Monroe asked.

'Yes, get a message out to the press. I want a statement released announcing that the man whose likeness we've issued may be going under a name starting with the letter J. We have to find Jason Elms, because whatever bizarre world he's inhabiting inside his head, I guarantee you, he's not done yet.'

Chapter Fifty-Six

Brian Perry was not proving to be DS Lively's favourite person. He'd tried the bathroom trip excuse and been hauled back down from a tiny window through which he was never destined to fit, pretended to fall unconscious, which had resulted in Lively pinching a circle of skin on Perry's inner thigh and twisting it hard, then resorted to screaming for help. After two hours, Lively had bound, gagged and threatened his life. Those weren't exactly the control methods Callanach had employed at Interpol, but then Lively wasn't his usual type of partner. Through it all, Perry's mobile had been ringing almost constantly. They let it ring, calls and texts remaining unanswered. If anyone wanted to speak to Perry today, they were going to have to visit in person.

It was nearly 5pm by the time the doorbell rang. Callanach had set up the lounge exactly as he'd needed it, coaching and threatening Perry to within an inch of his life. Their unhappy prisoner had been released from his bonds and moved to a more comfortable seat. Free of his gag he had complained and sworn non-stop until Lively had inserted the tip of a taser into Perry's mouth. Since then, the talkative Mr Perry had been remarkably quiet and compliant. Detective Sergeant Lively had proved extraordinarily inventive by cutting a hole in the back of an armchair through which he could poke his taser so that it remained in contact with Perry's back, concealing himself at the same time. Callanach was very nearly minded to forgive all the months of insults and piss-taking he'd endured at Lively's instigation. Checking the street from the bedroom window, Callanach positioned himself behind the open door between the lounge and the hallway.

'Say it,' Lively hissed at Perry. Callanach watched the man flinch as the taser was shoved hard into his back.

'It's open,' Perry shouted, his lack of enthusiasm not the least bit veiled.

The kitchen door squeaked on its hinges, then slammed. Footsteps came closer, muffled by the tackiness of the kitchen lino.

'You haven't answered your phone all day and the police are on their way to raid this address in connection with . . . what the hell are you doing with your eyes?' Dimitri asked.

Perry coughed.

'Get up, get some shoes on and disappear. Don't go to the club. The raid's not for another ten hours but they'll be watching well before they come in. Ramon doesn't want you on the street at all until we've figured out how to make this go away,' Dimitri said.

'I can't,' Perry muttered.

'You can't what, you idiot?' Dimitri asked.

'Can't get up,' Perry said.

'Like hell you can't. I said get some shoes on,' Dimitri marched forward, grabbing Perry by the shoulder and wrenching him up. Lively stood, raising the taser and aiming in Dimitri's direction.

'What the fuck are you doing?' Dimitri demanded. 'Do you have any idea who I am? Lower the taser, you moron.'

'You see, that's why I hate the brass. No humility. No under-standing of how to address lower ranking officers,' Lively said.

Perry was trying to shrink against the wall. Callanach stepped out of the doorway and pushed him back towards the chair.

'Sit down,' Callanach said. 'Both of you.'

Dimitri swung round. 'I know you,' he said.

'Then I won't waste time introducing myself,' Callanach replied. 'I want the paint flecks that were taken from Louis Jones' vehicle. The ones that mysteriously got lost in transit to the lab. Where are they?'

'Long gone, you idiot,' Dimitri said. 'And before you make any further demands, let's get a little more realistic. I outrank you, and my years of service to Police Scotland will make anything you have to say about me completely irrelevant. So this stops here. I'm leaving now. It's obvious that this raid was never going to happen, which means you have no evidence and no cause to make any arrests. I suggest you stop harassing this innocent member of the public who it appears you have falsely imprisoned, before he makes an official complaint or even sues for damages. You can regard your career in Scotland as having reached a full stop, DI Callanach. And whoever you are,' he said to Lively, 'you look like you've hit pensionable age already. Take the money and get out while you can or I will personally ensure that neither one of you ever sees another pay cheque.'

'Ach, would you get on and tell him, sir? He's making a right dick of himself. It's dreadful to watch,' Lively said.

'I want the gun that was used to kill Louis Jones,' Callanach said. 'And you can drop the pretence about the paint flecks having been destroyed. In your situation I would keep every bit of evidence against the men who were controlling me. Where have you put them? In a safe, I guess. Not in your office. If anything happened to you, other officers would find it eventually.'

'I'm done here,' Dimitri said. 'But I need a chat with Mr Perry before I go, so you gentlemen can leave now.'

'Oh, I can't stand this. You're on film, Chief Inspector. That mobile leaning on the plant pot there, the brown thing that's not been watered in an age, has been recording the conversation,' Lively said, walking over to the phone and handing it to Callanach.

'That won't do you any good,' Dimitri said. 'You've committed so many offences just being in here and mistreating a man not charged with any offence, that you'll both be in as much trouble as me. What are you going to accuse me of? Mishandling evidence?'

'We'll start with perverting the course of justice, and if I can tie you to the Louis Jones case, you're up on conspiracy to murder. I'd think that would be enough to persuade you to comply,' Callanach said.

Dimitri drew a gun from his pocket. 'You know, for a man who was supposedly one of Interpol's most lauded agents before his disgrace, you are remarkably ill-prepared. Did you think I would walk in here unarmed? Take the sim card out of that phone right now. You'll find that boiling both the phone and the sim card for a few minutes renders them quite useless. Perry, put the kettle on would you?'

'Actually, the area where Interpol really helped me was in constantly updating my knowledge and use of technology. The camera was sending a live feed to a social media site I'm registered with. At the moment it is passworded and completely private. All I have to do is change the settings and everyone will be able to see the conversation we just had.'

'You're telling me that because you want me to kill you. Is that right?' Dimitri asked.

'That won't help, I'm afraid. I've left a message on my desk for the attention of DCI Turner. If I fail to return to my desk to destroy that envelope, she will find a message from me complete with the necessary passwords to be able to view the recorded video feed. You'll want to lower that gun now,' Callanach said.

'Oh man, those boys totally fucked you over,' Perry whispered.

'Get out,' Dimitri told him.

'But where am I supposed to . . .' Perry said.

'Bedroom, now. Music on loud. Cuff him,' Dimitri told Lively.

Callanach waited until Perry was secured and beyond any chance of overhearing their conversation, then sat down. 'If I don't get the evidence I need to secure a conviction in the Louis Jones murder, we'll hand over what we have on you instead,' he said. 'I want it today. No delays.'

'You have no idea what you're getting yourselves into,' Dimitri said. 'This isn't your usual investigation. There are people involved that you don't want to mess with.'

'The St Leonard's police station extension number is on Louis Jones' incoming call logs, a landline you used shortly before the call out to the Jones crash. Did you threaten him? Tell him he was going to be arrested? Or was it a demand for payment from Trescoe?' Lively asked.

'I'm the one who told him to run, you morons. You think I want bloodshed on my patch? I thought I'd left all this behind when those lads got sentenced, only Ramon had different ideas when he was released,' Dimitri said.

'So why get rid of the evidence? The best thing you could do is help put them away again,' Lively said.

'You think it's that simple? The things we do when we're young leave stains. Some never fade. I did things back then that I'm not proud of, and I can't take them back. I have a family who'll pay the price. That's the way Trescoe operates. You have to let this go.'

'That's not going to happen,' Callanach said.

'For God's sake, Louis Jones was one of them. He was in it up to his neck. Why the hell are you so bothered about him? He provided the car your DCI was abducted in, and you're willing to do whatever it takes to avenge his murder? What the hell's wrong with you?' Dimitri shouted.

'It's not about Jones,' Callanach said quietly.

'What?' Dimitri asked.

'Lively, give the Chief Inspector and myself a moment, would you?' Callanach asked.

'Not while he's still got a gun in his pocket, with respect, sir,' Lively said.

'Hand it over,' Callanach told Dimitri, who held it out in Lively's direction without bothering to look at the Detective Sergeant. Lively smiled broadly in response and pocketed the weapon before leaving the room. 'I'm going to say this once and you're going to listen. You're right. I couldn't care less about Jones, but I did care about Begbie. That was another mess where you were first on the scene. Get me what I want, and do it today, because you are implicated in the death of a fellow officer, which will make whatever you did previously seem like child's play when it goes to court. I can tell you from experience that being a police officer in a prison is as hard as doing time gets.'

Chapter Fifty-Seven

'We got a hit on the DNA,' Tripp said, walking back into Ava's office. 'The report says it's a twelve million to one chance that it belongs to anyone except Jason Elms.'

'Right, update the publicity,' she looked at her watch. 'It's seven o'clock now so we've missed the newspaper print run and the early news programmes. That leaves the late news slots and online media. I'll have the press office draft a release to say that Elms may either be going under the name Christian or any name starting with J. It's a long shot but it's all we've got. Also, we'll have to upgrade the warning from wanted in connection with an incident, to potentially dangerous and should not be approached. Agreed?'

'Agreed,' Tripp said. 'We really could do with all hands on deck. I don't suppose there's been any word from DI Callanach or DS Lively, ma'am?'

'Nothing,' Ava said. 'But we can't worry about that now. I'll leave another message on Callanach's voicemail and let him know we need them back here as soon as possible. Other than that, I want officers on the streets. There needs to be a visible police presence. Every unit across the city must be notified and drafted in.'

'Already on it. Where will you be, ma'am, if I need to contact you?'

'Out with you, patrolling. Monroe will stay in the control room. I want to be in a car where I can respond if we get the call. I'm sick of the sight of this desk,' Ava said.

'Very good. I've organised a car from the pool. I'll let you know when it's time to go.'

Ava picked up her mobile and tried Callanach again. He'd been off the radar too long, and the problem was that she had no idea where to start looking for him.

'Luc,' she said quietly into voicemail. 'You haven't called in for hours. People are asking where you and Lively are. If you can't get hold of me, make sure one of you contacts the control room to update me. Just let me know you got this message. We have a positive ID on Lily and Cordelia's killer. I'll give you all the details later. For the remainder of tonight, I'll be patrolling with Tripp. We're giving the media the full picture. I hope you're okay. Please, call or text or something.'

Sean O'Cahill, fresh from a truly fabulous rehearsal, was lacing his boots and checking he had enough money in his wallet.

'Are you sure you don't want to join us? I'm meeting Mattie and Rex for a drink first, then we're off to The Lost Boys to meet this actor, Jackson, who I met at my last audition,' he called to Bradley.

'Jackson who?' Brad shouted from the bath.

'First name only. He was there when I got the part with the theatre company so it's another actor. I know you're rolling your eyes,' he said. 'Not all actors are egotistical bores.'

Bradley appeared in the bathroom doorway draped in a towel.

'True, it's only most of them,' he said. 'And no, honestly, I'm not up for it tonight. You go off out with your loveys. I'd only spend the evening looking at my watch and annoying you.'

'All right then, but don't say I didn't invite you when it's one in the morning and you're sad and alone. I'll be late, by the way, and hungover tomorrow. You'd better have bacon and eggs in the pan when I wake up or I will be unbearable all day.'

'Go on with you,' Bradley said. 'Why don't you leave your keys here? Just ring the bell and I'll get up and let you in.'

'Would you mind? Saves me carrying them all evening.'

'Saves you losing them again,' Bradley said. 'Just phone me when you're walking back so I have time to wake up properly.'

Sean kissed him. 'You're the best. Don't miss me too much. Love you.'

Bradley smiled, flushed a light shade of red, and waved him goodbye.

Christian showered, dried his hair, got dressed. They were the everyday movements of an ordinary man, and yet he felt so much more than ordinary. He wondered if he was a monster, decided he was overthinking it, not that it didn't matter, but simply that he didn't really care. Labels were for supermarket shelves. He wanted to turn the radio on but knew it would distract him. Earlier, in the news segment, they had said his name. His real name. Another label, one he hadn't used for many years. So they were closing in. It wouldn't ruin his night though. He could run, get enough of a head-start to board a ferry and begin again elsewhere, but then all of his hard work befriending Sean and Brad would have been for nothing. He couldn't bear the thought. One night was all he needed. Tomorrow he'd pack his things and go. Let Scotland cool off in his absence. Maybe in a year, maybe in a few, he could crawl back unnoticed. If the police had known where he lived, they'd have stormed the place by now. There was a sketch of him, too. With the morbid curiosity of a child who stamps on a spider then bends down to poke it, he had gone from radio to internet, seeing himself through the eyes of his pursuers.

It hadn't been flattering. There was a vacant stare to his eyes. His blonde hair had looked wild and unkempt, rather than California beach-dweller, which was how a hairdresser had once described it. Not much chance of him seeing California in the flesh now. Of course, there never really was, he grinned. Not on cash in hand and minimum wage jobs, and not with the start he'd had in life. The only person he'd ever loved had been stolen from him. Sent from children's home to temporary carer, to children's unit and back again, he'd been strapped into a rollercoaster that never stopped. Christian recalled the words a room-mate had imparted at one children's unit, shortly before stabbing a guard and being moved somewhere even less appealing.

'There are three things you need to know in here,' he'd said. 'The first is that to everyone else, you're just a problem. The second is that they always think you should be more grateful than you are. Finally, you'll never get any quiet.' Christian remembered his room-mate looking up, one finger crossing his lips as they listened to the sounds that defined institutions. Crying, shouting, disciplining, other people's music, other people's pain, the clanging of pots and pans in the kitchens, girls arguing over the bathroom, boys ranting, unable to find an antidote for the testosterone that made them growl and thrash. Never. Any. Peace.

That was why he'd learned to find his own quiet place. First in his imagination, then in small ways, with small people. His first attempt had been in a foster home. A remote place at the edge of a loch he could no longer name. He'd presented the family's seven-year-old daughter with her dead guinea pig. He'd found it like that in the cage, he'd told her, stroking its silky back, watching her eyes fill with tears. It had flopped in his hands as he'd held it, the break in its spine rendering it useless, but she hadn't noticed. The girl had sobbed on his shoulder, muttering the dead creature's name over and over, filling Christian with her grief and loss, until he'd felt something close to alive. Not all the way there, but better, half-fulfilled. Her parents had arrived to take the animal from him, peeling the girl from his embrace, exchanging suspicious glances, studiously not saying aloud what they were communicating to one another. A day later he'd been moved on again. He was never directly accused of any wrongdoing, but then as the stakes had got higher, he'd been cleverer about it.

There had been others before Lily, but hers was the first life he'd taken whose passing had caused such deep-rooted, heart-wrenching grief. That was what nourished him. He craved it as a man adrift at sea craved fresh water. The problem was that no amount of it quenched his thirst. He could kill a whole village and revel in the mourning the massacre evoked, and still the next day he would be left wanting again.

He felt a twinge of guilt at ditching Mina so abruptly, but she'd had nothing left to offer him once her initial horrific loss had been accepted. He required raw, immediate grief. Like tonight. Sean and Bradley. One little death. It wasn't so much to ask.

Chapter Fifty-Eight

In Brian Perry's lounge, Callanach was beginning to strategise. They had a limited window in which to make use of CI Dimitri's presence. Lively brought Perry back into the room to assist.

'Whose weapon was used to kill Jones?' Callanach asked.

'The gun belonged to Knuckles,' Perry said. 'I didn't even know he had it on him, and I never touched it, not once. I had no idea the plan was to kill Louis. I just get taken along to make up the numbers. Bit of muscle, that's all.'

Lively lowered the gun from where he'd pushed it into Perry's kneecap. 'Where's the gun that was used on Louis Jones now?' he asked.

'It's in the safe at The Maz. Knuckles won't keep it at home in case his kids get hold of it,' Perry muttered.

'What about the nail gun?' Callanach asked. 'Is that at The Maz, too?'

Perry was silent, but his eyes did the talking for him. He glanced nervously towards a cupboard then back at Dimitri's gun. 'Not sure,' he said.

'Bollocks are you not sure, son,' Lively said, walking to the cupboard and pulling it open. It was completely full. A variety of tools, overalls, wires and old electrical parts tumbled to the floor. 'I can and will pull out every single item, but it'll save time if you'll tell me where it is. Also, you'll still be able to walk tomorrow.'

'Fuck, all right, don't hurt me any more. It's wrapped in a rag, top shelf on the left,' Perry whined. 'I didn't use it though. They told me to take something to scare him. They wanted to know where the money was. It was Knuckles who did it.'

Lively took the nail gun out of the wrapping, photographing it then putting it into an evidence bag and labelling it.

'So now you're following procedure?' Dimitri asked. 'How are you going to explain what led you to Perry in the first place?'

'Because he's about to phone the police station and ask to speak to me. When I'm not there, he's going to leave his name and phone number so I can call him back,' Callanach said.

'You're frigging crazy, pal. Do you have any idea what'll happen to me if I do that?' Perry laughed.

Lively sighed and pointed the gun back at his knee. 'Pick up the phone,' he said.

'You've got to be shitting me. This goes on the record and I'm a dead man,' Perry said.

'In that case you seem to be stuck between a rock and a hard place, because we're not feeling all that charitable either,' Lively said. 'Now pick up the phone.'

Perry did.

Callanach took the unlit Gauloises cigarette from his mouth and crushed it beneath his boot. His phone had started buzzing when they'd arrived outside The Maz. He answered it as Lively got Perry out of the car and handcuffed him again, buttoning his jacket over the top to keep the cuffs hidden.

He listened to Ava's message, then Lance's voice came on the line as Callanach realised he hadn't finished listening to his voicemail the previous day.

'. . . leaving, a man walked past and handed me a flyer for The Maz. I didn't recognise him but I was concerned that he might have noticed me there. Just thought you should know.'

Callanach sighed as he switched his phone off. He'd established a clean connection from Perry to the nail gun. The last thing he needed was complications with Lance.

'Let's get on with it,' Callanach said. 'You're sure Trescoe isn't here?'

'I was told they were all out,' Dimitri said. 'They don't usually appear in the club until later in the evening. No reason they should be here now. Off we go.' He pulled out his gun and kept it pointed at Perry's back, as Lively rang the bell next to the club's main door. 'Not a word, now. Just act normal. Remember what we agreed, Perry.'

'Aye, like witness fucking protection is going to help me where these boys are involved,' Perry said. 'You might just as well shoot me right now.'

'Killjoy,' Lively muttered.

The eyepiece in the door shifted. 'Just me,' Perry said. The door opened.

So far so good, Callanach thought. Perry was behaving himself, not that he had much choice standing, as he was, at the business end of a gun. Dimitri's attitude had shifted substantially since Callanach had brought up Begbie's name. Perhaps it was a sudden rush of conscience, though more likely Dimitri realised that the only way he could remain a free man was if he helped get Trescoe arrested. It wasn't the best laid of plans, but it was all they had. Getting the gun out of Trescoe's safe would provide a solid link to Jones' death, and with that and Perry's testimony they could build a case. They needed Dimitri, a fact which stuck in Callanach's throat, but as long as the Chief Inspector believed the charade about the footage being uploaded and accessible at the police station, he would have to play along.

Dimitri stepped forward, gun in the side of Perry's neck as they hustled inside the club. Callanach followed with his taser on display and Lively brought up the rear, locking the door behind him.

The man who had opened it stepped back with his hands in the air. 'Chief Inspector Dimitri, we don't see you here often. And with your friends this time,' he said. Callanach recognised him as the club manager who'd taken such a keen interest in Ava. He fought the urge to punch him immediately.

'Straight through to the safe, Domo,' Dimitri said. 'Don't shout out. If we feel threatened, that'll be enough for us to use reasonable force and today that includes bullets.'

'I'm not stopping you. Go ahead. You know where it is,' Domo said.

'I think we'll follow you, if you don't mind. Who else is in?' Dimitri asked.

'Knuckles is in the cellar dealing with the barrels. A couple of the girls are in the changing rooms getting ready for opening later,' Domo said.

'Five minutes, in and out,' Dimitri said. 'That's all you've got. I'll wait here in case Knuckles comes up. Leave Domo with me.'

Lively and Callanach went with Perry through the VIP area to the rear of the ground floor, and into an office.

'Open it up,' Lively told Perry. He reached for the safe and turned the dial left and right a few times. The door didn't move. 'Don't make a mistake, lad,' Lively told him. 'Mess me around and we'll hang you out to dry with both your boss and the law courts. Pick a side, is my advice. Now hurry up.'

'It's not working,' Perry moaned.

'When did you last open it?' Callanach asked him.

'Couple of days ago to stow some cash we'd collected. Mr Trescoe transfers it all to his private safe upstairs at the end of the night.'

Footsteps came from the main area of the club towards the VIP section. Callanach grabbed Perry around the neck and put the taser to his temple.

Dimitri appeared in the doorway first, gun nowhere to be seen, with Domo and Knuckles behind him. They all moved aside to allow another person through. He was slim, with dusky skin and black eyes, and his smile made it clear that he was not the least bit surprised or perturbed to find Callanach and the others invading his space.

'I should've known we couldn't trust a bent copper,' Lively said. 'Was it greed or fear?'

'Shut up,' Dimitri responded.

'Will I hell,' Lively replied. 'It's not like we're getting out of here any way except wrapped in plastic. I might as well enjoy telling you what I think.'

'Lively, stop,' Callanach said, pulling Perry closer to him and looking Ramon Trescoe in the eyes. 'There's evidence against your men already, and I include Chief Inspector Dimitri in that. Evidence that implicates you. Even if Lively and I die, that evidence is admissible in court. You can't win.'

'I don't think you want to threaten me, DI Callanach. There are other people you care about involved in this debacle, and you don't want their blood on your hands,' Trescoe said.

'DCI Turner already met your men and came off rather better than them, as I understand it. I don't think she'd want me to back down because of her,' Callanach said.

'Oh, I wasn't referring to the lovely DCI Turner, although it's right to say I have her home address, front door in British racing green, isn't that right?' Trescoe said. Callanach stayed quiet. 'Actually, I was referring to your friend who I invited to stay here last night. He was good company for a while, then he found it all a bit overwhelming I'm afraid. Apologies if he's a bit of a mess. He took some persuading to explain who'd sent him to take photos of my car. We have a concealed CCTV system. Very basic really. Taking a note of his licence plate was embarrassingly simple. Not at all difficult to trace a home address when you have such good friends in the police. Knuckles, bring Lance Proudfoot up from the cellar, please.'

Chapter Fifty-Nine

Sean saw his new friend Jackson from a distance, leaning against the wall of The Lost Boys, running a hand through his hair, completely ignorant of the looks being thrown at him from passersby. He pointed him out to his companions.

'You're kidding me! Bradley let you out for the evening with him? He is gorgeous,' Rex said.

'Just because you can't keep it in your pants when there's a tall blonde nearby, doesn't mean we all behave the same way,' Mattie said. 'Sean and Brad are in love. You should try it.'

'If being in love means I stop fancying men like that, I'd sooner give it a miss thank you,' Rex replied.

'Knock it off you two, he'll hear. Anyway, he just wants to get to know a few people. I'm trying to be friendly. Play nice.' They approached Jackson, and Sean made the introductions. 'Shall we go in then?' Sean asked.

'I just need to get to a cashpoint. I wasn't sure where the nearest one was, so I thought I'd wait here for you first,' Jackson said.

'There's one a couple of corners down,' Rex said. 'We can go together. Won't take long.'

'Wouldn't hear of it, it's freezing. Give me directions. I'll find it,' Jackson said.

'You guys go on in, we'll meet up with you in a while. I know which cashpoint is closest. It'll give me a few minutes to tell Jackson who to avoid at the bar, as well,' Sean said.

'Stinky Barnaby,' Mattie and Rex said together.

'You two are evil,' Sean replied. 'Get on inside. We'll catch you shortly.'

'This is really kind of you,' Jackson said as they walked down the hill towards the junction. 'Sorry to be such a pain.'

'That's okay. It's just around the next corner,' Sean said. 'It's bitter though. That coat can't be keeping you warm.'

'I've got something better,' Jackson said, pulling a bottle from his pocket.

'Oh my word, Flaming Pig Spiced Irish,' Sean said, whistling as he took it from Jackson. 'I honestly can't remember the last time I drank this. I think it might have been at my friend's feature film debut. He was only on screen for four seconds and he didn't have any lines, but he was the first one of us with his name scrolling at the end of a movie and heavens, did we party!' He took the cap off and sniffed. 'Can you smell those cloves?' He smiled at Jackson. 'Do you mind if I take a sip?'

'Be my guest, take as much as you like, there's plenty,' Jackson said, pushing his card into the cashpoint machine.

'Do you taste the cinnamon in it?' Sean said. 'This is great. It's like every night out I ever had with my mates when we were teenagers. Someone always nabbed a bottle of this from their parents' cupboard. We were usually smashed by the time we got to the pub. Made it a cheap night out.' He took another sip and held the bottle out to Jackson.

'Give me a minute,' Jackson said, waving the bottle away. 'There's a problem with my card. I just need to check my balance. You have it. I've already drunk more than I should've!'

'Amen to that. It's so sweet, I've probably consumed my caloric allowance for the week. Warms the cockles, though, right?' Sean took another swig. 'You really can't beat spiced whisky for warming you up.' He puffed out hard.

'You all right?' Jackson asked.

'Sure, I'm fine. Probably shouldn't have mixed it with the red wine I had earlier.' He leaned against the wall.

'That'll just be the cold air getting to your head. I've nearly finished here. Have another sip. It'll get the blood flowing,' Jackson said.

'Promise you won't let me on the dance floor after this,' Sean laughed. 'I've made an arse of myself enough times already at The Lost Boys.' He took a final gulp and held the bottle towards Jackson. 'Take it away from me, you devil.'

Jackson grabbed the bottle as Sean began to slide towards the floor, hitting the wet pavement hard. 'You really shouldn't have mixed it with the red wine,' Jackson said. 'Come on, let me get you up.' He put an arm around Sean's waist and lifted.

'I'm so sorry, I've never got drunk that quickly. I'm not sure what's happening,' Sean slurred, opening his eyes wide before the eyelids began to droop again. 'I need to sit down.'

'Hold on,' Jackson said, 'my car's right here.' He held out his keys and clicked the lock.

'That was lucky,' Sean muttered. 'I think that's good idea. Just a sit for minute.'

'Come on,' Jackson said, holding one hand over Sean's head and lowering him into the front passenger seat. 'I should get you home.'

'You parked right next to cashpoint, s'funny. Didn't see it,' Sean said. 'Need to tell my address,' he murmured as his head fell forward to rest on his chest. Jackson secured the seatbelt for him.

'Don't you worry,' Jackson said softly. 'I already know where you live.'

Chapter Sixty

The control room put the call through to Ava's mobile.

'Um, hello, it's about the picture of that man, Christian Cadogan. I saw it online and there was a number to call,' a male said.

'Yes, thank you,' Ava replied, nudging Tripp with an elbow as he drove, and finding a notebook and pen. 'Could you give me your name?'

'Ben Miller. I work at a café on Broughton Street called the Nom de Plume. I do the 8am to 4pm shift Monday to Thursday.'

'About Christian Cadogan?' Ava prompted.

'I've seen him in there,' Ben said. 'I mean, I think it's him. The picture showed him with glasses, and I never saw him wear any. Some days he had his hood up when he came in, so it was harder to see his face. A couple of a weeks ago, though, he was in the gents when I went in for a pee. Hood down, I was right next to him. I'd swear it was the same man.'

'Did you ever hear him use a name?' Ava asked.

'No, it's always too busy to hear individual conversations and we respect our customers' privacy. It's important in a place like ours,' Ben said.

'Why is that?' Ava asked.

'I always assume everyone knows. We're kind of a focus for Edinburgh's lesbian and gay community, so we never ask names. It takes time to build trust. Some people are very shy.'

'And did you get the impression that Cadogan was part of that community for any reason?' Ava asked.

'I don't know about that, he always met up with the same guy when he came in. They had lunch together quite often. Cadogan's friend is definitely part of the scene because he's been in with other people before.'

'Do you know the name of the man Cadogan was meeting, so we can contact him?' Ava asked.

'I don't, I'm afraid. I can ask my boss, but it's sensitive, like I explained,' Ben said.

'I get that,' Ava said, 'but you've seen the publicity. This man might be dangerous. He's wanted in connection with serious crimes. Other people might be in danger, so the sooner we find him the better. I need you to make enquiries straight away and come back to me with any information you get. Will you do that, Ben?'

'Is there no other way?' Ben asked.

'You're our only lead. That means you might be the only person able to help us prevent further crimes. Do you understand?' Ava asked.

'Completely. I'll make some calls.' Ben rang off.

'I hope I didn't scare him,' Ava said.

'I hope you did,' Tripp replied.

Monroe called them minutes later. 'Ma'am, Ben Miller from the café called back. The owner of the Nom de Plume reckons the man seen lunching regularly with Cadogan has or had a boyfriend called Sean, Irish accent, no surname available. No information about Cadogan's lunch date himself as apparently he's much quieter. One of the staff members has a selfie with Sean in the background, which I'm forwarding to your mobile now.'

'Thanks, Monroe,' Ava said. 'It's a start.'

'It's more than just a start,' Tripp replied. 'It's the weekend, which means The Lost Boys will be packed out. If Sean's gay, then chances are that someone at the club will have met him, know him, or at least know of him.'

'Do you mind going in?' Ava asked. 'I know it can be difficult bridging the professional and the social when you're a police officer.'

'Not at all. Since I split up with my last boyfriend I haven't been out much, but that's only been down to the demands of work. Maybe I'll meet someone tonight, you never know.' Tripp smiled. He performed a tyre-shredding u-turn and headed back into the city centre towards the club, lights and sirens sending traffic to the sides of the road. Ava radioed for additional officers to meet them there, and instructed the control room to start circulating Sean's photograph to all beat officers. Inside The Lost Boys ten minutes later, they split up to cover the two floors more effectively.

Ava took the lower floor while Tripp went upstairs. She struggled through the dancing crowds, as more than one drink spilled down her trousers and spattered her back. Holding Sean's photo out in front of her, she began thrusting it into every face she passed. People shook their heads, tried to pull her onto the dance floor, all good natured but a waste of time. Her relief when she spotted Tripp waving frantically at her from the upper balcony was overwhelming. She sprinted up the stairs, shouting warnings at everyone else to get of her way. Tripp had pulled two perplexed looking men to one side.

'Ma'am, this is Rex' – Tripp motioned to the taller of the two – 'and Mattie. They've positively identified Sean from the photo,' Tripp shouted over the pulsing music. 'Sean's a regular in here, apparently. The barman up here pointed Rex and Mattie out to me as people he'd seen Sean with, so the ID looks dependable.'

'Sean's supposed to be here right now, so I don't think you'll find he's in any immediate danger.' Rex smiled. 'Me and Mattie came here with him. He just popped down to the cashpoint with his mate.'

'And Sean's surname is?' Ava asked.

'O'Cahill. He's Irish,' Mattie joined in. 'What is it you need him for? I can guarantee he hasn't done anything illegal. Sean's too nice for his own good.'

'We want to know if his partner can tell us anything about this man,' Tripp said, holding up the sketch of Cadogan. 'Do you know Sean's partner?'

'Bradley? Only to say hi to,' Mattie said. 'Isn't that . . .?' He squinted at the sketch then looked at Rex.

'It could be. Same hair. No glasses though. Definitely looks like him,' Rex said.

'I'm sorry, who are you talking about?' Ava asked.

'The man in this picture.' Rex pointed at the sketch of Cadogan. 'We saw him tonight. That's who Sean went to the cashpoint with. They should have been back here a while ago.' He checked his watch. 'Ages ago, actually.'

'Where did you last see them?' Tripp asked.

'Outside the club, about forty minutes ago. Is Sean all right? This sounds serious,' Rex said.

'We need to find them as soon as possible,' Ava said. 'Which cashpoint did they go to?'

'The one down the hill, outside the bank on the right,' Rex said.

Ava and Tripp ran for the door.

Chapter Sixty-One

Christian parked outside Bradley and Sean's flat, reaching over the sleeping man in his passenger seat to take a hypodermic syringe from a bag in the footwell. He rolled up Sean's sleeve, sliding the needle gently below the surface of his flesh and releasing additional heroin into his system. The oral solution he'd mixed into the Flaming Pig had been enough to render Sean senseless for a while, but not enough to do what really needed to be done.

He went round to the passenger's side while Sean could still be roused enough to put one foot in front of the other, and hauled him out.

'Come on,' he said. 'Bradley's inside. He can make you more comfortable.'

Christian manoeuvred him up the few steps to the door and rang the buzzer to the flat.

'Hello?' Bradley said.

'It's Chris.'

'Great, I'll buzz you in. First door on the left.' The outer door opened.

Christian half-carried Sean over the threshold and into the

corridor. Bradley opened the flat door before he could reach it, waving two wine glasses in one hand and a bottle in the other.

'Sean! Oh my God, what happened? How did you . . .'

'Where's the sofa?' Christian asked.

'Through here,' Bradley said. 'I'll get a blanket. Should we call a doctor do you think?'

'A blanket's a good idea, maybe a pillow too. I'll look after him,' Christian said, locating the landline phone while Bradley was out of the room, and turning the power off at the socket. Sean's mobile was still in his car to avoid distractions. All that remained was to disable Brad's.

'Here we go. Honestly, what a state he's in!' Bradley reappeared with a duvet and pillow set, making sure Sean was comfortable and running a hand over his forehead. 'I'm so sorry. He was supposed to be at a club with some friends. I wasn't expecting him back until much later. I've never, ever seen him this drunk. Where did you find him?'

'He was staggering up the road. I pulled my car over to ask if he was all right. When I heard the Irish accent I put two and two together,' Christian said.

'Thank goodness you were there,' Bradley said. 'He'd have ended up in a ditch for the night in this state. His breathing's very shallow. I'm wondering if a trip to the hospital might not be best.'

'We'll watch him together,' Christian said. 'Close the blinds and lock the door. It might be a long night. We might as well get comfortable. Could I use your mobile? I need to send a text and mine's out of battery.'

'Sure,' Brad said, handing it over. 'I'll put the kettle on. I know it's not quite how things were supposed to pan out tonight, but I'm glad you're here anyway.'

Christian waited until Brad was in the kitchen, then removed the phone's sim, leaving the mobile on a bookcase shelf. It wouldn't be needed. He looked at Sean. His respiration was even more shallow now. Christian lifted one eyelid, slapped Sean's face lightly and called his name. There was a brief response, a jerk of the head followed by an attempt to speak, then the eyelid drooped back over the pupil and Sean drifted back to whatever dream had taken him. It wouldn't be long.

Bradley brought coffee and they sat together on the sofa opposite Sean, sipping their drinks.

'You wanted to talk. I guess it's weird with Sean there, but I need to take my mind off the mess he's in. Since he joined the new theatre company it's felt as if we've drifted apart. He has so many new friends. When he first moved to Edinburgh, I was the only one he really had. We were building a life together, just the two of us. I'd assumed it was going to last, now I don't know. I love him, I'm not saying I don't, it's just that I can't see the future so clearly anymore.'

'I hope that's not because of anything I've done,' Christian whispered.

'No,' Bradley said. 'Well, maybe, a bit. But it's not your fault, I don't want you thinking that. You just opened my eyes to other possibilities, that's all.' He slid a hand over the top of Christian's and gripped it.

'Love is transient in all its forms. Don't feel guilty because your feelings for Sean have changed. Sometimes we all need saving.'

'I don't think I need saving, exactly.' Brad smiled. 'It's just hard keeping up with Sean at times. He's so outgoing and fun, people are drawn to him. He casts a big shadow, you know?'

'It's important to recognise when people aren't giving you what you need,' Christian said. 'And that you learn to let them go. Mourn and move on. It's a natural cycle.'

'You know what,' Bradley said, letting go of Christian's hand

and going to Sean's side, 'I really don't think he's breathing right. His skin's gone all waxy. What's that phone number for the NHS helpline? I'd be happier if I got some advice.'

'You're over-reacting,' Christian said. 'I've seen plenty of people in this state before. Give him a couple of hours to get it out of his system then we'll wake him up and fill him with coffee.'

'I think just to be on the safe side I'll make that call,' Brad said.

'I'm telling you, that's a mistake,' Christian said as Bradley reached for the landline.

'It's dead,' Brad said, looking bemused at the phone. 'Sorry, have you got my mobile?'

'You don't need it,' Christian replied.

'Look, I know this isn't what we planned, but I have to take care of Sean. If you want to go I'll understand. Maybe that would be best anyway. He'll be confused when he wakes up.'

'Bradley,' Christian said, 'Sean isn't going to wake up.'

'Don't talk stupid.' Bradley shook his head, frowning, his voice louder and higher in tone. 'Of course he's going to wake up. He's still breathing, he's just terribly drunk. The hospital might want to pump his stomach or something, but he's going to be fine.' He chewed a nail, laying his other hand on Sean's forehead. 'On balance, I think I'd be more comfortable if you'd leave. I need to be able to care for him my own way. Ah, there's my phone,' Brad said, grabbing his mobile off the bookcase and trying to dial. The phone didn't respond. 'What the hell's wrong with this one now?' he said. 'Right, I'm going upstairs to the neighbour's flat to use their phone. Do me a favour and watch him for one minute would . . .'

He looked up at Christian, ran his eyes down to the matt silver gun in his hand and mumbled into silence.

'You can't leave,' Christian said quietly. 'I wanted this evening to be perfect. I can't let you ruin it.'

Chapter Sixty-Two

'Let Lance go,' Callanach told Ramon Trescoe.

'I don't think so,' Trescoe said. 'Police Scotland needs to learn the art of compromise. I had hoped Chief Inspector Dimitri here would have that covered, but apparently all these years later he is still incompetent.'

Callanach looked at Dimitri who glanced away.

'Lance knows nothing about any of this. Release him. Dimitri will provide whatever alibi you need, not that Lance would be stupid enough to report you for kidnapping,' Callanach said.

Lance was on the floor in the corner, clutching the left side of his ribs and nursing an impressively bruised black eye that had spread to colour the entire right side of his face.

'What is it you want?' Callanach asked Trescoe.

'I want you to phone your office. Dimitri tells me there's a girl from his squad working there who should act sufficiently obediently. I want her to burn the contents of the envelope you left for DCI Turner without opening it, and I expect to see her doing that on video link. Police computers do use video links, don't they?' Trescoe said.

'That's not going to happen. Firstly, because Monroe will

immediately know something is wrong. Secondly, because that's my insurance policy,' Callanach replied.

At a flick of Trescoe's wrist, Knuckles moved forward to stand in front of Lively, pulling a crowbar from where it had been lodged between his belt and jeans. He grinned at Callanach. 'You get three chances,' Knuckles said, raising the bar above his head. 'You've used up the first one.' He swung the tool down onto Lively's left shoulder. The air exploded with sounds of splintering and Lively swearing in terms Callanach had never heard. To Lively's credit no scream escaped him, but he hit the wall and slid sideways, eyelids fluttering as he panted for oxygen to stay conscious.

'Do your friends here know who you're sacrificing them for? You've no doubt told them there's some higher purpose. That you want to stop the rise of a criminal gang, protect the community, same old tale. The truth's a bit muckier, though, wouldn't you agree?' Trescoe asked.

'The truth is that you ordered Louis Jones' death in a way that sent a clear message out to anyone who might dare fail to pay your protection money, blackmail fees or whatever other scams you're running at the moment,' Callanach said, assessing Lively's fitness to fight or flee.

'Sorry, should I not talk about DCI Begbie?' Trescoe asked. Lively looked up. 'I see I was right. You didn't fill the Sergeant in on all the details. What I find hypocritical is that you can accuse CI Dimitri of being a bent copper when you're defending the honour of a policeman who stole my money, then lived off the proceeds of prostitution and drug deals for years? Is it one rule for your friends and another for mine?'

'You forced Begbie to commit suicide,' Callanach said.

'Are you not curious about what he did?' Trescoe continued. 'I find it hard to believe that you're prepared to give your life without understanding why. You see George Begbie was party to plenty of useful information through his informant, Louis Jones. Jones was clever. A good driver, and a man who developed the skill of listening rather than talking. A man so quiet we often forgot he was even there. No doubt Jones pretended to be unwilling to give evidence against us, but the truth was that he'd been waiting for just such an opportunity. Putting myself and Mr McGill in prison meant he could clean up while we were out of action. Jones used to do the protection money rounds for us – pick up the weekly cash from local businesses. He continued doing that for no less than six months while we were on remand awaiting trial. Begbie knew about it and did nothing to stop it. They split the cash fifty-fifty. It all ended when we were convicted and sentenced. People realised they didn't need to pay anymore when it was clear we weren't coming back for years. Jones and Begbie made more money than they could have dreamed of – just too much to put into a bank account. I don't know why Begbie did it, but I can guess. You must know that the police only assigns officers onto vice squad for a limited period, before their minds get twisted by the filth and depravity they see. Money and sex operate exactly the same way. At first you're horrified by what you see, then you're intrigued. Soon enough you admit that you want it for yourself. Begbie went too long watching other people getting rich. It made him jealous and greedy. It killed him, and he's passed his misfortune onto you. Honestly, I think your precious former DCI got what was coming to him,' Trescoe finished.

'Whatever wrong he did, he spent his career putting men like you inside to make up for it. How did your boys do it? Did they hold a gun to the window while the car filled up with carbon monoxide?'

Knuckles laughed.

'So much drama, DI Callanach. You live by the sword, you

die by the sword. And George Begbie got off lightly, by the way. He died looking out at the sea, having gallantly pretended that all the money had gone in order to protect his dear wife. Then Ava Turner stuck her rather attractive nose in and everything became so much more complicated. I hope you don't mind dying to satisfy Turner's need to be proved right,' Trescoe said.

'Even if you kill all three of us, the envelope on my desk contains enough evidence to convict Mr Perry here of murder, and it also proves Dimitri's collusion. That investigation will lead directly to you.'

Trescoe raised his gun, flicked the barrel in Perry's direction and let off a shot directly into his chest. Perry hit the floor face down, cycling his legs against the concrete for a few seconds before giving in to the damage to his heart and lungs.

'I don't think he's going to be cutting any deals to give evidence against me now, and you have a form of justice. An eye for an eye. Does that feel better?'

Knuckles rolled his friend turned corpse over, checking for a pulse then risking a look in his boss' direction, saying nothing.

'Make the call, Callanach,' Trescoe said. 'I want that envelope destroyed.' He handed over a mobile.

'Don't do it, lad,' Lance said. 'We know how this ends. The call will change nothing.'

Trescoe nodded. Knuckles stood up and raised the crowbar once again. Lively lifted his head and smiled. 'Go fuck yourself,' he muttered.

The bar whistled through the air and made crushing contact with Lively's elbow, completing the devastation to the arm that had been struck before. Callanach kept his eyes open, watching Lively's face as he registered the pain then the damage that had been done.

'Last chance,' Knuckles said. Callanach stared at the mobile in his hand. The truth that he and Lively were all too aware of, was that the envelope with the passwords had been a bluff to get Dimitri to comply. There was nothing on his desk for Monroe to find. There wouldn't be any pictures of it burning to satisfy Trescoe. They had no leverage at all. 'Do you want to see how his skull looks with the crowbar sticking out of it?' Knuckles asked.

'I called our position in,' Lively bluffed through clenched teeth. 'I know you told me not to, sir, but I did it anyway. I didn't like walking in here without backup.' He looked up at Knuckles. 'If that envelope gets burned, your puppet Dimitri here gets off the hook, but the trail still leads the police straight to your door.'

Knuckles raised the crow bar for the final time.

Chapter Sixty-Three

'Ma'am, I'm sending the address to you now,' Janet Monroe said. 'We've identified a landline number registered in Sean O'Cahill's name that matches DVLA records. I've tried to call it but there's no response.'

'We're only five minutes away,' Tripp said, glancing at the address on the screen and putting on the sirens as he yanked the steering wheel hard left.

'One of Sean's friends from The Lost Boys tried calling his mobile but that went straight to voicemail, too. I'm assuming potential risk unless and until we can make direct contact with him. If you reach him before we do, Monroe, ask him to get to a secure location until we can speak with him in person. We'll check his home address out.'

The street was lifeless. Ava stood at the outer door to the apartments and looked around.

'Lights are on,' Tripp said. 'Can't hear anything though.' He stood with his ear to the glass of the apartment to the left of the door.

'We need to get into the building without putting Sean and Bradley at any increased risk. I'm trying the other apartments first to see if they'll give us access.' Ava pressed the buzzer for the second-floor flat. 'Good evening, this is Detective Ava Turner with Police Scotland. I wonder if you could . . .' The line went dead. Ava rolled her eyes skywards and grimaced before pressing the button to the alternative upper floor flat. 'Good evening, this is . . .' and the door opened. 'God help us, sublime to the ridiculous,' she muttered pulling the outer door wide and waiting for Tripp.

He was walking along the row of cars immediately outside, running his hands over the bonnets. He paused, holding his hand higher up on one vehicle, then took out a torch and went to the windows. Taking out his mobile, he called a number. Ava heard nothing, but a faint light shone from the passenger side window.

'Sean's mobile is on the front passenger seat of this car,' he said. 'It's not the vehicle the DVLA have registered to him.'

'Call it in,' Ava replied, wedging the doormat under the outer door to hold it open. 'Then get backup here with paramedics on a silent approach basis. I'm going up to check with the neighbours.'

She took the stairs two at a time, knocking gently on the first door she came to, holding up her ID badge as the door opened.

'Police,' she said. 'Please speak quietly. Have you seen anyone come or go from the flat below this evening?'

'Been watching the telly all night. Heard them, though, slamming the bloody door earlier. What've they done?' the woman asked.

'We're just making enquiries at this stage,' Ava said. 'Can I ask you to remain in your flat with the door locked until you're told that the situation is resolved?'

'Can you ask them downstairs to keep their voices down? I hear every bloody word at this time of night. Soon as I turn my TV off their nattering keeps me up for hours,' she said.

'Is it like that right now?' Ava asked.

'Listen for yourself,' she said, stepping backwards and letting Ava in.

The voices weren't clear but they were audible, both male, with one dominating the conversation. 'Could you get me a glass please?' Ava asked, putting it to the floor when the woman handed it to her. She placed it upside down on the wooden planks and knelt to put her ear to it.

'Why are you doing this?' Brad asked.

'Because you need me to,' Christian said. 'I'm here to comfort you. Sean wasn't right for you anyway, you told me that yourself in a hundred different ways.'

'I don't understand why you have a gun,' Brad said. 'He needs a doctor. Let me go.'

'Sit down,' Christian said. He pulled the syringe from his pocket and held it out towards Sean. 'If you don't sit down with me, I'll put this in him and he'll be gone in seconds. The way I had it planned was much more humane. He'll fall asleep forever hearing our voices as if he were just drifting into sleep. Wouldn't you prefer that?'

Bradley tried sitting, his shaking legs betraying him in the last second and dumping him onto the sofa. 'What did you do?' he asked.

'Don't speak to me so accusingly,' Christian said, perching on the arm of the settee near to Sean's feet. 'You wanted me to come here. If you'd agreed to go to The Lost Boys with Sean, none of this would ever have happened. I'd have known he wasn't meant to be taken from you. Sean didn't look after you properly anyway, going out with his friends, leaving you alone. I'm here for you, Bradley. I know how loss feels. I'm not going to let you suffer alone.'

'I don't want to suffer at all,' Bradley said. 'This isn't you, you're gentle and kind. Whatever you've gone through, we can talk about it after I've called for an ambulance.'

'That's not how this is going to work,' Christian said. 'It has to work like it did before. Sean won't suffer. My mother didn't suffer. I watched her. She just sort of faded. It took hours. I think it was hours but I was very young. Perhaps I lost track of time.'

'What happened to her?' Bradley whispered.

'Heroin overdose,' Christian said. 'Then I didn't have to go to school anymore.'

'That must have been an accident,' Brad said. 'You don't want the same thing to happen to Sean, do you? I'm sorry for your loss but we can still save him.'

'I'm afraid Sean's had a larger dose already than most people survive,' Christian said. 'I can hold you if you like?' He reached out the hand in which there was no gun, putting the syringe down on the sofa.

'Hold me? You are totally insane,' Brad said. 'I don't want you to hold me, or touch me or to be anywhere near me. I don't know how you got to Sean but you're sick and dangerous. This isn't some role-play where you get to use the man I love to reenact your twisted fantasy.' Bradley stood up. 'You're going to have to get out of my way, because I'm going through that door and I'm getting help.'

'You have to watch,' Christian shouted. 'That's how this goes!'

'I'm not going to sit here and do nothing.' Bradley moved to Christian's left, ducking to pass. The pistol came down hard on the back of his head, opening his skin with a stream of blood that he stared at as it dripped to the floor. Christian pushed him back down onto the couch.

'Police,' Ava shouted at the door. 'Open up immediately!'

'We need help!' Bradley shouted. Christian raised the gun to Brad's face.

'Stay away from the doors and windows,' Christian said. 'No one comes in or goes out. I have a gun.'

'You need to let me see Sean and Bradley,' Ava said. 'Once I know they're both still alive, we'll back off.'

'If you try to come in, I'll shoot them,' Christian said.

'Just open the curtains,' Ava said, 'so we can see that both of them are all right. Then I can give you more space and we can talk this through.'

'If I open the curtains, you'll shoot. You think I'm that stupid? I don't want to talk this through with you,' Christian shouted. 'This evening was meant for me. You weren't supposed to be here.'

'You don't need to hurt anyone,' Ava said. 'Just let me in on my own. You can lock the door behind me. No tricks, I promise. If you do that I can get the others to let the evening run its course.' She looked behind her to where twenty men and women in weapon resistant vests stood at various points around the property. She waved them back a few feet.

'Jacket off,' Christian shouted. 'Nothing except a t-shirt. Shoes off too. I'll unlock the door and open it, but you come in alone. Try anything and you'll get a bullet in your head. When you come in, turn around to face the door, get down on your knees and lace your hands behind your head.'

'Ma'am, you're just handing him an extra hostage. It's against protocol,' Tripp said.

'We need eyes in there to see what state those men are in and I can't negotiate with him shouting through a locked door. There's no choice. I'm putting you in charge out here. Keep all officers clear of the windows in case shots go through. Close off the road. No press. No one in or out. And no heroics, okay?'

'With respect, that feels like the speech I should be giving you. Are you going to conceal a weapon?' Tripp asked.

'No. If he finds it, he'll lose the plot. I'm going in,' Ava said.

The door to the apartment opened. Ava saw a pale-faced man with his hands in the air, his eyes darting between her and an unseen figure who must have been standing behind the door.

'Walk forwards,' a voice commanded. Ava did as she was told. 'Now get on your knees,' he said. She knelt down. The door slammed behind her and was locked. She attempted a reassuring smile at the man still stood with his hands in the air, noting the tears in his eyes. 'Take your clothes off.'

'Jason, my name's DCI Ava Turner. With respect . . .' Ava started.

'You don't respect me,' Christian said. 'Let's get one thing clear. I'm not Jason. I shed that skin a very long time ago. People move on, DCI Turner. They evolve. Please don't expect to come in here brandishing details of my past, that will suddenly make me break down and open my heart to you. This isn't some crappy B movie. It's real. The things I need are real. Right now, I need to check what's under your clothes, so strip down to your underwear. You can put everything straight back on as soon as I know there's nothing hidden.'

'Okay, that's fair,' Ava said. 'In your situation I'd make the same request. Could I just take a look at Sean first, to make sure he's breathing?'

'Clothes off, then you look.'

Ava stripped off her shirt and trousers, turning around slowly, getting a look at the man pointing a gun steadily at her head. He appeared remarkably calm. There was no shake to his hands, no looking away when she met his eyes. His brow was dry. Ava chose her tack as she got dressed.

'Is that Sean on the sofa?' she asked. 'Can I check him now?'

'Go ahead,' Christian said. 'You'll find his pulse is weak. I think the word is thready. Don't expect any response from him at this stage. He's too deeply unconscious.'

'You're something of an expert,' Ava said, laying her fingers across the inside of Sean's wrist. 'His pulse is extremely feeble. How much time do you think he has left?'

'Less than an hour,' Christian said. 'Of course, I had planned to spend that time privately with Bradley, but now we'll have to do things differently.'

'Don't worry on my account,' Ava said. 'What's Sean been given?'

'Heroin,' he said. 'I'm going to need you to sit on the floor, facing the wall. Hands laced on your head.'

'Jason, you're holding the gun. There's nothing to be gained by me sitting with my face to the wall. I think Brad will remain calmer if I keep eye contact with him. I'll sit on the floor though, if that's what you want.' She sat down next to Sean's head and laced her hands over her hair.

'His name's not Jason.' Brad sniffed. 'What are you talking about?'

'It's all right, I'm still Christian to you, Bradley,' Christian said. 'That's who you need.'

'You don't have to be Christian tonight. You can let Brad go, let Sean live. I understand what you must feel. We're all trapped in the moments in our past when our lives changed forever, and you suffered a trauma no child should ever have to experience. You were so young, Jason, the night you lost your mother. You don't have to keep reliving the awful things that happened,' Ava said.

'I didn't lose my mother,' Christian snarled. 'I was relieved of her. Is that why you were so keen to come in here? You wanted to talk me through my pain, let me know that you empathised about my mother's tragic death? What image did you have of her? Of someone who cuddled me at night, baked cakes and put plasters on my bloody knees? You and I didn't grow up in the same street, DCI Turner. I doubt we grew up on the same planet.'

'No parent is perfect, but seeing her die must have been awful. I understand there was no one there to protect you from Christian Cadogan. I read the police statements about the state of the place. Every child is entitled to expect better. The school, social services, your health care workers, someone should have realised something was wrong much sooner than . . .'

'You know what, you ignorant bitch, you talk a lot but you don't seem too capable of listening.' Christian walked across to stand above her. 'My mother didn't feed me for days on end because every penny in the house went on alcohol and drugs. She used to whore in front of me when she got short of cash. You think I was too young to remember that? The day Cadogan killed her was the best day of my life. He held me as she died. He talked to me. That evening, he went out and bought me fish and chips. He didn't hit me when I asked to go to the bathroom.' He grabbed Ava by the hair and hauled her up to standing, pushing the gun into her neck. 'Then you bastards hung him. He went into a police cell and he never came out. You took away the only person who was ever kind to me.'

Bradley began sobbing behind them. 'His breathing's slowing down. I can't hear it properly. Please, please, can you do something? Sean needs an ambulance. He's dying.'

'He's supposed to die!' Christian shouted. 'He was no good for you. He didn't value you, or treasure you. Can't you see that, even now? I was there when you wanted someone to talk to. I was coming here when he was off out with his friends. What the fuck is wrong with you?' He dragged Ava towards Sean's prone body, keeping the gun pressed against her as he picked up the syringe he'd left on the cushion.

'Christian, please don't,' Ava said quietly.

He swung his gun around to point at Bradley, shoving Ava roughly away. 'DCI Turner, make one move towards me and both men die. Stay back and there's a possibility that one of them might survive.'

Ava took a step further away, raising her hands and softening her face. 'No one has to die. Listen to me. You have a chance to turn this around. It's too late for Lily and for Cordelia, but you can still do the right thing for Sean.'

'He's turning blue,' Bradley shrieked.

'I was helping them,' Christian shouted. 'Do you have any idea how unhappy Randall Muir was when I met him? He wasn't getting what he needed from his family. They weren't encouraging him, weren't recognising his potential. And Lily? Perfect Lily who was happy to let her sister languish in her shadow. I helped Mina and Randall escape, and their grief was beautiful. They cried in my arms and clung to me. They needed me. You'll never understand how that feels, to be right there in that moment of loss.'

'Families are dysfunctional, Christian. Lily and Cordelia didn't need to die. The grief you witnessed never needed to exist. Don't do that to Bradley too. There shouldn't be any more victims,' Ava said.

'Are either of you even listening?' Bradley yelled. 'Sean is dying, right now.'

'Last chance, Christian,' Ava said. 'Let the medics in. You can keep me in here if that's what you need for now.'

'That's not what I want,' Christian said. 'It's over for me anyway, isn't it?'

Bradley screeched and threw himself forwards towards Sean. Christian raised both arms, sidestepping to intercept Bradley's manoeuvre. Ava launched herself in response, shoulders down low, aiming to push all the forward momentum of her body

403

into Christian's stomach. A misstep caught her ankle on the low coffee table and she twisted, her body falling towards the writhing mass of bodies. Bradley on top of Christian, both of them on top of Sean, hands flung out, grappling, wielding a gun and syringe of heroin.

Ava's head whipped back at the sound of the gun's report in deafening proximity to them all. There was half a second of silence, followed by a soft whump and a rush of air. Bradley collapsed at Christian's side, grabbing for the syringe as he rolled. The blood was a river, covering their faces and hands. Ava pushed up on one knee, driving one fist up into Christian's groin and following it up with an elbow to the side of his rib cage. Bradley brought a fist down onto Christian's neck with an odd half-hearted squeal of victory, his hand releasing as it fell to his side on the floor.

Then the flat door splintered apart and commands were yelled from all sides. Armed police came first, securing the gun, assessing the situation. The paramedics weren't far behind, allocating bodies between teams. Tripp barged through the lot of them to reach Ava.

'Gun shot wound over here!' a medic shouted.

'Heroin overdose,' Ava panted, pointing in Sean's direction.

'Just stay still ma'am,' Tripp said, reaching into a paramedics bag to take a wad of towelling, and wiping blood from her face. The sting made Ava realise it was her own.

'Sean will be okay, right?' she asked Tripp. 'Tell me we saved him.'

Then she blinked once, twice, her lines of vision closing in from both sides like some Hitchcockesque cinematic effect as she lost consciousness.

Chapter Sixty-Four

Callanach was taken into the cellar first with Lance behind him, and Lively given some assistance by Knuckles to account for the injuries to his arm and shoulders. Domo was finishing off upstairs, wrapping up Perry's body and cleaning the resulting blood stains off the tiled floor. Given the speed with which he'd gathered together towels, cleaning fluids and plastic wrap, it seemed a well-practised drill.

The cellar was large, damp, and it reeked of spilled ale and rotting fruit. Two small grates set high up in the walls let in cobweb-diffused daylight to accompany the few dim bulbs that swung from the ceiling. The floor had a vague tilt to it, all four corners leaning in to a centre point where a slatted iron hole cover lay waiting for purpose.

Callanach made eye contact with Lively who nodded at him.

'I'm sorry,' Callanach told him quietly.

'None of that,' Lively said.

'Last chance,' Ramon Trescoe said. 'You phone the office, have that envelope destroyed, or I take a life. Are you content to be responsible for that, DI Callanach? The trail might lead the police here, but you'll be gone by then along with every trace of your existence.'

'Everyone of us is as good as dead already. The least we can do is make sure you'll be convicted for it,' Lance muttered.

'Actually, that's not strictly true. I can kill any one of you in a second. What you don't know is that Chief Inspector Dimitri isn't the only person on our payroll inside Police Scotland. There are others. If PC Monroe doesn't get the order to destroy that envelope, there'll be someone waiting at her house later tonight. Her address will be easy enough to find for someone with access to police records. She might survive, it's possible, but I'll make sure her baby won't.'

'You evil wee scunner,' Lively said. 'Monroe's done nothing.'

Knuckles moved faster than Callanach had anticipated he could, bringing up an elbow as he span and ramming into the underside of Lively's jaw. A click reverberated around the stone walls as Lively's teeth connected on mass. His skull flew backwards, hitting the wall, and he slid into a heap in the filth on the floor. Small mercies, Callanach thought. At least Lively wouldn't be conscious to see the bullet coming for him. Lance was silent, staring at the floor. Knuckles was rubbing his elbow and grinning. Domo appeared from the cellar steps, wiping his hands on a rag that he shoved into his pocket.

'Didn't another officer lose a baby on your watch, Callanach? I seem to recall Dimitri telling me about it. Bloody mess, I think, would be a fair way to describe it. You must have felt terrible. I could let you live long enough to see the photos and hear all about it, knowing you had the power to save that innocent baby but elected not to, and for what? To secure a conviction against me? I wonder what PC Monroe would make of it if she was aware of the choice you were facing. Make the call.'

Callanach faced the inevitable. The second he made the call, even if he faked the instructions to Monroe about destroying the envelope, he would immediately be responsible for both Lively and Lance's deaths.

'I can't,' Callanach said.

Trescoe reached into his pocket and took out another mobile, speed dialling a number as he raised the gun to Lance's head. He listened for a moment as a voice answered the line, tinny in the electronic distance. 'This is Ramon,' Trescoe said. 'I've a problem that needs sorting out. Do you know a constable by the name of Monroe, was in Dimitri's squad, temporarily placed with MIT?'

Trescoe gave Callanach a wide, smug smile, cocking his head to the side, drawing out the moment. Callanach held his breath, hoping against the odds that Monroe would stay safe. The thought that he might be responsible for the death of another innocent baby was a prospect he knew he would never recover from.

'You do know her? Good. Are you able to find her home address?' Trescoe continued.

Dimitri jerked a hand from his pocket as he moved his left foot back to stabilise, gun poised to fire. Callanach threw himself across Lance's back, the cellar too small to guarantee any of them safety from bullets ricocheting off barrels, pushing the journalist to the floor as Dimitri's gun let go of its load.

Trescoe managed a couple of backwards steps before the ammunition opened a hole like a dam bursting in his chest. Trescoe's fingers fumbled their grip on his gun as he raised his free hand to investigate the place where his breast bone should have been. There was just time for him to mouth one last swearword at Dimitri before he lurched forward, staggering, then banging down onto the filthy floor. As Trescoe's legs thrashed their farewell, Knuckles grabbed a length of chain from a wall swinging it hard to one side.

Lance tried to raise his head. 'Stay low,' Callanach hissed at him, hearing the whistle of the chain wheeling through the air. As it smashed downwards onto Dimitri's gun hand, the weapon flying into some dim corner, Callanach launched himself up towards a stunned Domo. He cracked his own forehead into Domo's as hard as he could bear, and they recoiled in opposite directions. Beer sprayed across the room from a pierced barrel. Callanach's face was a river of red before he even registered the pain at his hairline. Through the ruby liquid he saw Knuckles' chain swing again, slashing Dimitri full in the face, dragging off a wide strip of skin as it fell away. Dimitri put a hand up to his face then brought it back down with a gelatinous white blob deflating in a sauce of blood.

Callanach reached out his arms to catch Dimitri, the full weight of the older man's body collapsing onto him and knocking him backwards, just as Lively sliced a bottle in a vicious arc through the air, planting it in Knuckles' skull. The glass smashed on impact, producing a fine red rain in its wake. Knuckles went down, drawing a knife from his shirt as his knees smashed into the concrete floor, slashing out indiscriminately at whatever was close to him.

'Sorry,' Dimitri muttered, as he slipped through Callanach's arms, rolling onto the floor, his one remaining eye a watery picture of regret. Lance groaned from the floor. Callanach staggered towards him, his vision an out-of-focus kaleidoscope of stars, holding his forehead, which seemed to be growing beneath his hand. He felt the slippery warmth of fresh blood on his friend's head and shouted for him to wake up. Running his hands over Lance's scalp it wasn't clear what had caused the injury – so many bullets, glass and weapons had flown around in the confined space – but his friend was still breathing, for now. Lively appeared from a corner clutching a gun. He pistol-whipped Knuckles across the back of the neck, knocking any remaining protest from him, before lurching towards Domo.

'On your knees,' Lively shouted. Domo, already cowering in a corner, was quick to comply, surrender written all over his panicked face.

'Get upstairs, call ambulances,' Callanach muttered. 'I don't know who's left alive.' He took off his jacket and spread it over Lance's shaking body, reaching a hand out to grip Dimitri's wrist although his own pulse was hammering so hard he knew it would be impossible to locate anyone else's. Time stretched. Lance faded in and out of consciousness. The cellar was a scene from a teenage sick-flick where the crew had gone overboard with the effects. Callanach kept one eye on Domo and the other on Knuckles, noting a shard of glass that was sticking like a landmark up out of the thug's skull. He closed his eyes a moment, the pain in his head too violent to fight. More minutes passed.

Then, finally, there were gentle hands on Callanach's shoulders pulling him up, a voice issuing instructions he struggled to understand. Boots rampaged above his head, instructions were yelled, then police and paramedics swarmed. Lance's limp body was lifted onto a stretcher as Callanach was helped back up the cellar stairs to a world he'd believed he would never see again.

Chapter Sixty-Five

Ava sat on the back step of the ambulance. Tripp was giving orders to forensic crews. Ailsa Lambert had arrived with her usual brusqueness, checking Ava's fitness in a matter of seconds before reprimanding her for the stupidity of inserting herself into a hostage situation. A body bag came out first. Paramedics were still in Sean and Bradley's apartment working their scientific magic.

Janet Monroe climbed out of a police car, her right arm wrapped protectively around her baby bump as she walked between cars, ambulances and forensics vehicles.

'Ma'am,' she said as she neared Ava. 'Are you all right?'

'Just a scratch,' Ava replied. 'Sean O'Cahill is being treated by paramedics to see if they can reverse the effects of the heroin.'

'Who's in the body bag?' Monroe asked.

'Jason Elms, also known as Christian Cadogan. He and Bradley ended up tussling over Sean's body. Bradley grabbed the syringe and shoved it in Elms' neck. He died almost immediately.'

'Maybe it's better that way,' Monroe said. 'I never know if the victims' families would prefer the killers to die or to face trial and imprisonment. Seems cleaner to me like this.'

'Not this time,' Ava said. 'Sean's partner, Bradley, was trying to stop Cadogan from giving Sean the lethal dose of heroin. He threw himself between Cadogan and Sean, and the gun went off. There was nothing paramedics could do to save him. If Sean lives, he'll wake up to a world where his boyfriend has been brutally murdered by a man he was trying to befriend.'

'I need a job with more happy endings,' Monroe said, patting her bump again. 'Sorry, I forgot, I came to tell you that we have reports of a large police presence at a club called The Maz in Glasgow. A former colleague let me know because it seems Chief Inspector Dimitri was involved. DI Callanach and I found something that might tie him to the Louis Jones death . . .' her voice trailed off.

'Where's Callanach?' Ava asked.

'Still no contact from him,' Monroe said. 'He's not answering his phone. Same goes for DS Lively.'

Ava put her head in her hands for a few seconds, then stood up. 'This is all my fault,' she said. 'Monroe, can you get in touch with your colleague now, on the phone?'

'Give me a few minutes,' Monroe said.

Ava wandered over to the ambulance where paramedics treating Sean O'Cahill were preparing to leave. 'How's he doing?' she asked.

'We've got him stable,' the medic answered. 'Remains to be seen what long-term damage has been done, but if I had to call it, I'd say he'll survive.'

'His family are in Ireland,' Ava said. 'He ought to have someone with him when he wakes up. It'll help him to know how bravely his partner defended him. Ask the doctors to inform me when he regains consciousness, would you?'

The medic nodded and shut the ambulance door, the blues lighting up as they pulled away.

'I've never really been sure if it creates more paperwork

when a suspect dies during a police raid or when you have to send them for trial,' Ailsa muttered from behind her.

'About the same amount,' Ava said. 'At least this way you don't have to worry that they might be found not guilty and end up wandering the streets looking for more victims.'

'Did you find out why he did it?' Ailsa asked, stripping off her gloves and tucking them carefully into a bag for sterile disposal.

Ava breathed out hard. 'He did it because society failed to protect him during his formative years. Then, just when we thought we were doing the right thing, we damaged him a little bit more. How many other monsters are we creating, Ailsa? Innocent children who get missed by the system, who suffer unheard and unseen, until it's too late.'

'If you and I really knew the answer to that, I suspect we might never get another night's sleep again,' Ailsa said. 'You just do your best, every hour, every day, and you help the ones you do know about. I'd best accompany these lost souls to my table. Come for dinner next week, dear. You look like you need a decent meal.' Ailsa walked away, toting a bag that looked too heavy for her tiny frame, her shoulders hunched in a way that reminded Ava that Ailsa was ageing in spite of her insuppressible nature.

'Ma'am, Sergeant Collins, at the scene in Glasgow,' Monroe said, thrusting a mobile towards Ava.

'Collins,' Ava said. 'Two of my officers are missing. Do you have any reports relating to either DI Callanach or DS Lively?'

'Sorry, ma'am, can't hear all that well, the ambulances are taking off,' Collins said.

'Callanach or Lively,' Ava shouted.

'I can check with the forensic pathologist who he's processed so far,' Collins said. 'They've brought out three body bags out from the club.'

Ava staggered, leaning against a car bonnet for support. 'Three dead?' she asked. 'What the hell happened over there?'

'Hang on, there's a man being taken to an ambulance now. Are either of your men in their fifties, thick set, argumentative by the look of him?'

'Lively,' Ava whispered. 'Confirm his identity then put him on the phone, Sergeant.'

'Ma'am, this is Lively,' he shouted a moment later.

'Thank God you're not in a body bag,' Ava said. 'Are you badly hurt?'

'Shoulder and elbow injuries, blow to my head, nothing compared to how bad I'm going to feel if I have to put up with hospital food for the next couple of days. You should know that there's been a police death, ma'am. The Glasgow brass are all over it already and the press are circling. It's going to get a bit muddy, I reckon.'

'Lively, just tell me. What happened to Callanach?' Ava shouted.

'From where I'm standing, I'd say he was enjoying the attention. There are at least four paramedics fighting over him, three of whom are female. He's currently taking his shirt off to reveal what I can only describe as a graze although no doubt he'll make a loud noise about the fact that it came from a bullet. In short, he's not badly hurt and everyone's treating him like he's royalty. Unfortunately, ma'am, his face is fine.'

'All right, Lively, that's enough.' Ava smiled. 'Who are the victims?'

When Lively spoke this time it was with a lowered voice. Ava could all but see his hand cupped over his mouth. 'Chief Inspector Dimitri, ma'am. There's going to be some difficult questions to answer. DI Callanach figured out that he'd been working for Trescoe all along. He stitched us up when we arrived at The Maz, but when Trescoe threatened to have Janet

Monroe attacked, he swapped sides. He was an idiot, I reckon, but not bad all the way through.'

'Lively, I've got to ask. Did Callanach tell you about . . .'

'The Chief?' Lively finished for her. 'It came up in conversation. We all do things we're not proud of, ma'am, and DCI Begbie was no different than the rest of us. He was a bloody idiot and he paid the price. No one else ever needs to hear a word about it. Ramon Trescoe is in a body bag. Dimitri's shot killed him. Trescoe's man Knuckles pulled a knife and caught Dimitri in the neck. I managed to persuade Knuckles to calm down with proper police training and the use of a bottle.'

'And the third dead body?' Ava asked.

'Brian Perry, Knuckles' little friend who I gather you're familiar with,' Lively said.

'I remember,' Ava said. 'Any others injured?'

'One of Trescoe's goons, Domo, got a headache courtesy of DI Callanach who performed a remarkably good French version of a Glasgow kiss. I'd never have imagined the boy would be so careless with his face, but credit where credit's due. The Detective Inspector's journalist friend isn't in great shape, having stayed in Trescoe's guest suite awaiting our arrival for several hours, but then . . .'

'What?' Ava asked.

'Dimitri chased up his motorbike licence plate, by all accounts. Led his boys straight to the man's address,' Lively said.

'A journalist? You had a journalist there for the whole event?' Ava hissed.

'Aye, thought you'd be pleased with that one,' Lively said. 'And there's some girl hanging around called Sugar who wants to know if she still has a job at The Maz. Did you want to speak with DI Callanach, ma'am, only his ambulance looks ready for the off.'

'No, Sergeant, don't worry about it. Just as long as you're all out of danger. DI Callanach and I will have plenty of time to talk this one through. Quite possibly when we're suspended together for the next few weeks.'

'Ma'am, you know I've never really seen eye to eye with DI Callanach, and that I'd sooner have had almost anyone else as my superior in MIT than him, right?'

'I was aware, yes,' Ava said.

'Then I should probably say that, actually, he's not a complete tosser. For the record. And in case there's trouble with Detective Superintendent Evil Overlord on this one.'

'Thank you, Detective Sergeant,' Ava said. 'No doubt your statement will reflect that. Preferably in more appropriate terms.'

'Where's the fun in that?' Lively asked. Ava hung up.

Three dead, Ava thought. If she'd just left it alone, those three men would still be breathing and that didn't take into account the trouble at the prison. Another visit to Glynis Begbie would be required and contemplating that made Ava's blood run cold. She could dress it up a thousand different ways, but it still boiled down to the fact that the Chief, for a while, had lost his way so badly that he'd been no better than the men he'd put behind bars. The money Begbie had stolen had come from endless victims: drug money, the proceeds of prostitution, protection rackets – who knew what else. It was dirty money, and Ava knew that Glynis would feel as if she would never wash her hands of it. Ava sympathised. Having broken every rule in the book for a man who'd betrayed everything Ava thought he stood for, it was a hollow victory knowing that Glasgow's streets were safer without Ramon Trescoe's malignant presence. Dimitri gone, too. Rough justice, Begbie and Dimitri dying for the same common bad deeds so many years after the event. Lively was right. Begbie had been a bloody idiot, but it was done. Least said, soonest mended. That was the phrase. Never truer than right then.

Ava stood up, stretched her back and flexed her shoulders. The world around her looked slightly less rosy. Police work was grim most of the time, but then most of the time you could sleep at night believing your team were the good guys. Begbie had rocked that solid foundation for her. It would heal, but it was going to take a while.

She sighed. You never really knew people, Ava thought.

Chapter Sixty-Six

A few days later, Ava wandered down Albany Street clutching tickets and a family sized bag of popcorn. It was dark already, although soon the evenings would start to get lighter. The street was tranquil in spite of the buzz up at York Place just a few hundred metres away. Passing the boutique hotels and family homes, Ava wondered if Callanach wouldn't be happier going back to his beloved France and trying to rebuild his life there. If nothing else, he could stop moaning about the rain. The problem now was that she would miss him. There were few people in life who truly had your back. Ava could count her closest allies on one hand with some digits to spare.

She stuffed the tickets into her pocket and hid the popcorn inside her coat as she climbed the stairs to his apartment, knocking on his door gently.

'*J'arrive!*' he shouted. 'I'm coming.' He pulled the door open, his eyes widening at the sight of her.

'I know,' she said. 'I should have called first. And I'm a mess, I get it. Just couldn't be bothered to dress up. Can I come in?' she asked, walking into his lounge and falling onto the sofa.

'I was going to call you. It took a few days for my vision

and hearing to normalise after the concussion. I won't be using my forehead as a weapon again. Sorry if work has been chaotic without me,' Callanach said. 'I heard about what happened with Cadogan. It was brave of you to go in there.'

'Ailsa may never speak to me again. She says I have a death wish,' Ava said. 'Sergeant Lively is back home. The hospital said he discharged himself after a row about how many portions of pudding he was allowed. Though I gather you were a big hit with the nurses during your stay.'

'Don't start,' Callanach said. 'Listen, about Lance. I'm sorry I got a civilian involved.'

'A civilian?' Ava laughed. 'You got a journalist involved, taken hostage and held at gunpoint under threat of death no less. Is he okay?'

'He's fine. Well, not fine. He's bruised, with lacerations, a couple of broken ribs and a concussion. But he's not dead.' Callanach looked at his watch. 'In a bizarre sort of way, I think he actually enjoyed it. Not being tied up and assaulted, obviously. He said it made him feel alive again when it was all over. I'm not sure I agree, but Lance is his own man.'

'He'll have to be careful,' Ava said. 'Trescoe's brother still has plenty of reach among Glasgow's finest.'

'I find generally that people are concerned about their own lives more than settling scores for others. With Ramon Trescoe dead, the old gang will lose its power. How's Mrs Begbie?' Callanach asked.

Ava took a deep breath in. 'Relieved the score has been settled, but terribly concerned about the injuries you, Lively and Lance Proudfoot suffered. She feels as if somehow she should have known what was going on and stopped it. I feel just as guilty.'

'How did you first find out that the Chief was involved? I know what was in Louis Jones' file, but there must have been more to it than that,' Callanach said.

'Between us, there was an obscene amount of cash in used non-sequential notes concealed behind boards in the Chief's loft. More than Glynis and I realised when she first discovered it. Then when Louis Jones went missing too, I did some home-work and everything pointed towards the recently released Ramon Trescoe.'

'Is Glynis Begbie going to be all right?' Callanach asked. 'That's a lot to deal with.'

'Actually, she's doing better than I thought possible. Originally the life insurance company refused to pay out on the suicide, so Glynis had her solicitors challenge the decision. Ailsa Lambert provided evidence about sudden police suicides from long-term undiagnosed post-traumatic stress disorder. The insurance company didn't want to be seen to be acting unfairly towards public servants, so they're paying out. There's been some recent case law that was helpful, according to the lawyers.'

'So, she'll cope financially then?' Callanach asked.

'She'll cope well enough that she doesn't need to rely on any of the money the Chief had stashed away. She's given it to Ailsa who'll ensure it goes to a good charity. Lucky, really, as that's where I'd said it had gone. Turns out it's one less lie I've told in the last few weeks,' Ava said.

'And you, how are you doing?'

'I hate the Chief, though I still miss him, and I can't help but wonder how many nights' sleep he lost thinking about what he'd done. The worst thing is that I'm sort of glad he's dead rather than dishonoured and living out the rest of his days in prison. Is that terrible?'

'Not at all. I think Begbie would have chosen that option, if he'd had the choice. Either way, he's at peace now. Lance will keep quiet about it, too. He's old-school, even if he is a reporter. Don't forget all the good George Begbie did, Ava. He saved lives, put himself in harm's way, balanced the scales. If

419

you're going to judge him, you've got to judge him on the whole picture, not just a snapshot.'

'You're right,' she said, smiling faintly. 'I guess that applies to your mother as well. I know I shouldn't have meddled. Have you and she . . .?' The question hung between them.

'We've talked, more than once, since she left. It's not easy exactly, but it is better. There was a lot I didn't know. If you hadn't decided to force the matter, things between us might never have improved. I don't think I thanked you properly,' he said.

'Or at all.' She grinned. 'Anyway, enough of that. I'm here to rescue you from your dull evening. There's a movie playing up the road, part of the late-night classics season. I saw it and thought of you.'

'Ava, I really can't . . .' Callanach muttered.

'Oh, come on. It's *The Liquidator*. From the book by John Gardner, Rod Taylor starring as Boysie Oakes? The alternative Bond? It has the best publicity poster. "His lips are on fire, his gun is not for hire, he fills girls with desire!" Honestly, if that isn't the most appropriate movie for you, then I'm going to struggle to find it,' Ava laughed.

'It's not that I don't appreciate the thought, it's just that the timing is wrong.' Callanach said.

'Look, we've both got a ton of paperwork. I still haven't faced Superintendent Overbeck in person. I'm not even sure how to start writing up the Trescoe case and I know you and Lively both put yourselves at risk, professionally and personally, on that one. But it's a problem that can wait until tomorrow. I just wanted an evening with you like it was before all this started. You refusing to eat popcorn at the cinema. Me refusing to let you speak until the credits have rolled. No one else there because apparently there's no other person in this whole city who'll come to the late-night showing of decades old films with me. Except you. And I may be a rank up, but I'd just like one evening with my friend. No police talk. No formalities. Anyway, you have to come because I've already . . .'

The knock at the door was brief, confident. Callanach was on his feet in a second.

'Hi, you ready?' a woman's voice echoed as she walked straight in. 'Oh, I'm sorry, I didn't realise you had someone else here.'

'No problem,' Callanach said. 'Selina Vega meet Ava Turner.'

Ava stood up, releasing the tickets she'd had in her hand and offering her palm to shake Selina's.

'Selina was the registrar present at Cordelia Muir's death,' Callanach offered.

'And you're Luc's boss, I understand,' Selina said. 'Sorry if I've interrupted a briefing.'

'Not at all. Just seemed like the right thing to do to check that my DI was in one piece following the week's events. I'll let you two enjoy your evening. It was nice to meet you, Selina,' Ava said. 'Make sure you're fully fit before you come back to work, okay?' she smiled at Callanach. 'There's no rush. The statements can wait, and you're due some leave in lieu of overtime if that helps.'

'Won't be necessary,' Callanach said. 'I'll be back in Monday morning.' Ava nodded and made her way to this front door. He followed her.

'Ava, if I'd known you were coming . . .'

'Have a wonderful evening,' Ava said. 'We'll have a team debrief Monday. Everyone's pleased you're safe.' She left.

'Shall we have a drink here or go straight to the restaurant?' Selina asked, appearing with a bottle of wine in her hand.

'Let's go straight out,' Callanach said, aware of the dents Ava had left in the cushions on his sofa, the covers still warm from her body. 'It'd be nice to go somewhere new.'

'That sounds good,' Selina said, walking forwards and leaning against him. 'Only can we get this over with first?' She leaned against his body, rising up slightly on her toes to kiss him. Callanach closed his eyes, back in The Maz, holding onto Ava as they almost kissed in the foyer. He forced his eyes open, brought himself back to the moment, back to Selina.

Slipping on his coat, he thought again of The Maz. It wasn't the first time he'd faced death. It was just that every other time he'd been scared of it. These days he was more scared of living. Callanach wrapped a scarf around his neck and ran a hand through his hair. Enough was enough, he decided. He couldn't be ruled by the past. It was time – finally – to see what Scotland really had to offer him.

Can't get enough of the
D.I. Luc Callanach series?

Then read on for a sneak peek
of the next book . . .

Chapter One – Zoey

Skin scraped stone. Gravel lodged in raw flesh. Still Zoey crawled.

Death was a ghoul in the dark, creeping up behind her one scraping footstep after another. Soon its freezing fingers would land on her shoulder. Then she would stop, but not until there was no blood left inside her. She was grateful for the pitch black of the autumn night. It meant she could not see the grotesque mess of her own body. What little strength remained in her upper arms deserted her. On her elbows, she dragged her body forward, hope still pulsing through her veins where plasma had once flowed.

Bad girl, she thought. The man had promised she would live if only she confessed. 'Bad girl,' Zoey whispered into the dirt. She did so want to survive.

The agony took her, planting her face down at the roadside, humbled by the devastating scale of it. Until that day, she had believed herself to be something of an expert on pain. There had been broken bones, a burst ear drum, a busted nose, but none of it had prepared her for how much torment the human body could withstand before death descended.

Picking her face up off the road, she forced her unwilling right knee forward a few more inches. Someone would come, she thought. Soon, someone would come. But she'd been thinking that for days. Where were those movie-screen nick-of-time rescuers when you needed them?

Ripped from her normal life on a Sunday afternoon, it had been a week since her nightmare had begun. Time had transformed as if in a fairground mirror, bloating grotesquely with slowness as she waited pathetically for her imprisonment to end, and splintering into nothingness when the end – her end – was finally in sight.

Zoey had lain for days on a cold, hard table in low light. The cruel joke was that she had been kept fed and watered, relatively unharmed until the end. The sickness was that she had allowed herself to believe she might survive. Years of watching horror movies, of smugly knowing which victim would die and which would live, and still she had fallen into the age-old trap. She had allowed herself to believe what she was told in order to get through the next second, the next minute, without terror consuming her.

Zoey had a new perspective on fear. There was plenty she could teach the other women at the domestic abuse centre now, not that she would ever get the chance. A bolt of pain dragged from her spine all the way through to her stomach, as if her body had been pierced by a spear. The scream she let out sounded more animal than human as it bounced from the asphalt and echoed down the country road. No one was coming. With that thought came a new clarity. She hadn't been dumped at the roadside in the middle of the night to give her a chance of survival. This was her final punishment. It was her grand humbling.

Her decision wasn't hard to make.

Zoey put her face to the pillow of road and allowed one leg

after the other to slide downwards until she was laid out flat. With the last of her strength she pushed herself over to one side, rolling further into the road, away from the trees at the verge. It didn't hurt. The good news – also the bad news, she supposed – was that all the pain had gone. All sense that her body had been torn in two had dissolved into the bitter October air. If there was nothing else left, she could stare at the moon one last time. Complete dark. She wasn't within the boundaries of the city, then. No light spilled to dampen the shine of the stars. Scotland's skies were like nothing else on Earth. Zoey might not have travelled much, but she never underestimated the blinding beauty of her homeland, never tired of the landscapes and architecture that had birthed endless folklore and song.

The stars had come out for her tonight. Perhaps they were doubled or trebled by the tears in her eyes, sparkling all the more through the brine, but it was a night sky to die for. She wasn't a bad girl, she thought. No point pretending anymore.

'I'm good,' her lips mouthed, even if there was no sound left to escape them. Had there been enough blood in her muscles to have fuelled the movement, she would have smiled, too.

Happier times. There had been some. Early days when her mother had doted on her father, before her brother had left home. A day when her father had pretended it was their six monthly trip to the dentist, only to take the family to a dog rescue centre. They had spent the afternoon cooing over every mutt until they found a scruffy little terrier forgotten in the last pen. They had called him Warrior, a sweet joke, although he had proved a fiercely faithful pet from that day on. Every day Zoey wondered if she would tire of walking, feeding and grooming him as she'd seen her friends grow bored of the neediness of animals they'd been given. Not so. Warrior had remained by her side from the age of five until she was twelve.

He had slept on her bed and quieted her crying when the big girl from over the road had bullied her every day for a month straight until her father had had a quiet word with the girl's parents. Warrior had let her carry him around the house like a doll when she was sad. He sat on the doormat of their house Monday to Friday at half past three waiting for Zoey to walk in from school. It had always astounded her that dogs could tell the time. And Warrior had pressed his furry muzzle into her face as she'd cried when her father's car had been hit by a vehicle containing a man with more alcohol in his bloodstream than anyone had a right to. There had been no trip to the hospital, no long farewell, only a police officer at the door, solemn-faced and softly spoken. Her mother had evaporated in grief.

Eighteen silent months later her stepfather had arrived. A year later her brother had celebrated his sixteenth birthday by signing up to join the army with their mother's consent. Zoey had hated her for it. She wondered if she would be able to find forgiveness with her last breath, but forgiveness required effort and concentration. It needed to be nourished by hope. There was none left where she was lying. Her brother's escape had been her entrapment. There was no barrier left between Zoey and her mother's new husband.

The fists her brother had tolerated until he could leave were turned to her. Her mother, a shard of broken china, said and did nothing. Perhaps she didn't care. Perhaps she was only grateful the blows did not touch her. The bruises were limited in their geography. Zoey's face remained untouched until the school summer holidays came around and then it was a free-for-all, the fear of prying teachers alleviated for a while. Zoey had cried her tears into Warrior's warm fur, and shivered into his skinny but comforting frame in her bedroom at night. Until her stepfather had found the love she had for the hound too much joy for Zoey's life. He had declared himself allergic, and the dog food too expensive, in spite of their large house and his good income. Letting out the odd, badly faked sneeze, he had said the dog must go.

That day had been etched in Zoey's memory like the scene from *The Wizard of Oz*, only Toto had not escaped from her stepfather's clutches to return to her. Warrior was pulled from her arms as she huddled on her bed, declaring that she would die if they took him.

'Stop making such a fuss,' her mother had said. Those five words had been a death sentence for whatever mother–daughter bond still fluttered like a fragile butterfly in the summer of Zoey's childhood. Her stepfather told her Warrior had gone to the dogs' home. He would go to a loving family better suited to him, he'd lectured. Zoey sat down that night and calculated how many days it was until her own sixteenth birthday, when she could flee as her brother had. Seven hundred and two. She had marked each one down in a notebook, ready to cross off with a red pencil as she waded through them.

What a waste of a life it had been, she thought. And the horrible truth now was that if she could have even a tiny percentage of those bruise-filled, hate-inducing days back, she would take them with a grateful heart.

By seventeen she had been living with a college friend until the girl's mother had lost her job and couldn't feed or house Zoey anymore. She had tried and failed to study and pass exams, but the constant moving between sofas was too exhausting. In the end she had given her mother one last try. Promises had been made. They were just as swiftly broken. Fists had flown once more.

At eighteen, Zoey had been wise enough to know when to cut her losses. She had walked out into the street to shout her opinion of her stepfather to the world, a safe enough place that even he wouldn't dare harm her. Then she had taken herself and her plastic bag of clothes to a shelter she'd heard about. Sporting the bruises that were her passport inside the safe haven, she had settled down while she waited in the endless list for social housing. Scars were examined. An offer to prosecute was made. Still Zoey couldn't be so cruel to her mother that she could put the man who kept a head over her house in prison. Even if he deserved it a thousand times over.

The sky came closer as she stared at the moon. A gust of wind danced through the branches of the trees above her, scattering a sheet of golden leaves over her body. A many-legged creature skittered over her neck, but Zoey didn't mind. No point flinching now. In a while, all she would be was bug food. The road was long and straight, unadorned by regulatory white lines. She was in the countryside, then. The next car might not pass until morning. It would be an awful discovery for the poor driver, Zoey thought. Imagine starting Monday morning with such a monstrosity. That was if the car didn't run over her.

The last seven days of her life had begun with a mistake. How many times were children told not to get too close to a car asking for directions? She had been distracted, wondering what to cook for dinner as she made her way to the local supermarket in Sighthill. Zoey hadn't noticed the car following her, although she knew now that it had been. There had been no sixth sense as she'd cut through a carpark between tenements. It hadn't occurred to her that the man who wanted to know how to get to the zoo might have a large knife up his sleeve, ready and waiting to poke into the side of her neck. Get into the car or bleed out in the parking lot had been her options. She wished she'd chosen the latter in hindsight. It would all have come out the same in the end.

In the passenger seat, knife pointed into her chest, he had told her to put on handcuffs. Her hands had shaken so badly that she hadn't been able to close the locks until the fourth attempt. Just rape me, she'd thought. Just get whatever this is out of your system. Use me, then let me go. But let me live. Please let me live. I crossed so many days off in red pen. It's not fair for me to die now.

The man had driven her further away, beyond the scope of roads she recognised as she lay across the rear seat. No bravery had been lacking. She'd slipped a foot under the door handle and tried to prise it open, only to find the child locks engaged. Dark windows at the rear of the vehicle had ruined her chances of waving for help. Even attempting to hit the man over the head with her bound hands had won her nothing but a contemptuous laugh and an elbow in her eye.

'Please don't kill me,' she'd said, as they'd finally pulled up into an overgrown driveway.

'I'm not going to,' he'd said. 'But you've been a bad girl.'

'What?' she'd asked, her mouth dry with fear and the shameful knowledge that her bladder had allowed its contents to run away, even while the rest of her couldn't.

'I need you to say it,' the man had said calmly. 'You've been a bad girl, haven't you?'

'You've got the wrong person,' Zoey had replied. 'I don't know who you think I am, but I'm not bad. I've never hurt anyone. If you let me go, I promise I won't say a word. I won't get you into trouble.'

'But you are a bad girl,' the man said. 'You're disrespectful. You're uncaring. You only ever think about yourself. Say it.'

'I'm not,' Zoey had cried, slinking away from him in the back seat. 'I'm not bad. You don't know me.'

At that, the man had climbed out of the front seat and opened the rear door. He was tall. His close-set eyes were such a dark shade of brown that Zoey couldn't discern pupils from irises. He smelled. As he leaned over her, grabbing a handful of hair to wrench her off the back seat, she caught the whiff of rotten matter.

'I'll do whatever you want. You can . . . you can have sex with me. I won't fight you. If you want me to be a bad girl for you then I can be. Okay? I can be whatever you want,' she had whispered, turning her face away as he pulled her to stand against him.

'You see? How many seconds did it take for you to show me exactly what you are. Say it to me,' he said.

'I'm a bad girl,' Zoey had muttered, as he pushed her to her knees on the driveway, a gesture that had signalled the end of hope. No one around to see what he was doing, if he was so confident so publicly. She had lifted her head to peer over the bushes. Not a building in sight save for the one she was destined to enter. No one to hear her scream.

An owl hooted in the trees above her. Zoey had always loved owls. A snuffling sound came from the verge beyond her line of sight. It's Warrior, she thought. Warrior's coming to sit with me, and I'll be with Daddy again. Nothing to be scared of anymore. The stars reflecting in her eyes went dark. Edinburgh's autumn was set to be long and cold.

Loved *Perfect Death*? Then why not go back to where it all started with book one of the D.I. Callanach series?

On a remote Highland mountain, the body of
Elaine Buxton is burning. All that will be left to identify
the respected lawyer are her teeth and a fragment of clothing.
Meanwhile, in the concealed back room of a house in
Edinburgh, the real Elaine Buxton screams into the darkness...

Welcome to Edinburgh.
Murder capital of Europe.

A dark and twisted serial killer thriller that fans
of M.J. Arlidge and Karin Slaughter won't be
able to put down.

History is repeating itself. How far will she go to stop it?

The million copy Sunday Times bestseller returns with a taut, compelling psychological thriller that will have you glued to the edge of your seat.

The truth won't stay locked up forever...

The bestselling Queen of Grip-Lit is back with a thrilling new novel, perfect for fans of Karin Slaughter and M.J. Arlidge.